**They Called Themselves F.E.A.R.
The Freedom and Equality Army
of Revolution . . .**

Charles sat staring at the TV.

The news came on. The Police Commissioner was interviewed. He was almost in tears. There were views of the shattered police car, of the victims being carried on stretchers, and of cops weeping at the station house.

Charles' face did not change.
Paula walked over. "There's thirty-two thousand of them. You fixin' to kill them all?"

Charles said nothing.

"I said are you fixin' to kill them all?"

Charles began cleaning his submachine gun.

TO KILL A COP

"Compelling!"

—Publishers Weekly

Also by Robert Daley
published by Ballantine Books:

STRONG WINE RED AS BLOOD

To Kill a Cop

Robert Daley

BALLANTINE BOOKS • NEW YORK

Library of Congress Catalog Card Number: 76-26924

ISBN 0-345-25945-9

This edition published by arrangement with
Crown Publishers, Inc.

Manufactured in the United States of America

First Ballantine Books Edition: September 1977

This book is for Sandra Warfield and James McCracken

Fear is an instructor of great sagacity and the herald of all revolutions.
—Ralph Waldo Emerson
Essays, first series

For the urban poor the police are those who arrest you. In almost any slum, there is a vast conspiracy against the forces of law and order.
—Michael Harrington

1

EARLY on the night of the assassinations two men came to the door of an apartment in a tenement in the Bronx. One was about twenty-five, the other younger. The older one, whose name was James Roberts, rang the bell.

"The bell don't work, James."

"The name is Charles."

"I know what you name is."

"Then call me Charles."

"I don't hear you calling me Mark D."

"You call me Charles, I'll call you Mark D. Get out of the way."

The apartment had once been broken into, and no professional had ever repaired the door. Charles lifted the door handle and at the same time shouldered into the apartment.

Inside was what had once been a living room. Now there were beds in the four corners of the room. Curtains hung from wires so that the room could be cut into cubicles. There was an old air conditioner in one window, but it did not work, and the room was pungent with body heat.

A girl, fully dressed, reclined on one of the beds. She had been watching the flickering TV set on the floor.

"I give you a key," she complained as the two men came into the room. "Why you always breakin' my door down?"

"Shut up, Paula."

"I gonna throw your ass out of here, hear? I call the police and have you removed."

But Paula, sinking back on the bed again, gave rapt attention to the TV set.

"Turn that thing off."

"It's the six o'clock news with Jim Jensen. I always watch the six o'clock news with Jim Jensen."

The man who called himself Charles bent and switched off the TV. "Where's Butch?"

"Him and Ida's in the back bedroom," Paula said, staring at the blank face of the TV. "I heard the springs going awhile ago. They's probably finished."

Charles said to Mark D.: "Get him out here."

Mark D. went down the hall. They heard Mark D. throw open the bedroom door. Then his voice said: "What you doing in there? Don't do nothing I wouldn't do."

There came a muffled curse in a girl's voice followed by Mark D. saying to someone: "Charles wants you."

"Charles who?" said a man's voice.

"You know, Charles."

"Oh, that Charles."

Mark D. came back into the main room, where he leaned in the doorway watching Charles.

Charles had set his satchel down on one of the beds. He had unzipped it and taken out a submachine gun. He held the submachine gun in his hands a moment, then placed it on the bed.

Paula glanced from Charles to Mark D., then back to Charles. Charles took four clips and some boxes out of the satchel and laid them beside the gun. Then he lifted the grease gun, threw the bolt back and peered into the slot.

"What you gonna do with that thing?" Paula asked.

"You ask too many questions."

Paula giggled. "I bet you ain't gonna shoot birds with it."

Mark D., leaning in the doorway grinning, said: "We going pig hunting with it."

"And you talk too fuckin' much," said Charles. "You talk all the fuckin' time."

The third man, Butch, came down the hall and into the main room. He was zipping up his fly. He was barefoot and naked to the waist. He grinned and said: "Is tonight the night? The big night?"

Charles said: "We just come back. They still there. Still sitting there. Waiting for us. Only they don't know they's waiting for us."

Butch explained to Paula: "Tonight we gonna off us two pigs."

Charles said: "You not gonna off nobody. You in the backup car."

"That ain't right, James. I belong in the hit car."

"You don't even know my name," said Charles.

"I mean Charles," said Butch.

"We took a vote," said Charles. In his hand he held an opened box of bullets. He was staring at the bullets. "You in the backup car."

"How come I didn't get no vote?"

"Because you was in the sack with that broad. You ain't no revolutionary. You just a mean stud with hot pants for that broad."

"We gonna ice some pigs, I want to be there."

"You can be there. You just ain't in the hit car."

Still reclining on the bed, Paula said: "What you bloods gonna do?"

A sleepy-faced girl in jeans and a blouse came out of the back bedroom. Her name was Ida and she was Butch's common-law wife. She stood beside Mark D. in the doorway. Mark D. put his arm around her, but she took his hand off her hip and handed it back to him.

Paula and Charles were staring at each other. Then Charles tossed a box of bullets and one clip onto the bed beside her. The box of bullets landed heavily. The empty clip struck the box with a tinny sound.

"Fill that clip," Charles ordered.

"What you bloods gonna do?"

"Damnit, sister, we gonna kill them."

After a moment Paula began to stuff bullets into the clip. On the opposite bed sat Charles with two other clips that were taped together at the closed ends. He had a second box of bullets beside his thigh, and he was slipping bullets one after another into one end of the two taped clips.

Mark D. went down the hallway. A closet door opened and shut, then Mark D. came back into the room with two rifles under one arm. He was also clutching three handguns to his chest.

"You fuckin' out of your mind?" said Charles. "Put them long pieces back in the closet."

"Okay, okay. Don't get excited."

Charles was stuffing bullets into the third clip. He heard the rifle butts strike the floor and the closet door shut again. When Mark D. came back into the room this time he had an automatic in his pants pocket. Its outline showed through the cloth.

The girl in the doorway, Ida, giggled and said: "That thing look like a hardon."

Mark D. grinned. "You want a hardon? I give you a hardon. I slap one in you that come out you throat."

The girl in the doorway gave him a cool look.

Charles said to Mark D.: "Put it in your belt and pull your shirt down over it." Charles was trying to force one last bullet into the full clip, but the bullet slipped out of his fingers and rolled across the floor. In the doorway Ida picked it up and bit on it. She grinned at Charles.

Charles got up and went into the bathroom. He came out with a laundry bag. He began dumping dirty laundry out onto the floor.

From the bed Paula asked plaintively: "What you doing there, Charles? Why you always makin' such a mess in my house?"

Charles placed his submachine gun in the laundry bag. He placed the four clips in after it. Then he began to stuff dirty clothes in on top.

Dirty laundry remained on the floor. Paula got up off the bed, picked up the laundry and carried it back into the bathroom.

"What car you in, Charles?" Butch asked sullenly.

"The grease goes in the hit car," said Charles.

"I been in the party as long as you. I got rights too."

"You got shit."

They stared at each other. Charles's face was hard. Butch's face was only sullen.

Charles said: "The backup car is the Riviera. That's the car you riding in, man. You a mean stud all right, but you ain't got no ideology."

Paula looked from one face to the other.

Charles slung the laundry bag over his shoulder.

Paula said: "Do I get my laundry bag back later?"

"Maybe," Charles said. "Maybe."

He moved toward the front door. Butch and Mark D. followed. Both now had guns in their belts with their summer shirts outside the belts.

Charles said to Paula: "We be back about nine or ten o'clock. You cook us up some pork chops. We gonna be hungry. And some of that apple wine."

"I ain't got no money."

Charles took out ten dollars. When she did not come forward to get it, he let it drop to the floor.

"And open some windows while we're gone," Charles said. "This place smells like a whorehouse."

The door slammed.

Paula picked up the money. She handed it to Ida.

"Go get a couple dozen pork chops. Get a gallon of Boone's Farm apple wine. That's what they like."

The other girl went out.

There was a phone on the floor between two of the beds. Paula stood looking down on the phone. It occurred to her to telephone the precinct. She wanted to get these men out of her house. Especially Charles. She could tell the police that Charles had a submachine gun in her laundry bag. The cops could be waiting here when the men came back.

But they might miss Charles. She knew they had been looking for Charles for months under another name in connection with another crime. They had not found him. Charles was too smart. Charles would elude them again, and if this happened she would not be safe.

Charles and Butch and Ida had moved into her house with their guns, and then every week it seemed more of them had moved in. About fifteen people lived in her flat now, off and on.

She decided she was too afraid of Charles to telephone anybody. She sat down on the bed again. She had switched the TV back on. She began watching the evening news with Walter Cronkite.

The hit car moved down Riverside Drive. In the back seat a man named Frank had a .38 police special on his lap. He had taken all the bullets out and was putting them back in again. A fully loaded .9-mm Browning automatic lay on the floor beside his left shoe. On the floor in front, between Charles's feet, lay the laundry bag containing the submachine gun. Mark D. was driving.

"There it is," said Charles.

The police car was parked on the grass between the northbound lane and the service road. It was facing the houses. It was about a hundred yards away.

The hit car, surrounded by light traffic, cruised on by.

At 110th Street Mark D. made a U-turn and they drove uptown on the service road. This time they passed the police car and the houses.

It was about nine o'clock. Across the river the sky was still gray above the Palisades, but the police car seemed to crouch in darkness under the trees. In the hit car no one spoke as they cruised in front of the police car. One cop was slumped in his seat, his cap pulled down over his eyes. The ceiling light was on and the other cop appeared to be writing on a clipboard on his lap. Neither cop looked up.

"How come them motherfuckers just sit there all day?" Mark D. said.

"They guarding the house of the big pig."

"Which big pig?"

"The District Attorney," muttered Charles.

They went on up and turned into 116th Street, where Mark D. pulled in to the curb. Charles lit a cigarette and stared out the window. The cylinder in Frank's revolver clicked into place.

"Get that fuckin' thing out of sight," snapped Charles.

People walked along the sidewalk.

"You want to go around again?" asked Mark D.

"We already circled them motherfuckers five times," said Frank.

"Where's the backup car?" Mark D. asked. He began peering about for the other car. "I ain't seen it since we made the first pass. That's an hour ago at least."

"I told you them studs had no ideology," said Charles. "When it comes to stickups, they're okay. But when it comes to something important they're not serious. Icing a pig don't interest them as much."

He reached down through the laundry and gripped his submachine gun. "Go down to 113th Street and come up alongside them real slow," he said.

Frank said: "Shouldn't we wait for the backup car?"

"We don't need them," said Charles.

They cruised south. At 113th Street, turn signal blinking, Mark D. waited for a break in the traffic. They could see the back of the police car under the trees a hundred yards away. The two police officers still had their ceiling light on.

Charles lifted his submachine gun out from the laundry and held it muzzle down between his legs.

Mark D. steered across the northbound lane and approached alongside the parked police car. His right wheels went up on the grass. He approached the police car from behind. There would be less than three feet separating the two cars.

Charles was remembering that he had been a political prisoner in the past, first for burglary, later for shooting three people. By concentrating on how much he hated the fascist state pig police, he was trying to maintain an icy calm. In about two seconds he would partially settle his own personal score, and he would also strike a blow for his oppressed people.

From the back seat, Frank whispered: "Them motherfuckers will never know what hit them."

Charles was so tense he was worried about squeezing off a burst before the grease came clear of the window.

Suddenly Charles cried: "Go on by, go on by."

A second police car was suddenly coming toward them along 113th Street.

Now Mark D. had seen it too. He floored the accelerator. One tire spit grass, then squealed as it bounded down onto the tarmac again. Mark D. wrenched the wheel left and they sped up toward 116th Street, where he turned left again, crossed the north-bound lane, and began racing south on Riverside Drive.

They had all seen the surprised face on the cop behind the wheel of the parked police car. He had looked absolutely shocked. Suddenly there had been another car on the grass beside him, two and a half feet away.

Mark D. had the car up to fifty. He couldn't go faster because of the traffic. They could hear the siren coming after them.

In the back of the car Frank was stuffing guns under the seat.

"Gimmie your piece," he said to Mark D.

Mark D. passed it back over his shoulder. Frank stuffed it under the seat.

"What about the grease?" Frank said.

"It's under the laundry," said Charles.

The police car was gaining on them.

The police car drew alongside. The cop in the passenger seat had his arm out the window. They had never seen his face before. During all their passes he had been dozing with his hat over his eyes. He motioned them to pull over.

Mark D. glanced at Charles.

"Do what he says."

Mark D. steered toward an empty bus stop, still rolling slowly. The police car was rolling alongside at the same speed.

Charles brought the submachine gun out of the laundry bag and up behind Mark D.'s neck. Mark D. gave a startled glance and ducked forward over the wheel. Behind his head the submachine gun erupted. The noise was stupendous. The air was filled with noise and dust and shattered glass. An empty bullet shell had stung Mark D.'s neck. Others ricocheted off the windshield.

The two cops had jumped and lurched in their seats. Smoke hid them. When it cleared, both had fallen out of sight. The car looked empty.

"Haul ass, man," said Charles. "I mean haul ass."

The police car was still rolling. It rolled into a parked panel truck and stopped. In it nothing moved.

The hit car sped down Riverside Drive.

"Jesus Christ," Frank chortled in the back seat. He was pounding Charles on the shoulders. "That's giving it to the motherfuckers. Them motherfuckers got the message that time."

Mark D. cried: "I can't hear. Why didn't you tell me? My ears are killing me. Jesus. That fucking grease might of burst my eardrums. My fucking ears are killing me."

"It was loud," said Frank. "Oh yes, it was loud."

Charles had stuffed the machine gun back into the laundry.

"Get over to Broadway," Charles said. He was peering out the rear window. Nothing was following. "Drive normal."

Mark D. made the turn. He was reaming his ears, first one, then the other. "My fucking ears."

A stench of burning filled the car. Charles reached into the laundry bag and pulled out a pair of nylon underpants. The nylon had started to smolder.

"Ah yes," said Frank. He giggled. "It hot in that laundry bag. Yeah man, it hot in there."

Charles dropped the scorched underpants out the window.

Frank said: "Them's the hottest underpants I ever seen."

Charles said nothing.

The car came out onto Broadway. Mark D. drove north in heavy traffic under the bright lights. The car windows were down. They could hear distant sirens.

Mark D. pulled the car in to the curb. There was a subway kiosk on the island between the north and southbound lanes. He did not look at Charles.

"I'm gonna split, man," he said. "It's time to split. This town's gonna be one hot fuckin' town in an hour."

"Too hot for you," muttered Charles. He stared at Mark D. with contempt.

"Gimme my piece," Mark D. said to Frank.

Frank handed it across into the front seat. Mark D. stuffed it into his belt under his shirt. He got out of the car.

Charles slid across into the driver's seat. The wheels squealed as he continued uptown. Mark D. watched them go, then went downstairs into the subway.

When Charles and Frank entered the apartment, they could smell pork chops frying. Charles walked over and turned on the TV.

"We's fixin' to eat," Ida said.

Charles ignored her. He sat staring at commercials. He was waiting for the news to come on.

The front door opened. In came Butch and two other men.

Butch walked up to Charles and gave him a slap handshake. "Congratulations, man. It's all over the radio. I mean *all* over." Butch was grinning.

Charles said: "Some backup car."

"We was there, man. We was close."

Charles took the submachine gun out of the laundry bag and hung it on a nail driven into the frame of the bathroom door.

Butch touched the submachine gun. He pretended it had burned his hand.

"That gun hot, man." Butch was laughing.

Frank grinned. "That grease so hot it smoking."

Charles had dumped the laundry bag out on the floor. He was picking through the laundry for his clips.

Paula, who had come out of the kitchen, stuffed the laundry back in the bag, and carried the bag into the bathroom.

Charles, the four clips lying beside him, sat staring at the TV.

The news came on. The Police Commissioner was interviewed. He was almost in tears. Then the Mayor was interviewed. The Mayor appeared very somber. He made a plea for gun control. There were views of the shattered police car, of the victims being carried on stretchers, and of cops weeping in the stationhouse.

All the men, grinning, came up to Charles and gave him a slap handshake. The expression on Charles's face did not change. He continued to stare at the TV.

Paula walked over and looked down at the clips on the bed. She rummaged among them until she found the clip that was empty.

She dropped the empty clip back onto the bed. She said to Charles: "I believe you done it."

"Shut up, sister," Charles said.

"There's thirty-two thousand of them," Paula said. "You fixin' to kill them all?"

Charles said nothing.

"I said, is you fixin' to kill them all?"

Charles only stared at the TV.

After a moment, the girl went into the kitchen and began frying more pork chops.

The news report had gone on to other subjects. Charles got up and switched the TV off. Then he lifted his submachine gun down off the nail. His face was without expression.

"Pork chops," said Paula, coming out of the kitchen with a plate of them. She set the plate on the table in the middle of the room. Everyone sat down to eat except Charles.

Charles sat on the bed and began cleaning his submachine gun.

2

THE Chief of Detectives, whose name was Earl Eis-chied, lay asleep on the leather sofa in his office in Police Headquarters. There came a timid tapping on his door.

Eischied sat up fast and, for a moment, couldn't remember where he was.

When the knock was repeated, Eischied growled: "What?"

A detective's head appeared in the doorway. "There's a Mr. Klopfman on the phone, Chief. He says you know him. He says it's personal and urgent."

Chief Eischied, rubbing his eyes, muttered: "Get his number."

"Right, Chief."

"No, wait a minute. Put him on."

Eischied barely remembered Klopfman, whom he had met at a dinner party some months before. A fat guy. Bald. Klopfman was chairman of the board and principal owner of one of the city's biggest department stores. That meant he was rich. Rich men could be useful. Therefore, the Chief of Detectives would talk to him.

On Eischied's desk stood three phones. One went directly to the Police Commissioner. One was Eischied's private wire. The third, which fed through headquarters switchboard, was equipped with buttons, one of which glowed. Beside this phone lay Eischied's gun in its clip-on holster. He rammed the gun into his belt, then grabbed up the phone and spoke: "Chief Eischied."

The words sounded like an accusation, and were meant to. An intimidated man was easier to deal with than one who imagined himself innocent. Eischied had been a policeman a long time.

"Oh, hello there, Chief. This is Myron Klopfman calling, and—"

Eischied, who prided himself on never forgetting the name of an important criminal, or an important citizen either, interrupted bluntly: "Do I know you?"

While Klopfman, a little too eagerly, was explaining when and how they had met, Eischied rummaged in his drawer for a cigar. Once the cigar was drawing properly, Eischied interrupted again: "So what can I do for you?"

"Well, you see, I have this son of mine. He's been taking treatment, but it hasn't been entirely successful yet, you know what I mean?"

"He's been arrested."

"You know about it?" asked the anguished father.

"I guessed."

"You guessed?"

"How many calls like this do you think I get?"

Klopfman, his voice husky, explained that his son had been arrested that morning for shoplifting.

"In your store?" interrupted Eischied.

"In another store."

Eischied almost laughed. When he was a younger man, and a younger detective, the aberrations of his fellow man had sometimes surprised, amazed, shocked, even pained him. Now they did not.

Eischied said bluntly: "You woke me out of a sound sleep."

"But it's almost noon."

"I was up half the night. We had two cops killed last night. It was front page in all the papers. I don't know if you noticed."

"Yes, a terrible thing. What can you do for my boy?"

Eischied had his feet up. He blew smoke rings at the ceiling. "Has the kid ever been arrested before?" This was always the first question to ask, and the answer was often a lie.

"I swear to God."

Eischied's gun was already digging into his abdomen. He pulled the package clear of his trousers and dropped it on his desk. "Give me the particulars."

As Klopfman spoke, Eishcied scribbled down details: time, place, kid's name, name of arresting officer. In his ear he could hear Klopfman's voice revert from supplicant back into businessman. It was as if Klopfman were reading numbers off an invoice.

"You got that detective's shield number?"

Klopfman did not. Eischied said: "I'll look into the case."

Klopfman said coolly: "It would be worth any amount to me if this thing could be taken care of."

There was a rather heavy silence.

"We're having a sale on suits this week," Klopfman said, "if you need a new suit. Why don't you come in and look them over?"

Eischied silently speculated. But he growled: "Did you ever hear about the laws of bribery?"

Klopfman said nothing. The businessman recognized an advantage when he held it. He neither retracted his offer nor apologized. He just let it hang there. At last he said: "Let me have your home number. I'll give you a call later tonight."

"I'll call you," said Eischied and hung up.

He buzzed immediately for his secretary. The detective who entered wore a red shirt, checked pants and a gun at his hip. He was a captain named Finnerty. He bossed Eischied's twenty-man office staff. Tearing the top page off his pad, Eischied thrust it at Captain Finnerty, saying: "Reach out for this Detective Smallwood for me. I want to talk to him. Get him in here."

Captain Finnerty stared down at the name. "Is this all you got on him, Chief? Do you know where he works or anything?"

Eischied, standing between his desk and his swivel chair, was forcing his holster and gun back inside his belt, but he paused to fix Finnerty with a baleful eye. "Somebody told me you were a detective."

"Yes, Chief."

"What detectives do is, they find guys."

"Yes, Chief."

"So you shouldn't have any trouble finding this Smallwood, should you?"

"No, Chief."

Chief Eischied might have instructed Finnerty to look in court, where Detective Smallwood no doubt still waited with his prisoner, Klopfman's son. But Eischied chose to say nothing. The less his staff knew about his business the better.

When Finnerty had gone out, Eischied dialed Criminal Records on his private phone. "See if you can get a make on this name. Kenneth Klopfman. I want to know if he's got a B number, and if he does, I want his sheet. Let me have the information as soon as possible. Have it hand carried up here in an envelope marked 'personal and confidential.' Got that?"

He did not want his staff intercepting this and connecting Detective Smallwood with the telephone call from Klopfman.

Hanging up, Eischied reached for the other phone again: "Finnerty, get my son on the line."

His cigar had gone out; he rolled it around his mouth. At last the secretary—a different detective this time—buzzed him: "Your son, Chief."

"Richie, how would you like me to buy you a birthday present? I'll send my car over to pick you up. About four P.M."

But the kid, who in two days would be sixteen, began to complain. At four o'clock he had a softball game with the guys.

Eischied, annoyed, said: "Tell them you've got to go out with me instead. How's your mother? Is your mother okay? Give her my regards." Without waiting for an answer, Eischied said: "Four o'clock," and hung up.

For a moment he remained standing behind his desk thinking: ungrateful little brat. Then he thought: at least he never got arrested for shoplifting.

The Chief of Detectives buzzed Captain Finnerty again: "Have my car brought around in front."

His in-basket was piled high with papers requiring his signature. Eischied was in direct command of three thousand detectives. Technically he was a three-star chief, one of four in the department. He reported directly to the four-star Chief Inspector, the highest ranking uniformed officer. On top of the Chief Inspector were the seven Deputy Commissioners, and the Commissioner himself, political appointees one and all.

Eischied began signing papers. Most were routine. He barely glanced at them: orders reassigning individual detectives from one squad to another; recommendations for promotion to second- or first-grade detective. There was also a request from the commander of the Police Academy for two detectives, one a burglary specialist, the other a homicide specialist, to be assigned there as lecturers for the duration of the next recruit class. Across this letter Eischied scrawled: "Find two guys for him." He slid it into his out-basket.

Eischied came to a pile of "reports of unusual occurrences"—brief synopses of yesterday's heavy crimes signed by whoever was in charge of each particular investigation. Eischied had no time to read them now. They went into his attaché case, where they reposed on top of the tools of his trade: his leather-covered sap, a box of .38-caliber bullets, a pair of handcuffs, a spare gun. These violent implements served to remind him each time he saw them of the nature of the business at which he made his living. He was an executive, not a street cop. He had not been involved personally in violence in twenty or more years. But this could change at any moment and he knew it.

Under his tools lay a thick file on revolutionary groups which he had ordered sent over from the intelligence division, and which he also had not yet had time to read.

The investigation into the machine-gunned cops was being directed at Eischied's orders out of the 24th Precinct stationhouse on West 100th Street. This was because the building was new. Many of the city's police stationhouses dated from the end of the last century and had switchboards to match.

Eischied had himself driven there. His unmarked car was a black Plymouth Fury. Unmarked it may have

been but every cop in the city, Eischied often reflected disgustedly, and also every criminal, recognized
it as a police car the moment they saw it. It lacked
decorative chrome, it was kept highly polished by
relays of detectives, and it bristled with radio aerials.
Aerials sprouted from three of its four fenders. Inside the car three mikes hung from the dashboard on
the passenger side, one for each of three frequencies:
citywide emergency, Detective Division, and the confidential band, a frequency restricted to the Police Commissioner, the Chief Inspector, the Chief of Detectives
and one or two other high commanders. Eischied's car
was assigned to him around the clock, as were the two
detectives who alternated as his chauffeurs.

The street in front of the West 100th Street stationhouse was crowded with citizens and also, Eischied
saw, with reporters and TV crews. His driver, Detective
Louie Malfitano, was not going to be able to approach
the curb.

"Put the siren on, Louie," Eischied ordered.

Siren wailing, the car nosed forward until its wheels
bumped the curb.

As Eischied climbed from the car, press and TV
crews converged upon him, pressing him against his
car. Cigar clamped between his teeth, looking neither
to right nor left, and preceded by Louie, who opened
the path, Eischied moved implacably toward the stationhouse steps. The reporters were all shouting.

"You got anything to tell us yet, Chief?"

"Give us a break, Chief."

Eischied went directly upstairs to the second floor,
where a number of offices gave off the squad room.
At the door to one of these waited Maloney, the two-
star chief of Manhattan North detectives, and a number
of lower-ranking detective commanders.

The big squad room itself was crowded with cops
and detectives. Some had been assigned to the investigation. Most were off duty but in their grief had turned
up and now waited there clamoring to be used. A cop
killing always brought more detectives and cops into

the stationhouse than commanders knew what to do with.

Eischied, entering the office, closed out the noise of the squad room.

"Whatta we got?" he demanded.

Inspector Gleason, head of the Major Crimes Squad, said gloomily: "Not much, Chief."

So Eischied glanced down at the detective in earphones who sat in front of the tape recorder in the corner. A special phone number had been printed in the papers, broadcast on all the stations. Tips from citizens, all of them tape-recorded on this machine, had been coming in all morning. Each conversation had been logged in a ledger, and now Eischied, thumbing back through the last three pages of the ledger, saw that most of the tips were as vague as always in cases of this kind.

So-and-so had a gun. So-and-so sells drugs. Nothing promising.

Teams of detectives would check out each tip. Perhaps one or another tip would lead to the machine gunner himself, but Eischied did not think so. He spun the book around and pushed it back toward the detective.

Why was he so pessimistic this time? he asked himself.

The only answer he could come to was not an answer at all: This one feels different.

Chief Maloney from Manhattan North said: "We typed up statements from the three so-called witnesses, got them to sign the statements, and we let them go home."

"Where are the statements?"

Inspector Gleason passed the statements across the desk. Eischied already knew what was in them for he had interrogated the witnesses before leaving here at dawn. All three witnesses claimed to have seen the getaway car speeding down Riverside Drive. Each, interrogated separately, had given a different make and model of the car. Two had called the car green, so maybe green was in fact its color. The third witness, an elderly widower walking his dog, had sworn that the car was red.

"The worst part," muttered Eischied, passing the statement back, "is that we're stuck with these descriptions in court. If we ever catch the son of a bitch with the machine gun, his lawyer will get him off on the grounds that all our witnesses contradict each other."

Chief Maloney pushed across the medical examiner's report, and the grisly photos that came with it. The photos showed the dead cops separately, lying on slabs in the morgue. Eischied looked down on the body of the twenty-two-year-old cop. The boy had lived till 4 A.M., meaning seven hours on the operating table. Once he died, they had washed all the blood off and sewn up all the incisions with what looked like fishing cord. The major incision was two and a half feet long, and had been loosely sewn with a single length of cord. It looked like someone had installed a zipper in the boy's body. The zipper started at his crotch and ended under his chin.

The other cop was somewhat older. He lay on the slab with his arms at his side and his eyes closed, and he looked like he was sleeping, except that his skin was too white. One of the bullets, Eischied noted, had torn away his penis. The others were in his armpits— in one side and out the other—and did not show.

Tears came to Eischied's eyes. These were not the first such photos he had looked at in his career, but they always moved him the same way. "We'll catch the sons of bitches," he muttered in a husky voice. He was making promises to photographs.

The other detectives glanced away while Eischied composed himself. After a moment, he said: "What has ballistics got to say?"

The ballistics report was passed to him, and he thumbed through it. Seventeen bullets had been recovered, some from trees, some from the bodies of the two dead cops. Most of the recovered bullets were so mutilated as to be useless for purposes of identification, but three contained clear markings and could be matched against bullets fired by this same machine gun, if it ever turned up.

"How come so few bullets are usable?" Eischied demanded.

Chief Maloney from Manhattan North said: "Most of them passed through the door of the car before they hit the cops."

The phone rang. The detective in earphones grabbed it, and the commanders fell silent. The tape recorder had turned itself on and the detective, hunched over his ledger, was questioning the citizen at the other end, and logging the call at the same time. The commanders, being unable to hear the citizen's voice, watched the spool turn, as if willing it to record the miracle they were hoping for.

When the detective had rung off they waited for him to speak but he had nothing momentous to say. They watched him complete the log entry. He did not even look up.

Presently Inspector Gleason said: "Ballistics did a good job. They were digging bullets out of trees all night. Some of those shots went through the car doors, through the guys and into the trees."

Eischied said: "I guess we're lucky no one else was killed but the two cops."

He picked up the ballistics report again. "Does this say what kind of gun it was?"

Inspector Gleason answered: "Their guess is a U.S. Army grease gun."

Again Eischied nodded. "Well, let's get to work. That gun is as good a place to start as any. Is Lieutenant McDonagh here?"

Lieutenant McDonagh was called in from the squad room. "Mac," Eischied said, "the gun is your job. You'll have to contact the Feds. Start with Alcohol, Tobacco and Firearms. Check the FBI. Check our own records." Eischied was thinking it out as he spoke. "How many men will you need to find that gun, or anything that could be that gun? Eight men? You'll have to check out of state. Maybe there are some states where it's legal to buy them. Does anybody remember any armories getting stuck up lately?" He glanced around the room, but no one answered. "Will eight men be enough? Start with eight men." Eischied did not believe that McDonagh could find the gun, not with eight men, not with fifty, but to tell him so would mean he wouldn't try hard. Giving him eight men would enhance his confidence. His lieutenant's rank was important too. It would ensure courteous treatment from the federal and state agencies he would have to contact.

When McDonagh had gone out, Eischied muttered: "That gun probably came from Vietnam. The city and the country are crawling with submachine guns and hand grenades and worse smuggled home from Vietnam. That war ruined us then and it's still ruining us."

Other jobs were apportioned. Two by two detectives were dispatched to investigate every person arrested by either of the two cops during the last six months—possibly the cops had been gunned down in settlement of a personal score, though Eischied did not think so. Detectives were sent down to the District Attorney's office to request wiretaps on certain known extremists. Eischied knew that most of these taps would be refused for technical, legal reasons, and that he would spend most of tomorrow with the D.A., pleading for them.

Every few minutes the phone rang, the tape recorder turned itself on and off, and the detective in headphones logged tips from citizens. Every few minutes the commanders called in a pair of detectives, briefed them and sent them out to check whichever phone tip had reached the top of the pile. Most addresses were in black ghettos and once, as a pair of detectives left bound for Harlem, Eischied commented: "Our guys are so uptight we'll be lucky if some law-abiding black citizen doesn't get shot before the week is out."

Citizens of the neighborhood of the assassination had been canvassed beginning about midnight, three hours late. Now Eischied arranged for the same area to be canvassed again tonight, at the exact hour of the crime, nine o'clock. The theory was that someone might have been on his way home from work or play just as the crime occurred; a detective might find the same person coming home at the same hour tonight, and that person might know something. Or perhaps someone passed by there only once a week at the same hour—meaning that a week from now the canvassing would be done again.

"If it's revolutionaries," Eischied said, "then we should be receiving a note. Those guys always brag about it afterward. There's got to be a note."

Eischied didn't know it, but this time there would be no note.

"Maybe it was a grudge hit," Eischied muttered. "Or maybe it was a maniac. At least if we get a message from them, we'll know a little better what we're looking for."

He felt a pervasive kind of hopelessness. He knew one felt this way nearly every time an investigation started. The perpetrator was out there in the world someplace and the detectives had no idea where to look. Normally the hopelessness disappeared as information came in, but this time he sensed it wasn't going to.

Stepping to the door, Eischied called for Louie, and when the chauffeur didn't appear, cried out: "Where's Detective Malfitano?"

Three other detectives hastened to locate the Chief's chauffeur.

Louie entered the office. "You wanted me, Chief?"

Eischied ordered a sandwich and coffee. The other commanders did too. Money fluttered to the desk top. Louie collected it all and went out.

While the commanders lunched, Eischied read to them out of the intelligence file. But when the names, dates and acronyms of past revolutionary groups piled up so fast that no one could keep them all straight, Eischied sent a detective for a blackboard. Once the blackboard was wheeled in, Eischied set his information down in columns: the SDS, the Weathermen, the Panthers. The gunning-down of cops was not new. The Weathermen were mostly white. The Panthers were black. The Armed Independence Revolutionary Movement was Puerto Rican. "Thank God we don't have Chicanos, Indians and Mexicans to contend with here," commented Eischied. He sipped his coffee. The Black Liberation Army had been broken up, its members killed or in jail. On the blackboard Eischied identified the FALN, the FURIA, the CAL. In an adjacent column he gave dates of birth and death of each extremist organization, where known.

"It could be any of these groups," he muttered. "Or none of them. It could be a new group. It could be a single deranged individual, but I don't think so. Probably it's a new movement growing out of an old one. That's the normal course of events. As each of these movements gets older it gets more talky and diffuse, more philosophic and less easy to understand. Violence is easy to understand. So the more violent dimwits in the group begin to break away and then they start killing cops."

Eischied wiped the chalk off his hands. The five commanders studied the blackboard, saying nothing. Chief Maloney took a big bite of his sandwich. Inspector Gleason pitched his empty coffee cup into the basket.

"It's all academic anyway, isn't it, Chief?" commented Gleason.

What could Eischied answer to that?

Gleason was not interested in theory, much less in philosophy. To him this case was a cop-killing case. The information on the blackboard provided no addresses; the address of the killer was all Gleason wanted to know, not the killer's ideology.

Gleason stared at his fingernails. He was Eischied's age but had white hair and a big red beacon of a nose. Gleason was a street cop grown heavy with rank. A case like this he was not likely to understand, but most other commanders were just like him, and it was his squad.

Eischied asked: "How many black detectives are still waiting out there in the squad room?"

"About fifteen, Chief."

23

"Let's spread them out over the various black neighborhoods," ordered Eischied. "Tell them just to hang around, ask questions." Unfortunately, fifteen wouldn't spread very far.

There came a knock on the door, and the precinct captain in uniform stuck his head in: "The press guys are driving us crazy, Chief. They want to know if you're going to make a statement."

Eischied followed the precinct captain downstairs. As they stepped out the door of the stationhouse, the press converged on Eischied, and he could hear the cameras begin turning. Questions came from all sides.

"The investigation is proceeding," Eischied began.

"Any leads, Chief?"

There were none. Had there been any, now was not the time to admit them anyway. The assassins might still be in the city. They also might have reached Ohio by now, or California. A good detective admitted nothing that might alarm them. At the same time the city—plus more than thirty thousand frightened cops—had to be reassured.

Eischied, looking somber, declared: "We have one or two leads that look promising. I can't announce more than that at this time. Let me repeat again the special telephone number. Detectives are standing by around the clock to take any tips that any concerned citizen might phone in. All information will be kept confidential. No one has to give his name."

"How many detectives are working on the case, Chief?"

Eischied growled: "A lot," and his face hardened, and he moved dangerously forward through the mob toward his car. The cameras tracked him all the way.

Detective Malfitano, who saw him coming, had the engine already running. "Let's get out of here, Louie," Eischied ordered.

"Where to, Chief?"

Thirty minutes later Eischied and his son were thumbing through racks of suits at Klopfman's department store. At the cash desk the Chief of Detectives said to the clerk: "Please inform Mr. Klopfman that Mr. Eischied is in the building."

He waited while the connection was made.

"Mr. Klopfman would like a word with you, sir."

Klopfman's eager voice came on the line: "Do you have some news for me, Chief?"

Eischied said gruffly: "I've got nothing for you. I've been tied up on the cop killings all day. When I have something I'll let you know. I'm here to buy my son a new suit."

"By all means, Chief. Pick out anything you like. Put the clerk back on the line. I'll explain it to him. Get one for yourself while you're in the store."

There was silence while Eischied digested the new fact: A phone call to the Chief of Detectives was expected to be expensive.

"All you do is sign the sales slip, Chief. Put the clerk back on."

"I sign nothing."

Klopfman became effusively apologetic: "Sorry, Chief, I didn't mean—"

Eischied handed the phone to the sales clerk: "The boss wants to speak to you."

Outside on the sidewalk in front of Klopfman's store, Eischied shook hands with and dismissed his son: "Give your mother my kind regards. I may not see you before your birthday, but you know I'm thinking of you."

As the Chief of Detectives' car sped down the East River Drive toward headquarters, Eischied had his attaché case open on his lap. He was leafing through the intelligence reports, some of them five years old, on revolutionaries. But I thought we broke that last gang up, he brooded. Was the whole thing starting up again?

As Eischied entered his office, Captain Finnerty said: "Detective Smallwood has been waiting here to see you all day." Finnerty also handed over a sealed envelope.

For a moment Eischied couldn't remember who Smallwood was, but when he had torn open the envelope and glanced down at its contents, he remembered. He was looking at the yellow sheet of Kenneth

Klopfman. The kid had been arrested twice before, both times for shoplifting. The dates, places and names of the arresting officer were given.

Eischied reflected: The next time somebody pulls this kid's sheet there will be a third arrest on it, and the arresting officer will be Detective Smallwood.

Eischied wondered who the kid's father had bought off the last two times, and also why the kid didn't shoplift in his father's place. It would make it so much easier for everyone.

"And the Commissioner wanted to see you as soon as you got back, Chief," Captain Finnerty added.

Across the room, Smallwood had risen to his feet. Tough-looking guy, Eischied saw. Unshaven. Wore a sports shirt and a baggy cardigan sweater that was unbuttoned. In Harlem they would make him as a detective immediately. To other people he might look like a retired fighter. In response to a mysterious summons from the Chief of Detectives' office he had now been waiting five hours. This often happened to detectives. Detectives were paid to wait.

Eischied looked across at him. "Come inside, Smallwood."

The detective followed Eischied into Eischied's inner office.

"Sit down, Smallwood."

Smallwood, who would probably have walked coolly into a gun battle, no longer looked like a tough guy. He looked extremely nervous. What had he done wrong to be called in here?

"Where did my guy finally find you today?" asked Eischied pleasantly, though he knew.

"I was in court with a prisoner."

"Something heavy?"

As if making idle conversation, the Chief of Detectives interrogated Smallwood. Smallwood had been in a department store trying to buy his wife a birthday present. He could hardly believe his eyes when the young thief, Kenneth Klopfman, began stuffing goods in his pockets. So he had made the off-duty arrest.

"The kid's a klepto, Chief."

Eischied nodded. "Good work. You've been doing a good job for me all along, Smallwood. What do you know about revolutionaries?"

"Black, Chief?"

"Black or white."

"I've always worked in burglary, Chief."

Klopfman could be expected to defend his kid with high-priced lawyers. There would be a number of pre-trial hearings. If the arresting officer—Detective Smallwood—failed to show up once or several times (because the Chief of Detectives had him busy on something else) then the judge could be relied upon to dismiss the case. The fine hand of the Chief of Detectives would be visible to no one.

"I want you to work on last night's killings. I'll have you reassigned to Inspector Gleason."

Eischied showed Smallwood to the door. "Sorry you had to wait around so long," Eischied said genially, patting the surprised detective on the back. To Captain Finnerty, Eischied called: "Ask if the PC can see me now."

The Police Commissioner in shirt sleeves came out from behind his big desk, and Eischied handed him copies of orders relating to the so-called inspectors' funerals for the two slain cops.

"I don't imagine you've seen these yet, Commissioner. They've just been cut."

The PC, scanning the orders, said: "I guess the funerals will be pretty big, Earl."

"The first one's tomorrow, Commissioner. The second one's the next day."

Very little police business would be conducted until the funerals ended. About five thousand New York cops had been assigned to attend each of them. Cops would fill the streets in front of the churches in both directions both days. The entire police hierarchy would stand out front, of course, plus the Mayor, plus most city politicians and some national ones. Units would attend representing about twenty other police departments from states as distant as Pennsylvania.

Eischied pictured the scene: the five thousand white

gloves flashing in salute as the coffin was carried into the church; the chilling notes of taps played by the department bugler.

Eischied saw all the police brass frozen in salute in front of the church door, and he thought: If it's revolutionaries, that's the time they ought to hit us. In a few seconds they could decapitate the Police Department. He heard the rattle of their guns and visualized the carnage in too rich detail. How many commanders could be cut down? There would be no one standing to organize pursuit, much less an investigation afterward.

"I'm seeing the Mayor in an hour, Earl."

Some of the five thousand cops would be killed too. The rest would have their guns out. It would be tough for the revolutionaries to get away. But in the confusion they might manage it.

Of course he didn't know if it was revolutionaries or not. But he decided he would put detectives on the rooftops; he would order the Bomb Squad to make sweeps of the churches an hour before each funeral.

Eischied wasn't really worried. With five thousand guns in the street, no one would have the balls. Would they?

"So, what do I tell the Mayor, Earl?"

Eischied thought: Tell him we're looking for a guy with a machine gun. But we don't know who we're looking for or where to look. The guy might have ditched the machine gun by now. He might not even be in the city anymore.

"So how is the investigation going so far?"

"Not good, Commissioner. Not good."

3

EVERETT WALKER was attired as always in recent years in an impeccable white caftan. His bright scarlet fez had not been faded by sun or by sweat either, and that was rare in this country. But the official behind the desk wore an ill-fitting and rather shiny European business suit. Most government officials Walker had dealt with had Persian carpets on the floors: this one's floor was bare.

Walker's years in exile had made him acutely sensitive to political nuance, though any fool could read the nuances here. The Arab across the desk, whose name was Abbas, did not even speak French, only Arabic, and an interpreter had to be sent for.

Walker had learned some French. "So how's your revolution going?" he inquired. He kept his voice bright, though it was an effort for him. In politics one began with small talk.

The interpreter said: "Monsieur Abbas notes that as president of your liberation movement you are a busy man, and he asks in what way he might help you."

Walker had brought his own interpreter, who was a twenty-three-year-old Dutch girl. Some weeks before she had asked him for an interview, claiming she was a journalist. Though she may have read his book, she was no journalist. All she was was a girl with a gorgeous body, a pretty face and a desire to experience everything.

But she did speak fluent English and French.

Walker said: "Tell him I'm holding a reception today to celebrate the opening of my new embassy. Tell him I have not yet received a reply from his government, and that I dropped in to ascertain the number of persons in his government's delegation who can be expected to attend."

It was quite a formal speech, and Walker waited while it was translated into French by the Dutch girl, and then into Arabic by the government interpreter. Then he waited again while the answer came back.

The Dutch girl sounded puzzled: "He says that it won't be possible for any government minister to accept your generous invitation because of the press of government business."

Walker must have been expecting this reply, for he attempted to give no reaction at all. Then he attempted a smile. For a moment all his teeth showed.

The Arab behind the desk seemed to become frightened immediately. Walker noted this. It proved he had that much power and reputation left at least.

Walker had a mild speaking voice. It was only in his speeches and his writing that the impact of the man came through. It was his reputation, not his voice, that was violent. He said: "Tell him I expect many gentlemen from the press."

Monsieur Abbas began to stammer in Arabic, but when translated his answer was adamant: "He says his government regrets the impossibility of accepting your most generous invitation," said the Dutch girl. She glanced at Walker in confusion.

Walker saw that he shouldn't have brought her. She —and previous girls like her—were props. They went with the grandiose role into which the world had forced him. Her presence these last few weeks had kept him sane. He did not wish to lose her because without her his days were empty, if not his life. There was no one and nothing else.

But now she would see him as powerless—as a mere supplicant. She would leave him for a film star or a bullfighter.

Walker slammed his palm down on the desk. "I wish to see Monsieur Habib." Habib was the highest official to whom Walker had ever had ready access.

"He says that he regrets it very much, but Monsieur Habib has been transferred to other duties."

"I will agree to see Muhammad Jamal."

"He says he regrets—"

With forced smile fixed in place, Abbas came around in front of his desk, hand outstretched. The hand was trembling.

Walker, who had regained control of himself, began the following speech. "Tell him the funds that his government provides are not sufficient. If an increase is not forthcoming, I may be obliged to denounce his government to the revolutionary peoples of the world. Tell him that I may even be obliged to move my seat of government to some other country."

Walker's voice was mild, but his black eyes never left the face of the little Arab, who seemed to become increasingly frightened. The Dutch girl kept glancing from the Arab to Walker and back again. Her pretty young face kept changing: surprise, disbelief. She saw clearly what Walker had realized for some time, and had sought to change. This government was tired of him. He had become an embarrassment. Walker was aware of her reactions.

The answer came back: "He says that you are at liberty to depart of course. But he fears no other country will accept you."

"Tell him I have no time for stupid men."

Walker strode out of the office, feeling empty, almost nauseated, but hoping that his departure had dignity. Behind him, the Arab gave a stiff formal bow to Walker's departing caftan.

Walker's "embassy" was a villa in a tacky seaside suburb. It was jammed in among other villas, each surrounded by high stone walls.

When he had first arrived in North Africa, Walker had been given half a floor in the downtown Grand Hotel. Government ministers had paid courtesy calls. Government press officers had led foreign journalists to his doors. His pronouncements had been front-page news in many parts of the world.

Later Walker's trips to North Korea, North Vietnam and Black Africa made headlines too. His speeches opposed colonialism, military imperialism.

But this afternoon's reception drew only thirteen people, including interpreters. There was a huge fat black man from the Angola Liberation Front, and a Basque separatist. There was a man from Kurdistan, and a man from the Chinese Embassy who smiled all the time. The thirteenth guest was a tall man of about thirty, obviously American—press, or CIA, maybe both. Walker, waiting to be approached for an interview, watched him covertly. At length Walker sent the Dutch girl over to find out—then for the next twenty minutes watched both of them covertly while moving among his guests, shaking hands, toasting revolutionary movements with glasses of orange juice and soft drinks —this was a Muslim country after all.

The words scarcely required translation.

"How's your revolution going, brother?"

"Excellently, brother, and yours?"

Has my force degenerated to this? Walker asked himself.

The revolutions of some of these men had further to go than Walker's, he tried to tell himself. Some had been in exile longer than he. None had been in jail more years than he, though.

After a time, unable to stay aloof any longer, Walker drifted over to the Dutch girl and the American, who introduced himself as a journalist based in Paris.

Walker gave a stiff, formal bow. He had learned that this was the best way to greet journalists. Political figures must allow no familiarity between themselves and a man like this, who was a mere scribe.

Walker waited to be interviewed.

The journalist—if he was a journalist—broke off his animated conversation with the Dutch girl and said: "I was in North Africa on another story, and heard about your reception. I thought you might have a statement you might care to make."

"See me after my guests leave," Walker said, nodding politely as he strode away.

The interview began as soon as the reception ended. They sat on two straight-back chairs set up on the stone-hard floor of Walker's little garden, in which nothing grew, not even weeds. The journalist produced some press clippings.

"There were two cops assassinated in New York last week. I wonder what you have to say about that."

Walker unfolded the clippings. He took in the photos: a riddled radio car, the police hierarchy lined up outside the church for the funeral of one of the slain oppressors. He felt elation—the revolution goes on— followed by anger—the revolutionary act had been bungled; according to the press clippings no note from the revoluionaries had even claimed credit. No political point had been made.

The journalist said: "There had been no attacks on the police for several years. Is this an isolated case, or is it starting up again?"

Walker in his mild voice spoke historical truth: "Historically all revolutions have always attacked the police as armed agents of the oppressors. As far as the so-called land of the free is concerned, the protests and demonstrations have again exhausted themselves. There is again nothing to do but escalate the violence."

The journalist said: "You've been here in Africa many years now. I was wondering if you might have re-evaluated your positon."

"There is nothing to re-evaluate except the choice of weapons."

The journalist's response—he was noting down every word—was quite satisfactory. So was his intensity. But Walker was wondering which group had assassinated the policemen. Was it men he knew? And why had no credit been claimed?

Eying Walker like an artist sketching his subject, the reporter noted down Walker's bushy black beard, the combat boots under the caftan, the single gold earring.

The reporter gestured toward the news clippings in Walker's hands and said: "Do you condone that kind of thing?"

Walker studied him. "The execution of policemen?"

"The killing of cops, yes."

Walker said thoughtfully: "Before I answer your question, let me ask you one." He paused, then said: "Did you ever go to see any of those old war movies?"

"Which war?"

"The war I had in mind," said Walker thoughtfully, "was World War Two."

"Sure. What's your point?"

"Let me describe a typical scene from one of the movies I had in mind. This Gestapo dude is on guard at night. It's dark, but you can see his uniform and his face. He's just some young dude. He's just standing there probably daydreaming about home or screwing his girl friend. All of a sudden this resistance fighter sneaks up behind him, throws a wire over his head and garrotes him."

"Get to the point." But the reporter's brow had darkened and it was clear he saw the point in advance.

"Do you condone that?" asked Walker.

"Gestapo? Sure."

Walker nodded thoughtfully. "Every time I ever saw such a movie scene, the audience condoned that. They applauded. Shit, usually they cheered." Walker glanced down at the clippings in his hand. "I wonder if you could tell me what's the difference between that scene and this one." He waved the clippings.

"Oh, come on," snorted the reporter. "America is not Nazi Germany. A New York cop is not the Gestapo."

"That depends on a man's point of view, doesn't it?" said Walker in his quiet voice. "Or at least that's the way it does seem to many people."

The reporter looked angry. Walker showed no emotion. They stared at each other.

"Sometimes," said Walker mildly, "a man's point of view depends mostly on what color that man is. If you are the wrong color all cops look like the Gestapo to a man."

The reporter, forcing himself to remain calm, said: "The reason one could condone an act of violence against the Gestapo, would be because violence—

murder if you will—was the only way to combat a police state."

"Yes, that's right," said Walker mildly. "I'm so glad you see it so clearly."

"America is not a police state."

"Not for some people, no."

They stared at each other.

Presently the reporter said coolly: "That caftan you sport is more usual in the eastern Mediterranean, and you're not an Arab anyway. So I was wondering why you wear it?"

"My garb?" said Walker. "My garb is not important."

The reporter said: "Then why do you wear it?"

"A revolutionary movement calls for unity," said Walker. He gripped a hank of skirt in his fist. "This garb is a way of showing unity with the revolutionary peoples of the Third World."

The reporter decided to goad Walker further. "Whatever happens in America, you're out of it. You're stuck here. You're a fugitive from justice. You can't move. You can't go back."

After staring the man down Walker said: "Given modern communications, I can direct the movement from here."

But he was unable to keep the wistful quality out of his voice, so that the reporter thought: Everett Walker was once the most dangerous of all the revolutionaries, because he had brains and he had eloquence. But this man here is a shell.

"Direct those cop killings the other night?"

Walker said nothing.

The reporter and Walker stared at each other. Then Walker gazed again at the clippings in his lap, clippings that filled him with a kind of homesickness he had not expected. The rich, heady action of the streets came back to him. The response of the populace. His people had needed him once, and still did. But he needed them, too. For every man needed someone to love, plus some cause to give his life meaning, and what was there for him here? What was there for him anywhere, except amidst the people he had come from? At one time in his own country there had been many leaders, himself among them, but the police had gunned down some and jailed others, often on trumped-up charges. Malcolm and even Martin, who was only an Uncle Tom basically, had been assassinated, until he himself had been almost the only leader left standing. The oppressors had zeroed in on him. The revolution was in tatters by then. To save his freedom of action (and probably his life; he had fled into exile, abandoning what was left of the movement to the thugs and killers who inhabit the fringes of any such movement and who are necessary, but who, being without politics, must be controlled.

Alive, though four thousand miles away, he could still be of some use, Walker had convinced himself. Dead or jailed he could help no one. He would wait only until the right moment came to return. But there had been no right moment in the years so far, and he suspected now there would never be. His only chance was to pick a certain moment—any moment—now, for instance—and somehow turn it into the right one.

He had read a great deal in prison and even more in exile. Ho, Mao, Castro, Ben Bella, Bourguiba—even De Gaulle—they had all been not only out of power but even like himself in jail. But they had had a constituency calling them back, and he was no longer sure he did. The American imperialism was the most insidious imperialism of all, because it was so hedonistic. It was so seductive. There was intellectual space inside Islam, even inside Communism, but in the urban ghettos of America only the flashy car, the quick deal counted. Walker's natural constituency, he feared, had already seen too much of the good life, and there was no intellectuality left there. His was a revolution without a constituency, and he didn't see what he could do about it. De Gaulle could go home to the French. He himself could go home only to a bunch of shiftless— His mind refused to complete the thought.

It was the children who needed him most, he reflected. Without him—or someone like him—they would grow up in their turn with swollen bellies and shrunken minds for generation upon generation to come.

"What motivates you, anyway?" said the reporter. "That's what I'd like to know."

"I don't think that's something we could talk about in any way that you could understand," said Walker.

"Oh for chrissake." The reporter decided to rephrase his question. "There are some people," he said, "who say you are nothing but an ex-convict twice convicted of armed robbery."

"Once that might have been an accurate statement," said Walker. "I was into stickups for their own sake. I was young and not politically astute at that time. I related to ripping off drugstores and supermarkets for its own sake."

"And served two sentences totaling nine years for it."

"And became educated," amended Walker.

"So what motivates you?"

"Let me ask you a question first. In the house where you grew up, did you ever see rats scurrying about your hallways? What city was it that you grew up in?"

"Greenwich, Connecticut," said the reporter.

"In Detroit we had rats in the downstairs hallway. Sometimes the upstairs hallway, too."

"Call the exterminator."

"I did that once," said Walker. "I acquired the funds to pay him from a drugstore. But he didn't kill the rats. That man just ripped us off."

The reporter laughed. "There's no justice in the world, is there?"

"What I'm talking about is human dignity," said Walker coolly. "Did you ever go down into your cellar in Greenwich, Connecticut, because it was winter and the boiler hadn't worked in three days and nobody knew how to find the landlord, carrying a candle because there was no electricity down there, and crunching across the backs of cockroaches all the way to the boiler and finding it froze up solid?"

"Now you're talking bullshit," said the reporter.

Walker studied the top of the wall surrounding what was his current prison. "The people I come from are so poor, and life is such a struggle for them, that they don't realize that without dignity life just isn't worth living. Their lack of dignity is a crime, wouldn't you say?"

"That business about the cockroaches is bullshit."

Walker was under no illusions. This journalist here could be counted on to mock and ridicule any statement Walker might make, Walker saw. The article, if it got printed at all, would make Walker out to be both a loser and a fool.

So Walker, bringing the interview to an abrupt end, sprang to his feet and entered the house through the garden door.

But the reporter, who was very skilled, followed. Walker's combat boots echoed through the house.

"You had a big thing going here with deserters and draft evaders during the war. It was almost an underground railroad. You sent them to Sweden and all over. But that war ended some time ago, so what do you do with yourself these days?"

Walker said nothing. He began looking into empty rooms. The reporter saw that two of the bedrooms contained one bed each; there were altogether three tables in the house, plus a number of straight chairs. Walker's mimeograph machine looked broken, as if it had not been used in years. In one room stood only two cardboard suitcases, two cartons of books and a typewriter.

"The royalties from your writings have been blocked by the U.S. government, as I understand it. Where does your money come from?"

The reporter waited for an answer.

Abruptly Walker's repressed rage exploded, and he began to denounce his hosts, their government and its ministers. Though former revolutionaries themselves, they had become fat and complacent, Walker said savagely. Arabs were untrustworthy, and had bilious yellow eyes. A new functionary class had sprung up here. The bureaucracy here was as stupid and inept as in Babylon—meaning America—itself.

When the reporter had gone, Everett Walker in his flowing robes went out into the streets. One or two neighbors saluted him, but he did not salute back. At the sea front he stood above steps that led down to a beach. For a long time he stood there staring at the sea. The sea seemed to him as empty as his life had become, and in his frustration he aimed a kick at the low stone and mortar balustrade at his feet. His combat boot stung the stones. Nearby, facing out to sea, was a bench. Grabbing it up, Walker swung it against the wall. The bench began to disintegrate, but the former stickup man, ex-convict and revolutionary kept swinging it until he had destroyed the bench, and a portion of the wall as well.

When Walker got back to his house, the Dutch girl was gone, leaving behind only a note. The note said she was tired of North Africa, and that she would try Torremolinos next.

In his hotel room the reporter was typing. His principal assignment here had been the Palestinians. That was the key revolutionary group now. The interview with Everett Walker had been an afterthought. But the article was working out well, he saw. The reporter had decided to slant it to show the son of a bitch bad-mouthing the government that supported him. They own that guy now, the reporter thought, as he typed. They put the food on his table and he can't make a move without their permission.

Chuckling, the reporter thought as he typed: There'll be hell to pay when the politicians here read what Walker said about them. Bilious yellow eyes. They'll cut off his funds, if not his balls. The bastard will starve to death.

In America a few years ago, the reporter remembered, all the papers took this guy seriously. His own paper and a few of the others built Walker up into a personage, and the word came down from the editors: kid gloves. But the kid-glove treatment was no longer required. Walker was now a has-been, and therefore fair game. He's like a comedian whose jokes have gone stale, the reporter thought. He's like a singer who's lost his voice. He's like a movie star whose tits have dropped. Screw him.

The reporter considered himself a studious, serious individual. The Arabs might kick Walker out, but they couldn't ship him back to America. Walker was under about six indictments. If he ever went back to America, they'd put him away for life. They'd reinstate capital punishment just for him.

The reporter thought: I wonder what the Arabs will do to Walker when my piece comes out?

After twelve days under guard in a remote village, Everett Walker was put aboard an Air Afrique flight to Havana, with intermediate stops at Casablanca and Caracas. With him was a Vietnam deserter whose name was Ulysses Brown, and who was the last of the band that had once surrounded him. The two were alone in first class, which was blocked off from the rest of the plane. "This is reminiscent to me of Lenin, crossing Germany in a sealed box car in 1917," said Walker to Brown. Walker could see the humor in it, or thought he could.

"Who's Lenin?" said Brown.

Who's Lenin? thought Walker bleakly. And this man Brown is, for the moment, my only disciple.

"Someone you might emulate," said Walker.

Brown is both a symptom and a result of the disease that afflicts my people. Walker brooded. I both love him for the injustice he has suffered, and hate him for his stupidity. The one political act of his life so far he committed without even knowing it was political.

But I expect too much, Walker brooded. Poverty destroys intellect, and for the poor there is no couch on which to make themselves whole. The thing I hate is that men like Brown become just what they are described as, self-reinforcing stereotypes. It isn't Brown's fault.

I love him, Walker brooded. He is my brother.

Though tourist-class passengers got on and off at

both intermediate stops, Walker and Brown were not disturbed. Brown managed to beg a bottle of champagne off one of the stewardesses, but Walker refused it. There was nothing to celebrate yet. Who's Lenin? Walker thought. Lenin was another who had had a constituency to return to.

The mohair bristles at Walker's back felt as unfriendly as the barely remembered whiskers of his father. From his briefcase Walker withdrew a yellow legal pad, on which he began to write down words.

Liberation
Violence
Army
Guns

Havana was this plane's destination, but not Walker's; he did not mean to stop there long. America had been born in violence; its rebirth would be more violent still.

Oppression
Slavery
Blood

America had known one revolution. He would show it now another. The first revolution had begun in Boston. This one would begin in New York.

He was trying to think up an acronym for his revolution. Acronyms were the tunes that modern armies marched to. The day of Yankee Doddle was over.

His movement must be called by a single word which would provoke terror each time it was heard. Walker was able to imagine several suitable acronyms: dread, revolt, arise, rage. But most had been used before, and he needed something new. What about fear? Yes, FEAR. A capable word. He drew it the length of the pad in bold capitals. The choice pleased him. The letters could stand for: the Freedom and Equality Army of Revolution.

He glanced at his watch. How much longer before this flight landed? And how would the Cubans treat him?

A revolution depended on guns, yes, he told Brown beside him. But also on words, because words mobilized minds. For every past revolution which had succeeded, holding mastery of guns and words both, a hundred others, lacking one or the other, had failed.

This was historically true, said Walker; every past revolutionary had recognized it.

"An unarmed man is a eunuch," said Walker to Brown, "but so is one who cannot speak."

But in the next seat Brown, with half a bottle of champagne inside him, had begun daydreaming about New York.

Walker, staring at his acronym, decided that he needed five men to start, more later of course, when cadres must be set up in many cities. Brown would be a good man, he was sure. To Brown he said: "Five men will be enough to administer the first harsh dose. Five will be enough to force the cathartic down the patient's throat. The medicine will be administered from the end of gun barrels. The body politic will shit blood."

Walker was bored and was perhaps practicing an essay or a speech.

Gulping champagne, Brown remained in his reverie. City buses floated by light as butterflies, and more blue. Girls strode the sidewalks wearing T-shirts and no bras, like in the magazines. He would lose this crazy dude beside him and . . .

The injustice and oppression of America were obvious to all, Walker brooded, but the fabric of American society was different, and called for a different revolution. America was not Cuba, nor China. Walker's revolution could not begin secretly in the mountains of some remote eastern province, nor could he hope to rally agrarian peasants. America was an urban society, and so there was no hope for any revolution that did not speak for the downtrodden masses of the cities. In addition, America suffered from over-communication —it swarmed with noise. The first job of any revolutionary, therefore, was to make himself heard over the rest of that noise, and Walker must do this in the cities. In one city. In New York.

From his billfold Walker extracted the now-tattered

news clippings pertaining to the funerals of the two machine-gunned policemen, and as he stared at these photos, an idea took root in his brain. There the mourners all stood in a row, the principal murderers of Babylon, and a good many politicians too, and no revolutionary leader in history could beg for a neater target than that. Suddenly Walker could hear the gunfire. He saw chiefs and commissioners falling.

When the seat-belt sign flashed, Walker obediently strapped himself in; he was often an obedient man.

Walker refolded the clippings, but went on considering his plan. It was of such calculated outrage that it would be heard around the world. Walker could think of no single act committed by Lenin, Mao, Fidel or any of the others that could match it. That one act by Walker would provoke uprisings by oppressed ghetto poor in many parts of the nation, or at least one could hope so. From there the revolution would enter its spontaneous phase.

The air got bumpy. They were flying through bad weather.

A war chest would have to be put together first. The place to collect money was from banks. The capitalist oppressor must be struck where he's most vulnerable, at the very roots of his system. Every modern revolutionary thinker has always preached that, Walker brooded. Hit the banks first.

To Brown, Walker said: "Tonight we stand ready to enter a new world."

Brown, who had begun swilling his champagne directly from the bottle, said: "Go, man, go."

For the rest of the flight, Everett Walker stared silently out the dark porthole. He would have to persuade the Cubans to put him ashore in Florida.

When the no smoking sign flashed, he obediently stubbed out his cigarette.

At Havana the plane door was thrown open. The night was hot. He breathed in the tropical air. To Brown he said: "Across the water is Florida, and beyond that—New York."

Brown said: "Gonna get me a woman first thing."

Walker, stepping down to the tarmac, sniffed the sultry night. He was almost home.

4

OFTEN you could judge how heavy the crime was by counting how many radio cars it had drawn. Eischied noted five empty cars double-parked in the street, plus the truck from Forensic. Which meant big. The fact that Eischied himself had come also made it big.

It was 7 A.M., and the unshaven Eischied went in past the neighbors who crowded the hall, past the uniformed cop who guarded the apartment door. The body was lying on its back in the front hall. The door, swinging closed behind Eischied, nearly brushed the feet.

In their bathrobes in the hallway, craning their necks, the neighbors had caught a glimpse of the corpse during the brief moment that the door was open. Eischied had heard the gasp go up.

There was no similar reaction from Eischied, to whom murdered corpses were normal. He gave this one a glance, registering all he needed to know about it at this point, and stepped over it. His mind had recorded immediate details in the same form that the official police report would later take: the body was that of a thirty-year-old white male wearing tan Levi's, suede loafers, and a pale blue open-necked shirt that had been unbuttoned all the way down, disclosing the knife wound in the solar plexus that had presumably killed him. The hole to Eischied resembled the punctures his wife used to make in the leg of a lamb to shove the garlic in, though no doubt this one was deeper—as deep as the man's backbone, probably. The hole was about the size and shape of a plum pit, and filled with blood up to the top. There was no other blood on the guy. His hands were practically transparent, waxy looking. Eischied had been routed from sleep by his duty sergeant's phone call, and briefed—the duty sergeant had only sketchy information. So Eischied had known an hour ago that the victim was dead, but he read confirmation now from the swarms of cops and detectives crowding the apartment, from the corpse's open, staring eyes, from the stab hole in the solar plexus. Without even realizing it, he took his principal confirmation from those transparent hands. There was no blood left in them. They looked as if there was nothing under the skin but water. That was the true look of death. All the rest could be faked by a movie director and his makeup men, but not the look of a murdered man's hands.

It took Eischied a moment to orient himself. Three rooms led off this foyer in which the corpse lay: living room, kitchen, bedroom. There were fifteen or twenty cops and detectives in the living room, and another fifteen or twenty in the bedroom. The kitchen was empty except for Inspector Gleason, head of the Major Crime Squad, who was on the phone there.

A voice said: "Would you mind stepping out of the way, Chief?"

Eischied glanced behind him at the police photographer, who had set up his tripod there.

Eischied stepped into the kitchen, and as he did so Inspector Gleason hung up the phone.

"Let me set the scene for you, Chief," Gleason said. Gleason wore his shield pinned to the lapel of his raincoat, and held his notebook opened in his hand. He lived nearby and had probably been here an hour already. "In the middle of the night, there were four people in this apartment, but not the two victims. This apartment belongs to one Joanne Cooper. You may remember that name, Chief. She was the girl friend of one Tommy Zumbo. One Tommy Zumbo was a real bad hood. He was machine-gunned to death in the lobby of this building three years ago. No perpetrator was ever found. The guy was literally riddled with bullets, and this was his girl friend."

"What's Tommy Zumbo got to do with it?" demanded Eischied. "Tommy Zumbo's dead."

"I'm just setting the scene for you, Chief. Tommy Zumbo gave this girl Cooper a kind of switchblade knife as long as your arm and as sharp as a stiletto. He gave her a whole set of cutlery apparently. The knife I'm referring to is good for nothing but killing someone with. There's the knife, Chief."

The knife lay on a piece of newspaper on the sideboard.

Eischied gestured toward the corpse in the entrance hallway. "Did you pull it out of the guy, or what?"

"No, Chief. When the first radio car team got here, this girl Cooper, this gang moll or whatever she is, whips it out of her underpants and hands it to them."

Chief Eischied nodded. So far he had neither seen nor heard anything that was in any way unusual. "Who's the second victim?" he asked.

"His name is Vinci. He's a known gambler. I've already run a check on him. He has twelve previous KG arrests, bookmaking, policy. He also was a friend of Tommy Zumbo. Tommy Zumbo once beat the shit out of him, as a matter of fact."

"Will you for crissake forget about Tommy Zumbo? Tommy Zumbo's been dead three years."

"Right, Chief. Well, this moll, Joanne Cooper, and this known gambler Vinci are boy friend and girl friend. Vinci is also supposed to be a loan shark and an extortionist, by the way."

Eischied was trying to keep it all clear in his head. Why could detectives never tell a story straight?

Gleason said: "Well, Chief, in this apartment in the middle of the night are four people: this Joanne Cooper, aged thirty; her girl friend Donna, also thirty, who is an airline stewardess; and two guys. One guy is named Genovese. He may be related to the organized-crime family of the same name. We're trying to check that out now, Chief. The other guy's name is supposed to be Rodger. That's all we got so far, Rodger. So at first there were four people in here, the two girls, Genovese and this Rodger. Then about four or five A.M. in come two more guys, the two victims, this man Vinci, who's on the critical list with a punctured lung, and that poor bastard on the floor there, Donald Dixon, the off-duty cop."

This was why he had come. In a low voice, Eischied said: "Tell me about the cop."

"He did a four-to-twelve, Chief. He's a scooter patrolman in the 19th Precinct. He lives on the third floor in this building." Inspector Gleason then gestured toward the two rooms on either side of the kitchen in which they stood. "We got the two girls one in each room, and we're interrogating them now. From what they tell us, Donald Dixon and Vinci come in here about five A.M., and there's a fight of some kind, and the moll is high on cocaine, grass, amphetamines—and Christ knows what else—and she pulls out the knife given to her by the deceased via machine-gunning, Tommy Zumbo, and she stabs her boy friend, Vinci, the policy guy, in the lung. She punctures his lung. He was still here when the first radio car team showed up. They say that for an hour or more he was spouting blood around and wouldn't sit down and refused medical attention. But finally they took him to the hospital, and he's critical. Anyway, after the moll stabs her boyfriend, the off-duty cop tries to take the knife away from her, and that's it for him. That stiletto was in and out so fast the cop probably didn't even see it coming. He said, 'I'm hurt, I'm hurt bad.' Then he dropped to the floor, and then he was dead."

At least it wasn't another assassination. This was what Eischied had feared—knowing only that another cop was dead—during the long drive over. He said: "Do you think we can call it line of duty?"

Gleason, as aware as Eischied of the unsavory information developed so far, grimaced. "Maybe we can, Chief. I don't know."

"Maybe they ran up to his apartment to get him.

Maybe somebody said get the cop down here to stop the fight, and he tried to stop it and got killed."

Gleason said: "It could be that way, Chief."

Eischied glanced out into the foyer at the unmoving corpse, and at the photographer who was packing up his gear.

Eischied said to Gleason: "Where's the cop's gun?"

Gleason frowned: "We didn't find his gun yet, Chief."

"Well, find it for chrissake. He should have had his gun on him but maybe he didn't because it was the middle of the night. Send two uniformed guys up to his apartment. Ransack the place until you find it. And get another uniformed guy in here to safeguard that murder weapon."

Eischied moved into the crowded living room. It looked exactly like a cocktail party. Small groups of people talked animatedly. There were even many half-empty glasses standing on low tables. But after a second it didn't look like a cocktail party anymore; it looked exactly like a crime scene. Why else were there no women present except for the lone besieged girl who sat with bowed head on the sofa while detectives with notebooks interrogated her? Why else were all of the men in the room still wearing raincoats, topcoats and hats? Who was that party goer kneeling on the floor in front of the coffee table dusting white powder onto the glasses?

"Getting anything?" inquired Eischied.

The fingerprint technician glanced up: "Lots of good ones, Chief. Glasses are easy."

The detectives parted to let Eischied approach the besieged girl. She was wearing a tight black cocktail dress which glittered with sequins. She was wearing eyelashes half an inch long, and the mascara had run in streaks below her eyes. Eischied listened as the detectives interrogated her. They were doing a competent, solid job. The questions were properly earnest. They were seeking only to help her, they kept explaining. What precisely had happened?

But the girl kept mumbling that, although she had

been seated on this very sofa at the time, she had seen nothing. Yes, she and Joanne had gone out earlier in the evening with two men. She named the bars they had toured. But she didn't know the names of either man. Both men had run away after the killing. Eischied, guessing, interrupted roughly: "You were Donald Dixon's girl friend, weren't you?"

The false eyelashes flicked upward, then covered her eyes again. "Yes," she admitted in a low voice.

"Did you live together?"

The girl shook her head.

The detectives watched Chief Eischied, who appeared to have taken over the interrogation. It was his as long as he wanted it.

"But you were fucking him regularly? Answer me."

The girl mumbled: "What kind of question is that?"

There was satisfaction in asking a woman a question like that. It was also the way you broke down her resistance to the interrogation.

"Just give me the answer. How often did you fuck him?"

After a moment the girl mumbled: "Infrequently."

The girl wore bangs as well as long eyelashes, and there was little Eischied could see of her downcast face She was pretty, she wore clothes well, and there even seemed a certain innocence about her. She had certainly got caught in a situation far beyond what she had bargained for: a corpse in the foyer, a stoned murderess in the other bedroom, and hordes of rough-talking men asking her personal questions. Though this thirty-year-old stewardess was perhaps no hardened whore, Eischied accepted the hard evidence. She must be one to run around with people like this.

Inspector Gleason was suddenly whispering in Eischied's ear: "We found some marijuana in the bedroom, Chief, and also what may be cocaine."

Eischied said aloud in a gruff voice: "Okay, we've found the narcotics, sister. Are you going to tell us your version of what happened here last night or do we lock you up on a narcotics charge?"

The girl sobbed. "I've told you all I know."

Eischied snorted. "You've told us you were out with two guys for four or five hours without knowing their names or where we can find them. You've told us that an off-duty cop gets knifed to death in the foyer there, and you're sitting here and you don't know what happened." Eischied said to Gleason: "Lock her up. Throw a drug charge at her. Take her back to the stationhouse and book her."

He thought the girl might start babbling now, but she did not.

He watched two detectives half lift the sobbing stewardess to her feet. One said: "Come on, honey, you've got to come with us now."

Eischied went into the other room. The moll, Joanne, was seated on the edge of the bed with detectives on either side interrogating her. More detectives stood in front of her. Joanne was wearing inch-long eyelashes too, and spike-heeled shoes. The heels were covered in mirror glass. Her bedroom reminded Eischied of a funeral parlor. It had a black bedspread and drapes. It had two enormous, pseudo-gilt carriage lamps hanging down from above the bed, and there were funereal-type frames around the pictures on the walls.

One of the detectives looked up. "She admits she killed him, Chief. She admits she stabbed the other guy, the one who's critical in the hospital, as well."

Eischied was not surprised. He merely in his mind shut the case off. Except for details it was over.

"Did you read her the Miranda warning first?" demanded Eischied.

"Yes, Chief."

"Which one of you read it?" The case was open and shut and Eischied did not want to see it lost in court on a technicality.

One of the detectives said: "I did, Chief."

Eischied studied the girl, who was alternately sobbing and babbling, and whose eyes were unfocused.

One of the detectives said: "She tells us Vinci went for her throat, and she was trying to hit Vinci with the knife, and she hit not only Vinci but she hit Donny Dixon, the cop."

Eischied said: "She hit two men without even knowing it. They both stood there and got hit. You tell that to anyone outside, and they wouldn't believe it." Eischied said to the hysterical woman: "Did Donny have his gun with him when he came in here?"

He had to repeat the question, and then listen hard for the answer which came in gulps. She didn't know anything about a gun.

Gleason in the doorway called, "They have his service revolver at the precinct, Chief."

Eischied went out into the foyer where Donny still lay dead. The medical examiner was crouched over him now. Eischied stepped over the corpse, opened the door and slipped out into the hallway into about twenty people. Most of the neighbors still wore bathrobes, or raincoats over their pajamas, but the reporters were dressed. There was the usual clamor from the reporters for information, but Eischield walked through them, saying nothing. Most trailed him out into the lobby. Two of them also trailed him up the stairs, but the others, torn between the Chief of Detectives and the crime scene, chose to stick with the crime scene.

Two flights up a uniformed cop stood guard in front of the dead cop's apartment. Eischied went inside, and closed the door on the two reporters trailing him.

The apartment was rather tastefully furnished, Eischied thought. There were books in the bookshelves, and reproductions of not bad nudes in nice frames on the walls.

He found two uniformed cops searching the bedroom.

Eischied said: "One of our guys phoned the precinct. They opened his locker, and they have his service revolver there. So what you're looking for is his off-duty gun."

Because the bureau drawers were all half opened, Eischied began rummaging through the dead cop's things. Under some shirts he came upon a number of loose capsules. He also found two prescription bottles filled with pills. He was beginning to know this Donald Dixon, who chased women, knew hoodlums socially and was a hophead besides—Eischied knew what amphetamines looked like when he saw them.

He pocketed all the pills.

One of the cops said: "His gun don't seem to be here, Chief."

Eischied said: "Where do you put your gun when you're home?"

The first cop answered: "I've got a lock box on the shelf in my closet, Chief. But there's no lock box in this room."

The other cop said: "I bury it under my shirts on a shelf too high for my kids to reach, Chief. But this guy wasn't married, and there's no such shelf."

Eischied said: "So where else would he hide his gun? Any sign of any false panels in that closet?"

No, but Eischied now noticed that the dead cop owned about ten pairs of shoes, including a pair of boots that would have come halfway up his calf. Bending down, Eischied lifted and shook the boots. Then he reached into the right boot and yanked out a short-barrel Colt .38. "You guys are some searchers," he said, disgustedly, and slipped the gun into his raincoat pocket. "The two of you can go back on patrol." He chased the two cops out of the apartment, told the cop on guard at the door to remain there until relieved, and went back downstairs and along the hall with the two reporters following him each step of the way, firing questions that he did not answer.

In the crime-scene bedroom Eischied said to the detectives interrogating the murderess: "Take her down to the stationhouse and book her for murder."

Inspector Gleason was crouched at one of the bedside tables. The drawers, which were out on the floor, were stuffed with photographs, bank books, letters. Gleason gave an audible groan: all of this stuff would have to be inventoried by detectives, however open and shut the case might seem.

Gleason said: "Christ, we'll be a week sifting through this stuff."

Eischied handed the dead cop's gun across to Gleason. "Take care of this too, will you?"

In the foyer, the medical examiner was unzipping the corpse's pants. As Eischied watched, out flopped Patrolman Dixon's dead penis. The source of life in death, Eischied reflected. But he looked it over carefully. Had it been engaged sexually an hour or two ago? If so, did this change the case?

In police work one asked all the questions, repugnant or not.

No. But there was an enormous stain at his crotch which could have been from wiping his bloody hand there. Or perhaps dying, he had peed all over himself.

The detectives were herding the two girls toward the front door. Both girls in their spike heels and sleek black dresses and their inch-long false eyelashes were forced to step over the body of Donny, whose pants had been undone. Eischied watched the stewardess, Donna, flinch and give a kind of gasp, which made him wonder what a woman felt at such a moment. Did she connect her own former lust to that dead—thing? Did she feel revulsion for herself, as if she had once made love to a corpse?

Before the door could be opened, Eischied ordered: "Cover him up first." The photographers outside would shoot into the room at the dead cop whose pecker was hanging out, and Eischied did not want this to happen. Eischied owed any cop more dignity than that.

The attendants had come in with a stretcher and a canvas body sheet. Eischied made everyone wait. The corpse was lifted onto the canvas sheet on top of the stretcher. As this was done blood bubbled out of the hole in Donny's solar plexus. It was as if they were hurting him. Eischied heard one of the girls give a sob, but did not look to see which one. When the four corners of the body sheet had been thrown over the corpse and belted into position, Eischied at last allowed the front door to be flung open. Detectives and girls stepped over the stretcher and out into the crowded hallway. The two attendants went out next, carrying the stretcher, and Eischied followed.

On the steps in front of the building Eischied submitted to a press conference. Inspector Gleason stood with him, and Eischied, using Gleason's notebook, read out the names of suspects and victims. He said nothing about the drugs he had found in the dead cop's bedroom drawer, and he made no reference to Tommy Zumbo, or any other mob name.

"Will there be an inspectors' funeral, Chief?" a reporter asked.

An inspectors' funeral could be pushed through, Eischied knew. He could claim that Donald Dixon, though off duty, had been attempting to stop a fight, and therefore was acting in the highest traditions of the police service. Eischied envisioned the five thousand cops in front of the church again, the five thousand white gloves in salute.

Eischied made his decision. "I don't think so. This was just a guy in a fight over some girls, and he got killed." Inspectors' funerals were prodigiously expensive, both in money and emotion. He couldn't see putting the department through an emotional orgy for a mug like this.

Additional questions tumbled one upon the other. Eischied waited immobile, as if intending to answer one or more, then changed his mind and strode toward his car. Although some of the reporters ran after him, he ignored them, for he was already brooding, and their questions seemed unrelated to the cop who had been Donald Dixon, dead on the floor in the foyer—the image was still fixed in Eischied's mind. Eischied, as he yanked open his car door, told himself he felt no grief for Dixon now; that he had felt no more emotion earlier than at any other homicide scene—how many murdered corpses had he looked down on by now, a thousand? Two thousand? But why had he felt no special emotion? Was it because Donny had not been in uniform? Was it the blue uniform that made the difference—that set cops off from other men and made the killing of one so tragic? There was a cop side in all of us, Eischied told himself, and it was the best side because it was the side that believed in right and wrong. So that, when someone killed a cop, he was attempting to destroy what was best not only in himself, but in mankind as well.

Did this make sense? Eischied asked himself.

The sun was high and the traffic clotted. As Detective Malfitano steered him through city streets toward headquarters, Eischied brooded about his profession, and about death, and about the meaning of both, but the answers he had sought for years were still not there. He was a man who approached life, events, people clinically, he told himself. There should be an explanation for everything. He was a detective, and could find any explanation he went after—if anyone could.

At headquarters, going through to his private toilet, he emptied the dead Patrolman Dixon's drugs into the toilet and flushed them away. The two prescription labels, he found, slid easily out of their bottles. He shredded them, and flushed them away also. He thought, That's the best I can do for you, pal.

Because his mind was on dead cops, Eischied got out the dossier on the machine-gunning case.

There were forty detectives still on the case, he saw, though there were no longer enough active leads to keep that many detectives busy. If it had been a bank robbery, or a rape, or an ordinary homicide, the investigating squad would be down to two or three men by now. But the machine-gun assassination of two police officers was not a normal crime. It was an atrocious crime, and it was, to policemen, entirely personal. Detectives did not want to give up yet. You could not let them give up yet.

The morale of the entire department demanded that they keep going.

The murder of Donny Dixon was a different thing entirely. Dixon had got killed in a fight over a girl. She had admitted it. Case closed. It wasn't even interesting.

Dixon's murder was like 65 percent of the homicides in this city, he told himself. The victim and the killer knew each other. That's the kind of homicides we solve. Most of the time the killer and the victim are still in the same room. The other 35 percent are the homicides we don't solve.

Eischied's hand stirred through the dossier on his desk, and photos of the two cops naked on the morgue slabs rose to the surface. Eischied stared down at them. Both faces still looked clean and peaceful. One cop was still stitched from crotch to chin. It still looked like a heavy-duty zipper.

Detective work plodded ahead, always in the same direction, methodically, implacably. Whereas the prey moved in leaps and spurts, obeying no discernible pattern. Each side had a method. But the two methods were not suited to each other. It was a wonder, Eischied thought, as he shoved the dossier back into its file drawer, that detectives ever managed to catch anybody.

5

EVERETT WALKER, hiding behind wrap-around shades, and wrap-around *Daily News* too, sat on a bench—in Needle Park in the middle of Broadway, and although sometimes he read the paper, mostly he watched the dry-cleaning store across the opposite sidewalk. Downtown traffic rolled by close to his knees, and uptown traffic close behind the back of his head, and the drowsy summer afternoon moved on toward evening, and he watched the store to see if it was under surveillance. It was not, and he was very happy. He could feel the thrust of the tall buildings all around him, and the rumble of the subway under his shoes, and he was happy to be back among his own people and in a real city again. The world seemed too focused and unfocused both, but delightfully so, and he felt as free and as joyous as on his first day out of jail.

Walker's beard was gone, and his gold earring. He wore a crisp, conservative haircut. He wore an open-necked white shirt and nondescript trousers, though his feet were still encased in the combat boots in which he had tramped through much of the Third World, a hero there though not here.

During the day an old man seated at the end of Walker's bench suddenly leaned forward and vomited. After studying the pool of vomit the old man went away, leaving the pool behind him, and Walker hurriedly changed benches, fearing the vomit might attract attention. About an hour later two junkies sat down on Walker's new bench and began to doze and nod, and Walker moved again for the same reason. But he was in no sense disgusted or offended. Destitute, sick old men and nodding junkies were normal—proof that he was home. They were part of what he wanted to do something about.

Everett Walker noted each police radio car that drove by, and whether or not the men inside took notice of him on his bench, and he was ready to move on if any did so. He did not expect to be recognized —certainly not from a distance from a moving police car. Many years had gone by, and he was supposed to be somewhere else. And he wore the dark glasses. Nonetheless, he could be recognized at any moment, by any pedestrian, a pleasant excitement in itself. Today was step one of his plan, and it was working perfectly. A first step must always be a simple one, he told himself, amd that was the case here. He was simply putting a dry-cleaning store under surveillance, the only job that faced him today, so as to notice if any forces of so-called law and order were doing the same, and they were not.

At five minutes to six Everett Walker deposited his folded *Daily News* neatly beside him, got up off his bench, crossed Broadway, and entered the store.

The store was empty. Walker stood between the counter and the plate-glass window. Behind the counter a curtain hung in a doorway. Walker heard bursts of steam. One burst. Two bursts. Three bursts. Then the steam stopped, and the pants presser, whose name Walker knew to be Albert Hoyt, stepped through the curtain and stood behind the counter. Hoyt looked prepared only to greet what he must assume to be the last customer of the day. You're in for a surprise, Walker thought.

"Yes?"

Hoyt was a big man and Walker's exact age. He stood in his sweat-soaked undershirt. It showed off his muscles. A handkerchief was knotted around his neck. His arms, shoulders and bald head gleamed with sweat.

Walker dramatically removed his dark glasses.

The pants presser said nothing. All of the blood left his face. His jaw dropped open.

A single word came out from between his teeth: "You!" Then the smile came on. "You!" Hoyt grasped Walker's hand and began wringing it.

Walker, grinning, said: "My name is Mr. King. Mr. James King. If you have occasion to mention my name to anybody that is the name you will mention."

The pants presser said: "The Big Man. That's who you are to me. The Big Man is back. Lemme look at you. You is a sight for sore eyes." His sweaty hand clapped Walker on the back. He was beaming.

But Walker kept glancing nervously out the plate-glass window at the street. People walked by, none looking for him, though one couldn't be sure.

The pants presser, noting Walker's nervousness and interpreting it correctly, led him through the curtain into the back, where Walker stood among racks of garments hanging inside plastic slips while Hoyt, out front, locked the front door and pulled the shade down.

Then the pants presser was back, shaking Walker's hand again, still beaming. He really looks pleased to see me, Walker thought, and was warmed.

"How are you?" the pants presser said. "I mean, how are you?"

Walker was happy to see Hoyt too. "I have need of a few things. A little assistance. You were a helpful kind of man, as I remember."

"Name it and you got it," said Hoyt. He pushed a switch and an air conditioner began to hum. He untied the handkerchief from around his neck. With a towel he was drying his arms and head. "Be cool in here in a minute," he promised. "What you need? You need some threads?"

He pushed another switch and the rack of garments began to revolve before them. The pants presser was peering through the transparent slips. He began unhooking garments from the moving rack. He had a suit in each hand and was holding the transparent slips against Walker, measuring the suits for size, while the rack continued to revolve.

"Try this here one. Brooks Brothers. Worth two hundred dollars." He ripped off the slip.

"What's the customer going to say?" said Walker, trying on the jacket. It fit him reasonably well.

The pants presser glanced at the name on the ticket. "He got so many he ain't even gonna miss it for a month or so." The pants presser's teeth gleamed. "Insurance gonna have to settle up. It done got lost."

Walker said: "A man wants to pass unnoticed, the best way is wearing a two-hundred-dollar suit."

"I didn't figure you made some deal," said Hoyt soberly. "I didn't figure you was walking tall."

Walker grasped Hoyt's wrist. "I'll walk tall again, Albert. We all will."

But Hoyt only frowned, and Walker noticed it. "What's the matter, Albert?"

"I'm just not sure I like that kind of talk. That kind of talk cost some of us too much in the past. It done cost you too many years and it cost me too many years, and it cost some of the brothers their lives."

Walker's expression did not change, but the cadence of his speech slowed, and he began choosing his words carefully.

"How are *you*, Albert? How is your life these days?"

The room was cooling off. The sweat on the pants presser's big arms was drying fast.

"I got this store now," said Hoyt, after a moment. "I got a woman. I got a car. I got an apartment on the top floor up on Lenox." Hoyt was watching Walker's face as he spoke. "I got a few other things going on the side. In the wintertime I take my woman down to one of them islands and live like a rich tourist for a while."

There was a silence. The pants presser studied Walker's downcast face.

"You want to get something going again," said Hoyt. "I know you."

Walker said: "You were one of the charter members of the party. You were head of the New York section."

"That was a long time ago," said the pants presser, still watching Walker's downcast face. "The party didn't do much good, did it? Nothing did much good. Everybody is dead or been put away for a long, long time. Rap don't get out until about 1982. Richard don't ever get out. Herman—did you know Herman? They called him Jonah sometimes. Also Sammy Penegard. Maybe you didn't know him. Well, Herman don't never get out neither. The party, what's left of it, is a shambles now."

"You and me together—" began Walker.

"I can't do it, man. I'm dragging too much weight. I'm dragging too much with me."

Walker nodded thoughtfully. "That's what I'll probably find. I've thought about it. Everybody's dragging either too much or too little. What about Stanley?"

"Stanley? Stanley's married, got a good job. The fire's out in that guy. I could sound him out for you. But I think I know his answer."

Walker nodded thoughtfully.

"I'm thirty-five years old," said the pants presser. "I still see all the social injustice. I do what I can." After hesitating a moment, the pants presser said: "I got a fencing operation on the side. I don't deal in no television sets. I don't deal in the poor ripping off the poor. I deal in high-class shit. I deal in art and carpets and business machines and shit like that. It's a way of ripping off the insurance companies, you might say. Maybe it's too subtle for you. It'll take a long time. But the way I see it, it undermines the capitalistic society just as much as ripping off a bank with a gun. Maybe more. And I got it rigged up so I can't get caught."

Walker nodded.

The pants presser said: "Everybody's thirty-five years old, more or less. Me, you, Stanley. Ain't gonna be many of the brothers you knew who will go in with you."

Walker nodded.

"I mean," the pants presser said, "fencing is safe. I could get caught. They just wouldn't have no evidence against me that would stand up. I never even see the shit I fence. I'm the broker, you might say. When I was off the street the last time, I studied a lot of law."

Walker nodded.

"I brokered, last year, maybe half a million dollars' worth of shit. Figure five times that amount retail value. That's what it cost the insurance companies. You might call it a kind of passive resistance. I'm through sticking up banks, and blowing up places. I'm through with the party. But I do what I can."

Walker might have read Hoyt a sermon: the movement failed because men like you laid down the sword. Walker might have declared: But I'm here now to pick up again. He might have shouted: I'm here to make you into a man again. Do you remember what it felt like to be a man?

He almost did begin shouting, but controlled himself. Rhetoric was for crowds, not friends. He understood Hoyt's point of view too well, he told himself.

And if I could walk the streets under my own name, Walker wondered, what choice would I make? Would I make the same choice Albert has made? Since he did not have the choice, the question was meaningless.

Hoyt said: "But anything else—you name it and it's yours."

From his billfold Walker removed the press clippings about the machine-gunned cops. "The blood who did this? Can you find him for me?"

Hoyt, glancing at the clippings, said: "Maybe. I know where to start asking anyway."

Walker almost put his arm around his former friend, but found he could not do it. "Thanks," he said.

"Thanks? I ain't done nothing yet. What else you need? You need some money? You need dinner, I guess. Let me go out and buy a few things. We gonna eat us up a feast right here. You wait. Only one thing I ask you. If the law comes while I'm gone, tell them you broke in and you ain't seen me yet."

The two men grinned at each other. Then Hoyt went out a side door into an alley lined with garbage cans, and Walker locked the door behind him.

With his new dark blue, $200 suit hanging over his arm, Walker explored the store. He found a door that opened onto a toilet, and another that opened onto a narrow, airless room that contained a cot and a small table with a lamp on it. This could be a good place to hole up, if he ever needed it.

The feast, cooked on Hoyt's hotplate and eaten from paper plates, was baked beans and frankfurters washed down with cold New York beer, and these were tastes Walker had not tasted in more than five years, and had longed for all that time. Dinner to Walker was delicious.

"I remember the first time you ever come to New York," Hoyt reminisced. He was smearing mustard on a hot dog. "You was just beginning to be talked about."

"The party was just beginning to be talked about," Walker corrected. "I was just an instrument of the party at that time."

"You was already the Big Man. Everybody could see that. That's when I first started calling you Big Man. Remember that?"

Walker, chewing his hot dog, nodded, smiling.

"You helped us set up the New York section, then you went home to Detroit and the first thing I know you was running for Mayor of Detroit. You was preaching violence, but you wasn't doing none of it yet."

Walker smiled again, for it was pleasant to remember all this. "I ran for election wearing two guns, one on each hip like some Western sheriff," Walker said. "Got me about forty thousand votes, too. Got everyone else so mad it gave them fits."

"Once the election ended, that's when the shit hit the fan."

"That's when the real harassment started," agreed Walker. "Not the penny-ante harassment we had all along. The real professional harassment. Seemed like every day one or another of us got busted on some trumped-up charge. We had real good lawyers though."

Then the day came, Walker remembered, when the entire Police Department, or so it seemed, came in shooting. Walker and two cops were wounded. Two brothers were killed outright. Walker, shot through both thighs, had been charged with attempted murder of police officers, and these events were less pleasant to remember. He was still under indictment in Detroit on that one, and his legs still ached in rainy weather.

"The party was so pure in those days," Walker said. "We were all idealists. There was a purity to waking up every morning and contemplating the ideals we were all fighting for. I used to lie in bed and just think about it and feel warm all over. Everyone scared shitless of us and wondering what we would do." His teeth pierced the skin of his hot dog, and the delicious juice sprayed the inside of Walker's mouth.

"In New York," Hoyt said, "we were planning to blow up a stationhouse and all the policemans that was in it."

"The party was too big by then," said Walker. This memory was actively painful. Someone had informed, and the plot had aborted.

"I wonder if we ever meant to go through with blowing up that stationhouse," mused Hoyt.

"Oh, yes."

"I'm not so sure."

"I said yes," snapped Walker savagely. "We had the guns. We had the explosives." But he calmed down quickly.

"Well," said the pants presser, "it would have been

63

nice to see all them blue uniforms go sailing through the air with pieces of arms and legs falling out."

"Yes, it would have."

Walker was mopping up juice from the baked beans with his hot-dog roll.

"The funny thing was they indicted you for it on a conspiracy charge," said Hoyt. "Nothing had even happened and you wasn't even there most of the time. You was running around to all the colleges speaking. You was very big in the colleges that spring."

"Yes, I was," agreed Walker, smiling again, but the smile faded as he realized the strain he was under tonight. Hoyt was warm and friendly, yes, but not his brother anymore, and Walker was digesting this fact, along with the franks and beans.

"You was big with the college kids, big with the liberals and intellectuals. The more indictments you was under, the more money came in. We had good lawyers. Every time you was locked up, they got you out."

Walker reached his fork into the pot and speared another hot dog. He folded the bun around it and smeared on American mustard. The mustard in North Africa was so powerful it burned the roof of your mouth, Walker remembered, hating the memory, but American mustard was only tart, almost sour, a taste out of his childhood that he had always loved.

Walker was trying to concentrate on the food.

"Them was good times," said Hoyt.

"Yes."

"We might have done something then," said Hoyt, watching Walker carefully. "The times ain't right for that kind of shit no more."

The rage that was always inside Walker, though usually tightly bottled, exploded. They were seated at a card table. Walker barely restrained himself from up-ending the table and its contents onto Hoyt's lap; he needed Hoyt, his only contact, and did not dare.

Instead he leaped to his feet, shouting: "That's bullshit, you hear me. Bullshit, bullshit, bullshit. It's not too late. It's never too late."

His fists were clenched, and he held his body so taut he seemed to be trembling. "The people who followed us then are worse off now than they ever were. They'll follow again, and together we will blow this country to shit."

He stood there trembling.

Hoyt eyed him. Presently, imagining that Walker's rage was spent, that this single outburst had voided it, Hoyt said. "Suppose you was truly to blow it to shit. Where do that leave you?"

"I'm not important," said Walker savagely. "I'm of no importance personally whatever."

"You want some more of them hot dogs?" asked Hoyt after a moment.

Walker, breathing hard, said nothing.

Hoyt began cleaning up. Over his shoulder he said: "You fixing to commit suicide? Is that it?"

"If it happens that way, yes," cried Walker fiercely.

Hoyt nodded. He went on cleaning up.

After a while Walker sat down again, and tried to light a cigarette. The hand holding the burning match was trembling, he saw. He had to grasp that hand with his other to light the cigarette. He sucked smoke in, and watched his trembling hand. He could feel the film of rage behind his eyes. The humiliating events of those years, the humiliating events of North Africa —it was all still there, still stifling him, cramping up all of his insides so that the pain was all but unbearable. He wanted to strike out, make someone pay, kill someone, but no one was within reach except his former friend Hoyt, whom he needed.

Hoyt had finished cleaning up. "Drink another beer," he suggested. "It will help you calm down."

Walker, seated at the card table, stared straight ahead.

"You want anything before I head on uptown?" Hoyt inquired.

Walker said nothing.

"You should sleep here tonight," suggested Hoyt. "You shouldn't go out in the street, the mood you is in.

You might do something bad and get picked up. I know you a long time."

Walker said nothing.

Hoyt opened the door to the alley. The grocery bag in his hand contained the used paper plates, the empty beer cans, and the packaging the food had come in. He stood peering out at the garbage cans in the alley.

In a flat, dead voice Walker said: "Find that blood for me, Albert." Walker's voice began to rise: "Tell him James King can show him how to strike a blow against oppression that will echo through history for all time."

"Well," said Hoyt, "I'm glad the Big Man is back, anyway."

The alley door slammed behind him.

And so on a cot in the back room of a dry-cleaning establishment whose glass store front faced out onto Broadway, Everett Walker slept. The store was situated approximately five blocks south of the 20th Precinct stationhouse, and about ten blocks north of the apartment building that housed Chief of Detectives Earl Eischied, who also slept. The store front was even closer to the radio cars that cruised back and forth outside all night, most of them en route to or from distant sectors of the precinct. Each cop inside each car daydreamed from time to time of the important arrest he hoped to make someday that would make him famous; no passing cop daydreamed that fifty feet away one of the world's most wanted fugitives lay unarmed and sound asleep almost asking to be taken.

6

THE promotion board met at 10 A.M. in the fourth-floor conference room. At the big table, while waiting for the first candidate to appear, Eischied made jokes with his peers—the three-star chiefs of personnel, patrol and inspectional services—while Chief Inspector Emerson and First Deputy Commissioner O'Connor studied dossiers. Eischied was wearing a gray pin-striped suit. Chief of Inspectional Services Palmer, a career detective like Eischied, was in civilian clothes also, as was First Deputy Commissioner O'Connor. The other three men were in uniform.

Because a deputy chief had retired the week before, it was the board's job this morning to interview seven inspectors for possible promotion to what, in the navy, would have been called flag rank.

"Are we ready?" inquired First Deputy O'Connor.

"Just a minute," said Eischied.

The third inspector to be interviewed would be James Gleason, and Eischied sought to disqualify himself in advance from having to vote on the head of his Major Crime Squad. "I've known the guy nearly thirty years."

First Deputy Commissioner O'Connor said coldly: "A commander has to exercise command responsibility. None of us can afford the luxury of passing the buck."

Eischied declined to lift his eyes from the table. He was trying to decide what answer to make, if any. The PC and the First Dep., both of whom were career prosecutors with no previous police experience, had taken over the Police Department about six months ago. The Mayor had sent them in with the usual mayoral mandate—increase efficiency; stamp out corruption. So far all they had done was force a good many older commanders to retire, replacing them with their own men, leaving most of the survivors jittery. Eischied had been safe—so far.

Eischied suggested: "A judge is allowed to disqualify himself from considering a case where he has had previous association with the accused. Like I said, I've known Gleason nearly thirty years."

"Nobody's accused of anything here, Earl."

One did not survive in the Police Department hierarchy by questioning the opinons of one's superiors. "Right," said Eischied.

First Deputy Commissioner O'Connor, mollified, added: "Everybody in this room has known most of these candidates nearly thirty years."

Except you, Commissioner, Eischied thought.

The board members sat along one side of the heavy oak table, and presently Gleason took his place in a single chair opposite. He looked like a man facing the Inquisition. Eischied, knowing his subordinate so well, saw immediately that Gleason had attempted to borrow this morning's supply of courage from a bottle.

God help the poor bastard, Eischied thought.

The First Deputy flashed a cold false smile.

"Why don't we start by having you summarize your career for us in your own words."

Gleason's career was already summarized in the dossiers in front of each member of the board.

"My career?"

"In your own words."

"These fellows all know me," suggested Gleason.

"I'm afraid I haven't had that pleasure before today. So if you'll please summarize—"

Gleason nervously wet his lips.

This would be funny, Eischield thought, if it wasn't so ghastly.

"Please continue," said the First Deputy.

Gleason attempted to do so, but only began to stammer.

Gleason's recital having petered out, First Deputy Commissioner O'Connor glanced up from Gleason's dossier and said in an almost affable voice: "Why don't you tell the board something about your work as head of the Major Crime Squad."

When Gleason said nothing, First Deputy O'Connor added in his false, affable voice: "As I understand it, you have about sixty detectives assigned to you, is that right?"

"Yes, sir, that is correct." Gleason, wasn't slurring his words. Rather he had begun spacing them too carefully.

"Nearly all those detectives, at present, are working on the case of the two machine-gunned police officers, am I correct?"

Gleason nodded. It was a strange line of questioning, and perhaps Gleason, like Eischied, had begun to wonder which direction it was about to take.

"Sixty detectives," said O'Connor. The career prosecutor was nodding thoughtfully. The witness, thoroughly cowed, awaited the next question. The prosecutor pounced. "So why has there been no solution to the case?"

Who's he trying to nail here, Eischied suddenly asked himself, Gleason or me?

"I don't know, sir," said Gleason.

"I would think," O'Connor continued, "that if sixty detectives proved unable to solve the case after so long, then something must be wrong. Wouldn't you say that?"

Gleason swallowed convulsively. "I wouldn't say that exactly, sir."

"No? What would you say?"

It's not Gleason he's after, Eischied thought, it's me. Is it just a casual attack or the first shot of an offensive?

"My own reading of the matter," said the First Deputy, "is that the detectives must be poor."

"Oh, no, sir. The men are good."

The prosecutor pounced again. "Then the leadership must be poor, wouldn't you agree? If the men are good but getting nowhere, then the blame must fall to the detective leadership. Yourself and"—the First Deputy paused thoughtfully—"and the commanders above you."

"The perpetrators must have left the city," offered Gleason desperately. "We can't find them if they're not here."

"If they're not here," pursued the First Deputy relentlessly, "then why are sixty detectives still looking for them?" He offered Gleason a bright smile.

"Not sixty," mumbled Gleason. "Not nearly sixty. More like, well, only maybe, say, forty."

"That's still forty detectives wasting their time and the city's money, wouldn't you say, Inspector?"

Gleason's eyes darted about, but Eischied avoided them.

"Don't you think you or"—O'Connor paused and gazed thoughtfully at the ceiling "—or one of your superiors should have put all or most of those detectives on something else, rather than wasting all that—that talent on an insoluble case? Tell me, Inspector, wouldn't that have seemed a sensible move?"

Eischied thought: I shouldn't sit here and let him hit Jimmy Gleason and do nothing in Jimmy's behalf when everyone in the room knows the real target is me.

But Eischied studied his fingernails and said nothing. I can't fight the First Dep., Eischied thought. A First Dep. has too much muscle.

There was a long vacant pause. Eischied, sitting with downcast eyes, trying to sort this out, could feel the other commanders staring at him.

"Well," said O'Connor casually, "let's let that matter drop for the moment and go on to something else." He began to sift through Gleason's dossier. When he glanced up, his false, affable smile was back in place, and he nodded at Gleason in a friendly way.

Gleason, Eischied saw, had grown more and more tense.

The First Deputy smiled across at Gleason and said: "Why don't you tell us some of the reasons why you think you ought to be promoted to deputy chief."

But Gleason had gone mute.

"In your own words."

"My own words," stammered Gleason.

"Just tell us in your own words," encouraged Commissioner O'Connor.

Gleason began visibly to sweat, and with that the aroma of his breath seemed to waft across the table. One physiological trauma had seemed to provoke another. He began to speak, stuttered, stopped.

"Is there something wrong?" the First Deputy demanded in a suddenly cold voice. They watched him sniff the air.

"No, sir," stammered Gleason. He attempted to flash a brave smile, but it failed.

Under other past regimes, Eischied reflected, there were rarely promotion boards. A man acceded to higher rank via seniority and the strength of his "rabbi." Eischied's rabbi had been a now deceased Chief of Detectives. Gleason's rabbi was Eischied himself. Under past regimes Eischied would have recommended Gleason for promotion. The recommendation would have joined other similar ones on the Police Commissioner's desk, and eventually, possibly without knowing Gleason personally or even having seen him, the Police Commissioner would have accorded or refused the great favor.

First Deputy Commissioner O'Connor demanded: "Are you drunk, man?"

Gleason shook his head vigorously.

"Answer me."

Gleason swallowed hard. "No sir."

"But you have been drinking?"

Thumb and forefinger an inch apart, Gleason admitted: "An eye opener. One drink, maybe. No more."

"At ten o'clock in the morning?" inquired O'Connor with distaste.

Gleason was sweating profusely. His stricken gaze moved from face to face, omitting only the First Dep.'s. Gleason was looking into the faces of his friends, begging help. But there was nothing they could do for him.

"You're excused," snapped O'Connor.

Gleason seemed unable to move. For Gleason, worlds had collided and now were falling in pieces.

"Get out, man."

Gleason shambled from the room. When the door had slammed, O'Connor snapped: "I want that man's shield on my desk immediately."

No one spoke.

Eischied commenced to shuffle through Gleason's dossier. "He's always been a good cop," Eischied suggested.

"He's a drunk."

"I see in here, how, when he was a young cop, he was in a shootout with two stickup men in a liquor store. Killed one and wounded the other."

"We don't promote men for marksmanship these days."

"I know him many years," Eischied said. He too glanced at his colleagues on the board, as if seeking support. "He takes a drink once in a while. We all do. He's not a drunk, you know."

"Probably only gets drunk when there's pressure on him," muttered O'Connor. "That still makes him a drunk. It's because of men like Gleason that the efficiency of this department has reached its present deplorably low state. I want his shield on my desk at once."

Eischied started to say more, but then allowed a silence to build up. He was hoping that one or another of the career cops at the table would decide to defend Gleason. But the silence continued.

First Deputy Commissioner O'Connor said to Chief Inspector Emerson: "I want his shield."

The Chief Inspector said to Eischied: "You better do it, Earl. It will be easier for him coming from you."

"Supposing he won't resign?" said Eischied.

"Then I want him brought up on charges," said O'Connor. "Drunk on duty."

Eischied nodded.

"Pass his folders over here," said O'Connor.

When he returned to his own office Eischied said to Captain Finnerty: "Reach out for Inspector Gleason. Get him in here."

Gleason, a shaken man, reached Eischied's outer office by midafternoon. Eischied kept him waiting an hour. He didn't want to face him.

At last Gleason stood shamefacedly across Eischied's desk.

"I guess I made an ass out of myself this morning," Gleason said. "I guess I won't be getting that star."

"No, you won't be getting that star. What's the matter with you anyway? Are you crazy?"

"I never had to face a promotion board before, Chief. I felt I needed something to relax me. So I had a drink."

"You had about five drinks."

Gleason said nothing. Eischied opened his desk drawer, rummaging for a cigar.

"I guess I'm not the first cop who's had a drink."

"You don't seem to realize how serious this is," said Eischied, staring at the cigar.

"Indeed I do. The star is out the window. For the time being anyway."

"Your career is out the window. That's what's out the window."

Gleason looked stunned.

Eischied bit off the end of his cigar, clamped his teeth on it, lit it. Then immediately stubbed it out in the ashtray.

"I think you better put your papers in."

"I—I don't understand, Chief."

"I'm asking you to put your papers in."

"But—I'm a cop, Chief. Earl, we've been cops together nearly thirty years. Earl, you're my friend."

"Times have changed. The Police Department's changed. The First Dep. wants your shield. I can't help you."

Gleason's face was red, but his jaw clamped shut. Then he said: "Screw him. I won't do it."

Eischied said in a gentle voice: "Think it over carefully, Jim. Think over what would be best for yourself, best for your family. You've been on the job nearly thirty years. You've got a big pension coming to you. It's no dishonor to resign as an inspector. There's all kinds of jobs out there you can get."

Eischied rammed the unlit cigar back into his mouth. Rummaging in his drawer for matches, he uncovered his gun and stared down at it.

"Earl, this is me, Jim Gleason. I thought we were friends."

Eischied said: "Don't call me Earl. I'm the Chief of Detectives, and you're an inspector, and if you don't put your papers in, O'Connor will bring you up on charges."

The two men watched each other across the desk.

"Let me explain something to you," Eischied said. "You hold inspector's rank at the pleasure of the Commissioner. He can flop you back to civil service captain for no reason at all, and if he doesn't have your shield by tomorrow that's what he'll do. After that he'll bring you up on charges for being drunk on duty, and if you lose that case, you go out on your ass without any pension. Now will you please see reason? Will you please put your papers in? Jimmy, I'm asking you for your own good, and for the good of your family."

Eischied, staring at the top of Gleason's head, thought: The job is changing. It's changing even faster than the world is changing. You either change or die.

Gleason mumbled: "How much time do I have?"

"The sooner the better. He wants your shield by tomorrow morning. If you need a couple of more days, if you thought you had a job lined up or something like that, maybe I could stall him. Maybe I could stall him a week. That's all I can do for you. I can't do anything more for you than that."

Abruptly Gleason strode toward the door. Eischied, coming out from behind his desk, had to hurry to catch up. He put his hand on Gleason's shoulder. "Do the right thing, Jim. Do what's best for yourself and for your family."

But Gleason shrugged his hand off, and rushed out the door, slamming it behind him.

Eischied went back behind his desk and sat down heavily. He would have to find someone else to take over the Major Crime Squad. The leather swivel chair swirled back and forth. For a while Eischied stared at his manicured fingernails—he had been to the barbershop that morning. Deciding to relight his cigar again, he pulled open his drawer for matches, and his gun once more caught his eye. He flipped the cylinder open, and let the bullets fall out onto the blotter. He counted them and there were five. It was as if he had stood in a firing squad and, now that the corpse had been dragged away, he was seeking proof that he had not fired the fatal bullet himself. See, none of his bullets had been fired.

Slowly, mindlessly, Eischied pushed the five bullets back into the cylinder, snapped the cylinder shut, and placed the gun back in the drawer. It lay there among paper clips, pencils, matches, stamps, rubber bands and other clerical junk.

Eischied began to mutter curses.

He cursed a Police Department now dominated by two men who were basically unsympathetic to cops. He cursed a system which sucked rough, ill-educated young men in at the bottom, which exalted and promoted them for physical bravery, but which then informed them as they approached middle age that entirely different qualities suddenly were necessary. Men like Gleason, former head of the Major Crime Squad, were being destroyed by the very whore they had given their lives to. It happened every day, and was in no way remarkable. It was as normal as a stickup. It was as normal as a victim dead on the floor. The Police Department was a whore, and Eischied was furious with it and with himself.

7

CHIEF of Detectives Eischied received a memo from the Police Commissioner: "Have you thought of Captain Cornfield as head of the Major Crime Squad?"

Eischied had not. He had been considering from among a number of inspectors. But if the PC wanted Cornfield, then Cornfield could have the job with Eischied's blessing—that was the political thing to do. Eischied buzzed Captain Finnerty and demanded Cornfield's personnel folder.

The folder, when it came, told little. Captain Cornfield's force card gave up his date of birth, date of appointment, dates of promotions, marital status, tax number, previous assignments, and addresses of the various places where Cornfield had lived. Eischied noted that Cornfield was extremely young for a captain, thirty-nine, and that he had moved six times during his eighteen years as a policeman. This was curious; cops were not normally nomads.

There were also several of the annual fitness reports. These had been instituted two police commissioners ago, and Eischied considered them useless. Each superior officer had been obliged to rate those men directly subordinate to him, but each had also been obliged to show each evaluation to the subordinate. Probably certain commanders had at first attempted to rate their men honestly, but very soon all had seen that there was no place for this type of honesty in an organization as political as the Police Department. Any honest evaluation would inspire bitterness and rage in the subordinate—who might one day be promoted over the man marking him.

An honest evaluation was out of the question.

As a result evaluation reports, these days, were not worth looking at. They contained nothing but praise.

Cornfield's folder failed to answer the principal questions in Eischied's mind: Where did Cornfield know the PC from? And how well did he know him?

At the moment Cornfield commanded 6th District Homicide—Harlem.

Chief of Detectives Eischied buzzed Captain Finnerty: "Reach out for Captain Cornfield. Get him down here."

Cornfield arrived that afternoon, and the two men smiled at each other across Eischied's big desk. Cornfield had been a sergeant on patrol in Queens ten years ago; Eischied, a lieutenant, had commanded the Robbery Squad in the same precinct. They reminisced.

"What was the name of that sergeant with the long nose?"

"And then Captain Lipschitz went and—"

Though he did not say so now, that had been Eis-chied's last field experience. Eischied had come from there into headquarters, and the rest of his time as a detective commander had been spent in headquarters. Once a man got to headquarters he fought to stay there. One did not become Chief of Detectives by stay-ing in Queens on the precinct level.

"Those were good days," Eischied said. An inane comment, but necessary at times like this. He lit a cigar. One kept a conversation going so as to glean what information one could.

"And a good precinct," said Cornfield, matching the Chief of Detectives in inanity.

"Nobody shooting at cops in those days either," Cornfield added.

They must have passed each other in doorways, on the staircases, in the crapper, Eischied reflected, draw-ing on the cigar. But he couldn't remember ever hav-ing seen Cornfield's face in that precinct—nor Cornfield his face, probably. More recently he had run into Cornfield during one investigation or another, but they had never worked in the same place or on the same level. They did not know each other.

In truth, Eischied reflected, personnel information in this Police Department was carried around not in dossiers but in people's heads. When you wanted in-formation on another cop, you went to guys who had worked with you and who now worked with him. Which, given the delicacy of this Cornfield matter, Eischied had not been able to do now.

Similarly, when you got into a position of authority, you promoted guys you had worked with and knew well. Outsiders were not even considered—and the rabbi system perpetuated itself.

"So how do you like working up there in Harlem?" Eischied inquired, knocking the head of ash into the ashtray.

"Busy, Chief. Busy."

Eischied waited to see if more inanities would be forthcoming, though why? And if they were forthcom-ing what would it prove?

"More murders up there than anywhere else in the city," Cornfield said. "Almost one a day now."

This was an inane comment too. Eischied knew the statistics better than Cornfield did; what he didn't know was where Cornfield knew the PC from. And he still couldn't ask.

"Small wonder," Cornfield said disgustedly. "Every buck nigger up there is carrying a gun."

Eischied registered the racism. He shared it—most crimes of violence were committed by blacks—but he had learned to keep his mouth shut on the subject. "It was worse in the old days," he said with a smile. "When I was a young cop up there, there weren't so many guns in circulation. The favorite weapon was the bread knife. Very messy. Blood all over the walls."

The two men chuckled at each other, then Eischied cut the chuckle short. The information he wanted would not be forthcoming. Get the job over with, he told himself.

"I've been considering you for a plum assignment," Eischied said. Realizing that he could not bring himself just to hand Cornfield the job outright, Eischied stopped and studied his cigar. The political thing was to give the job to the PC's choice, but Eischied's instinct was stuck like a record in a different groove. His instinct wanted to give the job to someone whose loyalty to the Chief of Detectives could be counted on. He did not need the PC's man in his personal entourage.

Cornfield sat with his knees together, prim as a virgin, a hand on each knee.

Eischied, stalling, picked up Cornfield's force card. "I see you've moved your place of residence a good deal. Why is that?"

Cornfield explained that during his first seven years as a cop he had acquired both a college education and a law degree. To save commuting time, he had moved first to the Bronx to be near Fordham College, then downtown to be near N.Y.U. Law School. Later, when he had made sergeant and got sent to Queens, he moved there.

The new fact registered: Cornfield was a lawyer. The PC would be partial to cops who were lawyers, you could depend on it.

"Saved a lot of hours that way," said Cornfield.

"You sound like a very efficient guy," said Eischied. He nodded as if to himself, and forced the words out. "That's why I've been considering you to take over the Major Crime Squad."

Across the desk the young captain looked first surprised, then delighted.

"I've been in communication with the PC about it," Eischied commented. He was studying his cigar because he could not make himself meet Cornfield's eye. "He has no objections," Eischied added, glancing now at Cornfield. "Apparently he knows you from somewhere."

There, the question, if that's what it was, had been spoken.

Any information Cornfield might give up now could be important, and Eischied waited for it.

"That was a Mafia hit when I was a sergeant," said Cornfield, looking pleased with himself. "He was the Assistant DA, and I was the cop who brought in the key witness. He convicted both those button guys, and Mafia convictions are rare, as you know. He got quite a lot of publicity for it. The funny thing is, I ran into the PC on the street the other day. I didn't think he'd remember me, but he said he did."

Eischied reflected: Of course he remembered you, shithead. He's been living off that one case for years. How do you think he got elected DA? How do you think he got appointed Police Commissioner? And now you're starting to live off that same case, whether you know it or not. As commander of the Major Crime Squad, you'll be a Deputy Inspector within a month, and if this PC lasts, who knows, you might be the next Chief of Detectives.

That's the way the system works, Eischied told himself. It's not something you can fight.

"Would you be interested in the job, if it should be offered to you?" Eischied's ash was an inch long. He studied it. In a moment it would fall of its own weight.

The young captain grinned. "Of course."

At present, Eischied reflected, Cornfield appeared to have no idea how strongly connected he was. And he isn't going to find out from me, Eischied reflected grimly.

Annoyed at what he was being forced to do, Eischied decided to take this annoyance out on Cornfield. Let the bastard sweat the appointment out. Eischied's face was inscrutable as he said: "I'll let you know my decision in due time. That will be all."

There was an executive conference in the board room the following day. The Police Commissioner, his seven Deputy Commissioners, his Chief Inspector and his four three-star chiefs discussed internal communications as related to management techniques for an hour and a half. There had been a great many of these conferences lately. The PC believed in them, or First Deputy O'Connor did. The First Deputy did most of the talking. A few others spoke to hear themselves speak. The PC moderated. Eischied, doodling on a yellow pad, let his mind roam.

This meeting, like all the others so far, ended without anything being decided.

"Well, at least we've identified the problem. Thank you, gentlemen," said the PC.

Everyone went off in different directions, yellow legal pads under their arms. Some of them carried handfuls of unused pencils. Eischied was disgusted. What a waste of time. He watched them go.

Eischied approached the Police Commissioner in the hall. "I've been looking into the record of Captain Cornfield, as you suggested."

"He once handed me a hell of a case," said the PC, smiling.

If he wants the favor, Eischied reflected, let him ask for it. "Do you want me to give him the job then?"

But the Police Commissioner avoided the trap. His smile vanished. "Only if he's otherwise qualified."

The two men eyed each other. Neither spoke.

"He's done an excellent job for me in Homicide up

in Harlem," Eischied said finally. "I was leaning toward him," Eischied lied, "even before I got your note. Let's consider it done then. Do you want to tell him, or shall I?"

But the Police Commissioner avoided this trap too. "Oh, no, he works for you. You should be the one. I have no obligations toward the man, nor him toward me. It was just a suggestion I made." The PC, after nodding coolly, disappeared down the stairwell. Eischied watched him go.

A week later Captain Cornfield, having assumed command of the Major Crime Squad, asked for an audience with the Chief of Detectives, and this was accorded him. Again the two men faced each other across Eischied's desk, but this time there was no small talk. Cornfield had brought studies and statistics. On Eischied's desk he spread out graphs marked with different-colored inks. The man's efficiency is incredible, Eischied observed with distaste.

"At the moment we have sixty detectives assigned to the Major Crime Squad," Cornfield began. The graph showed it. Cornfield was pointing with a pencil. "That's too much. We don't have superior officers to supervise that many detectives, and I estimate half the squad is not as productive as it should be. Now, what I suggest is this."

Cornfield came around to Eischied's side, the better to spread out his charts. He wanted to cut the squad down to five sergeants and twenty-five first- and second-grade detectives whom he would supervise himself, he explained. The other thirty detectives would be sent back to their original commands. As major cases occurred—"here and here," Cornfield said, pointing—the preliminary investigation would be done by Cornfield and his squad. As additional manpower was needed, Cornfield would "borrow" back detectives from field commands—he pointed out which ones with his pencil.

"A phone steal will do it," said Cornfield.

Eischied said: "Phone steals make field commanders mad. They never know where their guys are or when they're getting them back."

"Not necessarily, Chief."

The idea had some merit. What puzzled Eischied was that Cornfield was offering to diminish his new command by half. Commanders usually fought for more men, not less, for size was believed to equal importance, and they screamed like hell if you took men away from them. But here was Cornfield doing the opposite. Why?

Cornfield said: "I ran into the PC yesterday, and explained my idea to him, and he went for it. It's in line with his drive to tighten supervision and increase efficiency."

Eischied thought: Now I know why.

"Do I have your okay, Chief?"

Christ, Eischied thought, I've got a guy working for me who has direct access to the PC. This explained how Cornfield's voice and manner, in a week, had achieved such cool confidence. A week ago he didn't know how much strength he had or where it was coming from. Now he knew.

"For instance," Cornfield said, "we've still got nearly forty detectives working full time on the machine-gunning of the two cops, and there just aren't that many leads to check out. The guys are just spinning their wheels. All our wiretaps have expired, even. Yesterday I called up the Assistant DA who has the case to check out the wires and he said that there wasn't enough evidence coming in on those wires to support them. The machine-gunning is so far in the past that none of the subjects even mentions it anymore. He says their appeals bureau won't approve reinstating any of those wires. And you know something, Chief? He's right. I've been over the logs. I'll have to go along with him on that. Anyway, there we have thirty some detectives working on an investigation that isn't going anywhere. If it wasn't for the fact that the victims were cops, that investigation would have been put on the back burner a long time ago. Right now two guys would be just as effective as thirty."

Eischied, staring down at Cornfield's charts, said: "What about the morale of the department? Close down that investigation, and every cop on the street will know about it within a day, and they'll scream."

Cornfield snorted: "You know what this department has always considered the highest-priority crime there is?"

"The murder of a cop," said Eischied.

"Right, and frankly the public doesn't think that's the way it should be anymore."

Eischied, annoyed, stared Cornfield straight in the eye: "Fuck the public."

"I know," answered Cornfield hurriedly, "I agree with you. I'm a cop too. But we're getting a lot of pressure from the public these days, and frankly the public would rather have us concentrate on crimes that are of more interest to them."

Eischied knew well enough that Cornfield spoke for the Commissioner, for the Mayor, for the newspapers, for the liberal elements in the city, but he growled: "An attack on a cop is an attack on public order. It's an attack on the security of the state. It's a crime against society itself. It's an attack on the very viability of society."

"I happen to agree with you, but there are many other elements in this city, as I've said, who don't agree. Besides, we've hit a blank wall in every direction. Our stoolies haven't even heard any new rumors out there in the street. We haven't found any getaway car. No witnesses have come forward. We don't know if there was one guy in the hit car or twenty. We don't even know if they were white or black or green. I've about come to the conclusion myself that it was a single deranged individual. And you know how much chance we have of finding a guy like that in a city as crowded with maniacs as this one."

Eischied conceded. What else could he do? "Okay," he said. Was detective policy henceforth to be decided by a captain, with the approval of the Police Commissioner? Christ, the Chief of Detectives thought, I'm on shaky footing all of a sudden.

"The advantages of my plan," Cornfield said, "are—" He began to enumerate them, displaying more graphs, but the Chief of Detectives, though nodding agreement, did not listen.

When the young captain had concluded, Eischied said: "Sounds good to me."

"I have your permission then?"

"Of course," said the Chief of Detectives with a smile.

Wearing that same smile, the Chief of Detectives showed Captain Cornfield out. Standing beside Captain Finnerty's desk, gazing at Cornfield's departing back, Eischied muttered: "That fella will go far in this department, Finnerty. You know why, Finnerty? Because that fella is a very nice fella."

Finnerty, looking mystified, said: "You have Mr. Klopfman on the phone again, Chief."

Eischied frowned. "Tell him I'm in conference with the Mayor at City Hall."

"This is about the fifth time he's called. He says it's urgent."

Eischied said nothing.

After a moment Captain Finnerty said: "Do you want me to take a message?"

Eischied was thinking it over. Captain Finnerty waited.

Tomorrow orders would be cut reassigning thirty disgruntled detectives to their original commands. One of them no doubt would be Smallwood, who would return to Staten Island or somewhere, and to all his pending cases, one of them the charge of shoplifting against Klopfman's son. There was no ordinary way Eischied could prevent this. It would cause talk if he tried.

Eischied said: "Screw Klopfman. Tell him I'm gone for the day. Tell him you don't know where to reach me."

"Okay, Chief."

Standing behind his big desk Eischied, looking worried or perhaps only annoyed, rummaged in his drawer for a cigar. When the cigar was drawing properly he walked to his window and stood looking down at the traffic. It was raining. The cigar, clamped between his teeth, went out. He did not notice. He stood watching the cars go by in the rain.

8

MARK D. twisted the handle and at the same time shouldered the door open. Inside, the room was dimly lit, and a corner was curtained off. Everett Walker, following Mark D. into the room, did not know who or what might be behind those curtains. A television set flickered on the floor, and across from it on a bed sat the man Walker had come to see. Walker's gaze swept past this man onto the submachine gun that hung from a nail driven into the doorjamb. The submachine gun hung within reach of the man on the bed, whose face was expressionless. The eyes watched Walker. They were as black and cold, Walker thought, as the holes in a skull.

Walker turned to Mark D. "This is the brother you were describing to me?"

"Oh, yes, this is the brother. This brother likes to be called Charles."

Walker and Charles continued to eye each other. The monarch seated on the bed waited for the supplicant to state his business. The monarch's scepter hung there from the nail.

Walker turned again to Mark D. "I wonder if you would permit this gentleman and myself to conduct our business in private?"

As he waited to hear the door slam behind Mark D., Walker glanced from Charles's expressionless face to the hanging curtains that concealed one corner of the room. The apartment felt and sounded empty, but he could not be sure.

"I believe you have known Brother Mark quite some time," Walker began. Be careful, Walker told himself. You have to have this man.

Charles said nothing.

"I believe you were incarcerated together."

The black eyes never left Walker's face, but Charles said nothing.

Walker saw Charles not as a killer but as a doer. A man of action on the grand scale. The world was full of people who just talked. There was no problem finding talkers. But Charles was a walking murder weapon. Men like Charles had always been rare—not only here and now but historically.

"Let me tell you who I am," said Walker.

"I know who you is."

Walker had not expected to be welcomed with open arms, for killers were men who needed no one except, occasionally, victims. He said carefully: "Then you know my name is James King. If you should have cause to refer to me in the future, you will refer to me by that name."

"I got no cause to refer to you at all. What do I want to refer to you for? I got no cause to remember you even alive."

This is going to be harder than I thought, Walker noted. But his attention was distracted by the curtained cubicle in the corner. It made Walker increasingly uncomfortable. "Nice place you've got here," said Walker. Moving casually toward the curtains, he threw them suddenly apart. An unmade bed.

Charles, watching, laughed raucously. The humiliation burned Walker's ears, but as he turned away from the bed, he managed to keep his face inscrutable.

"You got something to say to me, say it," Charles snapped. "I ain't got all night."

Holding himself under tight control, Walker withdrew the old news clippings. "The man who performed this act," he said, "is the man I've come four thousand miles to see."

The two men eyed each other. I need this man, Walker cautioned himself. But his heart was beating fast as the humiliation and the need to strike back rose inside him.

The hanging submachine gun seemed a neutral topic, so Walker stepped toward it, trying to calm himself down with small talk. "And so this is the piece the history books will hear about."

But Charles leaped to his feet: "You stay away from that piece. That piece mine."

In an explosive silence, Charles's hand gripped the stock of the hanging weapon. At last the hand came away.

Walker waved his news clippings. "The man who did this act performed an act of revolutionary brilliance."

These words rang amidst the silence. They seemed to calm Charles and Walker both.

"Unfortunately," said Walker, "it seems to have been an isolated act, an act, therefore, of little political significance."

"Little political significance?" Charles gave a derisive snort. "Them two pigs is dead, man. That's two less. If that's not politically significant, I don't know what is."

"Then you don't know much about politics," said Walker. "Those two pigs have already been replaced by two more pigs. The car you shot up has been repaired or replaced. So what did you accomplish? There is no party behind you. There's no infrastructure. There's no program."

Charles's black eyes blazed. "That program shit don't work, man. We had years of programs. Where are the programs now? The program was a way of telling the pigs where you was at so they could come and get you. Pretty soon all the brothers was dead or in jail. I ain't interested in hearing about no programs. Programs is the past. You is the past. You is over the hill."

But Walker said: "You're the past, brother. You're the past because you have no future. Gunning down pigs is not the answer. It's what comes after that's important."

"Icing pigs is good enough for me. Pigs bleed just like anybody else. It does the heart good to see them bleed."

Walker's jaw muscles ached from the control he exerted over himself. "You think you're the only man hates," he said. "You haven't even learned hate yet. You don't know what hate is."

After a pause, Walker said: "You don't even know what it's like to be shot by them."

Walker saw himself forced to establish his credentials with the killer, a further humiliation. To a man as young as Charles, the name Everett Walker was perhaps just a name. Walker rolled up his left trouser leg to mid thigh. "I've been shot by them," he said.

Charles eyed the scars.

"The other leg is similar. The bullets were raining through the walls and doors. They were flat as dumdums and tumbling before they hit me and the other brothers."

Charles looked up from the scars.

"We had four or five guns to keep them out. They came at us firing ten times that many." Walker let his pants leg drop. "You don't know what hate is," he said.

For a moment he thought he detected respect in Charles's cold eyes. Then Charles said: "While you was living like a king over there, Mr. King, I was doing five years in the state penitentiary. I got a score to settle. I can't wait for no programs." But his voice was less hard.

Walker needed five men to fulfill the plan in his head, and he needed this man most of all. The plan itself still seemed solid to him. It was simple, grandiose, audacious. It ended in holocaust. Walker studied Charles. Walker needed five men and the necessary weapons. The weapons were no problem. A handgun could be bought on almost any ghetto corner. Most of the dealers, given a day or two, could come up with heavy stuff. The weapons were not the problem, the men were. The ghettos teemed with young men who talked endlessly of violence, but who limited themselves to sticking up Fanny Farmer candy shops. Walker's problem was the same as any executive's: to find and sign on the employee capable of bringing the project to the bottom line—in this case the man who could actually pull the trigger on an armed police officer. The man who could actually pull the trigger on a cop was rare. Any true killer was rare. This Charles was rare. Walker needed him. He stared into Charles's implacable black eyes.

"We don't need you," Charles muttered. But he sounded less sure of himself. "We don't need no programs."

Jabbing a finger at Charles's chest, Walker said: "Why was no attempt made to exploit your revolutionary act politically? No one ever claimed credit for it. The imperialists not only don't know who iced those pigs, they don't even know why those pigs were iced. Even the other pigs don't know why their brothers were iced."

"They know," muttered Charles.

Walker said: "In the past the party opened store fronts in many of the cities. There were public rallies with guest speakers. There was a newspaper. Defense funds were amassed. We ran our own candidate for president."

"You just gathered everybody together so the pigs could gun them down, which they did."

"That old method was futile," said Walker hastily. "I agree with you. There is no point going back to that futility. What I'm offering is something new and different. A small group, you and me and several others to start with." Somewhat hesitantly, afraid of spoiling the effect he had built up so far, Walker now brought forward the acronym he had been so proud of a short time ago. "We shall be known as FEAR—the Freedom and Equality Army of Revolution."

Charles only gave a derisive snort.

Walker continued hurriedly: "I'm talking about a series of acts of violence that escalate steadily. I'm talking about bloodshed spreading on the sidewalks of the cities until this entire country is in a paroxysm of fear, until FEAR is feared more than any other revolutionary army in history." Charles, Walker thought, had begun to look impressed. "I'm talking about a series of acts of violence which will put courage back into our people. Which will turn the former slaves into fearsome warriors against the slave masters. I'm talking about acts of violence which will lead to a general insurrection and to war in the streets."

In a low voice Charles said: "What you are saying is bullshit."

"What I'm preaching is urban guerrilla warfare."

An hour passed. Unnoticed, the TV on the floor flickered from image to image. Like a priest solidifying his most important convert, Everett Walker spoke earnestly on. All revolutions began with violence, he said. All oppressed people felt an uncontrollable desire to kill their masters. This force coud be unleashed and at the same time directed. That's what Walker and his band would do—direct it. Left alone, it turned in on itself and the slaves struck out only at each other; their mayhem turned inward because of fear of the armed might of the oppressor. But now FEAR would show men that with violence came freedom. FEAR would teach men to rise up and cut off the heads of their oppressors. FEAR would start with spectacular attacks on banks followed by similarly spectacular attacks on New York policemen, for the banks and the pigs were the natural enemies of the oppressed people. That was where the hatred was strongest and such attacks would make that hatred explode into fierce conflagration. Walker, attempting to fire up Charles, was firing up himself too. Spontaneous outbreaks of violence would begin to occur throughout the country, as the former slaves threw off their shackles. The true revolution would begin.

Charles, looking half convinced, said: "How you so sure it gonna work like you say?"

"Because the theory is historically sound."

"Never mind the big words," muttered Charles suspiciously.

"What do you think happened in Russia in 1917, in Algeria in 1954, in Cuba in 1958? In China, in Latin America. I'm talking to you about revolutionary history."

Now it was America's turn, Walker said. FEAR would put an unjust and repressive civilization to the torch. FEAR would start a conflagration that would never end. Not America the beautiful, America the blast furnace.

Charles's face split into a toothy grin. "I like it, man. I like it."

Walker said soberly: "No industrialized nation can survive against even a handful of determined urban guerrilla terrorists."

"I can see that," Charles said. "They won't know where we gonna strike next. They gonna be paralyzed."

The sound of a key in the front door startled Walker. He leaped to his feet.

"Mark D.?" he inquired.

"Paula more likely. She the only one uses a key to get into this place."

They heard her hang her coat in the hallway.

When she saw Charles she stopped in her tracks. Her gaze switched from Charles to Walker. "What you people doing in my house?"

Charles showed her all his teeth.

"Who this man, Charles? Where you come from, Charles? I thought you long gone, Charles. I thought I seen the last of you."

Charles said: "Paula, this here dude is Mr. James King. You be nice to him. You going to see a lot of Mr. James King."

Paula's apartment was on the ground floor of a four-story tenement at 831 Koch Street in the South Bronx. The top three floors had been condemned by the housing authority and sealed off.

Butch and Ida were the first to move back in with her. Two days had passed. Mark D., her boyfriend, had lived there off and on; now he moved in permanently. On the third night the man named Frank arrived with his "revolutionary wife," a girl named Marie. They carried mattresses in from a U-Haul van, and a number of rifles wrapped in blankets. Charles and his girl friend, Cookie, drove up two nights later in a gleaming, new Buick Riviera. Suitcases and sleeping bags were carried inside. Cookie then drove the Riviera away, and it was never seen by any of the others again, though Cookie herself was back in an hour.

Everett Walker did not move in immediately. Wearing his Brooks Brothers suit, looking regal, he came each night to see that his orders had been carried out, and to issue new ones. He wanted food stockpiled. He wanted extra blankets, boxes of candles and two kerosene space heaters brought in. He ordered sentry posts set up in each of the three front windows. A rifle, fully loaded, was fastened to the wall beside each window frame. At least one sentry post was to be manned at all times, and whenever the occupants of the house thought of it, this was done.

He ordered the ceiling of one of the closets broken through into the apartment upstairs. Access to the second floor was by ladder up through the closet ceiling. Upstairs Walker ordered the cinder blocks that sealed one of the rear windows broken out. In flooded light and air—and an escape route was suddenly provided via a length of heavy knotted rope, which Walker dropped to the floor.

Walker apportioned space. One room was the infirmary—he ordered a second hand operating table brought in, together with medical supplies. He ordered the women to study U.S. Army manuals, which he provided, on the emergency treatment of gunshot and shrapnel wounds when under fire from the enemy. They were now revolutionary nurses, Walker told them, for the violent stage of the revolution was near. "There will be men wounded in battle," Walker told them.

They gazed at him with solemn eyes. They felt as

loyal as nuns. Even Paula, who at first had resented all these intruders in her house, was under Walker's spell. She felt herself part of a movement that was bigger than she was. Walker saw this and was pleased.

At last Walker moved into the tenement himself, together with the Vietnam deserter Ulysses Brown. For himself, Walker took a sealed room on the second floor close to the escape route. This room was empty except for his sleeping bag, a pillow, his books, and a low table on which stood his typewriter and a candle in a saucer. He told them that leadership demanded isolation.

Each night a meeting took place in Walker's room by candlelight. His eyes were often fiery, and his voice moved them.

"A study of history's great revolutions," Walker intoned, "proves that every kind of miracle can be performed. We cannot fight the enemy with superior fire power. Our superiority is in the strength of our will and our purpose."

Walker sat cross-legged on top of his rolled sleeping bag. The others grouped around him on the floor, close to the combat boots, four women and five heavily armed men, a bigger group already than he had set out to form: Charles, Mark D., Butch, Frank, and Ulysses Brown. All were wanted by the police, and therefore could be trusted. So were two other youths, Floyd Fields and Leon Epps, whom Mark D. had brought by today and who were eager to move in, knowing only that something was about to happen and wanting to be part of it.

The candle at his elbow threw golden light onto a pamphlet by Chairman Mao that Walker read from. Candlelight danced across the teeth and eyeballs of the disciples at his feet, who sat mesmerized by his voice and messages. Only Charles, cradling his grease gun, looked restless.

Abruptly Walker spread bank diagrams out on the floor. "One week from today," he said. "Nine A.M. We go in."

Charles no longer looked restless. He leaned forward over the diagrams. His grin lit up the room.

Abruptly Walker decided to accept the applications of Brother Floyd and Brother Leon, and also of Brother Floyd's woman, a large, meaty girl called Sugar, for that would bring his followers to twelve and would provide spares in case the law wasted some. In any case, the number twelve seemed to Walker of considerable symbolic significance.

All the following week Walker drilled his men and apportioned jobs. The assault team would be composed of five men: Charles, Mark D., Butch, Frank and Ulysses Brown. The man Walker judged to be the weakest of the five would drive the getaway car: Ulysses Brown. To the two newest recruits, Floyd Fields and Leon Epps, went the job of stealing the needed cars the night before: one car to drive away in, the second car to switch to some distance away from the bank.

Walker had two problems. He worked out both.

The first was Charles. He did not control Charles yet, or trust him. Walker was confident he could gain ascendancy over Charles's mind in time, but not by next week, and Walker feared what might happen if Charles and that machine gun got inside the bank.

Walker foresaw carnage that would bring the entire Police Department down on top of them, and Walker's band was not strong enough to survive such a manhunt yet, or even the publicity of such a manhunt. Men would desert. Men would run to Florida and sign on as orange pickers, as Mark D. and Frank had done after machine-gunning the two cops last spring. This would break Walker's revolution in half. He would have to start again.

He had chosen a small store-front branch bank, lightly guarded. Success, at the start of any movement, was essential. He would stiffen their resolve with easy success.

The problem was to keep Charles out of the bank —or else make him leave that machine gun home, which was impossible.

Walker solved this problem by appointing Charles leader of the assault team, and making him responsible for covering from the car the escape from the bank; he had the only weapon suitable for the job.

Charles grinned. He was nodding his head. "I like it, man." He cradled his weapon, still nodding.

Walker, permitting himself a sigh of relief, said carefully: "You would fire only in an extreme emergency." He studied his words and Charles's face. "Otherwise the grease stays in the bag. We will strike them with increasing severity in the future, not now. Our purpose now is only to expropriate funds to finance future activities. It is not our purpose to attract too much attention yet."

Charles was still nodding. "I can see that."

"Good."

Walker permitted himself a single wistful thought: he wished he had Albert Hoyt, Stanley and some of the others with him, rather than this gang of brainless street criminals. A young Stanley, he amended, a young Albert Hoyt.

Still, he encouraged himself, other revolutionaries had had to work with worse clay than this. Even Christ had had to make do with a few dumb fishermen, even Christ. He, Everett Walker, would take this unpromising clay, mold it into shape, and fire it in the oven of the revolution.

Even Christ. He was writing legends for himself—and believing them.

Walker's second problem was the women.

All modern revolutionary thinkers taught that, to maintain security, new soldiers should be recruited only in jail. Security, Walker brooded, was the certainty that the enemy had infiltrated no spies or agents into your midst. Well, as far as the men were concerned, security was assured. All of the men had served time in the oppressor's dungeons.

But none of the women had.

The women, and the bourgeois consciences they were no doubt afflicted with, were the problem.

Walker found the solution.

All poor and oppressed peoples are susceptible to ideology, he reasoned, and the uneducated tend to believe absolutely in the truth of the printed word. In addition he knew that he himself exerted a powerful physical magnetism over these women.

His solution was to sit with the women in his candlelit room at night, the men having been dismissed (although some of them sometimes stayed) and to read to them from revolutionary literature, particularly from a tract called the *Minimanual of the Urban Guerrilla,* by Carlos Marighela, a Brazilian revolutionary ambushed by the police in São Paulo in November, 1969. From time to time he would stop to show them, by candlelight, where the words he spoke were written.

"The accusation of assault or terrorism no longer has the pejorative meaning it used to have," Walker read, his cadence slow, his voice somber. "It has acquired new clothing, a new coloration. It does not discredit. Today to be an assailant or a terrorist is a quality that ennobles any honorable man because it is an act worthy of a revolutionary engaged in armed struggle against the shameful dictatorship and its monstrosities. The urban guerrilla is characterized by his bravery and decisive nature. He must be a good tactician and a good shot. The urban guerrilla must be a person of great astuteness to compensate for the fact that he is not sufficiently strong in arms, ammunition, and equipment. The role of the urban guerrilla is to expropriate the wealth of the capitalists and the imperialists."

By flickering candlelight the women watched and listened in rapt attention.

"The urban guerrilla differs radically from the outlaw," Walker read. "The outlaw benefits personally from the action, and attacks indiscriminately without distinguishing between exploited and the exploiters, which is why there are so many ordinary men and women among his victims. The urban guerrilla follows a political goal and only attacks the government, and capitalists. The urban guerrilla is an implacable enemy who systematically inflicts damage on the authorities and on the men who dominate the country and exercise power."

The women looked at Walker, and were mesmerized by Walker's sonorous tones.

"The armed struggle of the urban guerrilla has two basic objectives, to kill the police and those dedicated to repression, and to expropriate the wealth of the capitalists and the imperialists. At the same time the urban guerrilla must avoid the outlaw's technique, which is one of unnecessary violence and appropriation of goods and possessions belonging to the people. He must use the assault for propaganda purposes at the very moment it is taking place, and distribute material explaining his objectives and principles."

Later Walker stood alone with Paula in the kitchen. It was Walker's habit to drink a cup of hot milk before bed, for it soothed his stomach and enabled him to get to sleep. Soon thirty thousand policemen would be looking for him, and he would be sitting in this kitchen drinking hot milk.

Paula, heating the milk for him, brought forth her thoughts with the hesitancy, he thought, of a child. "I always thought that taking money from people and banks and things was a crime," she said stubbornly. She had a little money in a bank herself.

She was annoyed at him, though he didn't realize it. She and the other women had jobs, earned money. The men preached revolution, but she and the other women were paying for it.

Walker attempted to give her childlike mind an explanation it could understand. "Being an escaped slave was a crime," he said. "Aiding and abetting an escaped slave was a crime. In the Warsaw Ghetto in 1940 to fight against the Nazis was a crime."

"I can see that them wasn't no real crimes," said Paula stubbornly. "But—" She was unable to phrase her thoughts. But what about killing, she wanted to ask, because that's where this was leading.

"The men who control the military and the corporations and banks," said Walker, "are men who live above the law. It is they who define the law. It is they who, in order to protect the money and possessions they have stolen from the workers and the people, have ordained what the law should be. They say it is a crime to take back what they have stolen. But it is not a crime, and the law that says it is, is an unjust and false law and must be stricken from the books."

Paula shrugged, thinking: There's no point talking to this man. But he is good looking.

There was adoration, Walker thought, on the face gazing up at him. "Your ear is pierced," murmured Paula. She touched it. "I never noticed it before."

Walker frowned. "You understand the true definition of crime?"

He ain't interested in me, Paula thought regretfully.

The milk was about to boil over, and Paula lunged for it. Her head was nodding as she poured the milk into Walker's cup. "I'm thinking on it," she said stubbornly.

She was typical of his people, Walker thought, as he sipped his milk. Her stupidity was their stupidity. She was typical of what he both hated and loved.

In the ghettos that he had come from his message should be believed without question. He had no illusions about how that message would be accepted elsewhere. The law, and the brainwashed public, would fit him into the mainstream of American crime along with all the other great bank robbers: Jesse James, Dillinger, Willie Sutton.

But mark how the styles and personalities have changed over the years.

9

ABOUT twenty detectives were assigned full time to the Police Commissioner's office, where their sole job was to cope with his daily avalanche of mail. Letters came in by the sackloads, and few ever reached the PC. Envelopes addressed to him by name and marked "personal and confidential" did go to his desk unopened usually; but ordinary envelopes, even those bearing the return address of reasonably important individuals or firms, got only as far as one of his four personal secretaries: a deputy inspector, two lieutenants and a sergeant. These four men perused such mail and in each case decided whether the PC needed to read the letter personally, or whether it could be forwarded for action or information to someone else.

The bulk of each day's mail was addressed simply: Police Commissioner, City of New York—as if he were a throne rather than a man—and such letters were opened by one or another of the twenty detectives in the outer office. Nearly all such letters contained suggestions, or complaints, or information about crimes, and some were solid enough to forward to the appropriate commander. But other times, it was plain, the signatory was some sort of lunatic. The twenty detectives got a lot of laughs reading these crazy letters aloud to each other.

Occasionally, even in the lunatic pile there was found a letter which deserved the prompt attention of the PC himself or of some commander. That is, the letter sounded, to the detective who sliced it open, solid.

Most detectives working in the PC's outer office had been there a decade or more while several police commissioners came and went. Most were first graders, drawing down salaries in excess of $20,000 a year, and they were no longer street detectives. They had become professional clerks, and they were among the highest-paid clerks in the world. Nonetheless they did wear guns, they did breathe the atmosphere of police headquarters, and their own early training was still there, though buried deep, and so most of them had an instinct, an immediate feel for the gravity of certain of these maniacal letters.

The letter that would later prove related to the machine-gunning of the two cops was one of a sackload dumped onto the desk of a first-grade detective named McCarthy. McCarthy had sorted through fifty or more letters already that day. He slit this one open, unfolded its contents, and automatically attached the letter to its envelope with a loud, swift punch at his stapling machine, for envelopes were clues too, and were saved. McCarthy then read the letter, and as he did so he stiffened slightly.

It wasn't really a letter. It was part of page three of yesterday's *Daily News*—the report of a bank robbery—on which the maniac, if he was a maniac, had overprinted with a red felt pen the message:

> The Revolution Begins Now.
> The capitalist oppressor will be struck where he is most vulnerable.
> This is the start of our autumn offensive.

The letter was signed with an acronym, printed in block letters: F E A R.

In parentheses underneath, Detective McCarthy read the explanation of the acronym: "The Freedom and Equality Army of Revolution."

This letter did not seem funny to Detective McCarthy. He did not read this one aloud to his friends. Acronyms were not jokes in the Police Department. Too many of these nutty organizations really existed, robbed banks and killed people.

With letter and envelope dangling, McCarthy walked through toward the Police Commissioner's office and waited for Deputy Inspector Ryan, the PC's chief secretary, to hang up the phone.

"What do you think of this, Inspector?"

Just then the Police Commissioner's office door opened and the PC himself stuck his head out. The clipping with its message in red felt ink attracted his eye, and he bent over Inspector Ryan's shoulder, saying: "What do we have here?" Ryan handed it to him.

The PC, after reading it, only looked puzzled.

Detective McCarthy asked: "What do you think we should do, Commissioner?"

But the PC had no idea how many such letters arrived each day, or whether this one was important. He was still relatively new in his role, and therefore fearful of making an ass out of himself in front of detectives.

So he spoke the first and safest words to come into his head. "I think Chief Eischied should see this, don't you?"

The letter suddenly acquired enormous weight. "Hand carry it to the Chief of Detectives," ordered Inspector Ryan.

In Eischied's office the letter was taken away from McCarthy by a Lieutenant Fitzgerald, who handed it to Captain Finnerty. Eischied, who happened to be standing in the doorway to his private office, observed all this without comment. When Finnerty held out the letter, Eischied took it, read it and said: "How many of you dummies have been handling this thing so far?"

Scowling, he glanced from face to face, but no one answered. "Have any of you dummies ever heard of the science of fingerprinting?" He was holding the letter and envelope between thumb and forefinger, almost daintily, as if it were on fire.

Finnerty, having stepped backward out of the line of fire, reached to answer the phone, and in his eagerness to change the subject quickly called out: "Phone call for you, Chief. It's that fellow Klopfman again."

Eischied, dismissing Detective McCarthy, said to Lieutenant Fitzgerald: "Give me a transparent plastic folder to go around this thing." To Finnerty he said: "I'll take that call inside."

Carrying the letter by its corner, Eischied retreated to his desk, where he read not only the message this time, but the news report of the bank robbery it referred to.

The call from Klopfman was on "Hold," and Eischied left it there until his lieutenant had reappeared with the folder.

At last the clipping lay under transparent plastic. Eischied jabbed at it with a forefinger and said to Fitzgerald: "There must have been an unusual on this bank robbery. Get it out and bring it to me."

Fitzgerald, red-haired, freckle-faced, thirty-five, asked: "Is this FEAR group something I should know about, Chief?"

"I don't even know if it's something I should know about. Get me the unusual, and don't ask so many questions."

He waited until Fitzgerald was gone, then jabbed one of the telephone buttons and barked into the mouthpiece: "Chief Eischied."

This produced almost a gasp of surprise at the other end. "Well, finally. Chief, I've been trying to reach you for days."

Klopfman seemed to feel at a disadvantage, and so Eischied determined to keep him that way. "Who is this?" he demanded.

"This is Mr. Klopfman, Chief. I've been unable to reach you all week. I thought you were going to help me. I needed your help, Chief."

After two sentences, the voice had become harder, more sure of itself. Eischied noted this. He said: "I've been very busy. The city is full of crime. I don't know if you noticed."

Eischied heard Klopfman suck in a deep breath, then say: "My son's case comes up for trial tomorrow. So what have you been able to do for me?"

Eischied was undecided on how to treat Klopfman. On the one hand, Klopfman was the father of a criminal. On the other, he was a rich man of vast influence.

"You told me your kid had no record, and I go out

on a limb for him and I find he's got a sheet as long
as my arm."

The father was all business. "Forget that. There isn't
much time. What can you do for him?"

Eischied was annoyed, and his attention was divided. Lieutenant Fitzgerald had come back into the
office bearing a copy of the unusual-occurrence report
on the bank robbery. Eischied wanted to read that
unusual, and he also wanted Fitzgerald, who loitered
in front of his desk, out of earshot before he said anything further to Klopfman.

"Hold on a minute," he barked at Klopfman, and
punched the hold button. To Fitzgerald he snapped:
"And what do you want, Red? Do you think I want
you standing around in front of me with your finger
up your ass?"

"Sorry, Chief," said Fitzgerald, scuttling out of the
office.

Eischied punched the phone button again.
"Yeah—" he said.

This was enough to start Klopfman pleading. The
tough businessman disappeared and the abject father
took his place. "You promised me you'd do something
to help my boy."

Eischied said brusquely: "I didn't promise you a
goddamn thing."

"You came to my store; you took two suits."

"You're lucky I didn't visit the jewelry department."

This produced a shocked silence on the other end.

"You're letting me down, is that it?" asked Klopfman in a low voice.

"I didn't let you down. Your kid let you down.
Speak to the Assistant District Attorney who has the
case. See if he'll give you a lesser plea. I can't do a
thing."

After a long strained silence, Klopfman said: "I'll
get you for this," and slammed down the phone.

Eischied put his own phone down. His hand was
sweaty, and he took out a handkerchief and wiped it
dry. After carefully cutting and lighting a cigar, he
picked up the unusual on the bank robbery and read

it through. A branch of the Kings Lafayette Bank on Fourth Street in Brooklyn had been stuck up by three men wearing ski masks and gloves. A getaway car had been waiting at the curb. In it the wheelman also wore a ski mask and gloves. The bank guard had been disarmed and his revolver taken. The robbers got away with approximately $2,300. The FBI had taken the film from the bank cameras and was processing it, but this was not expected to reveal much because of the masks. The following superior officers had responded to the scene. The unusual was signed by Lieutenant Schultz, who commanded the bank squad.

Eischied held the unusual in one hand and the message from FEAR inside its transparent folder in the other. There were sometimes three or four robberies of branch offices of banks in a single day—branch banks were small and poorly guarded, and as easy to stick up as any grocery store. And sometimes three or four letters from crackpots similar to this one, arrived in a single day, too. Possibly this letter was significant. More probably it was not. Why had the PC sent it over here?

The message did not even seem worth forwarding to the fingerprint lab.

Eischied buzzed for Captain Finnerty and ordered him to make out a dossier for the message and the unusual. "And then file the folder someplace where we can find it if we ever need it again."

"File it under what, Chief?"

Eischied said: "How the hell do I know what to file it under? You're the filing expert, not me. Wait a minute, file it under—" Eischied grabbed up the message and glanced at the acronym again. "File it under FEAR."

But after Finnerty had gone out Eischied felt slightly uneasy, though he said to himself, what the hell else was I supposed to do with it, give it to the newspapers? If this group wants publicity, let them give it to the newspapers themselves. And if they really want to attract attention, they ought to try knocking over a bigger bank. The news headline on the message just filed had read: THREE BANKS HELD UP; and the red-felt-pen printing had directed attention only to the one described in second place halfway down the column.

Was the PC really interested in this case or not? Maybe Eischied should have sent the message over to the fingerprint section, even if only to satisfy the PC.

Why? There'd be nothing on it but the prints of about eight dumb cops, most likely. There certainly wouldn't be ten prints belonging to some bank robber, and ten was what you needed if you were to have any hope of digging the perpetrator's card out of the hundreds of thousands on file.

The Chief of Detectives moved to the window and, as he stared down at the street, his mouth chewed ruminatively on his unlit cigar. He was trying to clear his mind, but thoughts of Klopfman—and of the PC —kept intruding. Eischied's seven detective borough commanders were due in approximately thirty minutes. These men were his immediate subordinates. Although the city was comprised of only five boroughs, for police purposes the two most active, Brooklyn and Manhattan, had been split in two. The detective commanders of Manhattan North and Brooklyn North were assistant chiefs, two stars. The others were all deputy chiefs, one star, except for Staten Island, which was still semi-isolated, almost rural, and relatively peaceful. The job there called for an inspector.

The subject of the conference was to be "Detective Evaluation and Advancement." A way must be found, Eischied had decided, to rate patrolmen for advancement to the detective division, and detectives for advancement in grade. A new system had to be constructed which would promise that each man's work would be measured accurately and objectively; the same system then would begin to distribute promotions on an equitable basis. The existing rating system was as big a failure as all the others which had gone before it, and this year's detectives were as cynical as the ones a generation ago. To detectives it wasn't what you did that counted, but who you knew. And they were right. How well connected was your rabbi?

Eischied at the window was considering the same basic problem most of his predecessors had considered. How can any detective ever be accurately evaluated? The classic test of cops up to now—almost the exclusive test of cops up to now—was an examination reduced to a single question: How many arrests has he made?

There was a detective up in the Bronx, Eischied knew, who in fifteen years had made about five thousand arrests. He stalked his ghetto precinct knocking heads together, which was illegal; he stopped citizens without probable cause and made them turn their pockets inside out, which was also illegal. Probably he had single-handedly turned that entire precinct into cop haters. He was a one-man Ku Klux Klan. But his methods worked. He came up with information. He came up with evidence. He had solved a number of big cases, and had once made one of the largest narcotics hauls in the history of the department.

But what sort of rating do you give a guy like that? Do you give him a medal or indict him?

How do you compare him to the detective in the forensic lab who is an ace at matching blood samples, or the black female detective who is invariably able to win the confidence of black female witnesses, worming out of them the information to convict their boy friends. And what about the detective who kicks in a door and rushes into a place under fire to disarm a gunman? How do you rate him? If you had an opening for one first-grade detective, who would you give it to?

Basically Eischied was as cynical as any of the detectives who worked for him, and the answer that popped into his head was this: None of them. You'd give it to the detective on the DA Squad because the District Attorney himself just called up on the guy's behalf. Each of the five district attorneys had between seventy and a hundred detectives assigned to his office full time. The detectives worked as legmen for assistant DAs preparing cases for trial, or were used to safeguard witnesses. They got to know district attorneys personally. There were an inordinate number of first-grade detectives working in the district attorneys' offices. Those guys had a softer life than most detectives too. But what chief of detectives was going to refuse a favor asked by a district attorney? The DA didn't outrank you, except that he did. He had political clout, and you didn't. Eischied had no illusions about himself. If a DA called him today, he'd promote the DA's guy for him.

Nonetheless, the system ought to be changed. It ought to be so formalized and stiffened that no DA could tamper with it—or anybody else either. If detectives could be made to believe in such a system, then gradually their cynicism would die out, their morale would improve and they'd work better. Morale and performance were directly related. A happy detective breaks his balls for you, Eischied reflected. An unhappy one goes through the motions.

Eischied was mulling over proposals to put to his borough commanders. They were all men of fifty or thereabouts. All had come up through the present system. Basically all were satisfied with the present system. They would see no real reason for the changes Eischied would propose. They would wonder why Eischied was proposing them. What was his ulterior motive? The Police Department was full of intrigue, and everybody had an ulterior motive. Otherwise why go out on a limb? Why not leave the old system alone? That way no one could take potshots at you.

Eischied's ulterior motive was that the present Commissioner, not being a career cop, had no basic sympathy with existing methods or systems. Or personnel either. Eischied, now that he felt in jeopardy, wanted to solidify his job. He sensed that this Commissioner would be a good deal more impressed by administrative reforms than by crimes solved. So that was the direction a man moved in, if he was smart. That was the direction in which survival lay.

In his mind Eischied was constructing a complicated

rating table. Perhaps a point system could be worked out. Each detective could be awarded, say, five points for each dangerous arrest effected, provided the arrest stood up in court; perhaps a detective could be awarded one point for each DD-5 turned in. In a lengthy investigation each detective was responsible only for a series of small pieces of the big puzzle. As he completed each day's assignment he was obliged to file a report on it. This was the report form numbered DD-5.

Eischied was still mulling over the possibilities when Captain Finnerty stuck his head in. "Chief Kincaid is here from Manhattan South, Chief."

Eischied had entirely forgotten the message signed "FEAR." He did not know it was connected to the machine-gunning, and he had too many things on his mind to bother with crackpots.

He had not entirely forgotten Klopfman. Still, what could the guy try?

"Send Kincaid in here. When the rest of the men arrive, send them right in too."

Stepping around in front of his desk, he shook hands with Chief Kincaid. Kincaid was six feet five, florid-faced, white-haired. Eischied decided to try his detective-evaluation idea on Kincaid first. If Kincaid was strongly against it, Eischied would be ready to let the idea drop. You couldn't accomplish anything in this Police Department unless your immediate subordinates were willing to go along with it. If they weren't, you could force the idea through, but it wouldn't work—they would sabotage it on you—and you would have made enemies. In a bureaucracy like this one you avoided making enemies at all costs. This was especially true at the very top of the department. There were various thrones in the ruling dynasty, but each was shaky and a single push by any enemy might unseat you. Eischied's ambition all his life was to be named Chief of Detectives, and the previous commissioner had given him the job. He meant to keep it as long as he could.

"I got an idea," he said to Kincaid. "Let me hear what you think of it."

High up in the dynasty, one treated even one's own immediate subordinates gingerly.

10

THE telephone bell rang. Eischied picked up the direct line to the Police Commissioner.

"Will you come in here please, Earl?"

In the PC's outer office Deputy Inspector Ryan invited Eischied to wait. "The PC's on the phone, Chief."

A panel of colored lights was affixed to the wall above Ryan's head, and the red bulb glowed. That was the telephone bulb. The blue and green bulbs were something else. Inspector Ryan plunged back into paperwork while Eischied, wondering why he had been summoned, watched the red bulb. At last he saw it wink out.

Eischied said: "I think he's off now."

After glancing around at the light, Ryan said: "You can go in now, Chief."

The Police Commissioner was wearing a cardigan sweater. He was a tall, cadaverous individual, sixty years old. He had served two terms as District Attorney of Queens County. Later he had served as Chief Counsel for one of the corruption commissions investigating the Police Department. Now here he was, PC himself.

"I just got another message from that FEAR group, Earl."

He was studying it on his desk. Finally he pushed it across to Eischied.

The PC hung his sweater on a coat tree, and slipped

one arm into the sleeve of his suit jacket. Evidently he was on his way out to lunch. "It's a telegram," he stated.

Eischied could see it was a telegram. It was addressed to the PC by name and bore four words only, plus the signature: "Chase Manhattan Lower Broadway." It was signed "FEAR."

"What do you make of it, Earl?"

Eischied didn't make anything of it. He had not been notified of any bank stickup on Lower Broadway —which didn't mean that one hadn't happened.

"I'll look into it, Commissioner."

Folding the telegram neatly in four, Eischied shoved it into his breast pocket and turned to leave the office.

The Commissioner's office had a back door and, outside it, a private elevator. With his hand on the doorknob, the PC said: "This is the second notification unless there were others I didn't hear about."

"No. Only two, so far as I know."

"What did your detectives turn up on the first one?"

But the first message had ended up inside a transparent plastic folder in a filing cabinet somewhere.

"Nothing significant, Commissioner."

"Any prints?"

The Commissioner had prosecuted a lot of cases, but seemed to have the general public's mentality on the subject of fingerprints—that they were both easy to find on any piece of evidence, and easy to identify once you found them.

Eischied said: "It's pretty hard to bring out prints on a piece of newspaper, Commissioner."

The Police Commissioner nodded but apparently was unwilling to let go of the subject. After a moment he inquired: "Any idea who this FEAR group might be?"

Eischied said thoughtfully: "Maybe now we'll be able to pick up a lead on them, Commissioner."

Eischied was watching the Police Commissioner carefully. To a man of Eischied's experience the symptoms were unmistakable. The PC saw himself personally initiating this investigation, and personally overseeing it to its conclusion. If arrests could be made, the PC would go before a press conference and claim credit.

"Well, keep me informed," advised the Police Commissioner.

"I'll do that," said Eischied, watching with narrowed eyes as the PC stepped out his back door.

With the door half closed, the PC ducked back. "Call me later in the day. Keep me informed."

To Eischied, there was nothing worse for a Chief of Detectives than to have the Police Commissioner personally interested in a case. Most cases, after all, were not solved.

Eischied said: "I may not have anything by the time you leave for the day."

"Oh. Well. Call me at home then tonight. You have my home number."

"I hate to bother you on something insignificant like this."

The PC, perceiving Eischied's reluctance, said: "I'll be anxious to hear. Give me a call about nine o'clock." Just before the door slammed, the PC added coolly: "Unless you have something before that, of course."

Eischied stood alone in the Police Commissioner's office. The red velvet drapes were half closed, but sunlight flooded across the rug toward his feet. Though the seat of so much power, this room, once its occupant was gone, was just a room like any other. Power had no odor. One could not smell it in the air. It had no color or sound. But the PC was the true boss of Eischied's three thousand detectives (not to mention the more than twenty-eight thousand uniformed policemen) and unfortunately the PC now wanted to play detective himself. The PC seemed to see himself smashing an important gang of robbers, personally, and if such a gang did not exist or could not be found, the PC was going to be unhappy. It behooved Eischied to have some facts to give him later in the day.

Suddenly the back door opened and the PC stuck his head back in. "Do you suppose the newspapers have learned about these FEAR people yet?"

"If they had, Commissioner, I think we would have read about it by now."

The PC's head nodded. "We can expect to hear from the press as soon as they get wind of it. We better have something to tell them by then."

"Yes, sir," said Eischied.

This time Eischied left the office immediately, and the empty room echoed with the sound of two doors closing simultaneously.

Back in his own office Eischied buzzed for Captain Finnerty. "And bring Lieutenant Fitzgerald in here with you."

The two detectives approached his desk.

"Did we have a bank stickup this morning on Lower Broadway?"

"We sure did, Chief," said Captian Finnerty. "They got away with—"

Eischied, beginning to pace, demanded, "Why wasn't I notified?"

"But, Chief," Finnerty complained, "you never told me you wanted to be notified about every bank robbery that took place."

"From now on, notify me, okay?"

"Every bank robbery?" asked the surprised Finnerty.

"Every goddamn one. Okay?"

"Right you are, Chief." The studious Finnerty was making a note of it on a stenographer's pad.

Red Fitzgerald, trying a joke, said: "Any he overlooks, I'll notify you on, Chief."

Eischied froze him with a glance.

"Sorry, Chief."

"I want that file we started the other day called FEAR."

There were filing cabinets along one wall of Eischied's office. Lieutenant Fitzgerald found the dossier quickly and handed it over. The Chief of Detectives withdrew the transparent plastic folder. Press clipping and blood-red message showed through. Eischied saw it not as a clue but as evidence in a trial: people's exhibit No.—No. what? He wondered if any jury would ever see it. If so, it would not look the same by then. It would not even look the same when it came back this afternoon after treatment, and so he sought to imprint a picture of it in his brain.

To Fitzgerald he said: "Put this thing in a manila envelope. Got that, Red? That's so no one will see you carrying it around. Once you have it in the manila envelope you are to hand carry it to the photo lab. You will have it photographed in color on both sides. Do you understand so far? I'm not going too fast for you?"

He was talking, chewing on a cigar and staring at Fitzgerald all at the same time. "I am giving you these instructions with what is termed childlike simplicity so that even a child's mind can follow them. No offense intended, Lieutenant Fitzgerald." Fitzgerald was suppressing a grin.

"After this thing has been photographed, hand carry it over to the fingerprint section. Have them check it for fingerprints, on both sides. They will probably find a number of clear prints, including yours, Lieutenant Fitzgerald, which means that after this thing has been treated, you're to bring a fingerprint technician back with you so he can take elimination prints from everybody who's touched this thing around here. That includes the PC, by the way."

But Fitzgerald no longer saw the humor of the assignment. "You mean I'm supposed to barge in there and ink up the PC's fingers for him?"

"That's right, Lieutenant Fitzgerald. For a man of your intelligence, wit and charm, such an assignment is a piece of cake."

"Right, Chief."

Fitzgerald still stood in front of the desk, no doubt waiting to hear what this was all about. The biggest part of the secret was still to come. But Eischied said: "Good-bye, Lieutenant Fitzgerald."

When Fitzgerald had gone out, Eischied dug in his pocket for the telegram, which he handed across to Captain Finnerty. "I want to know where this telegram was sent from, and exactly when. Find out what phony name the sender gave. You'll probably find out it was sent from a pay telephone. That's how dumb Western Union is. You give them the number of the pay telephone you're calling from, plus a phony address, and you can send telegrams anywhere in the world for nothing. Call up our contact at the telephone company. He can find out where the telephone booth is located. Tell him it's urgent. I wanna know by two o'clock this afternoon."

"Anything else, Chief?"

"Yeah. Reach out for Lieutenant Schultz who has the Bank Squad and get him in here. Now get me Deputy Greenberg on the phone."

Greenberg commanded the Narcotics Division under Eischied. When he came on the line, Eischied said: "Paul, I want you to do me a favor this afternoon. The PC is having his monthly planning conference at 3 P.M. I'm tied up on something else. I want you to sit in for me."

Greenberg said: "I wouldn't know what to say there."

"Don't say anything. All those civilians he has brought in will be discussing the latest management and efficiency techniques. All you have to do is sit there in silence and look wise." Eischied hung up.

Ten minutes later the Chief of Detectives' car pulled up in front of the Lower Broadway branch of the Chase Manhattan Bank. The first thing Eischied noticed as he stepped out onto the sidewalk was a bullet hole in the glass front door about three feet above the sill.

Striding into the bank, he glanced around. It wasn't really a bank; it was a store front. In another part of town or in another age the building would have been a saloon. The counter was the length of a bar. There were women behind its grilled cages. Eischied noted three cameras above the women's heads facing the few customers on lines. Toward the rear of the bank were the desks of the officers. Besides one desk a man sat interviewing one of the officers. He had his notebook on the edge of the desk. The bank officer was answering questions.

FBI agent, Eischied supposed. Bank robbing was a federal crime to which detectives and FBI usually responded simultaneously. After that they conducted two separate investigations and rarely cooperated with each other.

Eischied had come because he wanted to see what the bank had looked like to the robbers. When he turned around and looked out toward the street his eye was caught by the bullet hole again and this puzzled him. It was the only sign left of the violent act that had taken place there that morning.

Obviously the bank had reopened for business. The tellers were calmly working behind their cages, and there were about ten customers on the lines.

Out on the pavement again Eischied gazed across City Hall Park at the Gothic stone arches of the Brooklyn Bridge beyond. The bridge had been the escape route most likely. Eischied was trying to reconstruct the crime. He had been to a great many bank robberies in his life. He knew something about bank robberies.

In front of the bank was a bus stop with his own car parked in it and Detective Malfitano half asleep behind the wheel. Probably the robbers had parked in that exact spot this morning, Eischied reflected. Maybe they had picked this particular bank because of the bus stop. Robbers worry about parking too, or should, and these robbers had been assured in advance of finding a spot for their getaway car. It had waited right here, engine running, the wheelman's nerves probably in worse shape than the guys' who went into the bank.

With the proliferation of all these branches, bank robbery had become an extremely common crime. So what made this one different?

Because the PC is interested in it, Eischied thought cynically. That and the fact that the head robber is evidently very careful with details.

Climbing back into his car, Eischied ordered himself driven back to headquarters, where Lieutenant Schultz of the Bank Squad was no doubt already waiting.

Lieutenants did not converse every day with chiefs of detectives. On the other side of Eischied's desk, Schultz looked tense. Schultz wondered what this was about. The summons had given no clue. Schultz was twisting a pencil nervously in his hands.

Eischied, noting that Schultz was nervous, decided he should stay this way. Why not? Why should Schultz get off easier than anybody else? Eischied himself was nervous every time he got summoned by the PC or the Chief Inspector. Every man got nervous ten times a day. That was the price of being a man. That was why men died young.

Calmly, slowly, Eischied lit a cigar. When the cigar was glowing to his satisfaction, he said: "So tell me about that bank robbery this morning."

Schultz looked relieved. Schultz expelled a good deal of air. The Chief of Detectives just wanted to know about the bank robbery.

Schultz described a quite ordinary robbery. As Eischied had guessed, the car had halted in the bus stop. The wheelman waited. Three men had entered the bank. One had a long-barreled revolver. The other two had automatics, probably Browning 9 mm. There had been three girl tellers, two bank officers, and four customers in the bank at the time. The bank guard was in the men's room. By the time he came out the robbery was over.

Eischied said nothing.

According to Schultz one gunman stood near the door, back pressed into the corner. A second herded the customers toward the rear of the bank and held a gun on them there. The third moved along the counter with a satchel, ordering the tellers to empty the drawers.

The vault was to the rear of the bank, and it was open. There were some money sacks on the floor there. After the tellers had been cleaned out the robber in the back grabbed two sacks, as many as he could handle, and they all ran out of the bank.

Eischied thought disgustedly: And the bank guard was taking a shit through all this.

"Who fired the shot through the door? The bank guard?"

"One of the customers, Chief," answered Schultz. "According to the witnesses the robbers were out the door. Their car was probably halfway down Broadway, and this customer suddenly hauls out a piece and lets one fly right through the door. The line of fire was directly toward City Hall. It's lucky he didn't kill the Mayor."

"Illegal gun?" inquired Eischied. An illegal gun would mean a felony arrest at the scene of the bank robbery. The arrest would have nothing to do with the robbery, but the general public wouldn't know that, and the department would look a little better...

Schultz answered: "No, legal, Chief. The guy used to be in the job. He's a retired patrolman, and he kept his gun after he got out."

Nearly every ex-cop in the city was still armed. The few who stumbled across crimes usually managed to screw up. Either they got killed, or they managed to pull off a few wild shots after the crime was over.

"An ex-cop, and he lets one go straight toward City Hall," said Eischied disgustedly. "Do me a favor, don't tell anybody, okay?"

Schultz said: "The FBI was there. They took the film. They're processing it now."

Eischied, with equal disgust, said: "And when they have it developed, they won't let us see it most likely."

"I know, Chief. Maybe you could talk to them."

But Eischied had long ago given up trying to talk to the FBI.

"What about the getaway car?"

"A late-model red Chrysler, Chief."

"Who gave you that description, the ex-cop?"

"No, the bank guard. After he heard the shot go off, he came running out of the can holding his pants up with one hand, his gun in the other. He ran out into the street that way and fired three shots into the air. Christ, Chief. What a scene. All these pedestrians walking by on their way to work, and this clown is standing in the middle of Broadway firing his gun into the air and holding his pants up at the same time."

Eischied was laughing. It was indeed an amusing picture.

But he cut the laughter short. "Have you found the getaway car yet?"

"Not yet, Chief."

"You can't have looked very hard. Did you look on the other side of the Brooklyn Bridge?"

"What makes you think they went over the Brooklyn Bridge, Chief?"

Eischied sighed. Most detectives, he had found, failed to check out the most obvious possibilities. "Let me ask you something," he said to Schultz. "Let's suppose you stuck up that bank. Which direction would you go in?"

Schultz did not have to think it over long. "There's only one way to go, Chief. I'd go right over the Brooklyn Bridge, no question about it."

Eischied, tilted back in his swivel chair, was nodding at him.

"Right, Chief. I'll start a search there right away."

Eischied said: "Did that ex-cop notice anything helpful?" It was possible. Eischied wanted to believe that the ex-cop had done something useful to atone for firing a shot through the door.

"He didn't see nothing, Chief. He must have spent the whole time trying to decide how he was going to get his gun out, and what he was going to do with it once it was in his hand."

Eischied could visualize this scene too. To the ex-cop this must have seemed his last best chance of becoming a hero, though he was alone against three men. But the problem was too much for him. By the time he got it figured out the robbery was over, and so in his confusion, or frustration, or whatever emotion he was feeling, the ex-cop let one go through the door.

"Did the bank alarm go off?"

It had. Schultz gave the time, and Eischied noted it down: 9:07 A.M. The first radio car had responded at 9:12, but the robbers were gone by then. Still, that was a pretty good performance by the radio car at that time of the morning, when traffic was heavy and bank alarms were ringing all over the city. There was no urgency to a bank alarm at that hour. Nearly all of them every morning were set off by accident by left-footed bank officials. The radio car responding never expected to find anything.

The car this morning had arrived too late. Probably it was just as well, or some unsuspecting cop might have got killed.

"Okay," said Eischied, "so what do we know about the perpetrators? Were they white or black?"

"No way of telling, Chief. They wore ski masks and gloves."

Eischied nodded approvingly: the head robber was indeed a careful fellow.

Reaching into the folder labeled "FEAR," Eischied withdrew the unusual from the previous robbery. He pushed this across to Schultz, who glanced at it.

"Is this the same gang, or what?" Eischied inquired.

"Could be, Chief," said Schultz. "The perpetrators used ski masks and gloves both times. The M.O. was more or less the same."

"You never found a getaway car the first time?"

"Never did, Chief."

Eischied said: "Suppose you stuck up that bank this morning, and then took off over the Brooklyn Bridge. What would you do next?"

After a moment Schultz answered: "I'd dump the car in one of those narrow waterfront streets under the bridge. I'd have another car there waiting, and I'd transfer to it and take off."

It wasn't that detectives were unimaginative, Eischied reflected. They had brains. Most would have answered as Schultz had done. It was just that the system emphasized other qualities to such an extent that imagination rarely surfaced. Procedures had to be rigidly adhered to. As a result a detective like Schultz was extremely busy from the moment he arrived at a crime scene until many hours later. Statements had to be taken from all the witnesses. Forensic personnel had to be notified. The Chief of Detectives' office had to be notified. The commanding officer of the precinct had to be notified. If anyone had been wounded or killed the paperwork quadrupled. A detective like Schultz had no time at a crime scene for imagination. Besides, imagination paid off only if it was immediately and dramatically successful, whereas a detective could get in serious trouble if he forgot or overlooked even one item on the checklist of correct procedures at a bank robbery. Imagination was a luxury that a detective rarely had time for. The system ordained against imagination.

Eischied said: "Very good. Why didn't you think of that this morning? Why haven't you already canvassed that entire neighborhood over there? You might have found that getaway car three hours ago."

He glowered at Schultz across the desk.

After a while Schultz mumbled: "I was too busy, Chief."

Eischied could only sympathize. The system needed changing, and Eischied wished he was in charge and was man enough to try to change it. The system was like a lot of unmeshed gears. There was no way they could be straightened out without them grinding your fingers off. Or maybe your head.

In a more kindly voice Eischied said to Lieutenant Schultz: "I want you to go across the river immediately. Talk to the precinct commander. Tell him you're operating under my direct orders. Tell him when he turns out his cops at four o'clock that their first and only job, unless there's some emergency, is to check every street underneath that bridge until they find that getaway car. You're looking for a red car. That should make it easy. Every red car one of the guys sees he asks Central on the radio to run it through the computer. As soon as one comes up stolen, you've got your getaway car."

Was Eischied so sure the getaway car was there?

No, but if he wanted Schultz and the precinct cops to believe, then he better pretend he believed himself. If they believed, and if the car was there, they would find it. If they didn't believe they might not.

About an hour later Captain Finnerty came in with details relating to the telegram. Western Union intended to bill the telegram to a certain phone number —Finnerty read this number from his stenographer's notebook. "Then I asked our guy at the telephone company to locate the number for me, Chief. He just called back. It's a phone booth in the el station at Jerome Avenue and Fordham Road."

The other end of the city.

Eischied asked: "Did you get the exact time the telegram was phoned in?"

In his fussy, schoolteacherish voice, Captain Finnerty read it from his notes: "Nine forty-two, Chief."

The perpetrators couldn't have driven that far that quickly, which meant an accomplice phoned in the telegram. Eischied was calculating. Thirty-five minutes after the start of the robbery. Allow the perpetrators five minutes for the robbery itself and five more to ditch the getaway car. Five minutes after that they phone their accomplice in the Bronx and announce success. But the accomplice doesn't phone in his telegram right away, because he won't take the chance on his house phone. So he uses up twenty minutes to get out of the house, onto a subway train, and when he's far enough away from where he lives he phones in his telegram.

You could draw a circle fifteen minutes distant from that subway station. The whole circle would lie within the Bronx. Somewhere within that circle the gang lived. The gang was at least five people, and its leader was a very careful guy. Whoever phoned in the telegram might have been a woman. Hell, one of the robbers could have been a woman as far as that goes.

In any case, this fair-size gang, for reasons still unknown, liked to claim credit for its crimes afterward.

Soon Lieutenant Schultz phoned from Brooklyn. His voice was excited. "We found the car, Chief."

At the other end of the line Eischied's grin spread, until he lost control of his cigar. With his free hand he managed to catch it just in time.

"Tell me more," he purred.

Schultz explained that he also knew when and where the car had been stolen. "Here's where it was stolen. Here's the surprise, Chief. This wasn't an ordinary car clout. I mean the thief didn't just grab a car parked on the street. About eleven o'clock last night he walks into a parking garage in the Two-Four Precinct, sticks the place up and drives away in the car. And guess what, Chief? He's wearing a ski mask."

This information accreted like coral to information already planted in Eischied's head. But there were too many jagged edges. Eischied had had the gang leader pegged as a careful theoretician, which perhaps he was. But somebody in his band was a lunatic, which meant—what? Perhaps it meant only that the leader did not know what his men were doing behind his back—on their own time, so to speak. Because stealing cars at gunpoint made no sense. It was lunacy. Eischied thought: We get nearly 100,000 cars a year stolen off the street in this town. There is no crime easier than breaking into a parked car, crossing the wires, and driving away. But this lunatic converts the crime of grand larceny-auto into the crime of armed robbery. He scares the shit out of the parking attendant, and risks a confrontation that could end in a gunfight, just to get a car.

Hanging up on Schultz, Eischied barked into his intercom: "Finnerty, bring me the usuals from last night. And while you're at it, bring me the unusuals from the night preceding the previous bank job."

Captain Finnerty came in with two sheaves of flimsies, which he proceeded to arrange into two neat stacks on Eischied's desk. Eischied watched him step back to survey his handiwork, then step forward to pat an errant leaf into place. The piles were now as exact as two decks of cards. Finnerty had been in headquarters too long, Eischied decided. He had become compulsively precise. The former street detective had taken on the mannerisms of a spinster. It happened to all these guys in time, Eischied decided.

"Finnerty, you're too neat."

"How so, Chief?"

"You've become as fussy as an old maid."

"I don't understand, Chief."

Eischied dropped a heavy paw onto the nearer pile and mussed it up.

Finnerty flinched.

Eischied, laughing, mussed the second pile.

Finnerty said stiffly: "Will that be all, Chief?"

Eischied, grinning, said: "That will be all, Finnerty."

Eischied went through last night's batch first, and soon separated out the report he wanted. It was only six lines long and told him nothing he did not know already: a stickup man in a ski mask had taken a red Chrysler. But it did fix the time and place of the stickup: a garage on Broadway at 97th Street just before midnight.

Eischied was scarcely breathing as he thumbed through the second batch of unusuals. These dated from ten days ago. He went down through the stack. It was the last in the pile. He had almost given up. His confidence had gone flat on him; his hunch seemed obviously wrong. But then he found it: a similar stickup, a single car stolen, and the garage in this instance was in the exact same precinct.

When we find this guy, Eischied thought, we'll find out why he feels comfortable in the 24th Precinct. He probably used to live there or something.

And if there were to be more bank stickups, probably each would be preceded by a car stolen in exactly this way. Eischied congratulated himself. He now knew something that the gang didn't know he knew.

And then, late in the afternoon, Lieutenant Fitzgerald returned, bearing between two pieces of black cardboard, the newspaper clipping that had constituted the first message from the bank robbers, and which, by now, had been heavily dosed with chemicals. Fitzgerald was beaming.

"Look at this, Chief."

Fitzgerald spread the two cardboards. The clipping had turned crisp and brown. It looked toasted. But four distinct prints now showed.

"I watched how they do it, Chief. They spray it with this chemical. It's called ninhydrin, or something like that. All of a sudden the prints start to appear. Once the paper's been sprayed, if you leave it exposed to light it will just keep on getting darker and darker like photographic paper, until it's black. So I can only show it to you for a minute. Then I have to put it inside the black cardboard and take it back to the lab."

Eischied stared at the four prints. Three were clustered together. The fourth was alone in the center of a column of type.

With a pencil Fitzgerald pointed to each of the three prints in the cluster. "They all belong to Detective McCarthy, Chief. There's one of his on the other side too. I know you thought my prints would be on there too, Chief, but they're not."

Eischied said: "I didn't know you were so light-fingered. You ought to become a pickpocket or a cat burglar or something."

Fitzgerald said: "You're a great kidder, Chief. This one here"—he pointed with the pencil at the single print in the center of the column—"this one doesn't belong to any of our guys."

Eischied nodded. Those few whorls and lines were a man's signature. They were more incriminating than any signature, more incriminating even than a photograph or a confession. Some man somewhere owned that print. Eischied felt the owner's presence in this room, looking over his shoulder.

Eischied wondered if he should have got the FBI to work on this. He had no use for the FBI. But their fingerprint technicians were better than the Police Department's. Maybe the FBI could have found more on this clipping. Some of the smudges around the edges, for instance. Maybe the FBI could have brought up a usable print there.

"Congratulations," Eischied told Fitzgerald. "Now you can put it in my safe."

"The lab wants it back, Chief."

"My safe, Lieutenant Fitzgerald."

Eischied picked up his phone. "Reach out for the PC for me," he told Captain Finnerty. "Ask if he can see me."

Eischied had decided to inform the Police Commissioner about the partial print, and about the getaway car. Today's most significant piece of information was neither of those details, Eischied judged, but rather that these guys liked to stick up garages when they wanted to steal cars. That was the weakness. That was where the breakthrough was going to come. When it came. If it came. He decided not to tell the PC about the stickups. There was a kind of security to holding information no one else had. Eischied couldn't explain it, only feel it, and this security was something he had need of right now, though he could not have said why. It was—comforting.

11

ON Eischied's desk the direct phone sounded again. The PC's voice said: "Will you come in here please, Earl?"

Eischied for once was unworried. Oh, Christ, he thought, another bank robbery. FEAR strikes again.

He buzzed Captain Finnerty. "If there's been another bank robbery that you haven't told me about, Finnerty, you're going to find yourself patrolling the most eastern regions of Queens tomorrow."

"What bank robbery, Chief? There's been no bank robbery." Finnerty was flustered. "I'll check, but I'm almost sure—"

Eischied went down the corridor to the PC's outer office, where Inspector Ryan greeted him, all smiles. Ryan's smile further disarmed the Chief of Detectives.

"You can go right in, Chief."

Inside, drapes were drawn, and the office was as gloomy as a church. That was the first thing Eischied noted. He was unprepared, and the signals were fighting their way through, but slowly.

The PC wore a gray pin-stripe. He was not alone. The First Dep. was in navy blue with a starched shirt. He looked like the captain of a ship. Chief Inspector Emerson was in uniform, of course. The four stars on each shoulder caught light from the chandelier and reflected it upward, causing Emerson's ears to blush.

The next thing Eischied noticed was that all three men were seated on the same side of the PC's desk, facing him. Three against one, thought Eischied. What is this?

The PC directed Eischield to sit down opposite, which was ominous, and a part of Eischied's mind started whirring furiously. Another part was immediately terrified. A third part flashed a grin onto his face, forced his voice to demand almost lightly: "What is this, the Spanish Inquisition?"

The PC fiddled with papers while the other two men watched Eischied with hard eyes. Eischied used his own smile like a tennis ball; he lobbed one over and it bounced around there. But no one batted it back.

The First Deputy said: "The PC has received an allegation."

The PC, obviously uncomfortable, said: "Not an allegation, exactly. 'Allegation' means—"

Across the desk they began to argue the meaning of the word "allegation."

Eischied had gone immediately into a state of shock. Sweat already rimmed his hairline. His hands were pressed into his lap and he kept them there, for they were trembling. His voice was trembling too, despite himself, as he said: "What kind of allegation?"

The PC pushed forward a Xerox copy of a bill from the clothing department of Klopfman's department store. The bill was for two suits totaling $326.26, including tax. Eischied's name was scrawled across the sales slip, though not in his own handwriting, he noted, which was some comfort. He could hope to deny the whole thing so far. Eischied flipped up the bill and glanced at the letter stapled to it. The letter was signed by a man named Claude Muldaver, who identified himself as a sales clerk, clothing department. Muldaver's letter stated that on the date in question Chief of Detectives Eischied and his son were fitted for two suits for which Eischied neither paid nor signed a charge slip. It was apparently part of a payoff of some kind. It was the undersigned's impression that the Chief of Detectives had extorted the merchandise in exchange for an unspecified but probably illegal favor.

Eischied's eyes blurred, refocused, blurred again. He forced himself to read the letter again, while at the same time he fought down the urge to vomit. He knew that the color had left his face, and that, from his physical reaction alone, the men across the table were likely to find him guilty as charged. He didn't know what he could do about this for the moment. A man's physical reactions could not always be entirely controlled, however hard Eischied fought to regain control of his own.

He was a detective. He was trained to think in a series of postulates and questions. His mind began to work again. He doubted Muldaver had thought this letter up by himself. Klopfman was behind it. Klopfman had had to threaten the clerk, probably pay him. Probably the clerk was waiting somewhere terrified, imagining now that Chief of Detectives Eischied would turn the wrath of the Detective Division against him, would order him investigated, arrested, beaten, perhaps killed. That was the way people thought about cops. Whereas the exact opposite was true. Eischied had just been rendered impotent. Muldaver was absolutely safe from police harassment. To lift a finger against Muldaver would seal Eischied's doom.

His doom was perhaps sealed anyway.

The stricken Eischied found he could not raise his

eyes from the death warrant in his hand. His thumb kept lifting the sales slip up off the letter, then dropping it back, then lifting it again, as if he were reading first one page then the other, which he was not. Both were blurred and he could not see to read either one. Across the table he dimly heard the PC say: "Chief Inspector Emerson, perhaps you should read the Miranda warning to Mr. Eischied."

Mister Eischied?

Eischied's eyes focused on Emerson, who muttered that he didn't have the Miranda warning on him. Eischied heard the three inquisitors discuss sending a secretary for a copy—every street detective carried one. Lend us your Miranda warning, please. But under what pretext could one be borrowed? So far this terrible scandal was contained within this one room, and the three inquisitors meant to keep it here until they had more information.

Eischied had begun to count his strengths, if any, and this was possibly one. They weren't sure they had him cold, and weren't sure what to do next if they did.

Eischied heard himself say: "I know the Miranda warning by heart. It says that I have a right to remain silent. That I have a right to counsel. But if you try to read that thing to me I'm walking right out of this room."

So he was fighting back, though still unclear on how to do it, or with what.

He could not even decide on his demeanor. Should he be abject, irate, amused? What was the correct posture of innocence? Should he laugh at this thing?

Laughter was out, because he was trembling. He stood accused of extortion, a Class C felony punishable by up to fifteen years. The least charge against him that he could discern was acceptance of a gratuity, a misdemeanor punishable by a year in jail. Either way his career was over, his pension gone, his life ruined.

His muddled brain sought a method, an idea of some kind, and the only observation to seep through so far was that these men were at least as uncomfortable as he was. They did not know what to do next either.

Eischied, thinking as he spoke, gradually beginning to control his voice, said: "Let's assume that this is an allegation against me, that it is a terribly serious allegation, and that I am guilty. The crime would be extortion. That's a Class C felony. I go away for fifteen, and it's page one headlines tomorrow, and it smears the department and all of you." He paused. "Or let's say I only accepted a gratuity. That's a Class A misdemeanor. A year in jail. Same headlines probably. Big scandal."

He paused for breath, and because the possibilities were so awful.

"Next, consider that somebody's trying to do a job on me. That I've been set up. That I'm not guilty of anything."

This time he managed to look each of them in the eye, trying to plant the doubt. His gaze lingered longest on the Chief Inspector, because Emerson had been a cop as long as Eischied himself. Eischied tried to make his gaze say: Whatever I may be guilty of here, you've done the same somewhere in the past. We all have.

But the Chief Inspector's eyes showed no sympathy Eischied could discern.

The wheel was turning with Eischied's life savings riding on a single number. Eischied was betting that he could work out a cover story as he went along. This was his only chance, and at the moment it seemed a dim one. He wet his lips.

"The first question is did I, or did I not buy two suits in that store on that day. Well, I did buy two suits in that store around that time. Whether it was that exact day or not I don't know."

The lie sounded solid to him. It gave him confidence. But then a sudden memory flashed through Eischied's brain and it nearly undid him: There he stood, a brand-new recruit still in the Police Academy, hearing an instructor say, "You men have never been closer to going to jail than you are right this minute."

All the recruits had nodded soberly. Henceforth a whole new set of laws applied to them which did not apply to ordinary citizens. They could be found guilty of bribery, extortion, dereliction of duty and other crimes too numerous to mention. Henceforth they would be surrounded by all the paraphernalia of detection as well. Henceforth any court they might be dragged before would be rigid and harsh.

Eischied lied: "I may in fact have paid for the suits. I don't remember offhand and I don't have my checkbook in my pocket. Or I may have charged them. I know Klopfman socially, and he's got a kid who's always in trouble, and this may be an attempt by him to get even with me because of some favor I failed to do him or his kid. Now why don't you three talk over what you think you want to do while I go back to my office and look for my checkbook."

All he wanted to do was get out of that room.

They were confused. They were glancing at each other. Before anyone could stop him, Eischied was outside in the outer office, where Inspector Ryan made a remark about the weather. In the secretary's small talk Eischied perceived—or thought he perceived—his own possible salvation. Obviously Ryan, the PC's eyes and ears, knew nothing about the incriminating letter inside the PC's fingers. It must have reached the PC somehow directly. A grim Ryan would have been the most frightening omen so far, but the idiot was smiling.

"The long-range forecast is for a lot of snow this winter, Chief."

"The long-range forecast is for more crime, too."

If Ryan didn't know, that meant no one else knew —yet. Only three men to bluff, which was possible, not an entire Police Department, which wasn't. Eischied longed to wipe the fear and sweat from his brow but, in front of the cordial Ryan, couldn't.

Back in his own office Eischied shut off all calls, locked the door, and in his private toilet bathed his face. The idea came to him to type out a letter to Klopfman dated a month ago. It could demand a bill for the suits—he could stuff the carbon into his files somewhere. He could produce the carbon as evidence that his own conduct was aboveboard. If the bill hadn't come, it wasn't his fault. See, no extorted bribe here.

But this was too risky. Any such letter would have been dictated to a secretary, and the Chief of Detectives would be asked to produce this secretary. No good asking (or bribing) some loyal young lady to lie for him, as any big businessman could and doubtless would. All Eischied's secretaries were detectives who, instead of remembering the non-existent letter, would be figuring out exactly what the charges against Chief Eischied must be. In addition, said detectives had sworn the same oath as Eischied, and could go to jail just as fast. Official misconduct was a felony for them too. So was obstruction of justice.

Maybe Eischied should order up Klopfman's son's sheet, and show it. This would seem to prove that he hadn't helped the kid, and it suggested why Klopfman might now be out to set him up. But the date of the kid's last arrest, and the date on Eischied's sales slip would match, they were identical, and to those three men in there this "coincidence" was going to seem highly suspicious, if not absolutely damning. They might hang him with it, or try to.

But the dates were not going to change, and any investigation was going to dig them up anyway. Eischied had better produce them himself. Buzzing Finnerty, he ordered up the Klopfman kid's yellow sheet, and when it came, approached the PC's office again. He didn't want to go in there, but had to if he was to survive.

The drapes were still drawn. In the gloom they looked like men in a funeral home awaiting the arrival of the corpse himself. A fourth man was now present —Chief Palmer from Inspectional Services.

First Deputy O'Connor broke the silence: "Did you come up with proof that you paid for those suits yet, Earl? No canceled check?"

Eischied registered automatically the mood of the room. O'Connor was sure. Others too no doubt, which was neither here nor there, unless they could prove it.

"I don't find a canceled check," Eischied stated, "and I'm not going to tell you I paid for them in cash. I never pay cash for anything. I no doubt charged them." He pushed Kenneth Klopfman's yellow sheet across the desk at the PC. "The story's beginning to come back to me now. I took my kid around there to get him a suit, and while I was at it I bought one for myself. I found I didn't have my charge plate on me, or a check either, so I called up Klopfman and asked him to okay my charging the purchase. Naturally I expected to receive a bill. Presumably I never received one. Now, you will note from that yellow sheet that Klopfman's kid was arrested that very day. While I was talking to Klopfman about okaying the suits, he asked me if I could help his kid. I've got an anguished father on the phone, you understand. What could I say? Should I have accused him of trying to obstruct justice or something? I did what any one of you would have done. I told him I'd see if I could help him. Then I left and thought no more about it. You can check into the case all you want. You'll find out it went forward exactly on schedule. The kid got convicted. I did nothing whatsoever either for or against Klopfman's kid."

O'Connor snorted derisively, but the Police Commissioner, no more anxious than any other political man to expose a scandal inside his own administration, looked up from the yellow sheet. "I'd like to believe you, Earl."

First Deputy O'Connor said: "Frankly, I find your story farfetched."

Eischied shrugged.

The First Deputy pounced. "Let's see your charge plate."

Because Eischied had no charge plate for Klopfman's, physical panic took control again. The sweat began to pop out along his hairline, and he blurted: "I don't have any charge plate there. When I want something there I use my wife's." It was out before he had had a chance to test the way it would sound, and now, hearing it, he knew he had stirred up still more problems for himself.

The First Deputy said: "I thought you were divorced."

"We still see each other sometimes," mumbled Eischied after a momentary silence. He did not care how many personal secrets he exposed. All he was thinking about was staying out of jail. Did his ex-wife have a charge plate for that store? He hoped she did. Please God she did.

Eischied was made to wait outside the back door of the Police Commissioner's office on the small landing there between the PC's personal elevator and his personal toilet.

When he was invited to re-enter the office, the drapes were open, and the First Deputy and the Chief Inspector were gone. So was Chief Palmer. Sunlight flooded in. The PC informed him that an investigation would be conducted by Chief Palmer personally, beginning at once.

"You are free to go," said the Police Commissioner curtly.

Free?

Eischied went out past the genial Inspector Ryan, who still thought the weather unusual for this time of year. Not trusting himself to speak, Eischied only nodded.

From his own office he went through to his private toilet where his bowels voided themselves, and he was racked by hot and cold flashes.

Free?

He was amazed at the intensity of his yearning. Free for how long? Free to go where?

In his brain he heard his voice telling Klopfman: "You're lucky I didn't visit your jewelry department."

Suppose Klopfman had that on tape?

Suppose his ex-wife had no charge plate?

Suppose the clerk Muldaver had been bribed to "remember" some incriminating remark by Eischied?

Back at his desk the intercom buzzed, and Captain Finnerty announced Chief Palmer.

Chief Palmer, beaming with self-importance, stepped around Eischied's desk and flopped down in Eischied's swivel chair.

"I'll relieve you of your checkbook, if I may, Earl."

Palmer leaned back so Eischied could pull his desk drawer open. Eischied's gun was lying there among the cigars and clerical crap. So was the checkbook. Eischied handed it over.

Chief Palmer said: "There's no evidence lying around that I'm going to find, is there, Earl? If there is, you could save us all a great deal of trouble."

They stared at each other.

"Do you want a cigar?" inquired Eischied.

"No thank you."

Eischied, lighting one, said: "How long do you think your investigation is going to take?"

"Oh, a couple of days, Earl. A couple of days."

Eischied expelled smoke. "Do it as fast as you can, will you?"

It was a cry from the heart, one cop to another. It was a way of saying: If the news is bad put me out of my misery fast.

The smile disappeared from Palmer's face. Standing up, he patted Eischied on the back.

Eischied said: "Where will you go first?"

"Klopfman. I wouldn't try to talk to him before I do, Earl."

"You don't mind if I see my ex-wife before you do, do you?"

"I wouldn't, Earl."

"I've got about a million business problems to go over with her."

"Well, I can't stop you."

"No, you can't."

They went out of the building together. The two unmarked cars waited in front, engines running, armed chauffeurs staring out over the steering wheels.

Eischied went directly up to Washington Heights, where his wife lived in a fourth-floor apartment near Riverside Drive. He hadn't called first. If she wasn't there he planned to wait.

"Oh, it's you," she said uncertainly, standing in the doorway.

He had surprised her. Her hair was in disarray. She tried to smooth it with one hand, but failed. She was wearing plaid slacks and an emerald green sweater.

"You might at least have called first."

She looked middle-aged.

"May I come in?" Why so formal with someone with whom he had once been so intimate? He didn't like to visit his ex-wife. In her apartment he usually felt more uncomfortable than in the apartment of a perfect stranger.

"Are you here for some specific reason? If it's to see your son, he's out."

Eischied said nothing.

"Do you plan to stay any length of time? Would you like a cup of coffee?"

Her eyes swung this way and that, not meeting his. Finally Eischied said: "A cup of coffee would be nice."

He sat at the kitchen table and she served him. He had not even taken his topcoat off. Her sweater was tight. Otherwise she looked dowdy. While the coffee was heating, she had made several efforts to tidy her hair, patting it this way and that. Now she had given up.

She sat down opposite him, and they sipped from cups.

Presently Eischied asked questions about their son. He tried to keep his questions bright, and to appear good humored. But he watched her eyes narrow.

"You're in some kind of trouble."

He put his coffee cup down. "Maybe. I don't know."

She snorted. "What did you do?"

"There's a cop named Chief Palmer who's probably going to ask you some questions." He stopped.

In a more gentle voice she said: "Ed Palmer? What about?"

But he was having trouble requesting the favor he needed. She had no reason to accord him this favor, or any other. Probably she hated him.

He said: "You remember the day I took my son out and bought him a new suit? When Palmer asks you, I wish you'd tell him that the new suit was your idea, and that you sent me to Klopfman's with your charge plate. You do have a charge plate for Klopfman's, don't you?"

Instead of answering, she studied him through half-closed lids.

Her handbag lay on the sideboard. He reached for it, dumped it on the table, extracted cards from her billfold and began shuffling through them. She was angry. She had made an effort to pull the handbag away from him, but he had resisted. Now she watched him coldly.

Eischied had found no charge plate for Klopfman's store.

"You used to have one," he said.

She heard the panic in his voice and was perhaps pleased by it. "It's a shop I never liked."

Eischied gnawed his lower lip. Finally he said: "But you should tell Palmer you sent me there because of an ad you saw in the paper."

She watched him.

She had been a policeman's wife. She was as aware of the double standard as he was. A cop on someone's Christmas list was guilty of a crime. A reporter in exchange for an article could accept a free trip to the Caribbean, and that was no crime at all.

He told himself that, if she had wanted to ruin him, she could have done it years ago. He told himself he took no risk putting himself in her hands now.

She said grudgingly: "Maybe you better tell me what trouble you're in."

Eischied said nothing.

Her fingers raised the coffeepot. "More coffee?"

"No."

Eischied got up and moved toward the door. His ex-wife followed.

His hand on the knob, Eischied said: "I wish you'd call me. If he comes here I mean."

He waited, but she did not answer.

He went out. Behind him through the door he heard her fingers manipulating the locks and bolts. He heard her slide them home against him.

He got heavily back into the front seat of his car. It was early afternoon. A reading lamp hung there, attached by flexible tube to the dashboard. He pushed it out of his way.

"Move," he told Detective Malfitano.

He rode in front through long habit, and because the radios and microphones were there. Statesmen rode in the back seat. Commanders only wanted to be close to those mikes. A man in the back was at the mercy of his driver stretching a mike to him, a symbolic loss of power. A commander was one who commanded, who gave the impression of needing no one, though of course that was absurd. A commander was more dependent upon others by far than any cop on the street. A street cop made instant decisions on his own authority and, unless he shot someone or got caught in a corruption investigation, passed through life unnoticed. Many people thought cops corrupt or brutal, but a cop's life, it seemed to Eischied now, was a life of innocence. A cop was continually having to cope with ugly people, ugly sights, ugly events, and ugly temptations, but he was innocent nonetheless.

"Where to, Chief?" asked Detective Malfitano.

"Home, Louie."

If Louie was surprised, he did not show it. He tried to keep a light conversation, but Eischied stared out the window. Louie wasn't a real detective; he was a former traffic patrolman. His only qualification for detective rank was that he lived in the same precinct as Eischied. When Eischied was named Chief of Detectives he became entitled to two drivers assigned around the clock. The jobs carried detective rating. Since the Chief of Detectives' car had to be ready to roll day or night, his drivers had to live nearby, and so the computers in the Chief of Personnel's office went to work. The 20th Precinct on Manhattan's West Side was half luxury apartment buildings, half ghetto.

Cops didn't belong in either category, and so the computer turned up only four names. Eischied, having kept one of his predecessor's drivers, interviewed Louie Malfitano and three black patrolmen for the other job. Eischied had no desire to employ a black driver, fearing long racial discussions in the car. His principal feeling about blacks was that they committed about 65 percent of the violent crime in the city right now. That was fact. You couldn't change it. The criminals whom day after day he tried to hunt down and lock up were mostly black men. No, he had no need for a black driver.

So he chose Louie, who overnight found himself a detective, his life's ambition, formerly unattainable. Louie was just smart enough to drive a car, or to distribute parking tickets. Though he now had the rank, the gold shield and the extra money, he was no detective. That gold shield was the ambition of every patrolman in the city, and there must be twenty thousand of them more qualified than Louie, but Louie had it and they didn't and life is not fair, is it? Eischied asked himself again. Same question, same answer. For the millionth time.

Eischied, staring numbly out the window, found himself shaking his head.

"You say something, Chief?"

"No."

Eischied lived in a studio apartment half a block from Central Park. Stepping from the car, he glanced up at his building. What did he want to go in there for? Nothing was lonelier than four walls. Wrong. Prison was lonelier: three walls and some bars.

Abruptly he set off on foot toward the park, leaving Louie parked beside a fire hydrant. He had told Louie nothing. Why should he? A Chief of Detectives was not obliged to explain his actions to his chauffeur.

In the park, his feet plodded along, his mind too. The blacks were the city's criminal element this year. That was fact. It was a fact that do-gooders and liberals did not like to face. The Mayor refused to face it also. Black people don't commit the crimes, the Mayor liked to say, poor people commit the crimes.

Okay, thought Eischied roughly, but this year most blacks are poor people. That was fact, and fact was what a detective dealt with.

But Eischied's mind refused to stick with fact. It kept closing in on himself, his life, his suffering. He did not know what Klopfman would tell Chief Palmer. He did not know what his ex-wife would tell Chief Palmer. He wished he could sit down with Palmer, cop to cop, and say: We've been in this job together nearly thirty years. Give me a break. Depending upon the way you interrogate Klopfman, his clerk, even my wife, you can save me or ruin me. You can communicate fear. You can distribute fear. People are afraid of cops, and any detective can terrify a subject. You can watch their testimony break up, become vague. Whatever determination you bring back to the PC he is stuck with.

Eischied found himself standing in the park gazing south at the cliff face of buildings that reared up above the trees, a view as stunning and miraculous as any rock formation in any national park. It was a view of his city he had always loved, and he found that it gave him pleasure even now, though not much.

He plodded on, crossing the meadow where teams of boys kicked soccer balls about. Soccer was a game that didn't exist in New York in Eischied's youth. Maybe sissies played soccer somewhere, but a real boy didn't. Real boys played tackle football in the street. Tennis, another of today's popular games, was the same. Only fags played tennis then. If you saw a kid with a tennis racket, that meant he was a fag, unless he stole it.

This city was changing constantly, and everything within it changed, and people came into the city from other cities and took over the leadership of companies and dominated entire industries, and the people who were born here took lower jobs. Eischied was a New Yorker and proud of it, and had risen to the top of his profession in his own town, one of the city's few top-ranking executives born and bred here. Of course there was no competition from outsiders in law enforcement; cops were all New Yorkers together, watching over the city they had been born in, whose streets they had played on, guarding it for everyone, and this was part of cops' solidarity, part of their love for each other. If it was also part of their scorn for outsiders, opportunists, foreigners and, let's face it, minorities, this could not be helped. At least cops rarely turned against cops. It did happen sometimes though. In the police hierarchy, unfortunately, it happened often.

Once it was seen that Eischied was lost no top cop's voice would be raised to save him.

A wave of self-pity washed over the Chief of Detectives. It drenched him like sweat. He thought: I operate in a world that obeys no rules; so why expect me to? He felt like a man standing bound to the pole. The blindfold had already been tied on. Behind the rifles stood his "friends." He was waiting to feel the bullets thud into him.

He found himself peering up at the statue of Samuel F. B. Morse. There was a guy who made it big in life, Eischied reflected. Morse had come forward with an insane invention. Though his little tap-tap machine did seem to work when wires were strung from one room to another, applause should have been modest. Instead he had floated a scheme wherein millions of dollars were invested, millions of miles of wire were manufactured—and then strung coast to coast. Thousands of men were taught a crazy code consisting of long and short noises. How was this possible? To the men of his time Morse must have seemed a visionary, and consequently a lunatic. To say that he had come forward at the proper hour was insufficient. To say that his zany idea had "caught on" also explained nothing. Nonetheless, there he stood, commemorated in bronze, pigeon shit stuck all over him.

Eischied, shaking his head at Morse's streaked green face, was trying to put these ideas and others in perspective. It seemed to him that with clear thinking some of his fear would go away, his mortal danger would be less obvious to him, he would be able to face these next hours and days.

He found he envied Morse, nearly a hundred years dead but a hero for all time. Was not eternal heroship what all man sought, including himself?

He didn't know what all men sought, only what he himself sought at this moment, which was that he not be indicted, that he stay out of jail. He wanted to save his job if he could, but the other two projects came first.

He stared at Morse, glorified for all time for a single gadget which was not even significant in the world anymore; it scarcely even existed anymore. Morse had once been known for other inventions too, and also he had been a painter, Eischied knew, for he had once worked on the Art Squad. The acts and accomplishments by which a man was remembered diminished year by year. Time whittled him down. Time eroded all his accomplishments, until only one was left, the telegraph in Morse's case.

And in his own? Nearly thirty years' service to law and order would be forgotten. He would be remembered as a felon, a key figure in a spectacular scandal.

His life was about to be desecrated. Who had done this to him? Himself.

He walked on under the trees. He walked with downcast eyes but, being a detective, observed much, including that girl there, walking her dog. The dog was bounding away. The folded leash she clutched in her hand. Eischied watched her a moment. Pert profile, long hair. Nice breasts. If you wanted to pick up a girl, then to walk a dog in the park was one of the easiest ways. You struck up a conversation about your respective dogs. In fact, you didn't even need the dog, just the leash. Eischied knew of a rapist who used to pretend that his dog had run off beyond the trees. The girls never knew the difference. Gullible, romantic assholes. Several of the girls got killed. Eischied and two other detectives arrested the rapist and murderer, going in after him with shotguns.

Perhaps Eischied had become conscious too early in life of all of life's aberrations. It made certain of the more ordinary possibilities, like picking up strange girls, seem all too easy, and he had done it, and he was a divorced man now. Though he stood surrounded by privilege in the midst of thirty-two thousand armed men, though he knew a great many public figures, though he was an important catch for hostesses planning dinner parties, he was alone nonetheless. There was no one who loved him, he believed, or even liked him very much, no one who would mourn his fall for long.

He was alone, fighting for his life.

Coming out of the park on the other side he strolled east across 70th Street. The Frick Museum was on his left, one of the finest mansions and art collections in the world, though once the property of a single man, one Henry Clay Frick, a steel magnate. Frick, to Eischied, was one of the supreme scoundrels of all time. How many million dollars worth of goods and services did Frick extort in his lifetime, Eischied asked himself? How many murders was he responsible for, how many suicides? But no one ever indicted him, much less convicted him, and today he was known not as an arch criminal but as a patron of the arts. His memory was saluted by everyone who entered his museum.

Eischied thought: And I may go to jail for two suits.

He began to study the townhouses he passed. Some were brick, some stone. Some façades were ornamented, and a great many of the doorways were. He loved to walk the streets. He loved New York because it was his, because much of it was beautiful, and because for him it throbbed with life. Traffic moved, noise sounded, odors drifted by. Behind all those walls and doors and windows people ate, talked, worked. Beneath every street the ganglia of the city pulsed with juices, and the very manholes breathed.

They would take Eischied's city away from him, too.

On the corner stood Knoedler's art gallery. When he was a sergeant on the Art Squad that place had been burglarized, and though the investigation had seemed promising, it had soon petered out, and those paintings were never found. Eischied knew a great deal about paintings, including details other art lovers never dreamed of. He knew which type thief stole art, or fenced it, and which type collector bought and hung hot paintings.

To Eischied this neighborhood over here was an odd one. His own, being close to Lincoln Center, was prosperous and active. This one was tree-lined, sedate. It reeked of money. Its townhouses passed in rows, each with its wrought-iron balustrades and elaborate door knockers. The sidewalk was liberally plastered with stale dog business, which was another way you could tell a rich neighborhood. The rich liked dogs.

Ahead, double-parked, waited a black Cadillac limousine, license plate DA-10, the District Attorney's car. What was it doing here, Eischied wondered, when the DA lived not here but up on Riverside Drive, where the two cops were machine-gunned? But Eischied shut off his detective's mind. He was not investigating the District Attorney; the inquiry led nowhere.

Just then a door opened and the DA himself stepped forth. There was no way to avoid him.

"Earl, how are you?"

Eischied, taking the proffered hand, thought: This is the hand of the man who will prosecute me.

The DA offered a pleasantry. Eischied did likewise.

"Well, duty calls," said the DA, and jumped into his car. Eischied watched him go. The office paid only $40,000 a year—plus a city Cadillac and driver, plus the fun of all that power. People were wrong to think civil servants were underpaid. The Chief of Detectives got even less, and was not underpaid either.

At Madison Avenue, Eischied stopped. He didn't

want to walk further. He didn't want to go back either. Irresolute, he simply stood there. He heard a siren wail far off, a stimulant he was hooked on. Somewhere else he heard car horns honking impatiently, and that meant a different police problem. A young woman walked past carrying flowers wrapped in a cone of green tissue paper, and she was one of those he had sworn to safeguard.

He was a cop and this was his town, though for how much longer?

When he got back to his own building, Louie, standing beside the car, said excitedly: "They've been calling you on the radio."

He said nothing.

"I phoned in. The PC was looking for you. There's been another one of those bank robberies."

Eischied thought: Let him solve it himself.

Without speaking Eischied went into the building. Upstairs he smoked a great many cigars. He paced. His phone rang often, but he did not answer.

There was a woman he had been seeing with whom he had a dinner date that night. He thought of canceling but instead took her to a midtown restaurant. He was in no mood to act charming. He was in no mood to be alone, either.

The owner knew him, made a fuss over him, and later would charge him only about half what the bill should be. This too was against the law, Eischied knew. The owner gave the same break to film stars and opera singers who went in there, and it was not illegal for them.

The woman was ten years younger than Eischied, divorced, with an ample figure that pleased him. Her name was Florence Kowski. He had dated no one else for over a year now, and Florence, he strongly suspected, wanted to get married. But Eischied had been married, and was not anxious to be married again.

Florence was pleasant, intelligent and good in bed, but tonight Eischied found he had nothing to say to her, and she soon caught his mood of gloom.

When they came out of the restaurant Detective Malfitano was waiting with the car at the curb. Stolid as a tethered horse, he had waited there two and a half hours.

"I'm taking the car," Eischied told him.

He drove off with Florence, leaving Detective Malfitano at the curb.

Florence said: "You weren't very nice to him."

"He's a detective. I don't have to be nice to him."

"You haven't been very nice to me either, as far as that goes."

"I've got things on my mind."

"That doesn't excuse rudeness."

When he had parked in front of her building he turned toward her. "I'm coming up with you."

The police radio crackled between their knees. Central's bored voice said: "Report of a man down, Fifth Avenue at Four-Two Street. Emergency twelve to respond. Repeat, we have a cardiac arrest at—"

Not far away a man was dying on a sidewalk, but Eischied was watching Florence, who answered with annoyance: "Suppose I don't happen to feel like it?"

"Look, don't play games with me tonight, please."

"You think you can just walk in and out of my life any time you damn please. I'm getting pretty sick of it, if you want to know the truth."

Eischied was looking not for sex but for comfort, though the two were sometimes the same. He wanted to fall asleep with his head on someone's shoulder.

The radio blurted new news. Not bored Central this time, but a scared cop reaching one-handed back into his patrol car half the city away. "The perpetrators are running west along Charlton Street, Central. Send additional units."

Eischied, though he wondered what crime the cops had interrupted and what the outcome would be, leaned over and turned the radio down. "Usually it's quieter this time of night," he told Florence apologetically.

Florence said: "I don't know how you can go on living with such tragedy and violence."

The cop's appeal for help had become radio traffic

too dim to understand, though Eischied tried. To Florence he said: "I need you tonight." In what was for him a rare admission of weakness he added: "I'm in bad shape."

"It may be a wife's job to cheer her husband up under such circumstances," Florence said, "but I do not happen to be your wife, and cheering a man up is not a girl friend's job."

"Oh, for chrissake."

Eischied, who had taken both her hands, dropped them.

The ceiling light clicked on. With the door half open Florence hesitated. But Eischied stared straight ahead over the wheel.

Florence got out of the car. "Call me up when you feel better." Her voice sounded indifferent. Her words reflected her own bitterness, and the world's. "We'll go out and have some fun."

The slamming door ended Eischied's chances for tonight. He felt desperate. Under her short jacket, her ass wiggled as she walked into her building. He wanted to go after her, beg her, but could not make himself do it.

Now the interminable evening stretched ahead of him, and after that the interminable night. He turned the radio back up, but it had gone silent, the emergency —whatever it had been—already over.

He considered stopping at a bar, perhaps picking up some floozy, but this idea lasted only a moment. He could not face the effort it would take.

There was no friend he wanted to see. There was no one to whom he could explain the desperate trouble he was in.

If it was human warmth he sought, then he could find it in any precinct stationhouse in the city—he would go talk to some cops. This idea cheered him, and he drove up to the 32nd Precinct in Harlem, a sordid old building in a sordid neighborhood, and always busiest after midnight. In the second-floor squad room he watched the prisoners brought in and processed, all of them black, of course: junkies, prostitutes, car thieves, a burglar, two guys who had just bungled a stickup.

The prisoners were interchangeable. So were the detectives. He watched each bored detective in shirt sleeves fingerprint his prisoners, watched a seemingly endless supply of fingers get rolled across the ink, then get pressed down onto the card and rolled there. He watched each prisoner in turn sit beside a desk answering questions—they looked like job applicants—while detectives typed out forms with two fingers. By midnight there were eight prisoners in the cage across the squad room. One, a junkie, sat nodding on the floor against the wall. But others stood watching Eischied with dark, soulful eyes that seemed to accuse him of something, though what?

Later Eischied's nose became conscious of the unmistakable odor of human excrement. The Chief of Detectives glanced into the cage, where, in his corner, the nodding junkie nodded alone. All the other prisoners had moved as far away as the cage allowed.

A detective looked up from his typewriter, sniffed sharply, and barked: "Who shit in the cage?"

No detective wanted to drag the junkie out, so they sent for the uniformed cop who had arrested him. He was that cop's prisoner. It was up to that particular cop to drag him to the men's room and make him clean himself up.

The cop came into the squad room with his uniform blouse hanging open. Underneath he wore a red-and-blue plaid shirt. When he peered into the cage at his prisoner, his mouth curled with disgust.

Unaccountably, Eischied started to laugh.

By 2 A.M. he felt a little better, and he drove himself home and went to bed. In his dream Chief Palmer ferreted out every indiscretion of his life because Eischied's ex-wife had told Palmer where to look.

12

SHE was expecting him. As she stood in the doorway Chief Palmer saw that she was faultlessly dressed and groomed. It was midafternoon, but she looked dressed to go out to a nightclub. Even her hair was done. Palmer knew she would be looking down his throat. She would be ready for every question.

Every cop learned to dread Internal Affairs. So did every cop's wife.

Palmer gave his most disarming smile. "Hello, Betty," he said, beaming at her. "Long time no see."

He wondered if he should kiss her, but there was no answering smile, and so he did not.

That cops were members of a despised profession Palmer had long since recognized; they were loved only by other cops. They found welcome only inside police families. But even this solace was denied cops who worked for Internal Affairs.

She invited him inside, and in the living room asked if he wanted a drink.

Her demeanor seemed to him inscrutable. So was her face. This, plus the job he had come to do, left Palmer distinctly ill at ease.

"It's late in the day. I guess we can consider that I'm off duty," said Palmer genially. But it wasn't late in the day. He wasn't off duty either and they both knew it.

"What would you like?"

"Still Scotch on the rocks, Betty. Still Scotch on the rocks."

She frowned.

"You look great, Betty. How's the boy? How long is it since we've seen each other, anyway?"

Betty Eischied's eyes never left him. "It must be about ten years." She handed over his drink.

"I think the last time was when Earl and I were both working in Queens in Robbery, if I recall."

She did not answer.

"Then we both made captain and—"

She still said nothing.

"Well, here's looking at you," said Palmer. He swallowed a stiff dose.

Betty Eischied watched him.

"Time sure does fly," said Palmer. Her deportment was making Palmer nervous. He had hoped she would treat him like an old friend. Instead she sat with her rump against the arm of a chair. She had both arms crossed, and was watching him as carefully as a snake.

One began an interrogation like this with conversation that was more searching than it looked.

After taking another big swallow, Plamer remarked: "Earl said he was gonna stop by to see you." Had Earl come by? What had he told her? It was important to get this detail settled first. "I guess he's come and gone by now. Am I right?"

Betty Eischied said: "Would you like some more ice in your drink?" But she did not move to fetch ice, and her eyes never left him.

Palmer tried again. "Did Earl fill you in?"

It was almost the same question. Betty Eischied said: "Why don't you fill me in?"

Palmer forced a laugh. "Still a cop's wife, aren't you, Betty?"

She did not answer this remark either. It left Palmer not even sure she had been warned, much less how well. Discomfited, Palmer got his notebook out and began his interrogation.

There were rules for interrogations like this. One asked questions that required exact answers but which revealed little about the questioner—not his prior knowledge, nor the purpose of his questions, nor even the scope of the investigation. Bit by bit (one was not allowed to prompt or coach the witness), one forced from him or her the damaging information that was sought.

Palmer mentioned the specific date last summer. "Let me fix that date in your mind, Betty. It was the day after the two cops were machine-gunned. Did anything unusual happen on that particular day?"

But she parried the question. "Like what?"

"Well, for instance, did you happen to see Earl that day?" It would help him to know what type of relationship still existed between her and Earl.

"Whether I saw him or not would not be unusual."

Palmer, nodding, sipped from his drink. "Well, did you happen to see him that day? Or talk to him?" he added.

Betty Eischied's glance never left him. "Why don't you tell me what this is all about?"

Palmer picked up his drink again, thinking it over. She was a cop's wife. He was going to have to give up information if he hoped to get any. The question was, how much?

"There's been a minor allegation against Earl." He addded hurriedly: "A minor thing. Nothing to get excited about."

"There's no such thing as a minor allegation."

"Yes, there can be," Palmer protested.

"Not against a cop."

Palmer would have to tell her more. Depending on what relationship still existed between her and Earl she would either provide or not provide the answers he had come for.

He explained vaguely about the two suits. She said nothing. Her eyes studied him. He said it was his job to determine what this suit business was all about.

"You mean, did somebody give Earl some suits?"

"So my first question is, did he buy your son a new suit on that day, or not?"

The interrogation proceeded. Palmer brought forth his questions. She answered each in as few words as possible. Her answers were not exactly hostile. There was no emotion in them of any kind. Palmer worked hard. She volunteered nothing. But she did answer.

In the past Palmer had always liked Betty Eischied, and today he had even looked forward to seeing her again. However, this interview had turned as unpleasant as any he had ever conducted. Palmer, annoyed, decided to push harder, to push backward into the past.

"There's no reason why you should feel any great warmth toward Earl, is there, Betty? It wasn't a very friendly divorce, as I remember."

Betty Eischied, watching him, made no response.

"What's your relationship with him now, anyway? Is it friendly or what?"

Again she made no response.

"Earl's a great guy, isn't he?" offered Palmer.

"Not if you're married to him, no." She frowned. This was hopeful. Palmer composed his next question carefully.

"If there was something you wanted to tell me about any of Earl's activities, even something from the past that maybe we should look into, well, that information would be held in strictest confidence."

"You mean like taking ten dollars from a motorist when he was a patrolman?"

Palmer gave a false laugh. "Not that far back, and not that trivial. Something more important than that after he had attained a certain rank."

"About the suits?"

"About the suits, or about anything." He readied a fresh page in his notebook. "For instance, where did he get the money to buy that apartment he lives in?"

Betty Eischied watched him.

"I don't see where you owe Earl anything after the way he treated you."

"No," she said.

Sunlight, slanting through the venetian blinds, had crept across the rug onto Palmer's shiny black shoes. Cop's shoes, he thought, glancing down. Sunlight soft as a cat, and as insistent as questions. As the man

151

in the cop's shoes continued to interrogate another cop's ex-wife, Palmer felt shame, for it was a dirty job, though no dirtier than most jobs cops did.

Later, sullen as a girl, Betty Eischied led him to the door, where he made an attempt to salvage something of his own self-respect and of their former intimacy. Flashing his jovial grin he remarked: "You should never have married Earl, Betty. You should have married me."

Palmer bent to kiss her on the cheek, but she did not respond. He left. He had filled six pages in his notebook, for he counted them outside her door. Through the door he heard her hand pushing bolts home against him. The noise brought Palmer's shame rising up strong. But a dishonest cop sullies us all, he told himself. A dishonest cop undermines the very possibility of civilization.

13

EISCHIED looked haggard. He had not slept much, and in addition had cut himself shaving. He came downstairs and out onto the pavement. Sunlight slanted into him. It made one side of his face look as if he had been clawed. His other driver, Harold Stern, also a detective, waited at the curb. Harold apparently noticed neither the claw marks, nor the bloodshot eyes. Some detective.

"Morning, Chief."

Harold held open the car door for Eischied; then hurried around to the other side and slid under the wheel.

Harold was the strong, silent type. He never spoke unless spoken to, which was fine with Eischied, especially today. Without a word Harold aimed the car into the 65th Street transverse through Central Park, then sliced across the East Side. The car cut New York into segments, like a surgeon. Soon they were on the FDR Drive pointed toward headquarters. Harold, Eischied reflected, was like the proverbial horse that knew the way. Barring specific instructions to the contrary, inevitably, asking no questions, he steered straight for headquarters. But headquarters today was a place Eischied dreaded entering.

Abruptly he decided he wouldn't go there. The entire city came under his jurisdiction. He would choose some other place.

The *Daily News* lay beside him folded. Eischied unfolded it. There were big headlines for yesterday's bank robbery which had taken place on Jewel Avenue in Queens. A bank guard had been wounded; and a girl teller had fallen down, presumably from fright, and broken her arm. The perpetrators had had shotguns as well as handguns. They had shot up all the glass in the place. In the photos the glass looked thick as sawdust on the floor. They had escaped with over $50,000. An hour afterward messages had been hand delivered to the *New York Times* and to the *Daily News*. The rhetoric was the strongest yet, Eischied noted. Autumn offensive. Capitalist oppressors. Escalation of violence. Urban guerrilla warfare. The city would be brought to a standstill. Signed "FEAR."

Neither the PC nor Chief of Detectives Eischied had been available for comment, the reporter noted.

Refolding the paper, Eischied tossed it over onto the back seat.

There would be pressure for a statement all day today, Eischied knew.

Let the PC cope with that pressure by himself, thought Eischied. The PC would search frantically for his Chief of Detectives, but not find him. There was nothing the PC could do. You can't punish a man you are about to execute.

Traffic was gluey. As they inched past the UN

building, Eischied noted its geometric elegance: sweeping curve of the low building intersected by straight edges of the tall one. He noted also that the glass tower no longer glittered as it had when new. All that glass must be smudged over by some insoluble atmospheric filth. All the hope and promise the building had once inspired was smudged over too. Eischied sometimes thought that the world was getting old fast—it was aging as fast as he himself was, or faster, which it shouldn't, since its life span was different. But even the young did not exude the faith and innocence Eischied remembered from past generations. In place of grandiose visions men today pushed mean little schemes. Eischied recognized, or thought he recognized, a general absence of hope, and professionally this was important for it gave rise to anarchists and revolutionaries. Even the ranks of freelance petty criminals soared. In the absence of hope crime became a form of celebration, a kind of fiesta. Men celebrated the glorious release of tension that came from striking out at society.

Glare slanted up off the motionless river. A tugboat towing three barges moved downtown as fast as they.

Harold, still silent, steered the car arround the bulge in the lower part of the island. The bulge was like a growth, even a cancer, pushed outward by the fetid neighborhood which the river and the highway here curved around. The racially mixed ghetto neighborhood was known as the Lower East Side to New Yorkers; to specialists like Eischied it was the 9th Precinct, one of the most crime-ridden in the city.

The three great bridges soared into view, spanning the river: the Williamsburg, the Manhattan and Brooklyn bridges. They were almost side by side, and in the morning light the sun glanced off their beauty. From a distance their delicate nets tangled and intersected like some crazy modern sculpture. To Eischied this was the single most beautiful vision the city had to offer, and it perked him up a little, even today. How could anyone say New York was not beautiful? he asked himself. He had been to Paris, to London. New York, to him, was more beautiful than either.

"We're not going to headquarters, Harold."

"Where to then, Chief?"

He ordered Harold to drive across the Brooklyn Bridge. The vast police brotherhood was out there and he was still looking for comfort. He would spend the day in the field, as the euphemism had it. He would stand in squad rooms with detectives, as a good boss should. He would check the pulse of his men. He would watch detectives work. He had meant to do this for some time but had felt himself too busy at headquarters. He was not busy today. Today headquarters could fall to pieces as far as he was concerned. Today he would get at best an onerous but necessary job out of the way. At worst, he would look into some of the places which had meant a lot to him in the past. It would be a way of saying good-bye to them all.

In a Brooklyn tenement an hour later Eischied looked down on a black woman, the back of whose skull had been blown off. Close to the corpse forensic personnel worked busily, while in the other room detectives patiently interrogated the woman's out-of-work common-law husband, who was babbling hysterically that he had never meant to do it. The victim had been about twenty-two or twenty-three, Eischied judged, coffee-colored, rather pretty, and a few minutes ago her head had been not only all in one piece, but full of hopes and dreams—the same hopes and dreams that filled everybody's head.

Eischied, when gazing down at victims, always imagined himself unmoved, but this was far from true. Now his lips and teeth moved his cigar around, while his mind attempted to come to grips simultaneously with cosmic questions that were too big for it, and with the puzzle posed by the crime itself. Parts of the puzzle were always obvious. The pieces were spread out upon the floor. The detective merely had to put them together again—the job did not include fitting together the pieces of the victim's skull. The corpse never seemed to Eischied part of the criminal puzzle, but rather part of the cosmic one. Turn the clock back an hour and this woman would jump up off the floor laughing. How had that hairy, blood-clotted, mutilated shell managed to encompass so many thoughts, so much life, and how had all that life managed to leak out so fast, leaving—nothing? Leaving garbage. Time proceeded in one direction only, and not slowly. It marched fast, with human beings sprinting after it, never able to catch up.

A uniformed cop sat on the sofa, his black brogues six inches from the victim's outflung hand. The sofa was older and had seen more hard wear than the victim, Eischied reflected.

The cop was writing in his memo book. Eischied commented: "Nice-looking broad."

It was not something he had wanted to say, and it had nothihg to do with what he felt.

The cop, glancing up from his notes, said: "If you like them dusky."

Eischied gave him a sidelong lecherous grin. "Doesn't everybody? How long have you been working in this precinct? Haven't you had any of this dark stuff yet?"

But the cosmic questions remained, dark, unilluminated, baffling.

Later, in a high building in Queens, Eischied stood with Emergency Service cops as they attempted to talk a jumper in off a ledge.

It took an hour and thirty-five minutes. Eischied clocked it. For an hour and thirty-five minutes the same phrases wre endlessly repeated by cops leaning out the window as far as they dared.

"You don't want to jump. Why not come inside here, and we'll talk it over?"

No answer. Jumpers rarely answered. They seemed to realize that silence was part of their power. And most had never felt so powerful before.

"Is there somebody you'd like us to call for you? Do you have a wife?"

The ledge was six inches wide, the sidewalk nine stories below, but the power was so heady the guy wasn't even scared.

"Would you like us to get you a priest?"

It seemed obvious to Eischied, who had seen jumpers before, that this one had no intention of stepping into the void, though there was always the possibility he might lose his balance and fall. The only ones sweating it out were the cops who had to do the work.

In the street below stood crowds of upturned feces, parked radio cars, a fire truck with a half-extended ladder.

"What religion are you? Would you like to talk to a minister? A rabbi?"

It was like lies from a play. The speeches were entirely predictable, and so was the outcome. At length one cop began to crawl out onto the ledge. The jumper retreated along the ledge, but carefully. The other cop had the first cop by the shoes, which was probably all the guy would be left with if his partner lost his balance. But at last the cop on the ledge managed to take the jumper's hand and at length the two of them crawled slowly back into the apartment. Other cops on the roof put their gear away. The fire truck in the street drove off.

Inside the apartment, the cop who had been on the ledge sat in his undershirt, smoking and trembling. He said: "The guy never intended to jump."

Eischied answered: "He might have, if you guys hadn't been here."

After lunch Eischied responded with two detectives to an apartment which had been burglarized. The detectives were good. They asked all the proper questions, got down all the information. They were patient. They comforted the victim, a woman of about fifty. They did not inform her, and neither did Eischied, that the arrest rate for burglary was only 18 percent, and that the percentage of goods recovered was even lower than that. The woman would not see her silverware again, or her few pieces of jewelry. The facts and details compiled here would go into the computer, and would turn up a year from now as part of the FBI's crime statistics for major cities. That was the sole point of the exercise in most cases. But at least the woman was in better shape when they left than when they had arrived. She was under the illusion that someone cared, that the system was working to redress the injustice that had befallen her, though it was not.

By midafternoon Eischied was on a rooftop in the South Bronx crouched with two detectives inside a cardboard carton which had been placed close to the parapet. Through eyeholes cut in the cardboard the detectives had been keeping surveillance on a warehouse across the street for ten days. The warehouse, they believed, received stolen cars. They had binoculars and walkie-talkies to work with, but no camera, they told Eischied. They had tried to check out a 16-mm. camera. They had wanted to film cars entering the warehouse, because pieces of those same cars left later on the backs of trucks; but they had been told no camera was available. This might weaken their case in court. Still, they believed they had almost enough information now to raid the place.

"In ten days it only rained once, Chief," one of the detectives explained. "We didn't mind the rain so much, but our cardboard box melted around us. The next day we had to get rid of it and bring up another one."

As a young detective Eischied had many times sat on a place. He had sat in blinds like this one, and in parked cars, and in empty apartments. A detective sat for hours and hours, and nothing happened, but that was what detective work was all about, and if you had the soul of a detective you never got bored. A true detective knew, absolutely knew, that whatever he was waiting for to happen eventually would happen. A true detective was like a fisherman who was certain that the fish was there, and would take the bait. A true fisherman would wait for hours, and so would a true detective, and the pleasure that came when the line tautened was one of the keenest that it was given man to know.

Eischied was familiar with this case. The thieves took orders from body and fender shops for specific parts of specific makes of cars: fenders, trunk lids, nose clips. They then went out and stole the make and model car they needed and cut it up into pieces in this warehouse. They peddled the ordered piece to the customer and kept the rest on inventory. Once they had got rid of parts carrying serial numbers, they were safe from the law.

"This is a good case," Eischied told the two detectives.

They beamed. To them Eischied's meager comment counted as great praise, and now they would happily sit in this box surveying this warehouse for however long it might take, convinced that headquarters knew what they were doing, and cared.

Cops, like everyone else, needed praise, Eischied reflected. But they rarely got any, which was sad. A great many people hated cops, and almost no citizen ever praised them, and their bosses usually didn't either.

Still later in Harlem Eischied went with two detectives to an apartment in which an old man lay dead. The odor was already strong at the bottom of the stairs. It got stronger as Eischied and the two detectives climbed.

"Jesus," Eischied said, and concentrated on breathing through his mouth.

"This is a ripe one, all right," one of the detectives said.

Inside the apartment the odor was almost unsupportable, and Eischied gave his first order of the day: "Christ, somebody open the windows."

A neighbor had complained about the odor, Eischied supposed. Two radio car cops had responded, and had broken in through the door. At that the pent-up odor had expanded until it filled the entire building.

One of the uniformed guys was standing in the hall with his cap pushed back on his head. The other, Eischied noted, had vomited into the kitchen sink, and was now wiping his mouth on his handkerchief.

The corpse, bloated and blue, lay on the bedroom floor wearing pajamas. The pajamas had split in several places.

One of the detectives muttered: "I don't see any evidence of homicide, do you, Chief?"

He wanted to get out of there, and Eischied didn't blame him. If the Chief of Detectives had not been present, he probably would be gone already.

Eischied found this funny, and he laughed. "Don't you think you ought to examine the corpse before you decide?"

Eischied was rummaging in a closet. A makeshift smudge pot ought to be set burning, and ammonia spread around. In the meantime he had found a fan, which he handed to the other detective. "Plug this in, facing toward the windows. Maybe we can blow some of the stink out into the courtyard." Eischied thought: Let the neighbors get a whiff of it.

The stench must have been pretty strong even before the complaint was phoned in. This poor bastard on the floor had been dead a week at least, and must have become increasingly rank day by day. In a wealthy neighborhood the police would have heard the first complaint at the end of forty-eight hours, but in the ghetto different rules applied. The poor had learned to suffer in silence. Whatever went wrong in their lives, they simply put up with it.

The detective straightened up. His voice was muffled by the handkerchief pressed to his face. "There's no sign of a wound on him that I can see, Chief."

Eischied said to the two uniformed cops: "You'll have to wait here till the medical examiner comes. But there's no reason why you have to wait inside the apartment. You could wait in the hall, if you want to."

The two cops looked grateful. All five men trooped out of the apartment.

Eischied and the detectives left. Outside in the street Eischied invited them to have supper with him, and they accepted. In a crumby diner he bought them sandwiches and coffee, and for an hour he enjoyed their company, and they his, he hoped.

Occasionally he twitted them: "If the medical examiner finds it was homicide, you guys will have to go back there. I'll bet you're looking forward to it."

"Chief, please, not while I'm eating."

"Myself, I won't have to go back there. I'm Chief of Detectives."

In the street, after shaking hands, he watched them get into their car. He thought: For most people life is a terribly lonely place, but in his own city no cop is ever really alone.

14

THE Police Commissioner sat behind his big desk in shirt sleeves. The other three men, Chief Inspector Emerson in uniform, Chief Palmer and First Deputy O'Connor in civilian clothes, sat in a semicircle facing the PC across the desk. Palmer had his notes affixed to a clipboard, and as the others waited tensely for his report, he thumbed back through the notes, as if he had forgotten what was in them.

He cleared his throat. "Report on the Eischied allegations," he began.

Glancing up, he peered at the PC above the glasses perched on the end of his nose, and continued: "I went to see the clerk in the clothing department at Klopfman's, this fellow"—Palmer consulted his notes —"this fellow Muldaver. Muldaver is male, white, forty-five years of age. No criminal record. He's worked there twenty-two years. He's married and has three daughters. The oldest is of college age."

Again Palmer, glancing up from his notes, peered at them above his glasses.

"The interview took place in Klopfman's office. I had asked to see Muldaver alone, but Klopfman refused. Klopfman insisted on being there. He sat in on the entire interview. At first Muldaver merely repeated the allegations contained in his letter to the PC." Palmer, lifting the spring clip, withdrew the letter from his notes, and waved it. "This letter. Call it Exhibit 1. As he repeated the allegations, Muldaver glanced repeatedly across at Klopfman, who kept nodding encouragement at him. I noted that Muldaver was sweating profusely during the entire interview. Several times Klopfman prompted him. Once Klopfman said encouragingly, 'This is not a courtroom, Claude. You are not under oath. Chief Palmer is just trying to get the facts.' Briefly Muldaver said that Eischied walked in there, ordered suits for himself and his son, and was fitted. He then told the clerk he wasn't going to pay for them, that Klopfman would okay it. He then walked out."

Palmer, peering above his glasses, ignoring his notes for the moment, said: "That doesn't sound like Earl's style to me. Does it to any of you?"

No one answered. The PC was stone-faced. O'Connor, fists jammed in his pockets, began to pace the room.

Palmer continued: "It seemed strange to me that this clerk would allow Eischied just to walk out of there without consulting Klopfman, and I said so. But Klopfman insisted that's how it happened."

Chief Palmer folded back page one of his notes, exposing page two. "After Muldaver was dismissed, I prepared to interview Klopfman himself. I told him that these were very serious allegations, and that if it were shown that Chief Eischied had extorted a bribe, then a reasonable man could expect Eischied to be indicted, tried, convicted and sent to prison. I added that not only was the crime of extorting a bribe terribly serious, but that the crime of bribe giving to a public servant was equally heinous before the law."

Palmer glanced at them above his glasses, as if expecting applause, but no one spoke. "I judged Klopfman did not like the sound of this."

"Oh, shit," said O'Connor.

"I then attempted to interview Klopfman himself, but he said he would answer no questions without the presence of his lawyer, and he had me shown out. So that was that interview."

The First Deputy said disgustedly: "There goes the case against Eischied."

There was a half grin on Palmer's face. "Next I went to see Betty Eischied. She never remarried, you know. I don't know what her feelings are for Earl, and she volunteered no information whatsoever. In response to my questions she said that she had asked Earl to take his son to that store on that day to buy him a suit, because of an ad she saw. She had no charge account with that store. On the other hand, she used to have one when they were married, and Eischied may have thought she still did. He may have attempted to charge the suits to this nonexistent account as he claims. There's no way I can see whereby this possibility can be disproved."

O'Connor snapped: "What else?" The PC stared thoughtfully at his deputy, but said nothing.

"Next I ordered Detective Smallwood, who arrested Klopfman's son for shoplifting, to report to my office. He was terrified, naturally. Thought the subject of the investigation was himself. Took me twenty minutes to get him to talk coherently. The Kenneth Klopfman case turns out to have been a very banal case. Smallwood was in Macy's buying something for his wife, and he sees this kid stuffing goods inside his clothes, and he arrests him. As far as Smallwood is concerned, a very routine case. No one ever spoke to him about it one way or the other that he can remember. Not Earl, not anyone."

Palmer peered over his glasses at the others. O'Connor, who was at the window, showed only his back.

The Chief Inspector studied his fingernails. The PC stared at Palmer.

"Next Smallwood asks me what this is all about, and he's a detective, don't forget, and not all detectives are stupid, contrary to what one would think."

O'Connor snapped: "Never mind the jokes."

Palmer continued. "When I told Smallwood we were investigating allegations of attempted bribery by Klopfman, he perhaps was able to put two and two together." Palmer, studying his notes, studiously avoiding the eyes of the other officials in the room, added: "When you start an investigation of this kind, you take certain risks."

Palmer flipped over two pages of notes without speaking. Gazing down at the sheet now exposed in his lap, he added: "I went to see the Assistant DA who had the shoplifting case. Young guy named Gotbaum. He's new there. This was one of his first cases. He reports that it proceeded entirely normally. Smallwood showed up for each and every one of the pretrial hearings, six in number, which doesn't often happen in our Police Department, I understand. Most of our geniuses forget to attend at least one, and some miss all of them. So maybe we should give Smallwood a medal for devotion above and beyond the call of duty, or promote him to first grade, or something."

Palmer peered above his glasses as if expecting an outburst of laughter. But the other men were all staring in different directions.

"As far as ADA Gotbaum is concerned, the case went through the courts normally. It was the kid's third offense, he pled guilty to a reduced charge and was given six months' probation. Detective Smallwood spent altogether eight days in court. That's eight days of work that the Police Department lost in order for this kid to receive a sentence of six months' probation. Maybe one of us ought to be investigating whether or not the city got its money's worth. Was this a useful return on its investment in Smallwood, in

ADA Gotbaum, in the judge who heard the case, or was it not?"

Palmer allowed all the pages on his clipboard to flip back into place. "That's all I have, gentlemen."

The First Deputy glared at Palmer. "I thought you would come up with evidence. The tape of an incriminating conversation. Notes made contemporaneous to the event. Klopfman had nothing like that?"

Palmer answered: "I think if he had anything like that, he would have indicated as much."

The PC was drumming his fingers on the desk.

Palmer paged through his notes again. "There's certainly not enough here to support an indictment. This Muldaver would come to pieces on the stand. The first thing any defense attorney would ask him was what sort of pressure Klopfman put on him to write the letter. What it comes down to," Palmer concluded, "is an unsupported allegation."

The First Deputy said: "Oh, Eischied did it all right. I don't doubt that for a minute. We just can't prove it."

In the wake of this accusation, there was silence. Palmer was studying the top page of his notes, the Chief Inspector was studying his fingernails again, the PC was studiously stuffing a piece of chewing gum into his mouth.

The First Deputy glared at Palmer. "Are there any lines of inquiry you haven't followed up on yet?"

"No."

From behind his desk the PC said: "At least the press doesn't have wind of it yet. That's one good thing."

The First Deputy took charge. "For the moment, let's just say that the investigation is still open."

Palmer looked surprised. The Chief Inspector was expressionless. O'Connor ushered them both out of the office.

Alone with the PC, the First Deputy muttered, "We could order him to resign."

"And if he won't?"

"You remove him as Chief of Detectives."

The PC found this idea distasteful. "The allegation would come out. People would want to know why, if the allegation was true, Eischied wasn't in jail. And if it wasn't true, why was I firing him. It would be one helluva scandal. No one would believe Palmer's investigation. They'd say we were whitewashing the guy. There would be a terrific stink. None of us would look very good." The PC was thinking that he himself would be smeared as badly as Eischied, and perhaps would be forced to resign also.

In quiet voices they discussed what to do but got nowhere. For the time being they would be obliged to do nothing. Palmer's investigation had been discreet. He had thrown the fear of prosecution into both Klopfman and the clerk, Muldaver. Presumably both would keep their mouths shut. Young Assistant District Attorney Gotbaum could not possibly connect Eischied's name to Palmer's brief questions. That left Detective Smallwood who might suspect something, but surely not much.

"I wish there was some way to ease Eischied out," the PC mused.

The First Deputy said: "He's like all these career cops. He's a crook."

"Easy. Easy," the PC admonished. "You don't mean that, surely."

"It's an insulated department. They all protect each other. I don't like it."

"That's why you and I were put in here. To try to change all that."

After a moment the First Deputy calmed down: "The best thing is to try to ease him out in a month or so."

The PC said: "In the meantime, what do we tell him? It looks like he's in the clear for the moment, and he can't have got much sleep the last few nights. Do we relieve his mind for him?"

The First Deputy said: "Tell him nothing. Let the bastard sweat."

Eischied waited three more days, then could wait no longer. He telephoned Palmer.

"I'm not supposed to tell you anything, Earl."

"What the hell does that meaan?"

"According to the First Dep., the investigation is still open."

In this guarded reply Eischied read the outcome he had yearned for with such intensity. The investigation had reached a dead end.

He wanted it confirmed. "Why don't you tell me what's going on?"

"I can't, Earl."

Eischied took a deep breath. "Did I ever do you any harm? What do you think these last days have been like for me? Just tell me whether you're actively investigating any leads at this time."

"At this time? No."

"Thank you."

"Don't mention it. Watch your ass. They don't like you very much."

In his current state of ebullience the warning scarcely penetrated the grinning Eischied's mind. He put down the phone.

When Lieutenant Fitzgerald came into the room with papers to be signed, Eischied was lighting a cigar. His feet were on his desk, and he blew smoke at the ceiling.

"Red, how about putting your mighty powers of detection to their utmost use and make me a Scotch and soda."

Fitzgerald busied himself at the fridge in the corner. "It's nice to see you in a good mood again, Chief."

"What's happening out in the city, Red?"

Fitzgerald, handing over the drink, said: "The city's quiet, Chief."

"That's good." He had signed Fitzgerald's papers. Fitzgerald took them and went out. Eischied leaned back. He smoked his cigar. He sipped his drink. The late-afternoon sun cooked one side of his face. Since the city was quiet he could leave early, perhaps go see Florence, take her out to dinner. He breathed in and out, thinking, What fun it is just to breathe.

That was the evening before the bloodiest bank robbery yet perpetrated by the self-styled revolutionaries who signed themselves FEAR.

15

WILLIS HAPGOOD, the twenty-three-year-old bank guard, had loved guns as long as he could remember, particularly sidearms. From earliest childhood his ambition had been to own and carry a sidearm, to know its weight and comfort, to feel it hanging hot and heavy against his leg. Perhaps Willis even nursed a vague hope of one day wielding his sidearm in defense of lives or a payroll. Mostly he just wanted to have it.

As a teenager Willis had subscribed to all the cult magazines, and he saw all the best gun-slinging movies many times each, for he liked to study the techniques of the actors. He came to the conclusion that the slickest man with a gun he'd ever seen was Montgomery Clift.

As soon as he was able he joined the army, and in basic training the drill sergeants were delighted with him. Willis ran harder, did more pushups, marched with more precision than any other recruit, and when the sergeants put weapons into his hands he treated them with awe and with passion. The drill masters thought Willis the fiercest recruit they had ever trained. They thought they were training a killer, but Willis didn't think in terms of targets. It was the gun itself that interested Willis, plus the technique necessary to handle it with absolute precision. Willis's imagination stopped short of actual combat. Willis had a vision of himself leaping from cover, screaming his head off, firing his weapon with one hand. But no one ever fired back. Willis saw combat as a scene from a movie.

He reached Vietnam too late. The war, for Americans, was nearly over. On the night he realized he would never see action, Willis was close to tears. The only combat left seemed confined to the bars in Saigon, so when the opportunity came to transfer to the military police, Willis took it. This was the first time he ever wore a sidearm regularly, and the emotion it gave him was all he had expected. As far as American troops in Saigon were concerned, he, Willis Hapgood, had become the law. That sidearm was his authority.

Those parts of Saigon that Willis came to know intimately were both sordid and filthy, but Willis himself was impeccable. His uniforms were always immaculate. His creases were pressed sharp as the cutting edge of a tool. His leather shone. His lanyard always hung in disciplined loops. The sidearm itself, a U.S. Army issue .45-caliber Colt automatic, Willis took down and cleaned every night until the odor of oil under his nails seemed permanent. And he didn't walk his post, he strutted it, imagining that all the gooks watched him with admiration, even discussed the figure he cut, once he had passed by.

As a teenager Willis had been a tall, skinny, white-skinned boy, tortured by acne. The cursed acne had accompanied him even into military service. But once he became an MP all of the pustules disappeared. In Saigon his face was clear, though pocked, and he wished the high school girls who had mocked him could see him now.

He never fired his sidearm. It was never necessary. Nor did he ever use his billy. Some of the other MPs liked to swing their clubs, but Willis had found it sufficient merely to drop his hand to his sidearm. He had studied the rules and regulations. He knew how much force he was permitted, and how much would cost him his job and a court-martial, and he never overstepped the line. It was sufficient to let his hand hang there on his sidearm, finger still outside the trigger guard. Soldiers rushed to obey him.

When Willis was discharged from the army his world fell apart again, and almost immediately his pasty, pitted complexion filled up with more pustules. Though he squeezed frantically morning and night, spattering pus on the bathroom mirror, they would not go away.

Along with ten thousand others, Willis took the test for the Police Department, but he did poorly. It would be a year or two before they called him if they called him at all, and in his despair he settled for a job as an unarmed bank guard in the Southern Boulevard branch of the First National City Bank.

He was given an ill-fitting uniform, and a wide, dun-colored belt from which no sidearm had ever hung. This uniform Willis had restyled and tailored until it fit him as precisely as his army uniforms used to do. He knew how to rub life into old leather, and did so, until belt and shoulder strap almost glowed.

His deportment in the bank was as perfect as he could make it. He saw himself as a symbol of authority, and treated the customers accordingly. When customers questioned him he was precise, correct and aloof. His acne improved, and he was reasonably happy, though twenty times a day he cast envious glances at the shiny leather holster and flap that entirely concealed the sidearm worn by the old man, a retired cop, who was the bank's chief guard.

One day one of the bank officers called Willis over and asked him to sign some forms. The bank was applying for a pistol permit for him. The chief guard was leaving at the end of the month, and Willis would replace him, at least temporarily.

Willis was ecstatic.

Only a week ago he had acceded to his new rank. His new sidearm rode against his thigh, and each day he went to work with joy, and took up his station toward the rear of the bank. Within three days the acne on his cheeks had entirely disappeared. There was nothing left except a row of suppurating pustules across the nape of his neck. Over these he wore a white strip of bandage half hidden by his not-too-clean hair.

Newspaper reports of bank robberies Willis read avidly, and the latest ones fascinated him. Just the other day, studying the *Daily News* photos of a wounded guard, of glass all over the floor, Willis had remarked to the unarmed middle-aged man who had replaced him in the front of the bank: "I'd like to see those sons of bitches try to rob my bank." He had glanced meaningfully down at his sidearm. The middle-aged man had favored him with a funny look.

Willis was envisioning himself leaping from cover, gunning down all the robbers simultaneously, and perhaps the new, unarmed guard had perceived this. Willis had conceived another movie scene, and in the movies hero guards who perform such feats, like all movie heroes, do not get gunned down themselves.

When the first robber came through the door that morning, Willis was on station toward the rear of the bank. The vaults had just opened. Willis was watching two tellers coming from the vaults carrying sacks of money. In an instant two more robbers had sprung inside the bank. All three were wearing ski masks and brandishing guns. Willis didn't see them because he faced toward the vaults.

What he did note was the sudden change of expression on the faces of the two approaching tellers. He sensed what was happening even before he heard the voice near the door cry: "Don't any muthafucka move."

Bandits, thought Willis, who happened to be standing beside a large square pillar. Instantly he stepped behind it, and in another instant he had drawn his sidearm. From behind the pillar he could see none of the gunmen, of course, nor they him.

Two of them stood in the front corners of the bank, backs to the walls. They were not visible from the street. The third advanced toward the fear-frozen tellers and their sacks of money.

It took Willis less than a second to decide what to

do. This seemed enough. He had worked out his actions long ago. He knew exactly how to handle this. He felt a sudden rush of almost orgasmic happiness. Had he not trained all his life for this one instant? Although he did not even know how many men had entered the bank, or where they were placed, Willis made his move.

Screaming unintelligible sounds at the top of his lungs, he leaped out from behind his pillar. The scream was as shrill as a bugle call, as headlong as a cavalry charge. It signaled an event that was either heroic or irrational, depending on the point of view.

The third robber was about ten feet away. Willis shot him. He went down. Willis rushed forward, leaping over the corpse, and the gibberish Willis had been screaming turned itself into the command: "Drop your guns and reach for the sky." John Wayne might have delivered the same line, though in more of a baritone.

Willis could not tell what the two gunmen were thinking. Neither so much as twitched. The ski masks showed no expression. Like the head of a snake the muzzle of Willis's sidearm flicked from one to the other.

For a moment nothing happened. Willis, brandishing his sidearm, stood triumphant in the center of the bank. The two gunmen seemed paralyzed. The teller in number-one cage seemed paralyzed. So did the two officers behind their desks, the two customers on line —everybody seemed paralyzed except Willis, who felt such joy as a king must feel at the moment of his coronation.

Then the front door swung open, and a fourth robber jumped into the bank. This one had a submachine gun. His unexpected appearance totally disoriented Willis. The submachine gun and Willis fired virtually simultaneously. Willis's first bullet struck the teller in number-one cage in the head. His second perforated the plate glass window, passed between two moving cars in the street outside, and struck a woman on the opposite sidewalk who had just turned away from a shop window. The bullet broke both her mandibles and severed her jugular vein as well.

The bullets from the machine gun cut Willis Hapgood almost in half. He was stitched from hip to hip. The final bullet entered his mouth as he was falling, and came out the nape of his neck, carrying away the bandage which had covered Willis's few remaining pustules, and nailing it to the wall of the vault thirty feet away.

16

PATROLMAN Martin Delehanty, Shield No. 33214, had a problem, and as he steered his radio cab along Southern Boulevard that morning, he was trying to come to grips with it. Marty was falling in love with his radio car partner. Or perhaps all he felt was desire. He no longer was able to think clearly on the subject. He was reasonably certain that he would not have looked at Agnes twice if he had met her anywhere else but in a radio car.

Marty Delehanty, who in a few minutes would intervene in the bank robbery, was twenty-nine, married, the father of three small children, the youngest only ten months old. He had been a cop eight years, all of it, once he had graduated from the Police Academy, assigned to the 48th Precinct in the Bronx, and most of it spent riding in this exact same radio car, or in one of its predecessors, together with his partner, who had been, until a few weeks ago, a foul-mouthed patrolman of his own age named Sal Digilio. Sal was his best friend. Marty had moved his family from Brooklyn into an apartment in Queens so as to be close to Sal and Sal's family. Marty and

Sal went hunting and fishing together in the Adirondacks in summer and fall; they bowled together all winter. Their wives had become best friends too. Marty and Sal both belonged to the Patrolmen's Benevolent Association, of course. Both belonged to the Police Holy Name Society. The only difference was that Marty also belonged to the Emerald Society with other Irish cops like himself, whereas Sal belonged to the Columbia Society with all the Dago cops. Sal didn't mind when Marty called him a Dago. Sal was an easygoing guy, always the last one in ranks at roll call, often with his buttons still undone and his gun belt in his hand. Sometimes Marty would push Sal out the stationhouse door saying: "Get in the radio car, you slow-moving Dago."

Marty had found a security in the Police Department that had nothing to do with the steady paychecks or the twenty-year pension, and this security was the department's changelessness. It was a man's world. It hadn't changed for a hundred years, and looked good for another hundred. Sure, the precinct commanders changed, but the cops in the precinct did not, and a guy's partner did not. The radio runs changed each day, depending on what crazy things happened; but a cop's duty remained the same. The friendships a guy made were lasting, and the one thing you could count on above all others was another cop. Patrolman Delehanty had chosen to believe that the Police Department would never change, no matter what, at least during his twenty years, and in a volatile world this was comforting, and on it he had built his life.

But modern times, which had crept up so stealthily upon the world, had with equal stealth suddenly engulfed the Police Department. That women were suddenly claiming equal rights was a minor irritation elsewhere; it seemed catastrophic to cops. Female demands had struck the Police Department like a hammer blow. Among the rights women were demanding, it seemed, was the right to patrol precincts in radio cars, the right to get cursed, kicked, spat upon and beaten by their fellow citizens, possibly even shot and killed.

The Police Department had had its complement of women since long before Martin Delehanty was born, and had had them still when he was sworn in. The "matrons" who used to search female prisoners during the Gay Nineties were called policewomen now. In fact, in Marty's graduating class of nearly one thousand cops there had been four policewomen.

Marty subscribed to all the traditional police beliefs with regard to women. Female cops were not entirely useless these days. They were good at interrogating rape victims. They made excellent stationhouse switchboard operators. The best-looking ones were always grabbed by the headquarters brass as secretaries. And in fact the police career of Agnes Cusack, Marty's new partner, had been typical. Agnes was thirty, and in six years as a cop she had served as secretary to one Deputy Commissioner of Legal Matters, and two Deputy Commissioners of Administration. She had also worked two years in the Community Affairs Division, dealing with lost and abandoned children.

Only two policewomen had been assigned to the 48th Precinct at first; Agnes was one of them. The orders were to send them out on patrol, and obviously they couldn't go out together; too dangerous. Each would go out with a veteran cop. The precinct CO asked for volunteers, but didn't get any. So he grabbed Marty and Sal, partners these eight years, and split them in two, assigning a policewoman to each. Marty drew Agnes.

It had seemed hate at first sight. Agnes, sliding into the radio car that first day, accorded Marty a single truculent glance. He hadn't looked at her at all. He was furious. Marty let the clutch in so hard that the tires squealed, and Agnes lunged forward against the dashboard.

After a moment Agnes said: "Let's call a truce, shall we?"

Marty, though he said nothing, looked her over carefully for the first time. She wore no makeup. Her hair was jet black, and longer than it was supposed to be. She wore it knotted in a single braid twisted into a bun at the back of her head. The uniform made her look wide-hipped and chunky. Around her waist she wore all the gear he did: gun, handcuffs, memo book, whistle, extra bullets. She had a big bosom.

She lived in Staten Island, she told him. Her husband was a house painter. She had no children.

"Why not?"

"Why don't we confine our conversation to business?"

Radio cars were driven round the clock by pair after pair of cops, and acquired the odor of stale cigarettes and reawakened sweat. To Marty all radio cars had smelled the same until now, but in this one, over and above the male odor of patrol, his nostrils now detected the faintest whiff of perfume.

Agnes said: "Pull up at that trash basket on the corner. I want to empty this ashtray. I don't know how you guys can stand the stink of these cars."

Next she'll have a bottle of Airwick open on the dashboard, Marty thought.

But she asked no stupid questions, not that first day and not ever, she handled the radio well, and during the second four hours she drove the car competently. When meal period came he took her to the diner he always ate at, and afterward attempted to pay for her sandwich. She gave him a hard look, plunked her money down, and stomped back to the car. He decided she was a rather hard bitch—what else would you expect in a policewoman?—and Marty liked his women soft and clinging like his wife Kathleen.

"What does your husband think of you riding around with another guy all day?" asked Marty as he steered away from the diner.

"I don't see where he has anything to worry about," said Agnes coolly. "Do you?"

"The wives don't like it."

"I'm a wife," said Agnes grimly, "and I like it."

In the locker room after the tour ended, Marty and Sal commiserated with each other.

"Just our luck to get a couple of cunts assigned to us," Marty said.

Sal slid his hat onto the shelf, shield facing out. "Mine is ugly."

"Mine is not bad looking. You should see the size of her tits. Every time she gets in or out of the radio car I'm afraid she's going to slam the door on them."

After laughing uproariously at this remark, they became serious.

"Violence is inherent in street patrol," said Marty.

"Neither one of those cunts would be capable of handling a violent incident on patrol," agreed Sal. "They would endanger the public, and they would endanger us."

"In a real hard-core incident the cop would have to protect both himself and her," said Marty. For both of them the word cop had only one gender. A female police officer was not a cop.

"Just wait till the first time she's walking by, and somebody throws garbage down off the roof on her."

"Or comes back to the radio car and it's full of garbage."

Later Marty learned that Agnes was good at family fights. She seemed able to reduce tension. Almost the first run they went on together was a family fight. The wife was standing in the tenement kitchen with her nose bleeding. The husband was shouting he was going to kill her, and Agnes was somehow able to talk sense into both of them. Probably they just didn't expect her, Marty told Sal, trying to explain it away. When they saw Agnes they were surprised, and they stopped going at each other.

But Agnes's success at family fights continued. She didn't seem to need Marty there at all, and this annoyed him. Surely her success would fall off as the people of the precinct got used to seeing policewomen.

Looking back he could not decide when he had started to fall in love with her, or experience desire for her, or whatever it was he felt. His wife had a small bosom, and Agnes had this big one, which he found himself staring at all the time. He began to become consumed by a desire to put his face between Agnes's naked breasts.

Formerly he had saved his best uniform to wear to court. Now he found he wanted to wear his best uniform on patrol with Agnes. He was smoking less, and watching his language all the time.

One day he confessed to her that he had completed two years of college before coming on the job. Agnes seemed surprised, and asked why he had never gone on for his degree.

The question made Marty uncomfortable. "I plan to enroll in John Jay College next term," Marty lied. "I'm going to take a degree in criminal justice."

This seemed to please Agnes so much that Marty went down and enrolled, and a week ago he had begun attending classes again for the first time in ten years. He began to talk of making sergeant.

He still saw a great deal of Sal, and they still joked about their new partners.

"These cunts aren't cops," Sal said. "But I'll have to admit they put cooping in a new light."

Cooping was police jargon for parking the radio car in a dark lot during the midnight-to-eight tours and going to sleep.

"I wouldn't mind cooping with Agnes," said Sal.

Marty realized he wouldn't either, and he gave a sick grin.

"I guess we'll get used to them sooner or later," Marty said uncomfortably.

Sal said: "Remember a few years ago, nobody liked to team up with a black cop, but now they're accepted."

The logic of this comparison was not entirely clear to Marty. "Yeah," said Marty.

Sal was hanging his gun belt in his locker. He took the short-barreled off-duty gun down off the shelf, shoved it into the belt of his slacks, and slammed the locker door shut.

He said: "Still, it's odd when you think of it. I bet you never thought you'd wind up with a cunt for a partner."

Marty wished Sal would not refer to Agnes as a cunt. Sal would never have used that word to describe Marty's wife, for the husband-wife relationship was, to cops, sacred. Sal ought to realize that the relationship between partners in a radio car was sacred too. Marty spent eight hours a day closed up in there with Agnes, five days a week. He spent more time with Agnes than with his wife, Kathleen, and in many ways felt as close to Agnes as to his wife. He and Agnes were partners. They were responsible for each other.

"Oh, well," said Sal philosophically. "We'll have a great many more answers the first time one of these cunts gets caught in a shootout."

"Yeah," said Marty.

In the cops' pantheon of cosmic events the shootout ranked first. But shootouts were rare. Marty had never been in one. Neither had Sal.

There was tension in the car when Marty rode with Agnes now. They both felt it. They had begun to touch each other needlessly a dozen times a day. On several occasions Marty found himself holding open the car door for her. Whenever there was danger Marty wanted Agnes behind him, or otherwise out of the line of fire.

One night they answered a prowler run—possible man with a gun—on the roof of an apartment house. The superintendent cowered inside on the landing. Marty made Agnes get behind him, and instructed her to take her gun out.

Gun in hand, he kicked the roof door open. It banged against the wall and sprang shut again. Nothing happened. No one shot at it.

Most prowler runs were unfounded, and Marty was showing off for Agnes in any case. Pushing the door open, he sprang onto the roof and peered about. The roof was empty. He checked it out. Only then would he allow Agnes to step out beside him.

"Down in the street you wouldn't take your gun

out on a run like this ordinarily," Marty explained to her, ramming his gun back into the holster. "Too many people get alarmed when they see a cop with his gun out. Up on a rooftop you don't alarm anybody, because there's no one here except for the possible prowler, so you might as well have it in your hand in case you need it."

Agnes nodded soberly. She stood with her gun in one hand and their portable radio in the other. Taking the radio, Marty raised Central: "That prowler job is ten-ninety, Central—unfounded." To Agnes Marty said brightly: "You can put your gun away now."

Agnes snapped: "I don't need you to tell me that."

Inside on the landing the nervous super asked: "Can I lock up? Is there anybody left up there?"

"Only the man with the gun," joked Marty.

When they were downstairs getting back into the car Marty said: "Is that the first time you ever had your gun out?"

Agnes nodded. The experience had made her thoughtful: if you have it out, that means you're ready to use it.

"You'll get used to having it out," said Marty smugly.

Then came the bank robbery. The alarm went off at 9:03, meaning that by then Marty and Agnes were an hour and three minutes into an eight-to-four tour.

During their first thirty minutes on patrol they had driven aimlessly up and down the streets of their sector, eyeballing doorways and lobbies, studying pedestrians, looking for odd behavior that might signal either a crime in progress or a citizen in distress. At 8:30 they stopped to pick up coffee. Agnes rushed into a diner while Marty waited outside with engine and radio running. She came back with two containers plus a Danish pastry for Marty—the kind she knew he liked. Agnes never ate breakfast or pastries. The dieting cop was a new concept for Marty, and one he was still not used to.

Their post during the next thirty minutes was a school crossing. Agnes enjoyed stopping traffic to let gangs of school kids cross, but Marty thought the job demeaning to police officers. He thought school crossing guards should do it.

By 9:03 they were back in the car and Marty notified Central that they were resuming patrol. Thirty seconds later the radio crackled and Central announced in a bored voice: "Report of a ten-eleven, bank alarm, First National City Branch at the corner of Southern Boulevard and—"

Agnes, who was driving, had just turned onto Southern Boulevard. Marty picked up the phone and said: "Forty-eight Charlie to Central. K."

Central's still bored voice came back: "Forty-eight Charlie. K."

"We'll take that job, Central. We're right there."

The bank was about three blocks behind them. Agnes made a U-turn.

"Will you go, or will I go?" she asked Marty.

"We'll both go," said Marty. Marty was focused on Agnes, not the bank. He certainly was not worried about the bank alarm, and, as they pulled to a stop, he noted only vaguely the green car double-parked in front of the bank with no driver in sight. Its engine was running, for he perceived wisps of exhaust smoke, and there was some trouble on the opposite sidewalk too—his peripheral vision picked it up. A woman seemed to have fallen down, and someone was leaning over her. But the crumpled woman was not Marty's affair—at least not until after he had checked out the bank.

Both got out of the car. They started across the street.

Neither Marty nor Agnes carried portable radios. There had seemed no need to lug one along just to check out a bank alarm set off by some oaf of a teller. This was a mistake, for even now the frantic voice of Central filled the cavern of their empty car: "On that bank alarm job, Southern Boulevard First National City, report of shots fired." And then, on a rising note of panic: "Proceed with caution. Report of shots fired at this time."

The shots fired were already ninety seconds into

the past. Neither Marty nor Agnes had heard them.

Marty was concentrated chiefly on Agnes's arm, which he held, and on her flesh which he could feel through the cloth. Crossing the street through the traffic, he was guiding not another cop and his partner, but a girl. They had reached the yellow line and were waiting to dart across to the front door of the bank when suddenly the door flew open and the three gunmen erupted outside.

Marty noted the ski masks and was momentarily baffled. Then he noted money bags. Lastly he noted the submachine gun. It flamed and bucked—its dangerous mechanical orgasm had begun. It was pointed at him and Agnes. They were trapped in the middle of the street in a spray of bullets while the men with the money bags sprinted toward the green car.

Marty instinctively had gone down on one knee. He clawed at his service revolver. But even as it came clear his attention was divided. He was worried about Agnes, worried about being hit by a car, and he was shocked by the noise of the machine gun. He had no awareness at all of where its bullets went. The other two gunmen had reached the getaway car —one had dropped his money bags to the pavement in order to yank open the door, and he dived inside without picking them up. He was scrambling to get behind the wheel.

Other radio car teams were already racing toward the bank, sirens blaring. Marty could hear their distant symphony, punctuated by the sharp drum strokes of shots. The distant cars had no notion of what they were rushing toward and would arrive too late anyway. They would find money bags on the sidewalk, a streak of rubber on the street and, here and there, corpses.

Marty had ripped off three shots at the driver—stop him and you stop everybody—but the car lurched forward anyway, front door flapping, tires squealing. The machine gunner had run out of bullets or time and hung half out of the car trying to yank the door shut. The third gunman was out of sight in the back.

Marty kept yanking at his trigger, slamming more bullets into the car. Someone beside him was firing too: Agnes.

Marty's gun was empty. "Come on," he cried at Agnes, and sprinted for the radio car.

Both piled in, but more seconds were lost. Marty had to jump out again to stop traffic while Agnes made her U-turn.

Siren screaming, they began pursuit. Marty was trying to radio information to Central and at the same time reload his gun. Agnes tossed her own gun into his lap: "Reload mine too."

His mouth felt dry, his fingers thick. He had two guns, a dozen bullets and the telephone handle in his hands. Fumbling with all of them, he was being flung about as well.

Traffic hindered Agnes, but hindered the getaway car too. Marty saw flashes of it each time it sped out into the oncoming lane to pass. Agnes drove in lurches and spurts, swerving into the face of oncoming traffic, when she had to, avoiding cars only at the last second. Marty had finished with the guns. He had the radio phone in one hand and tried to brace himself with the other.

The getaway car crossed over the Cross Bronx Expressway, found the entrance and swooped down into the fast-moving flow of trucks and passenger cars, like a cancer invading the bloodstream of the city. Agnes swooped into the flow too—the city was rushing antibodies to the scene and would attempt to reject the sudden anarchy of cells.

Agnes had the accelerator floored, and was gaining. Marty radioed this news to Central. He had to repeat nearly everything because his own siren tended to drown out his words.

Ahead of them traffic closed up. Agnes could not get through. Though dome light urgently turned, though siren blasted, law-abiding motorists were impervious. In sunshine the dome light was invisible. Over rock stations the siren could not be heard. Then traffic opened up again, and they spurted into the clear. The getaway car must have been held up too, for there it was, only a hundred yards ahead. Arms and heads showed alongside it, and tiny points of flame danced like candles in a wind. Bullets came at them hard. The windshield turned to milk.

"I can't see," cried Agnes.

Marty hammered a hole through with his gun butt. Bits of glass stung his face and hand. When he glanced at Agnes, blood was running down both sides of her nose.

Instantly Marty forgot the chase and shouted, "Drop back. Drop back. Let them go. You're hit."

Agnes, brushing blood from her eyes, crouching low so as to peer through the hole, kept the accelerator floored.

The getaway car swooped up an exit ramp. Agnes swooped up too, closing fast. More shots rained back, pinging into the car. A front tire exploded, and Marty was thrown into the door, with Agnes almost on top of him. They careened across White Plains Road traffic. Brakes screeched, and cars barely missed them. Agnes, having clawed her way back behind the wheel, floored the accelerator again. Chunks of rubber whipped back and flew away. They sideswiped a parked car, bounced into the middle of an intersection and spun around twice. The engine stalled. They sat there facing out through a cloud of steam, siren still blaring. After a moment Marty reached over and switched it off.

He stepped out of the car. His knees felt so weak he was not sure they would support him. When he could catch his breath he walked completely around the radio car, counting bullet holes. There were so many that terror came on again and he thought he might vomit or faint. His gun was in his hand and hung against his leg, but he did not know it.

Remembering Agnes, he rammed his gun back, yanked her door open, and lifted her out. He held her in his arms. He could feel her trembling. With his handkerchief, carefully, tenderly, he wiped the blood off her face.

She said: "My face."

Marty said: "It's in the hairline. It's not your face. Your face is all right."

She clung to him, trembling.

Marty, holding her, said: "You are the most fearless broad in the entire Police Department."

She glanced up, and he watched a shy, contented smile come onto her face. He said: "We almost got them."

She had lost her cap. Probably it lay in the street in front of the bank. If so, some other cop would find it. There must be ten radio cars there by now. Reaching back into the car, Marty plucked out Agnes's gun, and handed it to her. Then he took the phone and informed Central of their location, and of the direction of flight of the getaway car.

"Are you hurt? K," demanded Central.

"Negative, Central. But we are immobilized. We'll need transport, and a department tow truck for the car."

He hung the phone back and stood with Agnes. Leaning their rumps against the fender of the wrecked car, they gazed at each other.

"Are you sure you're all right?"

She gave another tentative smile. "Yes. Are you all right?"

"Yes."

They stood thigh to thigh. Even so, it seemed to Marty that he could not get close enough to her. He wanted to climb inside her uniform, inside her very skin.

Agnes, who felt much the same, said: "I was so scared."

"You fooled me."

They were experiencing an emotion familiar to troops throughout history—the love of comrade for comrade once the fear and shooting stop. The only difference was that these two soldiers were of different sexes.

"How many shots did you fire, Agnes?"

"Three. How many did you fire?"

"I ripped off all six."

"I'm glad you didn't fire from the car. The crazy way I was driving, a shot might have gone wild and hit some innocent person."

"That guy was firing a submachine gun at you, and you kept right on going."

Agnes beamed with pleasure.

Marty, who had never been in combat before, felt such an outpouring of tenderness toward Agnes that he mistook it for love. Agnes, experiencing the same emotion, gave it the same name, though for her there was more excuse: both the shootout and her subsequent feelings were outside the normal experience of women.

"I guess you're the first female police officer to ever fire her weapon," said Marty.

"I guess so," said Agnes.

They luxuriated in what they had done, and in being alive.

"I guess we put nine bullets in their car," Marty said. "When it's found, that's how many holes it will have in it, I bet."

"If it doesn't, it will be pretty embarrassing."

"Maybe there will be holes in the guys inside it, too."

But Agnes did not want to think of this.

A crowd was gathering. Marty put his arm around Agnes. He had the absurd feeling that he had to protect her from them, too.

17

THE bank already swarmed with detectives and FBI agents. Eischied reached there about thirty-five minutes after the robbery, and was briefed by the captain who headed Bronx Homicide. The captain spoke in a low voice. Eischied listened, from time to time nodding his head. He wanted a precise scenario: how many robbers, how many corpses, who fired first?

Across the street a woman lay under a piece of tarpaulin. Eischied had already peered down at her. Her feet stuck out, and one shoe was off. At the moment a uniformed cop stood guard there; probably the medical examiner when he came would examine her first. No traffic moved by in the street; precinct cops were diverting it above and below the bank. The entire block was now a crime scene. No pedestrians moved in the street either. People hung from windows and stood in store doorways, all staring; you couldn't stop that.

Inside the bank Eischied watched people step carefully around or over the other three corpses, the torsos and faces of which were covered by spread newspapers.

"Which one is the bank guard?"

"That one there, Chief."

Hooking that morning's *New York Times* with the sole of his shoe, Eischied slid it back from Willis's face. Willis lay with his eyes open. His mouth was open too. He looked surprised. After a moment Eischied's shoe recovered him. To the Bronx Homicide captain Eischied muttered: "He fires three shots and kills three people. That's some bank guard."

Behind Willis lay the gunman. His hands protruded, fingertips already inked; in an hour or so the least important thing about him would be known—his name. The feet wore shabby sneakers. The socks were yellow, and the cuffs of the khaki trousers were frayed. Again Eischied's shoe pushed the newspaper aside, this time uncovering only the ski mask. Abruptly the Chief of Detectives knelt and peeled the mask back to the eyebrows.

He stared at a face he did not recognize. He thought: At least now we know what color they are. He was not surprised; he had expected it.

The face stared back. Dark eyes reproached him, because they did not blink. Smooth cheeks. On the chin some blackheads and a sparse stubble of beard. The youth was barely old enough to shave. Old enough to rob banks, though.

Eischied stood up. Another day's quest through the abnormal and the bizarre had begun. But he knew the outcome in advance. Once again every answer he sought would elude him. He kicked at the newspaper. As obedient as a window shade it slid into place, obscuring the too-harsh view.

There were two other sites to visit, and Eischied ordered himself driven to each in turn. En route to the first he radioed Captain Finnerty on the confidential band: "Any message from that FEAR group yet?"

"Not a word, Chief."

The shattered radio car waited where it had come to a stop. Two precinct cops and a handful of citizens were watching a police wrecker back up to it. Police Officers Delehanty and Cusack, Eischied was informed, were gone. Eischied counted the bullet holes in the car and thought: those were two very lucky cops.

He found them at site number two, the pillar under the el on White Plains Road that the getaway car had crashed into. Here uniformed cops surrounded the car, keeping the crowd back. Detectives milled about, as did press and TV crews. Eischied pushed close to the getaway car. More bullet holes. Inside were a number of empty shell casings but no blood that he could see. He saw a sheaf of money peeking out from under the front seat. At his elbow a detective told him that nothing had been touched yet; they were waiting for Forensic.

"The three perpetrators got away in a gypsy cab, Chief. According to witnesses, what happened is they crash into the stanchion, jump out carrying money bags and guns, flag down the gypsy cab—and they're gone."

"Just like that," said Eischied.

"Just like that, Chief."

Detectives would have to be assigned to contact gypsy cab companies. Maybe they could locate the driver, maybe not. Maybe he was a free lance. Maybe he preferred underprivileged bank robbers to establishment cops.

"Is there anything else you want me to do, Chief?"

Eischied said: "Where are the two cops who chased them."

Marty and Agnes were brought to him. He was surprised to find one of them a female officer. The fact annoyed him. He thought: As if four corpses didn't guarantee us headlines enough.

Marty and Agnes answered his questions. He interrogated them only briefly, for they told him nothing he did not know already. The emotional reaction, he could see, had begun to set in. They were in a state of exhilaration bordering on hysteria. They were coming down off a drunk. They were repeatedly touching each other, too, though neither seemed aware of it. The press, however, was very aware of it. Cameras were locked on them from all angles. In a moment they'd probably hold hands. Eischied considered ordering them to move apart, but it was their headache and the department's, not his. He said nothing. He had been against females in radio cars, and part of the reason was that messy divorce actions were certain to follow. Maybe one would happen here.

In any case, now the department would have to give that broad a medal.

Louie hurried over from Eischied's car: "It's them,

Chief. It's that FEAR group again. They delivered a message to the *Daily News*."

Eischied sighed. Four corpses, a female police officer hero, and now this.

Individual reporters were clamoring for a statement, and abruptly Eischied began to orchestrate in his head tonight's newscasts and tomorrow's headlines. Although he had always ignored the press in the past, he saw that he could force the press to serve as an ally now. Suppose he decided to ride this wave of bank robberies? He could announce to press and city that he was taking personal charge of the investigation, that he was in possession of secret information, that he could promise a break in the case shortly.

"How about a statement, Chief?"

"What can you tell us, Chief?"

Such headlines might give him a month's breathing room. If he could keep the city focused on himself and his investigation, then the PC and O'Connor would not dare move against him. He would seem to stand alone between the city and additional carnage. His survival as Chief of Detectives would be assured for a time. Time either to regain ground within the department or to find an outside job to move into. This wave of bank robberies was a terrible thing for the city. Properly used it might be the best thing possible for himself.

And so he stood in front of massed cameras and microphones, with the ruined getaway car at his back, with Police Officers Delehanty and Cusack on either side, and began to construct the press conference he needed. Those questions that served his purpose he answered. The rest he ignored. When he had made his headlines, he allowed Marty and Agnes to be interviewed each in turn, imagining that such added human interest could only enhance his own standing. But he was careful to step back out of camera range. Whatever rubbish they might utter he did not want associated with himself.

Now cameras and microphones were aimed at Police Officer Martin Delehanty, who, with one arm around Police Officer Agnes Cusack, was blurting: "She drove into a hail of bullets. It never fazed her. I want to tell you, this is one hell of a cop."

The praise made Agnes blush—and won the hearts of women all over the country.

Agnes in her turn described fighting to control the radio car after the tire had been shot away. Her face was still slightly stained with blood. She glanced at Marty. Ten million or more citizens tonight would interpret that glance as adoration, if not love. "My only regret," Police Officer Agnes Cusack said, "is that the perpetrators were able to make good their escape." The stilted police phrasing. For a moment she sounded a hundred percent cop, and Eischied warmed toward her. "But we'll get them. Chief Eischied will get them."

It made Eischied smile. Thank you, Police Officer Cusack, he thought.

18

CHIEF Eischied went back to the bank. There was a single small office, a kind of conference room, between the last of the tellers' cages and the vault, and this Eischied converted into his command post. It was airless, windowless. In it Eischied worked in shirt sleeves. He worked without lunch. Twice he sent detectives out to buy him coffee. He sat with his notes and papers while witnesses were brought in to him. Most had already given statements to detectives or FBI agents—the usual two separate investigations were already under way out in the bank proper, and Eischied's own made a third. Eischied interrogated each witness. He was looking for some detail, some minor thread that might give him the edge he needed. He was working hard. He sat mouthing his cigar, which was sometimes lit and sometimes not, asking the same blunt questions over and over again, his face betraying no expression or emotion whatsoever.

"Did the perpetrators say anything to each other?"

"I was still deaf from the noise of the machine gun, sir. You wouldn't believe the noise, sir."

"I believe it. What can you tell me about the shooter himself?"

"He was quick as a cat, sir. You wouldn't believe how quick he was."

"I believe it. What else?"

The bank itself had become a kind of glass prison. No one was allowed to leave. It stayed closed to business. The street outside remained closed to traffic. Once, between interviews, Eischied stood in the door of his room looking out through the bank past the detectives and FBI agents at a portion of empty street. The street looked both normal and not normal. It was eerie. Something which ought to be there was not there: movement. Outside the bank, city life had seemingly ceased to exist. It was as if a poison gas had descended and killed everybody.

"What can you tell me about the machine gunner himself?"

"Cold, sir. He was ice cold, and he moved like a cat."

"What was catlike about him?"

"I don't know exactly."

Eischied sighed. "Did you notice anything specific? His fingers, his ears?"

"He was wearing a ski mask, sir."

"Did you notice his eyes, his teeth? His voice?"

"It was a cold voice."

"I see."

Nonetheless, Eischied was able to form a picture of the man: about five feet six or seven, 140 pounds, dressed like his colleague, the corpse out there under the newspaper. But older by five or six years. Athletic, decisive, an artist with that submachine gun. Ruthless.

Then why had he been, at the start of the robbery, only the wheelman?

Because, Eischied guessed, he was obeying orders. The gang leader was someone else.

"Did either of the other two robbers appear to be the leader?"

Long pause. "I don't know what you mean, sir."

Outside in the bank, statements were being taken by Lieutenant Schultz and eight detectives from Eischied's Bank Squad, and also by ten FBI men ander the command of a special agent named Jim Kane. When it became clear to Kane that Eischied was conducting his own investigation, he phoned FBI headquarters on 69th Street. Two higher-ranking agents appeared at the bank within thirty minutes. They wanted to meet with Eischied. He told them he was too busy. He told them he would see them in his office downtown at 4 P.M., and closed the door on them.

Eischied's name was being blared in radio broadcasts. The afternoon editions of the *Post* carried it two inches high on the front page:

EISCHIED
PROMISES
BANK ARRESTS

Was it this publicity that brought the PC's favorite detective, Deputy Inspector Cornfield, formerly Captain Cornfield, to the bank? Cornfield wanted to know if he could help.

Eischied eyed him so coldly that Cornfield became uncomfortable.

Cornfield said: "I mean, I would think this case would automatically come under my Major Crime Squad."

After a moment, Eischied said: "Did I send for you?"

Suddenly unsure how much protection the PC could or would provide, Cornfield said: "No, Chief, you didn't."

Eischied got rid of him brusquely.

But he could not afford to make the PC too mad. Worry interfered with his interrogations.

Stepping to the door, he called to a detective: "Reach out for Cornfield for me." Cornfield was to attend the 4 P.M. meeting with the FBI in Eischied's office. Cornfield and the FBI fit into the same slot in Eischied's brain: supposed colleagues who couldn't be trusted.

There came a knock on the door. Eischied opened to Captain Rolfe, head of the Ballistics section. Earlier Eischied had instructed him to recover as many bullets as possible. The FBI would try to get them all, naturally, but Rolfe had enough rank and enough men to get some of them. Above all, Rolfe was to recover at least one reasonably unmutilated machine-gun bullet.

Now Rolfe reported that he had been able to recover only bullets fired at Officers Delehanty and Cusack in the street. These were four in number. Three had struck the opposite masonry and were mutilated. The fourth had gone in an open doorway and lodged in the staircase. Rolfe had cut it out personally. He opened his fist. Eischied looked down on the bullet. It was now the shape of a mushroom.

"The tail end of it is not mutilated at all," said Rolfe.

Eischied nodded. The undamaged stem of the mushroom would contain sufficient ballistics markings to match it to any other bullet fired from the same gun.

"There may have been others fired at the two cops in the street, but four is all we have been able to find."

"What about bullets that struck the radio car during the chase?"

"We're dismantling the car now, but I'm not hopeful. Most of them went right straight through it. Those cops were so lucky."

"Yes, they were," conceded Eischied, and he brooded for a moment about luck. What was luck exactly? Why had it never been measured? Did it even exist? The two cops had had marvelous luck today, but the four corpses had had none. The bank guard and the dead perpetrator were perhaps responsible for their own bad luck, but not the teller, or the woman across the street. Luck didn't make sense. The trouble was, nothing else made sense either.

The airless room reeked of cigar smoke and Rolfe's face showed distaste. "Christ, Chief, you should get some air in here."

Eischied, pleased with Rolfe, only grinned. "What about machine-gun bullets inside the bank?"

"The bank guard caught them all, apparently."

"That's some shooting," admitted Eischied, surprised.

"They all went in one side of him and out the other." Rolfe consulted his notes. "The poor bastard was hit five times. One of my guys recovered five shell casings, but the FBI took them away from him before I got here. The FBI also got all of the slugs, apparently. They went straight through the deceased and into the vault, I think. All the FBI had to do was pick them up off the floor. I don't know how usable they'll be. Very often they're unusable just from having gone through a guy. These went through him and then were stopped by steel. There's a possibility that one of them was stopped by the wooden table in the vault. The table has been worked at with a knife, like somebody was trying to dig a bullet out of there, but I looked it over pretty carefully and it's my impression that that particular bullet went in and out of the table, meaning that they picked it up off the floor too."

"What you're telling me," Eischied said, "is that the son of a bitch with the machine gun pulled off at least four shots out in the street and five in here but there's only one usable bullet, and we've got it."

"Right, Chief."

Eischied was grinning from ear to ear. "You're a great man, Rolfe. You know that?"

Rolfe beamed.

Eischied, staring at the bullet on the desk, said soberly: "The only trouble is, I see you too many times recently."

They both stared at the bullet. Rolfe said with equal soberness: "I know, Chief."

But it was not their job to remain grief-stricken over murdered citizens. Eischied pushed the bullet across the desk. "I want you to take that back to the lab. I want you to see if it matches the bullets dug out of those two machine-gunned cops last summer. I want you to do the work personally. If you get a match, I want you to come down to my office. I'll be there by three-thirty. I don't want anybody else to know what you're doing, particularly the FBI. Understand?"

Rolfe nodded. In the doorway Eischied patted him on the back, then hollered at the nearest detective: "Who's next in here, for chrissake?"

Much later, as he prepared to leave the bank, Eischied noted that Officers Delehanty and Cusack were still being held. They sat on straight chairs against the far wall in deep conversation with each other. So Eischied walked over there.

"Are you two all right?"

"Fine, Chief," said Agnes. Eischied was getting used to her rosy face above the blue uniform, though not to the gun belt around her waist. He thought: She's really not a bad-looking broad.

"The FBI guys asked us to stick around," explained Marty.

Eischied wondered if anyone had thought to bring them lunch. "Is there anything you need?"

"Not a thing, Chief," said Agnes, giving Eischied a smile.

"You were awfully lucky today," Eischied told her.

"I know."

They seemed happy enough sitting there with each other. "Well," said Eischied, "I'll see you again sometime," and he left the bank and drove to headquarters.

Reaching his own office Eischied was peeling his

topcoat off as he came through the door. "Finnerty, Fitzgerald, come in here please."

Eischied hung up his coat and lit a cigar. Captain Finnerty and Lieutenant Fitzgerald stood in front of his desk. Dropping into his swivel chair, Eischied put his feet up.

"Take this down," he ordered, and blew smoke at the ceiling.

Captain Finnerty flipped open the stenographer's pad.

Eischied said: "One: send a detective out to get me a tunafish-salad sandwich on rye bread and a cup of coffee. Two: I want the yellow sheet on the dead perpetrator from the bank." He stopped. "Fitzgerald, go get it."

As Fitzgerald hurried out of the room, Eischied hollered after him: "And I want the original of the message that was sent to the *Daily News* this morning from this FEAR gang."

Watching Captain Finnerty with narrowed eyes, Eischied continued: "Three: I want two copies of the late editions of the *Post*. Jesus Christ, why wasn't all this stuff on my desk already?"

"Sorry, Chief."

"Four: As of this minute you, Captain Finnerty, are in command of the Bank Squad. Call in Lieutenant Schultz and the sergeant and however many of the guys are working today, and get to work on that dead perpetrator. I want to know the name of every guy who was ever involved in a crime with him. I want to know where he did time and when. I want to know the name of every con who ever shared a cell with him in the can. And whatever information you come up with, I don't want to see it in any newspaper. Is that clear?"

Captain Finnerty, scribbling in his notebook, said huffily: "I'm not in the habit of leaking to the newspapers, Chief."

"Sometimes, Finnerty, I think you're too sensitive to be a detective." Eyes twinkling, Eischied watched him. Finnerty studied his notebook.

"When those Bank Squad guys get down here, take

them into a room and close the door. I don't want anybody overhearing what you tell them. I particularly don't want the FBI to know what you tell them, or what information they come back with either.

"Five: When you get all the names together, start narrowing them down. Forget about anybody still in the can. But I want to know the name of every possible current associate of this guy, and I want all their fingerprint cards brought in here. I want whoever is our best fingerprint technician brought in here too. People are gonna ask you a lot of questions. Don't answer any of them. This investigation is being run out of my office until further notice. Somebody wants information, you tell them to see me.

"Six: I want wiretaps. I want as many as we can get. That's your job. You get the facts together. You prepare affidavits on associates and relatives of this hoodlum, and you go down to the DA's office and you beg for wires. After that you are to make arrangements with the telephone company, and you set up teams of detectives to monitor the wires. Find a secure place. And tell our guys to keep their mouths shut. The trouble with detectives is they talk too goddamn much.

"Seven: Call up your wife and tell her she's not going to see much of you until this case is broken.

"Eight: Captain Rolfe from Ballistics is due here soon. Show him right in. I don't want him kept waiting.

"Nine: I got a meeting on with the FBI and with Captain, excuse me, Deputy Inspector Cornfield for four o'clock. Let me know when they arrive. I'll tell you when to show them in.

"Ten: Cancel any appointments I might have for the rest of the week."

Lieutenant Fitzgerald had re-entered with a copy of the dead gunman's yellow sheet, and with a copy of the message that had gone to the *Daily News*. The original was on its way over.

Eischied glanced at the two copies.

"The message was phoned in at 9:52, Chief. That's approximately forty-four minutes after the robbery."

"I can count," Eischied said.

The yellow sheet gave the dead gunman's name as Floyd Fields. Though only twenty years old, his sheet featured seven previous arrests. He had passed through the New York penal system twice already: The Tombs, Attica, Greenhaven. Finnerty would have a job checking all those places. The arrests ranged from disorderly conduct to armed robbery.

Eischied muttered: "This kid was one sweet fellow."

In each case the name of the arresting officer was given. To Finnerty Eischied said: "It might be worth your while to call down all these arresting officers and talk to them. Maybe they know something." He grinned at Finnerty and said slyly: "I don't know if the idea would have occurred to you. That's why I'm mentioning it."

Finnerty said fussily: "I had already thought of it, Chief. After all, I'm a detective."

Eischied only grinned at him. When Finnerty had gone out Eischied said: "Red, bring me all the unusuals from last night."

Left alone, the Chief of Detectives brooded. His feet were up and he was rolling the cigar from one side of his mouth to the other, but the thoughts did not come, possibly because his gun bothered him—it always bothered him when he tried to think, and a psychoanalyst would make much of that, no doubt. He stuffed the holstered gun into the desk drawer. The mental block was out of his belly, out of sight too, and now perhaps business could proceed. Eischied like to think of himself as an executive whose budget ran to $74 million a year, and who had three thousand employees. Executives running businesses of that size did not carry guns into meetings, and it sometimes seemed absurd to him that by law he was obliged to.

A civilian executive could legally keep whisky in his desk, too, which Eischied could not, though he did. The bottle came out of his lower drawer, the ice out of his miniature fridge. He poured Scotch over ice and sipped it meditatively.

Lieutenant Fitzgerald came in with last night's unusuals.

"Put them down on the desk, Red, and then get out of here. I'm trying to think, and when I look at you all I can think is that I wish I had become a plumber."

"You should take that routine on the stage, Chief."

When Eischied raised an ashtray to throw, Red, laughing, scampered out the door.

Eischied found what he was looking for at once: a car stolen at gunpoint from a parking garage in the 26th Precinct. This was one precinct north of the other car stickups. But the car stolen was not the getaway car. The getaway car—he checked the notes he had made at the bank—had been stolen in Queens off the street.

The pattern was clear, thought Eischied. Whoever is masterminding all this sends two guys out for cars the night before the robbery. One of these imbeciles likes to do it at gunpoint, which fact I doubt the mastermind even knows. But that is the weak spot in their organization, because sooner or later this stickup guy is going to run into a problem of some sort, and get caught or killed, and then we'll know a little more.

But neither Eischied nor the city could afford the luxury of waiting for this to happen.

The latest message signed FEAR was in Finnerty's handwriting—he had taken it over the phone from somebody at the *News*. Eischied read it.

This morning young Floyd Fields was brutally murdered by agents of the capitalist oppressors while engaged in the expropriation of funds needed by the army of the people in their fight to throw off the shackles of the oppressor. Floyd was the first martyr of the autumn offensive. His martyrdom will be avenged. The revolution will exact the lives of two fascist pig police in recompense. The revolutionary offensive continues. Long live the revolution.

Eischied was beginning to visualize the intelligence behind all this. The rhetoric of all the messages matched. The lines all came from the same brain. It was like lines from Shakespeare; you could recognize one the minute you heard it.

Each bank robbery had taken place in a different borough, all but one at approximately the same hour, which hour happened to be the most vulnerable hour for banks, since radio cars were chasing down bank alarms all over town at that time. Presumably the mastermind knew this, Eischied reflected, though how? Each branch bank had been a little more important than the one before it, and the amount of money stolen had increased dramatically each time, except for today when over $100,000 in money sacks had been left behind on the pavement. The stolen cars fit the pattern, and Eischied decided again that the mastermind surely did not know about the car stickups, or he would have stopped them.

Eischied contemplated assigning radio cars to every parking garage in what the car thief no doubt considered his lucky precincts. Cars could watch each spot between nine and midnight every night.

But could precinct cops be depended upon to keep their mouths shut?

The answer was no. Besides, radio cars would scare the guy off.

Suppose he assigned a detective to each garage?

He buzzed for Finnerty.

But by then Captain Finnerty was meeting with the Bank Squad in the fourth-floor conference room, and it was Lieutenant Fitzgerald who came through the door.

"Lieutenant Fitzgerald, I want you to do something for me. I hope it won't strain your intellectual capacity too much. I want a list of all parking garages in the 20th, 24th and 26th precincts."

"Thinking of going into business there, Chief?"

But Eischied ignored him, and went on brooding. He had no idea whether Fitzgerald would return with ten garages or a hundred, but it seemed worth assigning a detective to each, no matter how many there were, for this was Eischied's best lead, almost his only one, and he didn't have much time. The warning in the latest message was clear—this gang had pledged to assassinate two more cops.

Assassinating cops was entirely too easy. You could recognize them by their uniforms, Eischied thought bitterly, and those uniforms were not bulletproof. You strolled up behind one and started shooting. It had been done often enough in the past.

Eischied got out the dossier on recent extremist groups. Most were active from 1967 to 1972. They had killed some cops. They had bedeviled the city. All had called themselves revolutionaries, but Eischied, who had studied history, saw them as anarchists, one and all, for they had no program except destruction. They were no different from the killers and bomb throwers active in Spain in the early thirties, active in Russia before 1917, active in the United States three quarters of a century ago, which was when one of their number managed to gun down President McKinley. The anarchist movement went all the way back past ancient Rome to Greece. The black flag. Destroy.

And now, Eischied thought, we have them among us yet again, heavily armed, strong enough to hit four banks, promising next to kill cops.

The Black Panthers of the sixties had degenerated into the Black Liberation Army during the years when Eischied was a captain. In New York they had wounded a dozen cops and assassinated four. They had killed and wounded others elsewhere. They were the most dangerous gang Eischied remembered personally. Most had been jailed or killed. Some had fled the country. Today's dead gunman would have fit right in. Having missed that war, he had ripened in time for this one. But his leaders were perhaps left over from the last time. Eischied suspected that one or two of FEAR's leaders, if he could discover their names, would be in the dossier in his lap.

Crossing to his safe, he withdrew the heavy folder in which lay the scorched first message. Staring down at the single partial print, he thought: We have your other nine on file somewhere, pal, whoever you are.

In his mind Eischied was trying to form an image of FEAR's leader. A man of commanding physical presence. A voice that struck with physical force. Hypnotic eyes.

The name Everett Walker did not occur to Chief Eischied. Walker had never been active in New York, and besides he was supposedly in exile in North Africa.

Eischied saw a man who mixed superstition, religious faith and sonorous rhetoric to bend ghetto youths to his will, a man who was not so much a Christ as a conquistador, a kind of modern Cortez setting out to conquer the capital with a handful of dangerous men. To ghetto youths there was no more attractive political philosophy than anarchy. Violence is indeed lovely. Destruction does delight. Murder must bring an almost sexual high. The appeal was to the strongest and most basic of human emotions: anger, hatred, pain, fear, greed, lust, power, despair. Almost the only significant emotion left out was love. Maybe they even had that. Maybe they loved each other, the way cops loved each other.

No cop in the city was safe until they were caught.

Perhaps the leader, once caught, would prove legally insane, but he was sane enough now. He plotted well. The ripping-off of four banks in so short a time was no small feat. The city saw the mind behind this, Eischied judged. And was near hysteria as a result.

Lieutenant Fitzgerald announced the arrival of Captain Rolfe.

"You were right, Chief," Rolfe said soberly, as soon as the outer door had closed behind him. "The machine gun bullets match."

Eischied said nothing. He swallowed several times. Still without speaking, he glanced down at the latest message from FEAR. That it was in Finnerty's handwriting somehow made it seem less ominous. After a moment Eischied began reading the message aloud to Rolfe:

". . . The revolution will exact the lives of two fascist pig police . . ."

The meaning of the words did not change. Eischied

muttered: "They've already killed two cops, and now they're promising to kill two more. And the thing is I don't see how we can stop them."

"We could broadcast a warning to every radio car during each of the tours each day," Rolfe suggested.

He was a studious man, and more scientist than cop. He was at home in his laboratory with his instruments. In court, juries tended to accept his testimony without question. No defense attorney had ever managed to shake him. He seemed to have no interest in the political machinations within the Police Department, nor any desire for higher rank. Eischied had never heard him utter a word of department gossip.

He was one of the few men in the department Eischied felt could be trusted totally.

Eischied said: "Do you realize the state of panic any such announcement would throw our cops into? The city too, of course. But the cops. They'd be looking over their shoulders the whole time. They'd refuse to answer radio runs. They'd be gunning down citizens who made the slightest suspicious move."

The two men gazed at each other.

"I don't see how we can broadcast such a warning," Eischied said.

Rolfe said: "We can't send cops out in radio cars without telling them either. Is that what you're saying, Chief?"

For a time Eischied said nothing. When he spoke again his voice was barely audible: "Let me ask you something, Pete. Look at it from the point of view of the average citizen. Does the average citizen feel in more danger from this gang, or from thirty-two thousand frightened cops shooting at shadows?"

Rolfe only shook his head. "I'm just a captain, Chief. I don't have to answer such questions. I don't envy you."

Eischied said: "I can walk in there and drop it on the Commissioner's desk. Let him decide. The only thing is, he doesn't like cops at all. He thinks we're all thieves." After a moment Eischied added in a mumble: "I don't have any faith in his judgment."

Eischied led Rolfe to the safe and showed him the single latent print. "That's our guy, I think. Of course it could also be the print of the news vendor who sold the newspaper. We don't know. It's a crazy case, isn't it? On the one hand we really have a great deal of information. But on the other we have hardly any information at all."

The arrivals of Deputy Inspector Cornfield and the two FBI supervisors were announced.

Eischied said to Rolfe: "I'd like you to sit in on this. Just don't volunteer any information, okay?"

The five men sat around Eischied's conference table. Eischied said: "The purpose of this meeting is to exchange information. What do you guys know that we don't know, and vice versa." He gave what he hoped was a disarming smile.

Neither of the FBI agents smiled back.

Eischied said: "Let's assume that this Freedom and Equality Army of Revolution exists. You're the guys who are supposed to have infiltrated all these subversive groups. Do you have anything on this one?"

They did not, they said, and Eischied nodded. This was perhaps true. FEAR had surfaced only in the last month, and it took longer than that to infiltrate.

One of the FBI men produced the federal equivalent of the yellow sheet of the deceased Floyd Fields. He handed this across to Eischied like a Christmas present: "This may be of use to you, Chief."

This much information Eischied had already. In exchange the FBI would want only Rolfe's bullets. Eischied put the worthless sheet down without looking at it.

"My men tell me your guys picked up some bullets across the street from the bank," one of the FBI men said. His name was Morgan. Tall. Short haircut. Button-down collar. Rep tie. Brooks Brothers suit. "I'd like to have them, if I may." He added: "Bank robbery is a federal crime."

Eischied, annoyed, remarked: "Murder comes under our jurisdiction. At least it did the last time I looked."

"But this was a homicide committed during a bank robbery. Therefore it's federal."

He and Eischied stared at each other.

The second agent was named Taylor, also tall, short haircut, button-down shirt, rep tie, Brooks Brothers suit. Taylor asked: "What exactly did you guys pick up?"

Rolfe started to answer, but a glance from Eischied silenced him.

"We're still processing them," Eischied said blandly. "We should have some answers for you later on."

Morgan said: "We're all interested in the same outcome here, namely arrests, so we probably should have those bullets. Our lab probably could do a better job on them." Glancing at Rolfe, Morgan added hastily: "Not to denigrate the work you guys do, Captain, but we probably have more sophisticated gear than the Police Department."

This, sadly, was true. But Eischied had no intention of giving up the one identifiable bullet, or even mentioning it.

Across the table Deputy Inspector Cornfield was making diligent notes. So far he had said nothing.

Eischied asked if the FBI had any leads from informants. Unfortunately, said Morgan, they had none. Did Eischied?

"No," Eischied said.

Dealing with the FBI was always a one-way street. You gave and they took. Eischied was sick of the lot of them. None wore uniforms. None got shot in the back while out on routine patrol. And that was what was going to happen next.

The meeting broke up with promises on both sides to keep each other informed.

"Here's my home number," said Morgan, handing it across. "If anything comes up." In law enforcement home numbers were usually kept secret. So Morgan apparently was making a small concession in hope of winning a bigger one. "Why don't you give me yours?"

Eischied said blandly: "My office is open all night.

If you need me, call my duty sergeant. He'll reach out for me."

When the door had slammed on the FBI, the three policemen stood alone in the big office. Cornfield said: "Those FBI guys are awfully tight-lipped, aren't they?"

"That's right," Eischied said.

Rolfe said: "You have just witnessed a typical example of FBI-Police Department cooperation."

Cornfield wanted to help. Again he suggested bringing in the Major Crime Squad and himself. At least this time he was deferential about it. He sounded a good deal less brave than at the bank this morning.

Everybody wants to break this case, Eischied reflected. Cornfield, the FBI, the PC. Think of the pleasure. Think of the glory.

He thought: I want to break it too. I must break it if I am to survive as Chief of Detectives. He hoped he could break it before two more cops died.

He didn't want the Police Commissioner's spy in his entourage while he tried to do it, and so, choosing his words carefully, he told Cornfield that for the moment the investigation would best be handled by the Bank Squad. Cornfield's squad should continue with their other current investigations; especially that Mafia hit Cornfield was almost ready to hand over to the grand jury.

"You're doing a great job on that Mafia case. I'll call on you here as soon as we get a little more to go on."

When Cornfield went out, Eischied was alone with Captain Rolfe.

"There's no possibility of doubt, is there?" Eischied asked him. "The bullet from today's bank job does match the bullets fired into those two cops last summer?"

Rolfe nodded soberly. "No possibility of doubt at all, Chief."

An hour later Eischied was summoned by the PC. The PC demanded every scrap of information he had. The PC in his shirt sleeves stood importantly behind his desk, waiting.

On the PC's desk where Eischied could see it lay the afternoon *Post* with Eischied's name in giant headlines. Eischied had made his decision before entering the PC's office. The PC's attitude only confirmed it. He would tell the PC nothing.

And so he began to give a long-winded description of the robbery; he praised Officers Delehanty and Cusack. "You ought to consider a metal for that Cusack, Commissioner. You could pin it one one of those big boobs yourself. It might help you politically."

There—the chasm between cop and politician had been mentioned. Eischied's face was bland, the PC's impatient.

"Everything you've told me so far is in this paper, Earl."

The PC picked up the newspaper, waved it, dropped it with a splash on the desk. The back of his knuckles struck the headlines hard.

"I want to know about solid leads. I want to know what you've got."

Eischied was vague. He had no hard information yet. He would brief the Police Commissioner as soon as he had some.

"But you must have something, man," said the PC petulantly. Again the back of his knuckles smacked the newspaper. "You're promising to break the goddamn case within days. You must have something."

Eischied did not reply.

The two men eyed each other. Eischied stood in a position of strength, and knew it. For the moment the Chief of Detectives was a force that even the Police Commissioner would be afraid to meddle with.

The PC abruptly changed attitudes. "I suppose you're worried about that other matter."

They stared at each other. Klopfman. Two suits. It was as if Eischied waited for the Police Commissioner to explain the meaning of "other matter."

The PC said: "The preliminary investigation substantiated your explanation. For the moment the whole matter is on the back burner."

Eischied said only: "That's nice." Two suits were once again no more important than two suits.

Still they stared at each other. The PC was waiting for Eischied to hand across all information, and Eischied had no intention of doing so. He wondered what the PC would do now. Would he beg, expostulate, command, rant?

The Police Commissioner appeared to decide that any reaction at all was beneath his dignity. In a cold, suppressed voice he said only: "Keep me informed. That will be all."

Eischied nodded, and left the office.

When he was gone, First Deputy O'Connor came in via the back door. The PC was furious. "He defied me. He refused to tell me a word."

"He's got something," guessed the First Deputy. "He would have gone low profile otherwise. My guess is he's already got his hand on these thugs' shoulders. He's letting it build up in the press to make a hero out of himself. Once he's a hero, you won't be able to touch him. It's my advice to get rid of him now."

But the PC shook his head. He counted himself more politically astute than his deputy. He knew how to read a man's strength, and also a man's faith in his own strength. For the moment Eischied seemed to him invulnerable.

"If this FEAR case gets any worse, and if he breaks it," the First Deputy said, "they'll make him Police Commissioner by acclamation, if not Mayor."

19

IT was late afternoon before an FBI agent again next approached Marty and Agnes.

"I guess you two needn't hang around any longer."

It was so late, Marty observed, that the sun slanting through the window came halfway up the guy's pants leg. It was so late there weren't even any detectives left in the bank, for chrissake.

"We sure do appreciate your help."

At first Marty had felt like a hero. He had been proud to sit there with Agnes. But no one had interrogated them now in more than two hours. By now Marty felt like a patrolman again. Patrolmen got shat upon by everybody.

"Thanks a lot," said Marty in a surly voice. But he was afraid to talk back to an FBI guy. "Come on, Agnes."

Standing in the street with Agnes, Marty felt like he'd been released from prison.

They went back to the stationhouse and signed out. Except for a few clerical cops, the stationhouse was empty. It had been Marty's ambition all day to strut in there at four o'clock. The place would be jammed —one tour going off, the next one turning out. The guys would all cluster around. They would want to know about the shootout.

But now it was twenty after five. The place was practically empty. No one said a word to them. The shootout was the big event of Marty's life so far and no one seemed to know about it or care about it except Agnes. They went up to change.

Marty was waiting on the stoop when Agnes came out. It was beginning to get cold. She was wearing slacks and a heavy cardigan sweater. Her face looked scrubbed and her hair was down. Marty had never seen her hair down before. It's really long, he thought. She was wearing lipstick. Marty had noticed her after work a few times but she had never looked like this. Earrings peeped out at him. Are those earrings for me? Marty asked himself.

His heart had begun to pound. It was pounding almost as hard as during the shootout. He said: "You look nice."

Agnes, the thirty-year-old cop, blushed like a schoolgirl.

Marty said: "Well, what are you going to do now?"

"Well, I guess I'll go home to my old man."

After a moment Marty said: "I don't want you to go home."

"I don't want to go home either."

"We could have dinner. We could see the sights."

"Well—" Agnes peered down at herself. "I'm not really dressed for it."

"You look really nice. I'm the one who's not dressed for it." Marty wore an open-necked shirt. His T-shirt showed across his throat. The letters on the back of his bowling jacket read "Elmhurst Keglers."

Marty didn't want to let the shootout go, and he didn't want to let Agnes go.

"You could tell your husband we're not going to get off till late because of the shootout."

"You could tell your wife the same thing."

They smiled at each other.

Re-entering the stationhouse, they stood elbow to elbow while each in turn made the false phone call.

In Marty's car they drove down to Times Square and parked. Marty showed the garage attendant his shield: maybe the guy wouldn't charge them. In the streets they walked along holding hands, looking into the windows of the gift and curio shops.

"I feel like a tourist," said Marty. "I was born here, for crissake."

"I've never done this before," said Agnes.

Never done what? She gave his hand a squeeze, as if she suspected where the evening would end. But this was a new stage in their relationship, and she seemed to approach it as uncertainly as he.

They stepped into a necktie shop, where Marty bought a tie for a dollar, and put it on.

"Let me fix it for you," said Agnes.

"It's six o'clock," Marty announced, as Agnes straightened his new tie. Her fingers under the knot were buttoning his shirt. His heart was pounding again. Marty said: "I guess we're all over the TV news broadcasts starting about now." He was trying to keep his voice light. "We ought to hire a motel room and go up and watch ourselves on TV."

He thought he felt her stiffen. Her fingers drew the knot tight. She zipped up his bowling jacket for him, saying: "There!"

They went out of the shop together.

In the street, Marty said: "Now I feel well dressed enough to take you to dinner." He had planted the idea. He would let it work on her.

They chose Schrafft's on Broadway. They both had the special, lamb with gravy. They drank most of a bottle of sweet Portuguese rosé wine.

"That bottle is bottomless," said Agnes. She giggled. "It's good, though."

"What were you thinking when you were firing shots at them, Agnes?"

"I was worrying about them hitting you."

"I was worrying about you too," said Marty. He hadn't been. He couldn't remember any thoughts at all. He was just trying to stop them. He was trying to put bullets into somebody.

"My heart was pounding so much I couldn't even get my gun out at first," said Agnes.

"You did fine. My heart was pounding too." But he had got his gun out fast anyway, because he was a man. He had ripped off all six the way a cop was supposed to.

"We could have been killed," said Agnes soberly.

"I know." Tenderness for her came on strong. He put his hand down over hers on the tablecloth and was rewarded by another shy smile.

Outside they strolled along with the crowds. Forty-second Street was ablaze with light.

"Did you ever have occasion to work down here, Agnes?"

"No, I never did."

"I had occasion to fill in here a few times when I was a rookie. Times Square is full of degenerates. You wouldn't believe some of the degenerates I've locked up around here."

They stood under the marquee of a porno movie house, reading the titles to each other. Soon Agnes was giggling. They even discussed perhaps going in.

They stood on the sidewalk. The film was called *Slippery Cock*.

"It doesn't leave much to the imagination, does it?" Agnes giggled.

"I guess it doesn't."

"It's probably pretty dirty," said Agnes. Marty watched her. Maybe she was wishing Marty would step up and buy the tickets, but he wasn't going to.

"It probably is."

"Can you believe that I've never been to a dirty movie?"

"I can believe it," said Marty. It could be true. Female police officers, Marty had found, were not nearly as sophisticated as real cops. Marty doubted Agnes had even been unfaithful to her husband, for chrissake. This was an obstacle, and Marty was worried about it.

"Have you seen many, Marty?"

"Only one," lied Marty. "I went with Sal and the guys, just to see what it was like."

He had taken Kathleen to one, too, hoping it would make her hot. It had cost, like this one, five bucks a head. Kathleen had stomped out in disgust after about twenty minutes. She had refused to talk to him all the way home, and once they got there had not let him near her. He wasn't making that mistake again.

"Come on," Marty said gruffly, "let's go."

They strolled back toward where the car was parked. Beside the garage was a Howard Johnson's Motor Inn.

They stood looking up at a neon sign five stories high.

Marty had fallen silent. Time was running out. With an ordinary girl he would have been all right. But this was his partner.

He said: "I guess you could be home in time for the ten-o'clock news on Channel 5."

"Yes."

"Or we could watch it together in there."

Agnes did not look up.

Marty said doggedly: "I want to go to bed with you." He took both her hands.

It was a pleasure to hear it, of course, but Agnes didn't know what to answer, and so she didn't say anything.

Neither did Marty.

Then Marty said: "Let's go." His voice was rough.

As Marty signed in, Agnes stood beside him and her knees felt so weak she thought she'd fall. Up in the room he undid her blouse and buried his face in what he found there.

They stayed in that hotel room for hours. They stopped only long enough to watch themselves on the news at ten o'clock, and again at eleven.

20

IN the kitchen at Koch Street, Mark D. held one hand wrapped in a filthy blood-soaked handkerchief, and dripped blood on the floor. He moaned constantly that he had been shot.

Two satchels stood on the kitchen table. One held money. The other, which had held Charles's submachine gun, was empty. Charles, his face twisted with rage, gripped his grease gun with both hands.

Mark D. moaned: "They shot poor young Floyd. My hand, my fucking hand."

On the counter beside the stove a radio played. A disk jockey murmured commercials. His messages were punctuated by Mark D.'s pain.

Walker was trying to debrief the remnants of his assault team. "I want to know exactly what happened."

Instead of answering Walker's questions, the tight-lipped Charles at the kitchen table began field-stripping his machine gun. A burst of loud music came from the radio.

Leon Epps, near hysteria himself, said: "That cat jumped out and shot Floyd. Floyd never had no chance. He's hurt bad. I'm sure of it. We had to leave him."

"It's still bleeding," Mark D. moaned. He had unwrapped the handkerchief. He was staring at his torn hand. Walker saw that a bullet had passed cleanly through the webbing between two fingers. Mark D. moaned: "I'm losing blood. I can't use my hand. There's no feeling."

Walker was half listening to the radio. Newscasters had been breaking into programs for the last thirty minutes. They had spoken excitedly of holocausts and bloodbaths. They were enjoying this. It made them feel important.

To Leon Epps, Walker said: "Who shot all those other people?"

"The bank guard was spraying shots every which way."

"And who shot the bank guard?"

The disk jockey broke in with another commercial.

Epps glanced meaningfully down at the submachine gun. He did not answer. He did not have to. The gun was in pieces on the table, and Walker grabbed its clip. The clip was empty.

"You fired that piece in the bank?" demanded Walker incredulously.

Charles's black eyes fastened on Walker.

Walker said: "I told you not to use that grease gun inside a bank. I told you."

Charles raised the barrel to his eye and attempted to see daylight. Walker snapped the radio off.

"I gave you explicit orders," shouted Walker.

Charles said: "I ain't taking orders from you no more. I got my own score to settle with these pigs. I'll settle my own score my own way."

"Why didn't you leave your signature behind?" shouted Walker. "Or your picture. Did you ever hear of the science of ballistics? They will match today's bullets with the bullets taken out of those police officers you iced last summer. Every police officer in the city will be looking for you now."

Charles, working with an oil-soaked rag, said: "Every one of them was looking for me before. It don't make a fuck to me."

"They'll be trying to find this place."

Mark D. moaned: "I've gotta get me a doctor. I've been shot." He was holding his hand, sobbing. The tears were running down his face.

To Charles, Walker cried: "You have jeopardized the revolution." It was as if now he could see what the end would be. He was forced to confront his own future and it was bleak.

"I used to believe in ideology. But the only thing I believe in now is this." Charles thrust the machine gun toward Walker's nose.

Cold reason told Walker to pack a small bag while there was still time. Take his books, his new manuscript, wear his Brooks Brothers suit.

But the image of himself had by now fused with his personality. Fear was unworthy of him. A great captain could not run.

Mark D. moaned: "I'm shot. I've been shot."

Everett Walker, under extreme tension, batted Charles's machine gun aside with one hand, and slapped Mark D.'s face with the other. Staring at his torn hand, Mark D. began to sob aloud.

Charles, quivering with anger, had leaped to his feet. Leon Epps, grabbing for the gun in his belt, had leaped two steps backward and banged against the stove.

Walker saw that all three were on the edge of hysteria, and that his revolution was possibly in ruins.

Silence filled the kitchen. It seemed as cold as fear.

Slowly Leon Epp's hand came away from his piece. Charles lowered his half-reassembled grease gun. Mark D. stopped sobbing.

Dinner hour saw the Freedom and Equality Army of Revolution glued to Paula's TV set. Newscasts—and Walker at the set was switching stations repeatedly to monitor them all—showed a log jam of police radio cars in the street outside the bank. There were views through the glass at police and bank officials scurrying back and forth inside. Through the glass a long lens studied the corpses lying under newspapers.

"That's Floyd," said Mark D.

They recognized Floyd Fields by his sneakers.

"Floyd's on all the shows," said Paula with awe.

They babbled about Floyd while the camera lingered on him.

"He's famous now," said Leon Epps soberly. "He'd be happy. He always wanted to be famous."

Fame? thought Walker. You people don't know what fame is.

The men watched with grim, fixed stares as Floyd's body was carried out of the bank, but behind him Walker heard Sugar—Floyd's woman—sob.

An interview with Chief of Detectives Eischied commenced, after which Everett Walker's message to the newspapers—which had been hand-delivered by Cookie and Frank—was read: "In reprisal for the wanton murder of young Floyd Fields two police officers will be executed."

"Two?" said Mark D. His hand was bandaged, and he was acting like a man again. "Which two?"

Charles answered: "Any two. It don't make no difference. They all pigs."

"Targets of opportunity," said Mark D.

Everett Walker said: "Wrong."

All heads turned to stare at him.

He was thinking it out carefully.

The faces of Police Officers Delehanty and Cusack

filled the screen. Cheek to cheek they bragged of their part in the operation that had resulted in the death of Floyd Fields.

Walker was studying the TV screen.

Charles said: "What you mean 'wrong'?"

Walker said: "The time for random execution of police officers is over. The revolution must move on to specific targets. Two specific targets."

Charles sounded impressed. "Which two?"

On the screen Officers Delehanty and Cusack looked about to kiss each other.

Everett Walker nodded toward the TV screen: "Those two." The decision satisfied him.

Charles began to laugh. "Me and grease can handle that, can't we, grease?" His hands stroked the muzzle of his submachine gun.

Walker snapped: "Wrong."

All was clear to him. Though the politics of the revolution now demanded specific victims, the executioner could not be self-appointed, for this would be both to deny his own revolutionary primacy, and also to weaken the moral force which gave the revolution strength.

The logic was clear. The victims would be executed not by one man but by the entire revolution.

"The executioner will be selected from among us by lot," said Walker.

There was some grumbling. The execution of two specific police officers was too dangerous. It had never been tried anywhere. Better—and much safer—simply to rub out any two cops who happened by, targets of opportunity, as in the past.

But on the screen Officers Delehanty and Cusack continued to gaze lovingly at each other and the comments of the watching revolutionaries became ribald. "I bet that male pig been getting into the pants of that female pig," said Leon Epps.

Butch said: "They probably fucking each other right this minute."

Charles said: "When a man been doing a little

shooting, a man develop a powerful need for humping cunt, don't he?"

Walker saw that his decision had been accepted.

"By lot," said Everett Walker.

Upstairs in Walker's candlelit room the funeral service of Floyd Fields began. The men and women sat crosslegged on the floor. Walker took up position in front of the room's one table, which had been pushed against the cinder blocks that had once been a window. On this table two candles burned at either end, illuminating, in the center, stacks of bank notes. The table was like an altar weighed down by a tabernacle of money. Two guns, fully loaded, lay on this table also, muzzles trained toward the revolution's capital assets, as if protecting them. Walker had distributed thousands—Charles, tonight, wore a new offwhite suit and new wedge-sole shoes—but the bulk of the money belonged not to any of them, Walker had said. It belonged to the revolution.

In front of this candlelit altar Walker began his sermon: "Wherever there is struggle there is sacrifice, and death is a common occurrence. We have the interest of the people and the sufferings of the great majority at heart. And when we die for the people it is a worthy death."

A broken sob escaped Sugar. Soon Paula and Marie were crying too. The candle flames flickered on their tears. "Countless revolutionary martyrs," Walker intoned, "have laid down their lives in the interest of the people, and our hearts are filled with pain as we the living think of them. Can there be any personal interest then, that we would not sacrifice, or any error that we would not discard?"

Behind Walker stood the candlelit table that was either altar or bier, and its tabernacle that was indubitably money. The wailing of the women was punctuated by Walker's sonorous cadences, and the light from the flickering candles was not much different from the tribal campfires of darker continents. One tribe had suffered grievous hurt, and after this funeral service ended would inflict grievous hurt in its turn.

Young Floyd was the first martyr to the cause, Walker preached. There would be others. It was up to the women to be brave, to stand behind their men, and if a man fell then one of his brothers would take care of his woman. Each brother could rely on this, and go into combat without being worried about it.

With this statement some of the brothers began to eye Sugar. The candlelight, Walker noted, gleamed off their cheekbones and their suddenly moist lips. But he cut interest in Sugar short, intoning: "I offer the bereaved sister what solicitude she may be able to find in my tent tonight, and subsequently if she should so desire."

The eyeballs flicked toward Walker. The wailing and sobbing stopped. Paula looked shocked, then hurt, then perhaps jealous. Her eyes fell, but she did not speak. No one spoke.

Walker said: "We shall continue our revolutionary struggle, as the late lamented Floyd would have wished. Tomorrow we must contact Floyd's poor mama and offer our condolences." An odd thought for a self-styled "dedicated revolutionary," but to Walker at that moment a normal one. Walker's hate flowed only outward. To his own people he accorded compassion, even love, or so he believed.

"After that," he said in a harder voice, "we must make arrangements to acquire those weapons of combat which will be needed for the next phase of the revolution. In the matter of the execution of the two police officers already selected, tactical plans will go into operation at once."

He glanced down at Sugar. Her eyes were shining, though her face was still wet with tears.

Walker said: "Floyd is dead, but he died nobly and a hero fighting for the freedom of his people and of all oppressed people. No one could ask for a more glorious death than that which befell Brother Floyd today." Walker bowed his head over clasped hands. Then he looked up and said: "The memorial service is finished."

Silently all filed into the closet and down the ladder

until only Sugar and Walker were left standing in the bare airless room. The air was close from body heat, and from the guttering candles. Walker sniffed the odor of men and women, and of hot wax.

When all were gone but Sugar, Walker stretched out his arms.

Ten feet away, half hidden in darkness, Sugar seemed to catch her breath. Walker watched her hands smooth her dress down over her hips. She had big breasts and a meaty behind. Giving a sob, she ran forward into Walker's arms. For the moment Walker had saved the revolution, and knew it. He grabbed two handfuls and began kissing salt away from her eyes.

21

MARTY and Agnes were invited to a screening interview for the *Today Show*. A sergeant from the office of the Deputy Commissioner for Public Affairs accompanied them. Neither Marty nor Agnes understood that they must survive this interview and perhaps others in order to appear on the show. Both supposed that they had already been selected, and the interviewer said nothing to dispel this illusion.

"On the air," he said, "you'll be interviewed by Joe."

This pleased Agnes. "I think Joe's cute. I'd much rather be interviewed by Joe than by Wilma."

Only a few hours ago it would have seemed incredible to her to be interviewed by either. Now she was thinking of all the friends she'd have to call up to tell them to watch.

The interviewer, a young man of about twenty-five, asked first Marty, then Agnes where they had grown up and why they had joined the police force. He asked what assignments they had had before being made partners. He asked them to describe a typical day on patrol in the Bronx. He made copious notes. Although Agnes was taken by him, Marty was not. Marty's answers were careful and brief. Marty watched him through narrowed eyes.

"What's Joe really like?" asked Agnes.

"Well, you'll meet him on the show."

Now the interviewer began to ask Agnes her opinions about the women's liberation movement. Did she see herself as a token woman in an experiment, or as a real cop, or what?

Marty saw that the star of the show was going to be Agnes. This was nice for her, but where did it leave him? What would the guys say in the stationhouse when the show was over? And who was this fag interviewing them?

Marty, watching the interviewer carefully, asked, "What day do we go on?"

"That hasn't been decided upon," said the young man suavely. Marty noted that he reeked of some kind of perfume. "You'll be notified in plenty of time."

After the interview Marty, filled with misgivings, stood on the sidewalk with Agnes. Traffic went by in the street.

Marty said: "We're gonna get ripped off by these people. I'm telling you."

"Oh, Marty, you're exaggerating."

"You'll see," said Marty, and went home. Agnes went straight to the hairdresser's and had a permanent.

At an executive conference later that day a number of potential guests were considered, and the pros and cons thrashed over. Approximately five minutes were devoted to Marty and Agnes.

"Well, they have certainly had a lot of ink recently," said one assistant producer.

The producer said: "Nobody wants to hear a cop come on and talk about apprehending perpetrators."

The young interviewer, looking up from his notes, said: "The women's lib aspect of it looked good to me. She talks real well on the subject."

"Yeah, if she doesn't choke up and go silent on us once she sees the red light wink on."

The producer was thumbing through news clippings on Marty and Agnes. "Okay," he said after a moment. "But let's let Wilma handle it, rather than Joe. Tell her to dig into this women's lib business."

Marty and Agnes were ordered to report to the studio the next morning in uniform. They would meet the sergeant from Public Affairs on the sidewalk in front at 5:45 A.M.

That night Marty made his wife press his best uniform three times before he was satisfied with it. In Staten Island, after taking in seams to make a better fit, and then pressing her uniform, Agnes put it on and studied herself in a full-length mirror. She certainly looked better without all that gear around the middle, she thought.

The sergeant from Public Affairs had been ordered to put them on camera without their guns, but next morning, as 6 A.M. approached, the producer absolutely demanded that guns not only be worn, but that they not be hidden by a desk or any furniture. Marty and Agnes were to sit in open chairs with guns and all other gear around their waists showing.

They had been handed releases to sign that absolved NBC from all possible potential legal consequences of their appearance. Being police officers, both had had a great deal to do with lawyers, especially Marty, and Marty, now having read the form through, announced to the producer: "I'm not signing this thing."

The producer, all smiles, informed him that he couldn't go on the air unless he signed it.

Marty, Agnes and the sergeant sat in an anteroom. The producer stood in the doorway. Out in the studio the show had already started. "So you see, you have to sign it," said the producer cheerfully.

"No sir," said Marty.

The producer had evidently been through this before and knew how to handle recalcitrant guests at 6 A.M. Gathering up the forms he said: "Well, I'm sorry you see it that way, but in that case we won't be able to use you. Sorry to have put you to the trouble of coming down here so early in the morning."

Offering a false smile, he awaited the predictable result.

Marty glanced at Agnes. Agnes looked stricken. Marty thought: She really wants to go on. It means a lot to her. Marty didn't care for himself, but Agnes had everyone she knew watching the show this morning.

Marty looked to the Public Affairs sergeant for advice. "What do you think, sarge?"

But sergeants, Marty had found, were experts at avoiding responsibility where possible, and this one rose to his feet saying: "Let me see if I can find some coffee around here. You'd like a cup, wouldn't you, Agnes? I know I would." And out the door he went.

Marty read the form through again. It still read the same. He was still assuming legal responsibility for his part of the program.

Unsure of himself, Marty said to Agnes: "What do you think?"

"I don't mind signing it, if you don't," said Agnes in a small voice.

Abruptly he pulled a pen out of his belt and signed the form. Beside him Agnes sighed. Her own pen moved across the paper.

After that, both were led into makeup. They sat side by side in barber's chairs and men worked on them. The guy's fingers on his face made Marty tense up.

Later they were led out onto the sound stage. Their guide, an assistant producer, repeatedly cautioned them not to trip over all the cables. He acted as if they were dummies, and Marty was annoyed. Marty saw strong lights, chairs, and a technician who, as soon as they had sat down, affixed microphones to their ties. The chair between them was empty. They waited. The makeup was caked to Marty's face, and he felt like a fairy. The makeup man's touches had not been unpleasant, and Marty was feeling twinges of guilt mixed with vague doubts about his own virility. The lights beat down on his forehead. Sweat began to pop out. His forehead felt like it was bleeding.

Marty was focued entirely on himself.

Two chairs away Agnes was focused entirely on herself also. She could not keep her hands away from her hair. Did it still look its best? She fiddled with her blouse, arranging it over her bosom, and she readjusted the microphone that tended to pucker her tie. Should she have put on more lipstick, or less? She had made herself up heavily before leaving home, and the makeup technician had barely touched her. Sweat had begun to run down her breastbone. She could feel it begin to work its way through her makeup. She wished they'd start.

Two enormous cameras on dollies were wheeled toward them. Though ponderous, they made no noise. The nearer camera was stationed only about three feet away.

Both police officers stared at it, transfixed. Agnes began to get extremely excited. Marty began to get scared.

On another set across the sound stage the show proceeded without them. A discussion ended. A commercial was read. Marty and Agnes, focused on the nearest lens, were scarcely aware of this. Marty kept wetting and rewetting his lips. Agnes patted her hair.

Suddenly the interviewer advanced toward them, circled the camera dolly, and slipped into the seat between them. Agnes realized that the interviewer was not Joe, it was Wilma, who gave them a smile and shook hands with both.

"Not nervous, are you?" inquired Wilma.

"Not at all," said Agnes, flashing a bright smile. But she glanced past Wilma at Marty, and saw that he was terrified. This filled her with concern. How could she help him? Her job was to aid her partner, and she began frantically trying to think of a way.

Wilma, ignoring both of them, was waiting for her cue. Suddenly the red light winked atop the near camera. Marty, seeing it, swallowed convulsively. Agnes, not seeing it at all, leaned across in front of

Wilma, blocking her, and squeezed Marty's knee, whispering: "Don't worry, Marty, there's nothing to worry about."

Wilma had gone into a kind of convulsion herself. She was canted far to the side, trying to deliver her introductory remarks past Agnes at the camera.

Hearing Wilma's voice, Agnes straightened up fast, her head, as she did so, colliding with Wilma's. Both women saw stars. The noise resounded in kitchens and breakfast nooks across the nation. People had noticed Marty's terror, had heard Agnes's stage whisper. Now they watched the blinking Wilma trying to refocus her eyes. Many experienced mirth, a rare emotion so early in the day. Bodies shook inside bathrobes. Coffee sloshed over into a million saucers.

Though her eyes were still glazed, Wilma began to interview Marty, whom she had never met before this minute. But his answers were both monosyllabic and uttered in a choked voice. Wilma, still in a state of shock, turned to Agnes and flung out the only question that came to mind. Why had Agnes become a cop?

Agnes said: "I wanted to do good with my life, I think." Agnes was not flustered at all. "I wanted to devote my life to the service of others, almost like becoming a nun, you might say."

It gave Wilma time to recover. "Nuns don't carry guns," she pointed out. She was breathing hard but was again in control.

"I never thought I'd have to use my gun," Agnes said in a low voice. "I never did use it before the other day."

Wilma turned back to Marty, giving him another chance. "Tell us about that," she purred.

Marty managed to speak. He blurted: "All I can say is, I wouldn't like to be in the shoes of any perpetrator that meets up with Agnes."

In a living room such a remark might have provoked an embarrassed silence. But this was television. Silence was not permitted.

Flashing her bright smile Wilma returned to Agnes. "Is there sexual tension in the radio car?"

Agnes considered this with the detachment of a scientist. It was not her radio car Wilma was asking about. The question in no way related to her and Marty. It was not personal.

She answered: "I'd be surprised if there wasn't, wouldn't you?"

Wilma nodded. It was a knowing nod. A suggestive nod. It entered the consciousness of every viewer—including Agnes's husband and Marty's wife.

When Agnes had fired on the getaway car the other day, what was she thinking, Wilma asked.

"I was trying to stop the perpetrators from getting away," Agnes began, "and—"

"And what?"

"It's complicated," answered Agnes earnestly. "But I felt I represented all women trying to find a foothold in what had been a man's world. For me the Police Department symbolized that man's world, and I wanted to be part of it, and at that moment I wanted to do my job as well as any man could have."

Wilma purred: "Were you scared?"

"I was afraid of failing to do my job and—"

"And what?"

"And of—" Agnes turned those big earnest eyes on Marty. Marty was staring straight ahead, locked inside a world of his own, for he recognized himself as a failure on TV, hated himself for being here at all, hated everyone connected with this program. At the moment he hated even Agnes, who was doing so well.

"Go on," encouraged Wilma.

"—and I was afraid for Marty. I was more afraid that one of those bullets would hit Marty than that I would be hit myself."

The camera now closed up on Wilma, until she filled the home screen from ear to ear, and with her professional smile fully in place, she murmured into the lens: "Thank you so much for being with us this morning, Police Officers Agnes Cusack and Martin"—she had to hesitate to read Marty's name off her notes—"Delehanty, who so bravely shot it out with bank robbers here in New York City only a few days ago."

An instant later the camera's red light winked out and an instant after that Wilma was gone. Agnes and Marty sat in stunned silence, an empty chair between them.

Marty muttered in a thick voice: "What did you have to say crap like that for."

Agnes was having second thoughts herself. With ghastly clarity her own words still rang in her head. But her immediate problem was Marty. Marty needed bucking up. So she said with false enthusiasm: "You did great, Marty. You were really good. I was proud of you this morning."

Marty muttered: "I'd like to lock that broad up. I'd like to put handcuffs on that fucking Wilma and take her down to the stationhouse and book her."

Ten minutes later Agnes and Marty stood on the sidewalk outside the RCA building. There was no sign of the sergeant from Public Affairs. Cars went by. Marty muttered: "I'd like to throw her in the cage with all the other degenerates."

"Don't you want to get some breakfast, Marty?"

"No," said Marty, "I'm going home." Agnes watched him stalk off toward the subway.

Agnes got into her car and drove back to Staten Island. By the time she reached her house it was past nine o'clock and she was surprised to find her husband still there.

"You were beautiful," he snarled at her. "Oh, Christ, weren't you beautiful? What's going on between you and that cop?"

Agnes found herself blushing. "What—what do you mean?"

"Don't hand me that shit. I saw it in your face. Every goddamn idiot in America who was watching that program saw it."

"But, darling——"

He slapped her. It made her eyes water. She had gone into a crouch from the first blow, and as soon as she straightened up he swung another. And another. And another.

She was trying to think what to do, but at the same

time she was standing apart from herself watching this scene. She recognized it as a classic family fight, the type that cops on patrol responded to every day, and she thought with a kind of panic: If I were the police called in here I'd know just what to do. Isn't it ironic? Would weapons show next? She knew how incredibly quickly weapons could appear, called forth by simple pain or by blind rage, or panic, or despair. She felt all these emotions, plus guilt as well, and her face stung, and for a moment she considered pulling her gun on her husband.

But that would only escalate the violence. She had never pulled her gun in a family fight yet. She could not do it now, and she had her hands to her cheeks trying to protect her face, while her gun stayed in its holster at her waist. The blows—punches now—were raining down on her head and neck and shoulders, and she realized she was weeping. The police officer in uniform was weeping.

"Tell me, you bitch."

He had backed her halfway down the hall. She felt so guilty that a part of her wanted just to stand there and take it. Abruptly, she turned and sprinted for the bathroom.

She got the door closed and locked just in time. Her husband's fist beat on it.

"You bitch, you stinking bitch."

Relief, rage, and who knew what other emotions welled up inside her, and she shouted through the door: "He's twice the man you are. Ten times the man you are."

The minute the words were out she wanted to call them back. From the other side of the door came only heavy silence. Then she heard his footsteps diminishing, and when she pulled the window curtain aside she saw him getting heavily into his truck. She watched him drive away. Now the tears welled up. She realized that she was in love with her husband, in love with Marty, in love with being a cop on patrol. In addition she saw herself as a symbol for all women everywhere trying to find and hold a place in a man's world, and all this responsibility seemed to come crashing down on her, so that, suddenly, it seemed to her that she wasn't tough enough, wasn't woman enough to handle it all at once. The police officer sat on the toilet lid sobbing into her hands.

22

THE gun dealer, Vincente Cuomo, wore a cream-colored cashmere topcoat over a dark blue business suit. His felt fedora was cream-colored too. He wore it with the brim snapped down on one side. On the coat tree beside the booth he hung his coat carefully, but he slid into the seat still wearing the hat. His brief-case lay on his lap under the table. He sat with both hands on top of it.

Charles, already seated, said: "Put that fucking briefcase on the seat."

"What'll you have, gents," asked the barman.

Leaning over he wiped the tabletop with a wet rag, leaving behind a glistening sheen.

"It was better the way it was, for chrissake," Cuomo told him. Cuomo plucked napkins from the dispenser and began wiping the table down. "You ought to wring that rag out once in a while."

The barman, waiting, said nothing.

"I'm wearing a two-hundred-dollar suit, for chrissake."

Charles sipped wordlessly at a beer.

Cuomo said: "Bring me a fucking Americano. And use Italian wine."

Cuomo glanced around the saloon. He noted that a dozen rough-looking men stood at the bar. Charles's eyes never left Cuomo.

"Well," said Cuomo cheerfully, turning back to Charles. "How's tricks? How's the wife and kiddies? What do you think about the situation on Wall Street?"

Charles said: "You got something to sell?"

"I need a vacation," Cuomo said. "This city's going to the dogs. These urban-renewal projects are turning the city into a hotbed of crime, for chrissake."

"I said, do you got something to sell?"

"What are you interested in? Are you interested in the Grand Canyon? The Grand Canyon is lovely this time of year."

"You know what I'm interested in."

"I got some pictures to show you. Got them right here in my fucking briefcase."

As his hand plunged into the briefcase, Charles stiffened, and, under the table, clutched something hard. "Take them out slow, muthafucka, real slow."

The barman put a drink in front of Cuomo. When the barman was gone, Cuomo laid some brochures on the table. "Take a look at these."

They were travel brochures. Watching Charles carefully, Cuomo pushed them across the table. "How about a Caribbean cruise? Very popular right now. Just the thing for the wife and kiddies."

Charles, expecting photos of guns, found photos of beaches. He swept the brochures onto the floor. His voice was as cold as his eyes. "I said, do you got something to sell?"

Cuomo said: "I'm a travel agent. You leave word that you want to see me, naturally I think you're interested in one of my tours. How about a week in Egypt?"

"You got nothing," said Charles. He slid out of the booth. "You wasting my time." He had a satchel with him, and dragged it out from under the table. To Cuomo the satchel looked heavy.

Cuomo grabbed him by the arm. "Talk to me, pal. You want something, maybe I can get it for you."

They stared at each other. After a moment, Charles slid back into the booth.

Cuomo was pleased with himself. He was like a

used-car salesman applauding his own technique. The first job was to establish how badly the sucker wanted your merchandise; the second was to learn how much he had to spend; the third was to unload the ripest merchandise you could get him to go for.

Charles said: "You a cool piece of work, man."

Cuomo accepted the compliment. "What did you have in mind?"

"You got access to hand grenades?" Charles imagined them being pitched down off a church roof as the coffin was being lifted from the hearse.

"Two Ks a box."

"You got anything heavy?"

"What do you want, an antitank gun?"

"Something like that, maybe." Charles imagined the panic of cops under rocket attack during a funeral.

"What are you going to do, start a fucking war?"

Charles's eyes went flat. "You ask too fucking many questions."

Cuomo in his mind was putting two and two together. He thought: I bet this is the guy.

He said coolly: "That grease gun I sold you, I see in the paper you've been using it."

Charles lifted his satchel off the floor and dropped it heavily on the table. "I got it right here and I'm thinking of using it right now."

Cuomo blanched. He peered around the edge of the booth. There were still a dozen or so men at the bar.

Charles saw sweat on Cuomo's brow. Cuomo hissed: "You must be out of your mind to tote that fucking piece around with you." Cuomo was mopping his brow with a folded handkerchief.

Cuomo said: "Anybody catches you with that thing while I'm with you, I go away too." But his voice was under control again. He said: "I don't like that. The guys I work for don't like that."

Charles's eyes bored into him.

Cuomo said: "Grenades, antitank gun. What else you want?"

"What else you got?"

Cuomo set the hook a little deeper. "Take a look at this."

From his briefcase he extracted the photo of a tommy gun.

After glancing at it, Charles passed it back. "I already got one." He patted his satchel.

"Not like this one you haven't. This here gun is a very special gun. How many rounds does that grease of yours hold at one time, twenty? This drum on top of the barrel"—Cuomo pointed at it with a pen—"it holds one hundred sixty-seven rounds. They are twenty-two long rifle slugs. No recoil. This gun won't climb on you. It fires twenty-five rounds a second. Twenty-five a second, I said. Know how long a second is? Notice the telescopic sight. Notice this thing under the barrel. It's about the size of a carton of cigarettes, right?"

"I can see it," said Charles. But he looked interested. The sales pitch was getting to him.

"It's a laser beam," said Cuomo. "You know what a laser beam is? They use it in eye surgery. That's how accurate it is. On this particular weapon it's an aiming device. You point that laser beam and it makes a red bead appear on the target. You lay that red bead on some guy, you hold the trigger down for one second, and you put twenty-five rounds into that red bead. In under seven seconds you empty the fucking drum, and all 167 bullets go right where you put that red bead."

Charles, studying the photo, was silent.

"It's made by a factory called American International," said Cuomo. "The only people have this gun is the FBI. It's been used operationally only once. There was a prison riot in Utah, and the ringleader is out in the yard announcing his demands, and all of a sudden he glances down and there's this red bead in the middle of his breastbone.

"He says: 'What the fuck is this red bead?' The FBI calls out to him over a bullhorn: 'That's where twenty-five bullets are going to hit you inside of one second if you don't surrender?' So the stupid prick surrendered. What else could he do?"

Charles was imagining himself spraying 167 bullets down on massed policemen.

"How much you want for that piece?"

"That piece will run you three Ks."

Charles said: "You get me that piece."

Cuomo said, "How do I know you got that kind of money?"

Charles unzipped his satchel and lifted out a paper bag, which he tossed onto the table top. It landed like a packed lunch. Cuomo unfurled the bag and peeked inside. Money. His hand disappeared from view and thumbed bills.

Standing up, he said: "Excuse me."

Charles's eyes followed Cuomo into the men's room.

When Cuomo came back he dropped the paper bag on the table, saying: "Two Ks. You want me to take that?"

"How long it take you to deliver?"

"Two nights from now."

"Where?"

"Same place as last time."

Charles understood that he should park his car alongside Yankee Stadium at midnight. Cuomo would pull up behind him. The merchandise would be transferred from Cuomo's trunk to Charles's trunk. The money would change hands, and both cars would wait until it had been counted out under the dashboard light. Cuomo would have a colleague riding shotgun. So would Charles.

"How many grenades in a box?" asked Charles.

"You want twelve, you can have twelve. You want twenty-four, you can have twenty-four, but you better have another guy along to help you lift the box."

"Twenty-four," Charles said.

Cuomo nodded. "Six Ks. I'll fill an order to that amount. Satisfaction guaranteed. I need a deposit."

Charles, his eyes never leaving Cuomo's face, pushed the paper bag across the table, saying: "You be there. Because if you not there, I come looking for you."

Cuomo's face darkened. Fucking creep, he thought, screw you. But he controlled himself. Cuomo was in the process of selling valuable but hard-to-move merchandise. In two years it hadn't moved. It was part of a munition truck shipment hijacked and lying in a warehouse ever since. There would be a nice commission for Cuomo, and his boss would be delighted.

"I'll leave first," Cuomo said.

"You will go second," said Charles. "You will leave after I leave."

"Be my guest," said Cuomo.

EISCHIED poured himself out a Scotch over ice and paced his office, brooding. The PC was for the moment as off balance as the city itself, and Eischied's job, temporarily, was safe. He could not be removed while sitting on a case this big. The public might scream. The PC would never risk it.

If Eischied's own talents could be weighed, he thought he would be marked above average as a detective. But his real skill, he told himself, was his ability to gauge political forces. He had managed to stay alive and afloat all these years, though many other earnest and dedicated cops had not, and now he was Chief of Detectives. Though a concerted attempt had just been mounted to remove him—it might have destroyed him—he had managed to blunt it. He had bought time. Flushed with this imagined triumph, he felt confident. He could hang on indefinitely.

All he had to do was break this case.

He sipped his whisky.

So what else did he know about this gang of bank robbers?

Well, the three men who had entered the bank were amateurs. They were small-time stickup men. One had walked straight into the bank guard's bullet, even though the bank guard was an amateur too. The other two, though armed, had frozen into paralysis at the sight of the bank guard with his single revolver.

Small-time gunmen like this existed by the thousands in New York today. Their existence was to be deplored, and to be contained insofar as possible by a vigilant police department, but they in no way menaced the heartbeat of the city.

Eischied sipped more whisky.

The guy with the machine gun was another story. He had killed two cops last summer, and in the bank had manipulated that same machine gun with deadly efficiency. What did Eischied know about him?

That he was cool, ruthless.

That he was able to make, and then act upon, abrupt decisions. Without a sign of panic or hesitation he had recognized a deteriorating situation, and reversed it.

But there were other facts about him which, to Eischied, were even more significant.

1. Although he had presumably gunned down the two cops last summer, he had sent no messages to the police or press then. The messages had begun only this fall. He—or someone behind him—now was bragging about every bank robbery. Why?

2. At today's bank robbery he had been only the wheelman. What did this mean?

Eischied kept returning to the notion that the killer was under orders to serve as wheelman. That the brain behind this wave of bank robberies must be someone else.

If it was someone else, then it was someone with a substantial reputation for so-called revolutionary acts.

Eischied came to the conclusion that he was dealing with two separate and distinct forces here: the brain and the gun. The gun knows how to use that thing, Eischied reflected, and likes to use it, probably too much, and the brain tells him, no, you are the wheel-man—and makes it stick. The brain controls the gun. The gun is a substantial fellow in his own right, so what does that make the brain?

The answer to Eischied was: It makes him even more substantial than I might have feared.

Eischied walked to his safe and opened the heavy door. Lifting the black cardboard, he stared down at the single scorched fingerprint.

I bet that's the guy, he told himself. But who?

Each time he looked at the print the page seemed darker. The photos of it which had been made in the lab could be used by detectives for eventual identification, but this darkening piece of newsprint was the true evidence. Its continued existence was vital to any case against this gang that might someday be presented in court.

Eischied let the cardboard drop into place, closing light off from the evidence. He pushed the heavy door shut.

As he turned away from the safe Eischied thought: Maybe I should hand this print over to the FBI. Their technicians on the whole are better than ours. Maybe they can find out who it belongs to.

The answer came back: If they did find out, they probably wouldn't tell us.

He knew he wanted the evidence where he could see it and feel it. It had become an emotional need with him. It was like the photo of a beloved. He took strength from it, and almost life. He needed to look at it often.

He brooded again about the identity of the brain behind the gun. To control somebody like this machine gunner, Eischied thought, he must be one hell of a guy.

Inside the Koch Street tenement in the South Bronx, TV news blared every night. Drinking Boone's Farm apple wine, playfully jostling for position, they crowded around the set, and they chortled with delight when mention of their handiwork came on. They saw plenty of Officers Cusack and Delehanty, who were being turned into heroes. This was fine with them, for that made them heroes too, and, watching, they made jokes and obscene remarks. These were particularly numerous during interviews with Police Officer Agnes Cusack. They liked to boast about which parts of her anatomy their bullets would soon rip into.

Everett Walker studied the TV intently. Each detail from the lives of the two police officers he noted down. He was especially alert for clues that would tell him where they lived. Phase II (the assassinations of Officers Delehanty and Cusack) could not go forward until Phase III was also in place. Phase III was the funeral. There was no point killing them until he knew which churches they would be buried from. The day he could fix addresses beside their names—and the addresses of their parish churches—was the day he signed their death warrants.

He culled the newspapers with the same religious zeal. He was like a seminarian studying for ordination. He was as devoted as a priest. He was like a bishop about to lay on hands.

He was like a hunter quartering the terrain, and he was closing in on their separate lairs.

In a TV interview Officer Delehanty had mentioned the name of the Queens emporium where he bowled, which, to Walker, was a place where the ritual of execution could be played out. A photograph in the *Daily News* showed him playing basketball in a Queens schoolyard near his house. He lived in Queens, then, though where? Clues were thick. His house lay under one of the glide paths serving La Guardia Airport. It was a policeman's ghetto only one rank up from the ghettos Walker was used to, but he didn't know this. It was within walking distance of the tennis stadium at Forest Hills, a rich man's sport and place, and as alien to Delehanty as to Walker.

As far as Police Officer Martin Delehanty was concerned, map references were almost complete.

Walker knew also that Officer Agnes Cusack lived in Staten Island, that her husband was a house painter, and that she could see the Verrazano Bridge from her bedroom window. The house painter worked out of a construction firm in Stapleton, but Agnes's home phone number and address, like Delehanty's, was not listed. Cops' phones were never listed, Walker realized. Cops had feared reprisals since before Walker was born.

Press clippings about the two police officers Everett Walker Scotch-taped to the walls of Paula's flat. Over the two biggest photos—these had run in the centerfold of the *Daily News*—Walker superimposed hand-drawn targets with bull's-eyes over the hearts. The targets made it clear to all: the high priest had selected sacrificial victims. It remained only to lure them to the altar—or to bring the altar to them—and then put them to death. The gods being momentarily appeased and Phase II fulfilled, it would be time to prepare the final details of Phase III.

Interviews with Chief of Detectives Earl Eischied were clipped also, but Walker studied them apart. This was personal. Eischied in these interviews made no mention of machine-gun bullets recovered from the bank or of matching them to those dug out of last summer's cops, and perhap he had never made the connection, but Walker believed differently—that Eischied knew, but was holding the information back. Why? What else did Eischied know but conceal? Walker had begun to see Eischied as his own counterpart, as the man he himself must outwit. This concept was flattering to Walker, for Eischied wore three stars and Walker had never held official rank anywhere.

Walker realized that Eischied was managing to communicate calm to the city. Eischied intimated that he knew exactly whom he was looking for, and where. The city could count on arrests at any hour.

Walker wondered why. Was it not risky to promise success that the Chief of Detectives could not deliver?

Or did Eischied in fact know? If so, how much time did Walker have? How close were detectives?

Not close enough. Destiny had breathed on Walker, he had convinced himself. He could not be stopped. The future was inevitable. On the night before the Great Funeral Massacre he would give orders to his people, send them out to conduct revolution in other places. Maybe he would hold a last supper—okra, turnip greens and—

What about himself?

Some days he saw himself riddled with police bullets, immolated, a finale to match any crucifixion. His death would send his revolution beyond these times and people into the hearts of all men everywhere, always. But it is impossible for anyone to believe in his own death. Walker, like everyone else, saw his own death as a scene from a play. One jumped up afterward and removed the makeup.

He would certainly attempt to escape. And if he succeeded—what?

At times Walker saw himself stepping back into exile, leaving the revolution in the secure hands of his disciples, Charles and the other survivors. It was possible to imagine a hero's welcome for himself in North Africa or Cuba or any Third World capital. There he would be courted by the world's dignitaries again, and would write his memoirs.

But all this was fantasy. The attack was not fantasy. It was real, inevitable. It was a wall, a turning in the road. He could not see past it.

At last Walker was able to nail down Agnes Cusack's address.

On the *New York Times* food page there appeared a photograph of Police Officer Cusack, wearing a dress, standing in her kitchen. There was also a photo of the exterior of her small frame house. According to the article, which was careful not to give an exact address, this house had been painted lavender by Officer Cusack's husband, and was the only lavender house in that part of Staten Island.

Walker tore the page out of the newspaper.

Mark D. complained: "I haven't read that paper yet."

"You and me, we are taking a trip to Staten Island today."

The house was easy to find. It stood on Tompkins Avenue, two blocks inland from the water and about eight blocks from the bridge. The house painter's truck was in the driveway.

Mark D. had slowed as they drove by so that Walker could study the house. After a moment Walker said: "Keep going straight ahead till I tell you to stop."

He had his Catholic Directory open on his lap, and he was matching the Tompkins Avenue address to the nearest Catholic church. "Turn right here," he ordered Mark D. "Now pull in to the curb."

The church was called St. Robert Bellarmine. From the opposite sidewalk Walker studied it. Agnes's funeral would draw between three and five thousand cops, plus the usual political figures. Walker's imagination began to fill the street in both directions with rank after rank of uniformed targets, their thousands of white gloves holding a salute. The hearse would park just there, slightly past the steps of the church, and the pallbearers would lift Agnes's coffin up onto their shoulders. At that very moment the grenades and the automatic weapon fire would come crashing down from the church roof.

No, not this church roof. Walker saw that it was too steep. It was slate and came to a peak. There was no cover on it, and no way off it. But the roof of any of the apartment houses across the street, he noted, should prove suitable.

He had two tremendous details to work out here. Access to a suitable roof was one of them, and a successful getaway route was the other.

Leaving Mark D. in the car, he stepped into the church. He wanted to get the feel of it. What would it be like inside as the grenades fell outside? What would God do?

It was a bright church. The stained glass was modern, and the floor was dappled in multicolored light. The pews were white oak. The kneelers had foam rubber on top of them. Except for the stations of the cross the walls were bare. Several people knelt in pews close to the altar and a woman in black was lighting candles at a shrine up there.

Afterward he crossed the street to the apartment

building opposite. The lobby door yielded to his hand. In the daytime it wasn't even locked. Why should it be? This was a low crime area over here. People were not afraid. This was practically the suburbs. He rode the elevator to the top floor, encountering no one, then mounted a service staircase to the roof. At the top of the staircase was a door. It was not locked either. Walker stepped out into sunshine. Bed sheets hung, worried stiff by wind. Ducking under, he moved to the parapet and glanced down five stories. A grenade dropped from here would bounce off the hearse roof.

Excellent, he thought.

On the morning of the funeral of Police Officer Agnes Cusack, arriving early, the necessary number of revolutionaries and weapons would mount to this roof and conceal themselves.

It was a pity the attack could not be done from the roof of the church, though. Walker saw the symbolism of churches. To the superstitious it would seem that God had blessed Walker's work. The revolution would gain many recruits.

He ducked under other bed sheets blowing on lines, and surveyed the street to the rear. Fire escapes snaked down the back of all seven apartment buildings in this row. One could leap across any of the adjoining rooftops and take one's pick. The rooftops were like a bank of elevators. Going down? Excellent, Walker thought.

Of the thousands of cops in the street, many would be dead and the rest would not react in time. The revolutionaries would leave the roof via the back fire escapes, landing in another street. The getaway car would be at the curb.

And then?

The escape route proved better than he dared hope. He spent half an hour checking it out.

Less than a quarter of a mile away Walker found an entrance to the Staten Island Expressway. There would be a single right turn to make onto Hylan Boulevard, and two blocks after that a choice of entrances onto the expressway. A change of cars could be arranged a short distance farther on.

Excellent, Walker thought.

Beside him in the car Mark D. said: "What you grinning about? What did we come out here for anyway?"

Walker said only: "Drive me back to Koch Street."

Mark D. grumbled: "You never tell me nothing."

"If I did, probably everybody in that poolroom you play at would know about it by now."

The final pieces were falling into place.

At sixty miles an hour the car leaped over New York Bay. Walker stared down at slate-gray water far below, and was silently jubilant. He could see the Statue of Liberty. Her torch seemed to be waving at him.

24

VINCENTE CUOMO, having arranged to sell his merchandise to Charles, saw no reason why he couldn't sell that same merchandise a second time. The second customer would be the FBI.

The FBI agent, Pat McGovern, was thirty years old and beginning to hate his job. McGovern had a B.A. from Fordham College and a degree in accounting from Fordham Business School. He had paid his way through graduate school by serving as assistant sports publicity director, and he already had two children when, in a romantic moment, he decided to join the FBI. Lately he had convinced himself that he was working at a dead-end job. There was no place he could go with it. He worked long and irregular hours and his wife had begun bitching all the time. Investigatory work did not suit him. The FBI, he had found, kept secrets even from its own agents. Agents were rarely told how the overall investigation was shaping up back in headquarters. As a result, McGovern usually had no confidence in how to approach a subject, or what questions to ask.

Dangerous moments, exciting moments, had proven to be exceedingly rare. They always caught McGovern unawares and unprepared, and he did not like them. He had come to the conclusion that, although he was a member of the police establishment, he had the soul of an auditor, and some weeks ago he had applied for a job on the auditing staff of Equitable Life.

Most of the other agents—there were about a thousand assigned to the New York office—were roughly his age. Most, like himself, had come out of Catholic colleges. Irish Catholic names—just as among New York police detectives—predominated. It sometimes occurred to McGovern that the average detective and the average agent were the same guy, except that the agent had more education and was required by Bureau regulations to dress in coat and necktie at all times. But police work to McGovern was largely drudgery. You harassed petty criminals for information. You endlessly followed up meaningless leads. McGovern sometimes wondered if the average detective, being less well educated, was not better equipped to deal with such a life than was the average agent.

All FBI agents were obliged to cultivate strings of informants, and Vincente Cuomo was one of McGovern's. Three months previously Cuomo had been indicted in federal court as part of a scheme to market stolen airline tickets. McGovern, who worked on the FBI's Fraud Squad, had been sent around by his supervisor to see Cuomo. He was to explain to Cuomo that, in exchange for "cooperation," the Bureau might be able to help him get a lighter sentence, or perhaps even avoid jail altogether.

This meeting took place in a chic midtown bar. Cuomo, who had not had a good night's sleep since his indictment, shouted: "Are you crazy? Are you trying to get me killed?"

McGovern soothed him. The idea had been planted. McGovern pressed his home phone number into Cuomo's hand, and left.

Thereafter McGovern went looking for Cuomo at least once a week, learned all the man's haunts, and drank a succession of coffees and beers with him in seedy places.

It had seemed to lead nowhere. But now Cuomo had phoned promising something big, and they had arranged to meet in the last row of a 42nd Street movie house.

The theatre, when McGovern got there, was showing homosexual pornography. Christ, he thought, and hesitated. But Cuomo presumably was waiting in there. McGovern glanced furtively around, plunked his money down and ducked inside.

In the dark McGovern slid into the seat beside Cuomo. Neither acknowledged the other. Both pretended to watch the movie. McGovern, waiting for Cuomo to speak, scarcely absorbed what he saw, though it was seeping through to him slowly.

Cuomo whispered: "I think I got something on the guy who's been pulling those bank jobs."

McGovern turned sharply in the darkness. "Which bank jobs?

"The guy with the machine gun."

McGovern, careful to let no excitement show, turned back to the movie, where one actor was unzipping another actor's trousers. Out of the side of his mouth McGovern said: "Well, which machine gun?" But he knew immediately, and his heart had started pounding. The biggest case in the city—in the country—might be about to drop into his lap.

On the screen one homosexual was massaging another to erection.

McGovern imagined himself breaking the case, then resigning from the Bureau in triumph and joining Equitable Life. What a case to go out on! He saw his name in headlines for the first time.

One actor, naked, was bent over a piece of furniture. The other actor, also naked, was buggering him.

McGovern saw himself, for a few days, the most famous accountant in the city. Cuomo would want money, which the Bureau would be happy to pay him, if it wasn't too much. McGovern would have to try to beat Cuomo's price down or the agent in charge might refuse, and the whole thing could fall through.

One actor was reaming the other, really reaming him. A third actor entered the picture and began sucking the first guy's tool from underneath.

McGovern, suddenly aware of what was happening on the screen, felt his lunch rise up toward his throat. He thought he might be ill. Then he became furious. Beside him in the dark Cuomo was silent, but McGovern had forgotten Cuomo, McGovern wanted to arrest someone. He considered arresting every employee in the theater. He wanted to take them to the nearest precinct and book them. He knew it would do no good. They would be out on bail in an hour. The charges would never stick. McGovern wanted to do it anyway.

Cuomo said: "He's trying to arrange to buy munitions."

With an effort, McGovern jerked his eyes around and saw Cuomo's face in the gloom.

"Munitions?"

On the screen one man was ejaculating into another man's face.

McGovern could not keep his mind on munitions. He wanted to fire shots at the screen. He wanted to arrest every pervert in the theatre.

To Cuomo he muttered: "Let's get out of here. I can't stand this."

Cuomo refused to go out into the street with him, so they headed for the men's room. As the door slammed behind them, McGovern saw that they had walked in on an elderly man who stood in the center of the floor with his pants down. He had a twenty-dollar bill in his hand. A younger man was kneeling on the floor lapping the older one's crotch.

These two degenerates McGovern could arrest, and

it would stand up in court, eyewitness testimony by himself and Cuomo, and he was so outraged and offended that he almost did it.

But he couldn't afford to. That was not what he was here for.

Frozen and aghast he stood staring while ideas that had been churning around in his head for months suddenly focused, and he knew why he hated police work. Because it was so degrading. Day after day he was exposed to scum like this—and Cuomo was no better.

McGovern dragged Cuomo out into the lobby, and there they conversed in low voices.

"He showed me this grease gun he has. He said he knocked over that bank."

"Who sold him the grease gun, if I may ask?"

Cuomo answered: "Don't look at me. I'm a travel agent."

"Sure. What kind of munitions is he looking for?"

"Hand grenades. A bazooka. Automatic weapons."

"Christ. Why did he come to you?"

"How the fuck do I know?"

McGovern eyed him.

Cuomo said: "Some people get a reputation that's undeserved."

McGovern wrenched his notebook out of his coat pocket and demanded: "When is the drop, and where?"

Cuomo did not answer. Cuomo eyed him shrewdly. McGovern's ballpoint remained poised to start.

"What's the guy's name?" demanded McGovern.

Cuomo said: "That kind of information, friend, will cost you five big ones."

McGovern fought for control of himself, and presently achieved it. The bargaining began. McGovern suggested that Cuomo would be better off to give his information free; in exchange he would have the FBI in his corner when he was sentenced. Cuomo said he wanted help at sentencing too; that was part of the deal. The five big ones were to pay his lawyer.

"Where else am I going to get the lawyer's fee? Do you want me to go out and stick up stores?"

"I would think that the organization you work for has a defense fund."

"What organization?"

McGovern said he would talk to his supervisor.

Cuomo wanted $2,500 down, the balance when the arrest was made. McGovern asked how the merchandise was to be handed over, and where. Cuomo told him how—two cars coming together at night at a deserted spot—but not where, not when.

McGovern went back to Bureau headquarters on 69th Street, and the director of the New York office called a conference at which it was agreed that the Bureau would consent to Cuomo's terms, except that the front money would be cut to $1,000, the rest to be paid upon the arrest of the gunman. The Bureau would round up half a dozen automatic rifles to serve as Cuomo's merchandise.

There was no talk of the ethics of paying money to a man like Cuomo. There was no talk of morality at all. They were businessmen coolly discussing a deal. McGovern was disgusted with all of them.

"We ought to let the bastard furnish his own rifles," he said. "You know goddamn well he's got them. He deals in everything, that guy."

The director of the New York office glanced around at McGovern. No one else reacted to his suggestion in any way.

Cuomo would drive up in his own car to the rendezvous point, the director continued. An FBI agent, presumably McGovern himself, would be sitting beside him, pretending to be riding shotgun on the shipment of illegal arms. A second FBI agent would probably be secreted on the floor in the back seat. Teams of FBI agents in cars could cordon off the entire area of the drop.

They were making plans that involved McGovern's personal safety without asking his opinion, without knowing where the drop was or what the area would even look like.

The director chortled. "That fucking Eischied has

been popping off to the press every day. I'd like to see his face when we break this thing."

McGovern said: "Suppose Cuomo won't agree to the reduced front money, and to taking part in the arrest himself."

The director said coolly: "That's your job, Paddy, my boy. Bring him around. That's what you get paid for."

It took McGovern most of the next day to bring Cuomo around. It was also McGovern's job to get Cuomo to sign a receipt for the front money, and he expected difficulty, but got none. Cuomo, after counting and pocketing the cash, signed the chit without comment.

McGovern waved it in the air. "Suppose I show this to the guys you work for, Cuomo. That would mean concrete overshoes for you, wouldn't it?"

"Nah," scoffed Cuomo. "We don't want these fucking creeps robbing banks any more than you do. It's bad for business. It gives everybody a bad name."

McGovern had to give a wry laugh.

All of crime is interrelated, he realized, just as all of law enforcement is. Crime and law enforcement are interrelated too. The whole system is intimately, mutually interdependent, one piece upon the other. No wonder it works no better than it does.

He wondered in exactly what way Cuomo was setting this deal up so as to take a profit out of both sides. There was nothing McGovern could do about it in any case. For the moment, as far as these bank robbers were concerned, the entire Federal Bureau of Investigation was totally dependent upon one small-time gun dealer.

25

THE hours passed, and young Leon Epps, sent out to steal a car, did not come back. Walker paced nervously. Charles watched him with those cold dead eyes. Walker was smoking—he had begun smoking too much. His fingers were turning yellow. He was like a man waiting for a signature at the bottom of a gigantic deal. But he had waited too long. He had put months into it. The signature seemed assured, but for Walker the waiting had become excruciating. Tonight he was waiting for Epps to come back with a car. After that he would wait for Charles to come back from meeting Cuomo. Phases II and III could not go forward until Cuomo's munitions were in this house.

"Something's happened," said Walker, and ground his cigarette out on the floor.

"He probably met a broad. Either I take Hoyt's car, or we blow the meet."

Walker had been borrowing the pants presser's car from time to time, and had it now. Walker said: "Suppose it's a setup?"

"I dealt with this dude before. The pigs want him bad as they want me. Besides, he got a reputation to live up to. He supply half the guns in this city."

Walker said: "Hoyt's car can lead them to Hoyt—or straight back here."

Charles patted his satchel. "Hoyt's car can lead them nowhere."

They stared at each other. From his pocket Charles removed the car keys. He jingled them in Walker's face. Then he went downstairs. A little later, together with Mark D., he left the house. Scrupulously observing all traffic regulations, driving with extreme care, he crossed the bottom of the Bronx toward the rendezvous point.

Suddenly Yankee Stadium loomed up out of its parking lots. They came under the Jerome Avenue el and there it was. It was as if someone had plunked down a huge wedding cake on a table.

Charles carefully circled its luminous walls. He saw a number of empty parked cars, none Cuomo's. He looked each over carefully as he drove by. The sub-machine gun was in its satchel at his feet. From time to time he reached down and touched the bag's bulk. It always reassured him. He felt ready.

Making a right-hand turn he drove into Ruppert Place, and then turned right again onto 161st Street, slowly circling the wedding cake. He had the car radio turned low. He was listening to songs by James Brown on WLIB. At the same time he had the windows down and was listening for abnormal night noises. Once a taxicab, speeding up, passed him. He watched it. He saw a couple embracing in the back seat. Give it to her, man, he thought, but he watched the cab carefully. It continued straight down Gerard Avenue, crossing 153rd Street. He watched it go. It did not slow down, it did not stop. Only when it was gone did he feel himself relax.

Beside him Mark D. began playing with the radio dial. Charles slapped his hand: "Leave it where it is, man."

Charles steered up Walton Avenue, passing a police radio car parked outside a diner. He looked it over. Empty. He was still circling.

For the third time Charles passed by the rendezvous point. This time Cuomo's car was there, pointed out toward the Major Deegan Expressway. Charles saw no other car nearby. He had noted nothing suspicious.

Charles pulled in behind Cuomo. His wheels bumped the curb. Leaving the engine running, Charles unzipped his satchel on the floor. His hand fitted around the stock and he gripped it. His finger was inside the trigger guard. He freed the stock from the bag.

To Mark D., Charles muttered: "Get out and talk to him."

Charles watched Cuomo and Mark D. approach each

other. They stood on the sidewalk conversing. They stood approximately halfway between the two cars.

Mark D. came up to Charles's window. "He wants to talk to you."

"Get in the car," said Charles. He sensed something was wrong.

Mark D., surprised, rounded the car and slid in on the passenger side.

Charles was trying to decide what to do. Cuomo came up to his window. Charles looked through his windshield into the back of the other car. The cat riding shotgun for Cuomo was twisted in his seat, staring through the intervening glass at Charles's face. Charles guessed the man had a gun in each hand.

Cuomo said: "Relax. You're among friends."

Charles said: "Where's the fucking merchandise?"

"You got the money?"

Charles said to Mark D.: "Show him the money."

Cuomo reached across in front of Charles and took the paper bag of bank notes out of Mark D.'s hands. They watched him get back into his own car. His ceiling light came on. He took his time counting the money.

Presently his door opened, and he came around and opened the lid of his trunk.

Charles said to Mark D.: "Get out and transfer the merchandise." His voice was tight, but he was less nervous than before. However, he still gripped the stock. His hand squeezed it reassuringly. His finger inside the guard patted the trigger several times. He had only to pull that slim bit of steel and—

Mark D. staggered past him with the box of hand grenades. It looked heavy. He heard the thump as Mark D. dropped the box in the trunk.

Next Mark D. came past carrying a second heavy box, and after that what looked like a rolled-up rug.

Cuomo stood at Charles's window chatting. "You got a box of twenty-four fragmentation grenades. You got an antitank gun. It's called a bazooka. Wait till you see it. You got rockets for that bazooka. What can I tell you?"

Charles's suspicions focused in. "Where's the automatic pieces?"

"You want the automatic pieces, you come back tomorrow night. Same time, same place. No extra charge."

Charles yanked his submachine gun out of the satchel, but Cuomo said coldly: "You try anything and my guys will blow you to pieces. You think you're so fucking smart, but you're surrounded. We've been in this business a long time. We don't take chances."

Charles, not knowing whether he was surrounded or not, didn't know what to do.

Cuomo said to him in the same hard voice: "We're not trying to cheat you, pal. I couldn't get them on time. I'm sorry. I can have them for you tomorrow night. Five M-14 rifles and the piece I spoke to you about."

Charles said: "I pay on delivery, not before." The trouble was, Cuomo already had the money and Charles saw no way, short of shooting it out with both of them, to get any back.

"Sorry, pal, the price is the same, whether you come tomorrow night or not. It don't make shit to me. Personally I think you should come back. You're getting a bargain, five M-14s and the most tremendous weapon I ever had the privilege of selling. Think of that laser beam. Think of laying that red bead on some guy's chest. Think of a drum holds a hundred sixty-seven rounds. Think of a piece that delivers twenty-five rounds a second. It's a sweetheart, that gun. Me, I'd come back for it."

Turning casually, Cuomo sauntered to his car, slid in behind the wheel, and drove leisurely away.

The trunk lid slammed, and Mark D. climbed in on the passenger side. As soon as Mark D.'s door closed, Charles left there with a squeal of rubber.

"That Dago is a cool piece of work, ain't he?" said Mark D. admiringly. "I thought you was going to blow him away."

Charles muttered under his breath.

Back at Koch Street, Charles and Mark D. carried

the box of grenades up from the car. Then they carried up the box of rockets. Outside, the street was empty. Pools of lamplight illuminated the roofs of parked cars. Along the sidewalk nothing stirred.

Lastly, Mark D. carried up the bazooka itself, wrapped in an old rug.

In the candlelit room upstairs Charles forced a screwdriver under the lid of the box of grenades. Under pressure from his screwdriver the wood split, and he ripped off pieces with his hands. Inside, the grenades nestled like eggs.

Walker's teeth gleamed.

All of the men reached in, sifting them like handfuls of jewelry. Palms and fingers clasped the rough metal surfaces. Grenades passed from hand to hand, even among the girls.

Everett Walker pried the lid off the case of rockets. The rockets were dull black. They were smooth, sleek, more sexual in appearance and texture. They too made the rounds.

"Unroll the carpet," ordered Walker.

Mark D. grasped one end. With a flourish, he spilled the carpet across the floor, and the bazooka tumbled free. Several hands reached for it, but Charles grabbed it up and sighted on the opposite wall. "This mutha is mine," he cried, and gave one of his rare grins.

Walker asked: "Where are the automatic pieces you spoke of?"

"They coming tomorrow," said Charles in a flat, cold voice.

Walker looked at him. Charles said: "Did that mutha Leon come back yet?"

"No," said Everett Walker.

26

EISCHIED and Florence went to the theatre, but the Chief of Detectives sat there two and a half hours and couldn't keep his mind on it. He had his beeper in his belt. He kept fingering it in the dark. He kept expecting it to go off. He had left Louie monitoring the radio outside—with instructions to come in and get him if necessary. Eischied was convinced something would happen tonight, though he didn't know what—or why he knew, either.

Louis was standing on the curb beside the car afterward.

"Anything come over?" Eischied asked him.

"Not a thing, Chief."

Eischied dismissed him and drove Florence home. She was happy and talkative, but Eischied kept fiddling with the radio. Every time it went silent he imagined it was broken. Mostly it played its usual disorderly song: disturbance in front of such-and-such an address, prowler on a rooftop, cardiac arrest in a restaurant.

In Florence's apartment he prepared drinks, which they sat on the sofa sipping, at the same time necking like teenagers. He hadn't seen her in two weeks. Although so far tonight she was being nice to him, getting her into bed he considered no sure thing. Any false move by him and she was capable of turning off the charm and telling him to leave. He was not at ease with her anymore. He supposed she still wanted to get married; he knew he still did not. Tonight he was determined to seduce her, though he hardly knew why, for half his mind was elsewhere. He still wore his beeper—it protruded into his abdomen worse than his gun—but he had no faith in beepers. For all he knew it was out of order. He was still vaguely listening for radio calls too, though the radio was downstairs at the curb and there was no way he could hear it if it sounded.

"Anything happening?" he asked. He had phoned in.

"Nothing heavy, Chief."

"Well, I'm out of my car. You can get me on my beeper."

"You want to give me a phone number, Chief?"

"No."

Why did he expect something to happen tonight? He began undressing Florence and she let him.

Then for a while he forgot everything. He forgot that he clung to his job by improvising scare headlines from day to day. He forgot this nagging instinctive conviction that tonight something would happen. He forgot that Florence only wanted to marry him.

Still, he did not enjoy it much. He sensed she was feigning passion as much as he was. He felt only enough to perform, not enough to be transported. In one way this was good. He was able to play her to a climax, a job he concentrated on long enough to accomplish, after which he slid himself into the snug slippery place and allowed her to concentrate on him for a change.

Presently, after lighting cigarettes for them both, he padded naked into the living room, where he eyed the telephone for a moment, before moving to fix fresh drinks.

They sat up in Florence's bed sipping Scotch, smoking, chatting, but Eischied found himself listening only for the phone.

"Everything's quiet, Chief," the duty sergeant told him. Unable to resist any longer, he had got up and called his office.

His duty sergeant added cheerfully: "One of our guys killed a stickup man in a garage an hour or so ago, Chief. But that's not something you'd be interested in. Fourth District Homicide responded. The stickup man was trying to steal a car, apparently."

Eischied, standing naked beside the phone, had found a pencil. He took down the address. To the duty sergeant he said: "Wake up Louie. Have him meet me there."

To Florence, sitting heavy-breasted against the headboard, Eischied said: "Sorry, but I've got to go."

She pouted at him while he got dressed. When he had put his topcoat on, he kissed her on the forehead, and on each nipple, but he was no longer thinking about her, and she knew it. He said: "I'll call you. Okay?"

Ten minutes later he was looking down on the body of Leon Epps, though he did not yet know Leon's name. The kid looked about seventeen years old. He looked small, frail, very young and very dead. He looked exactly like the other one in the bank. We're nibbling at them, Eischied thought.

In the office beside the ramp the detective who had killed Epps was giving statements to superior officers and to an assistant district attorney. Eischied glanced from the corpse at his feet to the lighted office window, and back to the corpse again. It wore sneakers, ragged Levi's and a windbreaker. The gun Leon had carried still lay beside him. Eishied picked it up. A chrome-plated Saturday Night Special. Fire it once, he reflected, and the barrel gets so hot that the next bullet is likely to explode in the chamber.

A single bullet had been fired, he saw. The detective, Eischied understood, had fired five times.

Stupid kid, Eischied thought. But Leon wasn't a kid anymore, he was a corpse. This corpse was like all other corpses: in an instant, hopes and dreams had become cooling meat. What I see of life, Eischied thought, is always death. There is no variety. I see only one side. Then he told himself: Everybody sees only one side. I'm no different from skiers who think it is always winter, or prima donnas who think it is always opera houses, or whores who think it is always night. You take what you get, he told himself. You learn as much as you can under the illusion that knowledge makes life easier, which it doesn't.

A number of detectives stood some distance off, silently watching Eischied. "Did we lift his prints?"

"They went downtown about an hour ago, Chief. We should be hearing soon."

"Do we know his name?"

"He didn't have no identification, Chief."

"He didn't have any identification," Eischied corrected. "If you guys would try to speak decent English maybe people wouldn't think detectives were so dumb."

Eischied called over the Homicide lieutenant. "Get a photo of this guy, and take it around to all the other garages in these precincts that have been stuck up lately. See if they can identify this as the same guy."

"Now, Chief?"

"Now."

"But it's two o'clock in the morning, Chief."

"Wake people up if you have to." Though the lieutenant waited for an explanation, Eischied gave none.

There would be other jobs to apportion in the morning, Eischied reflected. He touched the waxy corpse with his shoe as if trying to wake Leon up. Presumably the corpse was older than it looked and had been in prison. Eischied would want to know every prison he'd been in, and every cellmate. He would want to match this guy's cellmates with those of the perpetrator killed in the bank robbery.

"Did he have anything on him at all?"

The lieutenant said: "Just this, Chief."

It was a cash-register check from a luncheonette in the South Bronx. Eischied, fingering the check, visualized the area and said to himself: They're in there somewhere.

To the lieutenant he said: "I'll take care of this." He put the receipt in his pocket.

Tomorrow he would send detectives up to the luncheonette to show mug shots of the deceased. Maybe someone knew where he lived. This cash-register check might lead somewhere. Or it might not.

The detectives were watching him. None spoke. Eischied thought: I knew something would happen tonight, and I was right. I wonder how I knew. Then he thought: But stealing a car has to be a preliminary to something else, because it always was in the past.

Preliminary to what?

In the past this kid would steal a car at gunpoint, and the next morning they would stick up a bank. Possibly they planned to stick up another bank tomorrow—or to assassinate the two promised cops tomorrow.

A detective came out of the lighted office, calling: "A sergeant from Press Relations is on the phone, Chief. He wants to know what to give out to the press."

Eischied got on the phone. "You give nothing out to the press. You make believe this never happened." He hung up.

Whatever their plans, the gang would be waiting for this fellow to come back with a car. He would not be coming back, and they would get very nervous waiting for him.

They would read tomorrow's papers to see what happened to their guy, but they wouldn't find anything. They would worry more. Eischied wanted them to worry.

He wanted them confused enough to make a mistake—a bad mistake. He wanted them to imagine that this kid was in custody and singing his head off.

Perhaps they would get some other car somewhere else and go on with tomorrow's plans without him. Or perhaps they would postpone the robbery or assassination or whatever they had in mind.

In the garage's glass-enclosed office, which was crowded with detectives, Eischied searched his address book for the unlisted telephone of Chief of Patrol Dan Duncan, a man he despised. Though Eischied's equal in rank, Duncan was a much younger man who had been promoted over scores of men senior to him as part of the new Commissioner's shakeup of the department. Obviously Duncan was on the PC's team; Duncan had shown himself eager to support any idea the PC came up with, however asinine.

If the PC decided to get rid of the Chief of Detectives, this Duncan could be counted on to applaud him for it. But now Eischied saw a way to use Duncan.

Eischied woke Duncan up.

"Dan, something's happened. I wish you'd get down here right away. How soon can I expect you?"

Duncan, half asleep, was struggling to come to grips with the summons and its source: should he obey, or not?

"Can you brief me on what this is all about, Earl?"

"No, I can't."

Duncan hesitated. "Can you at least give me a hint?"

"No, I can't. How soon can I expect you?"

In the Police Department mystery equaled strength. Eischied, dealing out mystery, was dealing from strength, and Duncan, unsure of himself, soon capitulated: he would come as soon as he could.

The Chief of Patrol was driven up by his chauffeur about half an hour later.

Stepping over the rope hung with the crime-scene placards, he entered the garage. He saw a corpse there, but corpses to cops were normal.

"What's it all about, Earl?"

The two high-ranking policemen stood gazing down at the late Leon Epps.

Eischied said: "I want you to do me a favor, Dan. I want you to contact every patrol precinct in the city. I want you to ask every one of your precinct commanders to be in his stationhouse for roll call when the eight-to-four tour turns out tomorrow morning. I want each commander to deploy his cars to cover as many banks as possible during the first hour that the banks are open."

The Chief of Patrol realized he was being asked to accept orders from the Chief of Detectives, who was not his superior, and he did not like it.

"What shall I tell them is the reason for such action?"

"Tell them nothing. And don't send a T.O.P. out either, because some reporter will get hold of a copy, and then there'll be all sorts of questions. If I were you I'd phone each of my seven borough commanders right now. I'd instruct them to phone their division commanders. Each division commander then phones each of his precinct commanders personally. That way nobody knows that it's citywide except you. Down on the precinct level, nobody knows that any other precinct is affected."

The Chief of Patrol, staring down at the dead stickup man, said nothing.

Eischied said: "At the same time I want each precinct commander to warn his men to be especially vigilant for assaults against police officers."

The Chief of Patrol said: "Don't you think I need a little more information to go on?"

Eischied said: "No, you don't."

After a moment the Chief of Patrol said: "Does it have something to do with this guy?" He pointed with his foot at the unmoving Leon Epps.

Eischied said: "No, I just like to get out of bed in the middle of the night and come down to garages to look at corpses. That's how I get my kicks. It turns me on sexually. Some men like to look at bare tits. With me it's guys like this." And Eischied too pointed at Epps with his foot.

But the Chief of Patrol was still fighting to regain political equality with the Chief of Detectives. "What do you expect to happen tomorrow morning, Earl?"

"I hope nothing."

Eischied had not answered a single question yet, and the Chief of Patrol, realizing this, was furious. Unwilling to let his emotion show, he said: "I need a little more to go on, Earl."

"You want to know what I expect is going to happen?"

"That's right."

Eischied nodded several times. A friend he would have told. Duncan was not a friend. "If you do what I ask you, I'm reasonably certain nothing will happen. If you don't"—Eischied shrugged—"then whatever happens is on your head."

The two men stared at each other. After a moment the Chief of Patrol sighed, and Eischied knew he had won.

"Okay," the Chief of Patrol said.

Eischied's face displayed no gleam of triumph. He said: "I'd advise the Staten Island precincts to be especially vigilant. That's the one borough they haven't hit yet."

The Chief of Patrol said: "That's a lot of phone calls. I better get started."

Eischied went contentedly home to bed. He had won a test of strength with the Chief of Patrol, the PC's handpicked boy, and therefore with the PC himself, and so his job seemed to him for the moment slightly more secure. For a long time Eischied lay awake gloating over this supposed triumph. It was as if he had won a shootout with the Chief of Patrol— and this kind of shootout was as fraught with peril as the other kind, make no mistake. The PC would hear about it. The Chief of Patrol would be in there at 9 A.M. to tell him, and the PC would recognize the strength Eischied was dealing from, and would feel unsettled and uncertain himself, and his hand would be stayed a while longer.

Eischied lay awake wondering what other crime tonight's attempted car theft was supposed to be connected to. Somehow he did not think it was just another bank robbery. He also wondered if FEAR stole cars at gunpoint because this particular kid was an inept thief, or deliberately, so as to show contempt for society. It would take a deep thinker indeed to relate stealing cars at gunpoint to a general contempt for authority, Eischied decided. He was willing to rule that out.

As he was dropping off to sleep it occurred to him that no more cars would be stolen this way—which meant Eischied would not be forewarned again.

27

AT roll call Marty glanced out of the corner of his eye along the line of cops standing beside him at attention, and he was as surprised as always to notice female bosoms sticking out farther than any guy's chest.

The eight-to-four tour was about to go out on patrol. Sunlight streamed in the door.

Most days most sergeants had something to say before turning out the troops. Some liked to read off stolen-car numbers, and some just liked to hear themselves talk. But today's sergeant had a new twist. He began reading off the addresses of banks and assigning a radio car to each one. Marty and Agnes drew the First National City Branch on Southern Boulevard.

The sergeant looked at them over his glasses. "I trust you know where it is?"

It made Marty smile. "Yes, sarge."

"And you, Officer Cusack?"

"Yes, sarge," said Agnes.

And so twenty-two cops poured out into the sunshine and climbed into their cars. An hour passed.

Marty was parked beside the fire hydrant squarely in front of the bank's doors. He and Agnes talked over why they were there. Marty guessed, accurately, that a warning of some sort had been received at headquarters.

"Somebody downtown got some information," he told Agnes. "They're expecting a bank to get knocked over this morning. It's probably the same gang."

Agnes said: "I can't imagine them coming back here, can you?"

Marty decided to kid Agnes. "They wouldn't

dare," he told her. "They'd have to figure you'd be sitting on this bank. They wouldn't want to tangle with you. You're the toughest broad in the Police Department."

Agnes frowned. She did not like being called a broad.

When she remained silent, Marty realized she was annoyed at him. Marty decided Agnes lacked a sense of humor.

He decided to kid her further. "I heard a funny story," he began. "It's a true story. This really happened. It happened in the Seven-Three Precinct in Brooklyn."

Agnes watched him.

The story Marty was about to tell was perhaps fictional. He had had it from Sal this morning. Sal heard it from a cop in the Seven-Three. Sal swore it was true, and it had a ring of truth to Marty.

"Well," he continued, "there's this policewoman in the Seven-Three, and the other day she comes in to see the precinct commander. She wants to speak to him alone. She wants to close the door to the captain's office so they can have privacy. Well, the captain begins to get nervous. He asks himself: What the hell is this?

"The policewoman is obviously distraught. She's practically crying. The captain begins trying to calm her down. She tells him she has a problem. He asks what it is. She says she can't tell him. She can't bring herself to utter her problem. The captain is really worried. He says to her: 'Nothing is as awful as that.' She tells him: 'Well, yes it is.' The captain fears the worst so he says to her: 'If you're pregnant, that's not so bad, you can get maternity leave.'

"The policewoman says: 'Well, I am pregnant, but that's not my problem.'

"The captain says: 'If you're not married, that's not so bad either. You can still get maternity leave.'

"The policewoman says: 'Well, I'm not married, but that's not my problem.'

"The captain's eyes get narrow, and he says: 'Is the father a cop in this precinct?'

"The policewoman says: 'Yes, but that's not my problem.'

"The captain hollers: 'Which one?'

"The policewoman says: 'I don't know, and that's my problem.' "

Behind the wheel of the radio car Marty was laughing. But Agnes beside him sat stony-faced.

Marty said: "When I heard that story, it broke me up."

Beside him Agnes stared straight ahead.

Marty said: "I guess you don't think it's funny."

Agnes in a tight voice said: "Who made that story up?"

"Nobody. It's a true story."

"It's not true at all," said Agnes fiercely. "Nothing like that ever happened. Not in the Seven-Three, not anywhere."

Marty was silent. "Some idiot like Sal made that story up," said Agnes. "That's what all you he-men would like to believe. That all police women are sluts. That women don't belong in this job."

Her wrath was so genuine that Marty had begun to squirm.

"I didn't mean to offend you," he apologized.

"You'd like to believe it too. You're no better than the rest of them."

Marty said: "I'm sorry, Agnes."

"If you ever repeat that story to anyone, I'll never speak to you again."

She turned away from him. For the next hour Agnes studied the people who went in and out of the bank. Marty studied the hard line of Agnes's jaw. He tried to talk to her several times, but she did not respond.

By then Eischied was at his desk studying material that had come in during the night, principally the mug shot of Leon Epps, his yellow sheet and an address in the 24th Precinct.

"What address is this?" Eischied demanded.

Captain Finnerty at his elbow said: "His mother, Chief. She's a cleaning woman in an office building in the Wall Street area."

"Has she been notified yet?"

"Not yet."

"Good, don't notify her. Don't notify anybody."

Finnerty said: "But she's the deceased's mother, Chief. Shouldn't we—I mean—I have two detectives ready to send up there now."

Eischied said: "You've been watching too many soap operas, Finnerty. The only detectives we'll send up there is detectives to tap her phone."

Eischied studied the mug shot of Leon Epps alive. To Finnerty he said: "Get fifty copies of this made." From his wallet Eischied fished the cash-register check that had been recovered from the corpse. "Get two detectives who don't look too much like detectives and send them up to this lunchroom in the Bronx. Tell the detectives not to identify themselves as detectives. We don't want to put that whole neighborhood in an uproar. Cut the numbers off Epps's picture before you give it to them. Spread the other forty-nine photos among the narco guys who work that area. Tell them to show it to their informants. Maybe one of the informants will recognize him."

Eischied was still staring at the lunchroom check, which was for thirty-six cents, and which represented —what? A coffee and a piece of pastry? The kid's last meal? He thought: Well, we'll all die with undigested food inside us. There is a last meal for everybody.

But what the hell did Epps save such a check for?

Eischied passed the check to Finnerty, then continued: "I want a wiretap order on his mother's phone. I want you to go down to the DA's office personally and get it. I'll call the DA for you myself. Have two guys standing by to put it in the minute you get the order."

Eischied lifted the mug shot from his desk and stared at it a moment. Thinking aloud, he said: "This guy didn't come back last night, and his friends are going to wonder what happened to him. They're going to call up his mama to find out if she's seen him. I want to know what they say to her. Maybe she'll start calling around to all his friends. I want to know who she calls and what they tell her."

The dutiful Finnerty was making notes on his stenographer's pad.

Eischied had opened the dossier, and was comparing Epp's yellow sheet with that of the deceased Floyd Fields. He saw that they had never been in prison together, for the dates did not match. To Finnerty, Eischied said: "Put as many detectives as you need on finding out who Epp's cellmates were over the years. Find out the name of every con he was friendly with. Make up a list. Then compare that list with the one we already got on the late Floyd Fields. Somewhere in those lists you're going to find a common name. I want to know what it is."

"Anything else, Chief?"

"Yeah. Send a detective out to get me a regular coffee and a seeded roll buttered on both sides."

A few minutes later Eischied was in conversation with the District Attorney, who was sixty-five years old and had held office for two decades. Early in his career he had been a crusading crime buster, but as the mood of the city turned toward civil libertarianism, the DA had become increasingly civil liberties oriented. That was how he stayed in office, Eischied thought. What could you expect?

Eischied said: "After that perpetrator was killed in the bank robbery I asked you for some wires. Your guys weren't too cooperative."

In a mild voice the DA explained that there were laws his office was obliged to adhere to. Those requests for wiretaps which had seemed to have the most merit according to law had been accorded. The others had been denied.

Eischied said: "Last night one of my guys killed a stickup man in a garage. I have information that the deceased was part of the same gang. And this gang has promised to assassinate two cops, as you know. I'm only asking you for one new tap. I'm asking you for a tap on this deceased stickup man's mother's phone."

There was silence at the other end of the phone. Eischied considered explaining his theory to the DA —that the other gunmen would phone the mother. But the DA had been in office twenty years. One did not have to draw pictures. To draw pictures would be to insult him, and then there would be no wiretap.

The District Attorney said: "Is she part of the continuing criminal conspiracy, do you think, Chief?"

Eischied said nothing. Here comes the legal terminology, he thought.

"Because if you had information to indicate that she lives with them or buys guns for them, or drives the getaway cars, that would support a wire. But being the mother of a deceased gunman is not, legally speaking, being part of a continuing criminal conspiracy. It wasn't the last time I looked, anyway."

That's what I need, Eischied thought, a lesson in wiretap law. He considered pleading, but his dignity would not allow it. Even if he did plead it would do no good.

The DA said: "In addition I suspect this woman is one of the minority groups. Am I right, Chief? Ethnically speaking, I mean?"

Eischied said: "I wish you'd think it over."

"I'm thinking it over as I talk to you, Earl. Thinking it over out loud, you might say."

"This is a matter of gravest importance."

"The felony crime, yes. But the mother is not part of the felony, as I understand it."

"I wish you'd try to see it from my point of view." He's got me begging anyway, Eischied thought.

"I'm trying, Chief. But it's hard."

"My guy will be down there to start on the affidavits in a few minutes."

"That's the problem," the DA said. "The affidavits. We would have to make out two affidavits and a court order. That's thirty to forty pages of paperwork.

It would tie up a lot of my people for a lot of time. For about two days, in fact. For instance, the affidavits would have to allege that all other leads are futile. Is that accurate, Chief, are all other leads futile?"

Eischied said nothing.

"The affidavits have to be very specific, you know. That's in order to minimize the intrusion. The affidavits would allow detectives to eavesdrop only on conversations between Party A, the mother, and certain other specific parties—and, as I understand it, you don't have the names of any other specific parties, do you, Chief?"

"We do have some possible names, yes."

"That's something, anyway," the DA said. "But it still leaves us short of the bottom line. The bottom line, I'm afraid, is that probable cause would not be sufficiently alleged. The judge would deny the order."

"Find a friendly judge."

"The few that are friendly we like to keep friendly."

Eischied said nothing.

The DA said: "From a police point of view I can see that the tap you want is entirely justified. But legally it seems to me that your reasoning is tenuous, to say the least. I can put the matter to our Appeals Bureau, but I think I know how they'll reply. Any evidence that you might gather on such a wire would be inadmissible, by the way."

Eischied burst out: "I'm not looking for evidence, I'm looking for information."

"But legally speaking you can only have one for the purpose of gathering evidence."

Unperturbed, the DA continued: "And if the *New York Times* got wind of such a wiretap, I'm sure they'd denounce all of us. Not only my office, but your office as well. I could stand the static better than you could, Chief. My term has three more years to run. Whereas you—"

In a flat, emotionless voice Eischied urged the District Attorney to reconsider the matter, if he could, then hung up. He knew there would be no wire.

He could order a detective to install a gypsy wire, of course. Tapping a phone was no difficult thing for the older detectives, and even after the strict wiretap law came in one or another of them had continued to install wires when they thought they could get away with it.

But a gypsy wire was an illegal wire, and the detective who got caught was guilty of a federal felony and would go to jail.

So would the commander who gave the order.

Eischied, much as he wanted that phone tapped, was not brave enough to give such an order now.

Of the taps Eischied had been accorded so far, the only one that seemed productive was on a pants presser on Broadway. The guy was an ex-con, and into something, though perhaps not this, for he made no outgoing calls at all. Many of the calls he received were from suspected burglars; others were from people who used code names: Mark D., the Big Man, Charles. Eischied had supported the tap with information about the pants presser's known activities as a fence of stolen goods, not his past associations with men serving time for assaults on police officers.

A character like that, Eischied reflected, is sometimes accorded less than his legal rights, even by a civil libertarian like the incumbent District Attorney of New York County.

Eischied wondered who Mark D. might be, or Charles, or the Big Man. These names corresponded to no known suspects in bank robberies or attacks on police officers. This wiretap had given no indication yet that the pants presser was in any way involved with the bank robberies, with this FEAR, with this so-called autumn offensive.

Maybe detectives monitoring the pants presser's phone were wasting their own time and the city's money. They had collected not even enough evidence to arrest the guy for criminal receiving. This tap would run out in a few days and probably the DA would refuse to renew it.

In movies, or TV cop shows, the detectives always

managed to narrow the suspects to two or three. In real life a criminal was not one of two or three suspects, he was one of eight million New Yorkers. He did not wear a sign. He did not froth at the mouth. He looked as normal as anyone else. In fact crooks and honest citizens looked exactly alike.

It is amazing under the circumstances, Eischied reflected, that we ever manage to arrest anybody at all.

The voices of Mark D. and such people talking to the pants presser were down on tape, but maybe they were not even criminals. If Eischied could get a tap on Leon Epps's mother, perhaps one of these same voices would phone her. That would link the pants presser to the investigation, he could be put under twenty-four-hour surveillance, Eischied would be one step closer to breaking this case. But at the moment Eischied had no idea what he was up against. These people were turning him in circles. They were giving him headaches, and there was nothing he could do about it.

Eischied went over to his safe and lifted the black cardboard cover protecting the first message signed: FEAR. He stared down at the single partial print. Maybe it's him, he told himself. The brain behind this case.

This case is driving me buggy, he told himself. Dropping the lid on the print and closing the safe, he resolved to concentrate on some other case today. There was a good one about to break, and he buzzed Lieutenant Fitzgerald in his anteroom: "Reach out for Lieutenant Maher, Red. Get him in here."

Lieutenant Maher headed the Hotel Squad. There had been a rash of robberies along the southern edge of Central Park. The thieves liked to wear Halloween masks and they worked with Band-Aids on their fingertips. They invaded hotels in the middle of the night, handcuffed employees and hammered open safe-deposit boxes. They had made several stupendous hauls, but one of their members had got himself arrested on an unrelated charge, and had offered to

271

give up his colleagues in exchange for immunity from prosecution.

Lieutenant Maher said he was ready to make his arrests at any time. "The only question now, Chief, is when do I take them?" added Maher, seated respectfully beside Eischied's desk.

Eischied put his feet up and blew cigar smoke toward the points of his shoes. He saw another headline for himself here. He saw himself before a press conference announcing that he had smashed the hotel ring. He visualized some of the recovered jewelry on the tabletop. He was himself speaking into a thicket of microphones.

Unfortunately the city was too focused on these bank robberies right now. He would have to give the bank robberies a day or two to cool down, if the hotel case was to have any impact.

"Don't make any arrests until I tell you," Eischied said, and dismissed Maher.

There were no reports so far today of bank robberies anywhere in the city—or about assaults on cops either, though other crimes were occurring or being discovered at their ordinary rate. During the course of the morning Eischied was advised of two truck hijackings, and of a hoodlum with an Italian name found in the trunk of a car in the Park Slope section of Brooklyn with half his head blown away. Other robberies, burglaries, muggings, rapes—mere statistics to Eischied—were taking place normally and were not even brought to his attention. A lieutenant had been indicted for corruption and Eischied was obliged to order a captain out to arrest him.

So far, just another turbulent day in the life of the city, Eischied noted.

But for Marty and Agnes the day was proving not ordinary at all.

They had just come off meal period when the call came over: disturbance in a hallway on the southern edge of the precinct where it abutted on the Four-One. The street given was a shabby row of tenements.

Marty and Agnes, responding, were out of their sector, the regular sector car having gone on meal period in its turn.

Marty by then was glum. Since early this morning Agnes had spoken to him only in monosyllables. As he double parked in front of the tenement, Marty reviewed in his mind the story of the policewoman with the "problem." Women had no sense of humor about themselves, they were all the same, he told himself. An inoffensive story had put Agnes in this mood. Marty had since gone through some moods himself. He had tried to win Agnes around with reason, anger, affection, humor. None had worked. Now he was merely glum.

They entered the dim, sour-smelling hallway. Marty pushed through the front door first. Agnes was about two paces behind him. It was Agnes who carried the radio.

Directly ahead, halfway up a steep narrow staircase, stood a psycho. He was a black man. He was big. At first Marty thought the guy's eyes were merely rolling in his head, but now Marty saw they were unfocused too.

The man had a gun. It was pointed right at Marty's chest.

"The lord sent me to clean up this neighborhood," the man shouted. "Move, you muthafuckers."

Marty's eyes were fixed on the gun. The barrel looked seven inches long. Marty's heart had begun to pound. To Agnes, Marty snapped: "Get behind me."

The man on the stairs shouted: "Give me liberty or give me death."

Marty said: "Drop that weapon."

The man shouted: "I shoot you now."

Marty's knees had turned to jelly. His hand was six inches from his revolver, but would not move any closer. He had begun swallowing convulsively.

On the staircase the psycho started laughing. "I'm gonna shoot Sidney," he cried.

Thoughts began to reach Marty's brain in some

sequence. This was not his first psycho, and there were techniques that sometimes worked. In a quiet voice he said: "You can't shoot Sidney. I already shot Sidney." Marty also forced himself one step closer to the staircase.

Suddenly the psycho turned and ran upstairs. They heard him stop on the landing. The landing hid him. "Come and get me," he shouted. "Ah's waiting for you. I gonna blow off the first head shows above this landing."

Marty yanked out his gun and started up the stairs. Behind him Agnes had not reacted at all. Now he heard her sharp intake of breath. "No, Marty," she cried. "He'll shoot you."

Marty had been terrified many times as a cop, never more than now. But slowly, carefully, he began climbing the stairs.

Out of sight on the landing the psycho was cackling and laughing. Marty forced his shoes to climb. The landing was getting closer. He couldn't see the psycho, but in a moment the psycho would see him. Marty's head would rise above the level of the landing, and the psycho would pull the trigger of the cannon he was holding. Marty's legs were trembling. So was the hand that held his service revolver. But he had to keep climbing. The alternative was to admit to Agnes that he was afraid.

The psycho shouted: "One more step muthafucker, and I blow your head off."

Marty kept climbing.

Abruptly Marty heard the psycho's feet running away. The psycho's mad cackle diminished along the hallway, and in a moment a door slammed.

Marty sprinted the rest of the way to the landing. The hall was empty. Marty ran in the direction the psycho had run. He came to a door. Behind it he could hear the psycho laughing.

Agnes had run up behind Marty. "What are you going to do?"

"Go in and get him," said Marty tightly.

"Wait, Marty, please wait." Agnes tried to raise

Central on the radio, but no answer came back. "We'll call in emergency service," Agnes said to Marty. "They have bullet proof vests and shotguns. Let them go in after him. I'll go down and call Central from the car. Please wait."

"No," said Marty.

He drove his foot against the door. The doorjamb splintered. A second kick swung the door open all the way, and Marty ran inside, expecting a shootout, hoping to get off the first shot. He was crouched, holding his gun in both fists, ready to shoot.

The psycho was sitting on the floor, laughing and bleeding. The psycho's gun was on a table.

The psycho had slashed both wrists. "Now look what you made me do," he whimpered, waving his wrists at Marty. "Now look what you made me do." He began laughing uproariously.

Marty, soaked in sweat, heart still racing, swung his gun barrel and laid open the psycho's head.

"And now," murmured Agnes behind him, "we've got a case of police brutality on our hands."

Marty, still trembling, holstered his gun. The psycho, bleeding profusely, was still laughing.

Agnes managed to raise Central on the radio: "On that psycho run, the psycho has been disarmed, but we'll need an ambulance. He has slashed both his wrists, and he also seems to have fallen down and cut his head open."

Marty had picked up the psycho's gun. He gave a broken sob. "It's a cap pistol," he said.

Marty and Agnes gazed at each other. After a moment Agnes stroked his cheek.

Though the PC and Chief of Patrol Duncan were doubtless on edge all day, alert for word of trouble from the precincts, the city stayed quiet. No bank robberies were attempted or foiled. No cop was shot. Any moment now the PC would become confident enough to summon Eischied to explain this morning's extraordinary precautions. But Eischied wouldn't be there. Ordering his car brought around, he had himself driven up to Rodman's Neck in the northeast Bronx, site of the Police Department's outdoor target range, a safe place to disappear to. It would take the PC an hour to find him. Like all cops from patrolman to chief, Eischied was obliged to qualify with his two guns twice each year, and he would get that out of the way today, while the PC burned.

For a man of his rank Eischied considered this training a waste of bullets, not to mention time. Each year about seventy-five cops engaged in gunfights. Each year one or two were sergeants. All the rest were patrolmen and detectives. Eischied could not remember the last time a man of his rank had fired shots on duty, and most cops, Eischied included, never fired shots during their entire careers.

It was a warm sunny day, and Eischied's car drove into the police reservation under brilliant fall foliage. The range officer, having been warned when the Chief of Detectives passed the guard post, was at the parking lot to yank open Eischied's door and to lead him promptly to a firing position.

The qualifying cycle for an ordinary cop took all day: hours of lectures, instruction and dry firing left cops comatose. The brief bombardment of targets woke them up, quick spasms of pleasure succeeding interminable foreplay.

But chiefs were royalty. They drove up, were helped from their cars and began shooting.

Eischied was led around a row of Quonset huts. The range itself came into view. There were about fifty fire lanes, and cops wearing sound barriers crouched in each, firing at targets only seven yards away.

When Eischied was a rookie, targets were fifty feet distant. But when the Police Department at last began to analyze its statistics, it was found that almost all shootouts took place with cop and perpetrator in the same room—at arm's length so to speak. After that the targets were moved up close and cops were taught to aim their guns like flashlights, and to empty them quickly. The idea was to empty one's gun into a perpetrator's life-support system, not to try for the single perfect shot.

The noise as Eischied approached the firing line was stupendous. Behind each lane stood other cops waiting their turns, but the range lieutenant quickly cleared three lanes for the Chief of Detectives, and all other firing soon ceased as Eischied's name passed down the line.

Eischied extracted his snub-nosed .38 and said to the range lieutenant: "I don't even have my big gun with me. You'll have to borrow one for me." Like all cops, detectives or not, Eischied was obliged to own the standard service revolver with its four-inch barrel, though he never carried it. It was supposed to go with the uniform, which he was also obliged to own though he never wore it.

The range lieutenant hooked a fresh paper target in place. It bore the image of a crouched gunman firing back. A loaded service revolver was handed to Eischied, who put his own gun back in its holster.

Casually the Chief of Detectives walked up to the line, but when he reached it he dropped into a semi-crouch, grabbed the gun with both hands and emptied all six shots at the target.

Holes appeared in the dangling paper. Eischied noted that he had shot out the target's left eye, hit him twice in the left elbow and once in the groin. The other two shots hit to the side.

He could feel the cops nearby whispering among themselves. They were watching him. The range lieutenant said nothing. Eischied ejected his empty shells into the can and asked for more bullets, which were handed him. He reloaded the gun, and went through the same performance a second time. There were now twelve holes in the paper, but it was difficult to remember which were newest.

Eischied reloaded and fired again. He was concentrating hard, unwilling to make an ass of himself in front of all the onlooking cops. After the fourth time he switched to his own gun, perforating the paper target in only five new places now, for the short-barreled revolver held only five shots, not six. He reloaded and fired his own gun five times.

The regulations stipulated fifty rounds, and Eischied had fired only forty-nine, but he had had enough. Turning to the lieutenant, he said: "Satisfied, Lou?"

"You did fine, Chief. If you'll come on over to the office, we can sign you in and out."

Eischied had to wait several minutes while his driver, Louie, finished firing. Louie was being rushed through the program quickly too, in courtesy to Eischied, but Louie was not a chief, and so it took somewhat longer.

Back at headquarters, as Eischied had expected, there was a summons from the PC.

Eischied went in there.

By then it was late afternoon. The heavy red drapes were drawn, and the only light came from the lamp on the PC's desk. He was in shirt sleeves as always. Over in the corner in the shadows sat the First Dep. The PC said: "Well, the city seems calm, Earl."

Eischied knew he would now have to give up some of his information, but he meant to make the PC beg for it. He said only: "It seems calm, Commissioner."

The PC seemed to be choosing his words carefully. "You had the Chief of Patrol put the Patrol Forces in a state of alert this morning."

The PC waited for an explanation, but Eischied said only: "Yes, I did, Commissioner."

After a moment the PC was forced to ask: "Why was that?"

"We had information, Commissioner." Information, hell, Eischied thought. We had a dead perpetrator in a garage. They must have wanted that car for something.

But maybe they just wanted to drive to Florida in it. Maybe they needed it to transport guns, Eischied thought, guessing closer than he knew.

From the corner gloom the First Dep. said harshly: "What kind of information did you have, Earl?"

The PC said firmly: "We'd like to hear the story, Earl."

After a moment Eischied explained how he had staked out detectives in selected garages, and in one of them last night a gunman was killed.

"You're sure that this Leon Epps was part of the gang?"

"Absolutely, Commissioner."

"You may be closer to them than I thought."

The PC looked impressed. Even the First Dep. was silent. The PC asked: "Do you suppose that deploying our radio cars according to your orders this morning scared them off from hitting another bank?"

Eischied said: "Your guess is as good as mine, Commissioner."

The First Dep. and the PC eyed each other. Then the PC said: "What other information do you have on this?"

But Eischied decided he could cut it off here. "Just a lot of bits and pieces, Commissioner. Nothing solid."

He stared blandly across at the Police Commissioner. The PC unwilling to surrender, was forced to ask: "What happens next?"

Eischied decided not to answer this question either. Instead he said: "I'm trying to put in some wires. I've talked to the DA but I don't think he's going to give me any."

The PC, Eischied saw, still wanted information. More than that, he wanted to keep Eischied friendly. If Eischied was really about to solve this case, then the PC was about to look very good indeed.

"Is there anything I can do to help, Earl?"

Eischied decided to say: "The FBI, Commissioner. They won't tell us anything. I had a couple of their guys down here. They wouldn't say a word. The only one can put heat on the FBI is the Federal Attorney for the Southern District. You know the guy. I was wondering if you could call him up and get him to order the Bureau to cooperate."

After a moment the PC said: "I'll see what I can do."

Eischied was standing in front of the desk. The PC rose to his feet and came around. Clapping Eischied on the shoulder he said: "That other business. I think you can forget about it."

Eischied didn't trust this man, and it would be foolhardy to believe him. Eischied felt not relief but power. He thought: He really believes I'm about to break this case for him.

Nonetheless Eischied said: "Thank you, Commissioner."

In the corner gloom the First Dep. sat silent as an owl. His expression never changed.

The PC said in a friendly voice: "I'm getting a lot of static from down there—" He jerked his thumb in the presumed direction of City Hall. "The Mayor keeps asking me what we're doing up here. They think all you have to do is snap your fingers and scoop up these perpetrators."

"Perpetrator" was a cop's word. On a cop's lips it sounded normal. On the lips of the PC it sounded grotesque.

"What I'd like to know is, do you have some other fairly big case that you're about to break? I thought maybe we could make our arrests in such a case, and then go public with it. Put on a big press conference. That would serve to keep the Mayor quiet for a while. It would buy us time for this other thing."

He beamed at Eischied, man to man, friend to friend.

Eischied cautioned himself: Inside the police hierarchy, no one's your friend. Particularly this man.

But Eischied, who had only a moment to make up his mind, decided to throw the hotel case onto the PC's desk. It would mean giving headlines to the PC that he might have kept for himself. But, if the PC meant to act friendly, the thing to do was to keep him that way. Eischied could always find another big case for himself.

"As a matter of fact, Commissioner, my guys are

about to break this ring of hotel thieves." Briefly Eischied described the case and the prospective arrests. "If you announced it at a press conference, Commissioner, I'm sure you would get big exposure in the media."

The PC, after thinking it over, said: "All right, if you think that's the way to handle it, Earl, I'll go along with you on that."

The PC walked Eischied to the door, patting his shoulder all the way.

When Eischied was back in his own office, Captain Finnerty came in beaming. Finnerty was wearing rimless glasses and looked more like a schoolteacher than ever. He handed over two lists of names.

"The first list, you will note, Chief," said Finnerty in his fussy way, "is a list of the known prison associates of the late Leon Epps."

There were about twenty names on each list.

"So?" Eischied growled.

Finnerty permitted himself a smug smile. "Did you note one name that is common to both lists, Chief?"

"No, I did not note one name that is common to both lists. What are you being so mysterious about, for chrissake? What are you trying to tell me?"

Finnerty came around the desk and pointed with a pencil. "The one common name is that of Mr. Jonah Daniel Bell, Chief."

"Fine," said Eischied, "who is Mr. Jonah Daniel Bell?"

Finnerty looked pleased with himself. "I have here his sheet, Chief."

Eischied scanned Bell's sheet. He had been arrested only three times. Armed robbery, assault, armed robbery. Hundreds of street hoodlums had more impressive sheets than that.

Finnerty said smugly: "Note the aliases, Chief."

Eischied read them: Jonah Daniel Bell was also known as Jonah Daniels, Jonah Danielson, Daniel Bell, Mark Daniels, Mark D. Bell—

Eischied "Mark D.—who's Mark D.? Isn't that

one of the names came off the wiretap of that pants presser on Broadway?"

"That is correct, Chief," said Finnerty smugly.

Eischied grinned. "Why, for chrissake, Finnerty. What's come over you all of a sudden? You're acting like a real detective, for chrissake."

"I thought you'd be pleased, Chief."

"What does this Mark D. look like? Do we have an address on him?"

"No address, Chief, unfortunately. He's on parole and his parole officer hasn't seen him in months." Finnerty, looking pleased, thrust a mug photo in front of Eischied. "But this is what he looks like, Chief."

Eischied glanced down at the photo. "Mean-looking bastard."

Eischied rose to his feet and began pacing. There was a cigar in his shirt pocket. He took it out and bit off one end.

"Give me a light, Finnerty."

"Sure, Chief."

Finnerty was awaiting instructions. Presently Eischied said: "That tap we got on the pants presser should be about to expire. This ought to be enough to get it renewed for another thirty days. Take care of that first, okay?"

Finnerty had opened his stenographer's notebook to a fresh page, and was making notes.

"Next, have somebody go over the tapes of the tap on the pants presser. Put Red on it, or someone you can trust. Have him scour those tapes for some detail we may have overlooked. Especially any hint of an address."

Eischied blew smoke at the ceiling. "I want round-the-clock surveillance on that pants presser. If it's too late to find him tonight, pick him up when he comes to work tomorrow. Don't let him out of our sight. I leave it to you to find detectives bright enough to do the job without getting made. I want to know everything that pants presser does, everyone he sees. If this Mark D. shows up, follow him. If he makes the tail, grab him."

"On what grounds might he be arrested, Chief?" asked Finnerty.

"What are you, Finnerty, a civil libertarian all of a sudden? Just grab him. We'll worry about the grounds later."

Finnerty asked stiffly: "Anything else, Chief?"

"Yeah. Make me out scrapbooks on all known criminal associates of this Mark D., both in prison and out, and the same on this pants presser. I want to see scrapbooks of at least twenty photos each by morning, okay?"

Finnerty would be up all night, but all he said was: "Right, Chief."

As Finnerty was leaving the office, Eischied called: "One more thing, Finnerty."

"Yes, Chief?"

Eischied, after blowing smoke at him, said: "You done good so far, Finnerty. You done very good so far."

Finnerty beamed.

28

MIDNIGHT. A car parked near Yankee Stadium.

FBI Agent Pat McGovern wore a leather windbreaker, a battered snap-brim hat pulled way down, and a two-day growth of beard. He hoped he looked suitably Mafia. Beside him Cuomo, who was Mafia, wore a cream-colored cashmere overcoat. Cuomo looked dressed to go dancing.

Cuomo had both hands on the wheel and stared straight ahead. McGovern's radio lay on the floorboard. On it he could hear the other units being radioed into position.

Yankee Stadium shone white in the moonlight. McGovern watched the electric signboard high on the wall. It blinked on and off. Time and temperature alternated with the message: the Giants would play the Eagles there Sunday. As a child McGovern used to go to games there free. His father, a police sergeant, would show his shield and take his kid in by the hand without paying.

McGovern was nervous but trying not to think about it. He was surrounded by friends who would protect him—provided they got there in time. They would protect Cuomo too, but they were not friends of his and would protect him second, and no doubt this made a difference as far as Cuomo's peace of mind was concerned.

Now Cuomo muttered: "That fucking guy has got a fucking machine gun."

"How do you know?"

Cuomo sounded almost nervous enough to mutter: Because I sold it to him. But he said only: "Because he showed it to me. He carries it in this Scotch-plaid satchel."

"What makes you sure this guy is the guy who's been knocking over the banks?"

"I'm not sure. But how many guys you know in this town got a machine gun?"

On the stadium wall time kept advancing.

Cuomo said: "If there's any shooting, I get caught in the middle. I got both sides shooting at me."

McGovern laughed. The laugh sounded solid to him.

Cuomo muttered: "I don't know why I agreed to become the fucking pigeon."

"Because you love your country," McGovern answered.

The car filled up with silence.

"He's not coming," said Cuomo. Cuomo had banked the FBI's front money this afternoon. The front money was safe.

"Is he usually on time?"

McGovern glanced at the stadium clock again. It now read 12:15.

"How do I know if he's on time or not?" said Cuomo. "You think I sold him stuff before or something?"

"Like that machine gun you're so afraid of."

"Fuck you, friend." If Charles didn't come, the FBI would pay no additional money. But there would be no shooting either.

McGovern went over the plan again in his head. As the merchandise was transferred into the other car's trunk, FBI cars would zoom up from all directions and surround it. A dozen of McGovern's colleagues would jump out pointing shotguns. Conceivably there would be shooting, but McGovern did not think so. Even a guy with a machine gun was not crazy enough to open up on that many men and that much artillery.

McGovern studied the stadium. People think that what goes on inside there is a team sport, he reflected, but it's not, it's cold-blooded business. People think that crime is cold-blooded business, but it's not, it's a team sport.

The signboard clock ticked off what could be the final minutes of McGovern's life.

It was sometimes a dangerous sport; on one team or the other men sometimes got killed. The risk was out of all proportion to the profit, and they were all in it not for money, which was usually small, but because crime was the most exciting game in town. It was the game of games. McGovern told himself he had the soul of an auditor, which was what he would soon become; still, he was not immune to the pleasurable tingle in his hands as he sat beside Cuomo, waiting to meet a killer. What game could be more exciting than tonight's game?

Cuomo said: "Fucking guy's not coming."

McGovern answered: "We'll wait a little longer though."

In fact they waited until 2 A.M. Cuomo, who had pulled his hat down over his eyes, fell asleep, snoring gently. McGovern began dozing himself, every once in a while jerking awake, expecting to see a gun pointed at him.

Once, gazing over at Cuomo, McGovern thought: One of the things they don't tell you as a kid is that the bad guys are brave too. Sometimes braver than the good guys. Cuomo should be a churl, according to the book, but McGovern felt reasonably certain that Cuomo was a braver man than himself.

For a while McGovern sat watching the imperceptible movement of the dashboard clock. It was two minutes slower than the one high on the stadium wall, he noted, and he wondered which was correct—and if either was in sync with whatever clock the gunman was operating on.

Cuomo, though he did not move, had stopped snoring.

"You awake, Cuomo?"

"Are you crazy. You think I could sleep waiting for this creep to sneak up on me?"

"Of course not," said McGovern.

For thirty minutes the radio on the floorboard had been silent.

"I don't think he's coming," said McGovern at last. He picked the radio up.

"I coulda told you that two hours ago."

McGovern, having raised his supervisor, said into the radio: "What do we do now?"

The answer came back: "What does the informant advise?"

"That's you, Cuomo. What do you advise?"

"What can I tell you?" said Cuomo.

"He thinks the guy is not coming."

"Let's abort then. Bring the informant in."

McGovern signed off.

Cuomo said: "What does he mean? Bring the informant in where?"

"Headquarters, Cuomo. You are in trouble, I would say."

"I'm going home."

"Not right away, Cuomo. Not right away."

At FBI headquarters, Cuomo was unmercifully grilled. The interrogation room was crowded. Even the director of the New York office, worried about the $1,000 front money, was there. The questions and accusations were heated, though Cuomo did not respond.

"What kind of shitheads do you take us for, Cuomo?"

"You owe us one thousand bucks, Cuomo, and you better come up with it or you're in trouble."

"Cooperation, Cuomo, that's the name of the game. You fuck with us and you wind up behind the eight ball."

McGovern, watching, said nothing. Cuomo was his informant, which made McGovern, according to the peculiar rules of the FBI, responsible for Cuomo's conduct. Cuomo had failed. Therefore McGovern had failed. McGovern's turn would come next.

"Something scared them off. What scared them off, Cuomo?"

"What can I tell you?"

"We know you deal in guns, Cuomo. We want to know everything you ever sold this guy."

"I never even sold him a tour."

"You sold him that machine gun you say he has."

"I'm a travel agent."

"We want to know everything you know about this guy. When did you first meet him? What does he look like?"

"I've seen him around a few times. He never goes anywhere without that fucking grease gun. He takes it out and shows it to you in bars. He gives me the creeps."

"What's his name?"

"Charles."

"Charles what?"

"How the fuck do I know?"

Nonetheless, Cuomo began to provide a rough description of Charles, and he also mentioned Charles's car.

"You didn't get the plate number of that car by any chance, did you?"

Cuomo was sick of being pushed around. He said: "I might be able to remember it—for one thousand bucks."

This produced dead silence in the interrogation room.

After a moment the supervisor of the Bank Squad said to the director: "Would you step outside with me a moment, sir?"

Presently the supervisor re-entered the room. He said in a low voice: "If you can remember that number, Cuomo, and if it checks out, you can forget the thousand bucks you owe us."

Cuomo said: "I think it's coming back to me now."

The license number went down on a note pad— the car would prove registered to one Albert Hoyt, a pants presser—and the page was ripped off and thrust at McGovern. "Put this on the Telex, and see what comes back."

By 4 A.M. McGovern held in his hand Hoyt's name and mug shot, plus an address at which Hoyt perhaps no longer lived.

"Is this the guy, Cuomo?"

"No, that is not Charles."

"Who is it then?"

"What can I tell you?"

McGovern stared at Hoyt's photo. "This isn't much for a thousand dollars, Cuomo," he commented.

Cuomo was shown photos of known bank robbers and after that political extremists. He recognized no photo. "It's your fault, not mine," said Cuomo. "A guy like this you should have in your book."

The supervisor of the Bank Squad laughed derisively and said: "Go on home, Cuomo. Just get out of my sight, okay? Move."

"What's the matter with you?" inquired Cuomo indignantly. "Can I help it you don't have his photo."

When Cuomo had gone out, the supervisor said tiredly: "Let's all go home. Let's get some sleep."

Tomorrow they would try to run down this Albert Hoyt.

Cuomo had promised to call if Charles made contact.

"We were pretty rough on him," said McGovern. "Do you think he'll call?"

"He's your informant," answered the supervisor. "You ought to know."

Another agent said: "He'll call, now he knows the color of our money."

They were getting ready to break up. The coffee containers were emptied. Men stood up and knotted loosened ties.

McGovern, studying his notes, said: "We got a guy trying to buy heavy artillery who perhaps has stuck up several banks and killed a bank guard. We don't know why he wanted the artillery, nor if he's really the bank robber—"

The supervisor interrupted sarcastically: "Nor even if he exists. The only one says he exists is your pal Cuomo."

McGovern continued. "—plus a car registered in the name of an unknown man which may or may not be the car that this guy was driving—if he exists." McGovern shook his head dubiously. "We got a very small piece of a puzzle. Maybe the cops have more. Maybe they know Hoyt. Or Charles. Maybe if we got Cuomo together with them we could figure something out. Maybe the first picture in the first book they show him would be this Charles."

The supervisor said: "Screw the cops."

McGovern, whose father had been a cop, felt vague loyalty to the Police Department. But his principal loyalty was to the Bureau.

"Are we going to tell them what we have, or not?" he asked.

The supervisor said: "Would they tell us? In a pig's ass. Tell them nothing. Screw the cops."

McGovern said: "Okay. Screw the cops. What the fuck do I care? Let's go home and go to bed."

29

THREE men rode in the front seat: Charles, Mark D. and the man known as Frank, who was driving. In the rear seat, as alone as any potentate, sat Everett Walker.

For an hour they had cruised the streets of the 48th Precinct looking for Police Officers Delehanty and Cusack in their radio car.

Mark D. said nervously: "Maybe they not on duty tonight. Maybe we wasting our time." Mark D. was nervous because he was the man who had drawn high card.

After supper Everett Walker had produced a deck of cards. "To the man who draws high card goes the privilege of executing the two enemies of the people."

The drawing was done almost casually, around a table crowded with clotted dishes. The girls watched in awe.

Frank drew the deuce of clubs. "Shit," he said. But he looked relieved.

Mark D., whose turn was next, turned up the king of diamonds.

His tongue passed back and forth across his lips, as rapidly as a snake, while the deck was passed in turn to Butch, to Charles, to Walker himself. Butch drew the jack of diamonds, Charles the eight of hearts, and Walker the ten of spades.

Mark D. then.

They had all crowded around. They had clapped Mark D. on the back. He had professed jubilation. But, as the car bore him toward the 48th Precinct, as they joined the traffic moving along under the bright lights of Southern Boulevard, his boastful conversation approached the thin edge of hysteria. Once they had turned off and begun to cruise the dark residential streets he lapsed into total silence.

They swam through the precinct, searching: they were like a single shark with a mouth full of dangerous teeth. They had so far come upon eight different police cars, several of them twice. Walker had a clipboard in his lap and was noting down cars' numbers. All eight they ignored. A quick glance was sufficient to show that none contained a woman. None contained Agnes.

"There's another one," muttered Charles.

It was double parked, empty, outside a tenement. As they drew close Walker jotted down its number. He said: "That's one we haven't checked out as yet. Drive on past it. Good. Now park right here."

The parked radio car was now approximately fifty yards behind them. They waited there almost twenty minutes. Through the rear window Walker watched the empty police car. Then two police officers came out of the building, one short, one tall. They stood on the sidewalk talking animatedly to each other. The street was dark. Very little light fell on their faces. Walker said aloud: "Walk under the light, goddammit, so as I can tell." He said: "It could be them." He watched them climb into their car.

The ceiling light went out as the doors slammed. But after a moment, though the door stayed closed, it came back on again. The cop on the passenger side seemed to be writing something in a notebook.

"It's her," said Walker.

Agnes had removed her cap. After a moment Marty did too. Presently the ceiling light went off.

"Here they come," said Walker.

The police car came past them. Agnes threw them only a glance, for she was busy on the radio phone.

Walker said to Frank: "Fall in behind them."

The radio car turned out onto Southern Boulevard. Frank asked over his shoulder: "What do I do?"

Walker's voice was flat and cold. "Just follow along behind till I tell you otherwise."

Two blocks down Southern Boulevard the radio

car swerved into a bus stop. As the hit car came abreast, the two police officers were getting out of their car.

"Keep going," Walker told Frank.

Watching out the back window, Walker imagined that Officers Delehanty and Cusack were strolling toward a diner.

"Go on around the block again, fast," he ordered.

The side streets were dark as tunnels. They drove in and then out again. Then came the lights of Southern Boulevard a second time.

The radio car was still parked in the bus stop. There was no sign of the two police officers.

"They've gone into that luncheonette," said Walker. "Pull in to the curb."

Parked, they could see into the luncheonette. A few people were seated at the counter, but none were cops in blue.

Walker said: "They must be seated in a booth in the back. Back up into the bus stop in front of them."

Frank backed the car up against the police car until the bumpers met.

"Can you see them?" whispered Frank.

"Yes. I can see his hat on the pole," said Walker. He leaned over the seat and squeezed Mark D.'s shoulders.

"It's up to you, Mark."

"Yeah, man," Frank said, encouraging him.

"Right on," said Charles.

Mark D. had his hand on the door handle, but seemed unable to lift it. His head was canted sideways, and he seemed incapable of speech.

Charles said: "Get out of the way. I'll do it."

Mark D. stammered: "I'm going. I'm going. Just let me check my fucking piece."

He had a Browning .9-mm automatic. They watched him withdraw the clip and test the spring that would push fresh bullets into the chamber. He slipped the clip back into the handle and slapped its bottom with the heel of his hand. It clicked home.

Walker started to say: "Mark—"

But Mark D. threw the door opened, climbed out of the car and dashed into the diner.

Charles ordered Frank: "Keep the engine running." He had slid over into Mark D.'s place. The door was still open. Charles had unzipped his satchel and had both hands down inside it on the floor.

Walker whispered to Frank: "Pull forward a bit so we can see directly into the diner."

Frank did so.

They could see Mark D. seated at the counter. Once he glanced toward the rear of the diner. Otherwise he sat staring straight ahead, stiff as a statue.

They watched a cup of coffee being placed down in front of him.

Frank gave a nervous laugh. "What's that mutha gonna do, order dinner?"

Charles said: "I'm going in there."

"Wait," cautioned Walker. They watched tensely.

At the counter Mark D. had forced himself to his feet. They saw him plunk money down on the counter, paying for the coffee he had not touched. He pushed back from the counter with both hands. They saw his hand dig his gun out of his belt. The barrel came clear.

Everett Walker breathed a sigh of relief. "There he goes."

To Frank, Charles said: "Get ready to haul ass, man."

30

THE luncheonette in which Agnes and Marty were eating dinner was about two blocks down from the First National City branch bank that they had risked their lives to defend. This event, though to them as fresh as yesterday, was already stale news. Under the impression that they were permanent heroes, both had become slightly arrogant, a condition Agnes would have described as "swell-headed." They thought they were permanently important to the city, when in fact they were already forgotten. Modern society has no room for permanent anything. They didn't know this. Nor did they know that interest in their names was about to be revived. There would be one more flurry of headlines about them, after which they would be forgotten again, this time forever.

It was then shortly after 10 P.M. Their tour would end at midnight, but their turn at meal period had come late tonight, and both were ravenous. Their dinners had just been placed down in front of them— big hot cheeseburgers, and Agnes, already munching on a succulent bite, watched Marty reach for the catsup bottle.

They sat in a booth at the rear of the diner. Marty sat facing the cash desk, counter and plate-glass windows, and from time to time, Agnes noted, he glanced out at that portion of Southern Boulevard he could see, eyeballing it, the way a good cop should. Agnes sat opposite, facing the doors to the rest rooms, pressing her knees against his under the table, knobs to knobs.

"You have sexy knees, Marty."

He smiled at her, then resumed trying to bang catsup out of the bottle.

Agnes, chewing contentedly, leaned her head back, her bun pressing against the plastic booth, and watched Marty prepare his cheeseburger for eating. He was so meticulous, she noted. He always had to put salt, pepper and then catsup on first, and he never varied the sequence or the amounts.

For her this love affair had all started with that family fight in the tenement. The 48th Precinct was not one of the city's worst, but it had its bad spots, and most were down near the border with the 41st Precinct. The Four-One was called Fort Apache, and was one of the most crime-ridden in the city.

They were working a four-to-twelve that day, too, and this particular job would probably be their last run of the tour. They stepped into the tenement apartment and found the husband, a carving knife in his fist, circling a sprung sofa, trying to put the knife in his hysterical wife.

The husband was a black man, about six feet four. He was crazed with drink and something else, perhaps drugs, perhaps jealousy, perhaps even grief—it was always so difficult for a cop to size up the situation and know how to deal with it. But, with tears streaming down his face, he was lunging across the sofa, sometimes kneeing the springs back under the material, and he was trying to stick that knife into his wife.

Immediately stepping in front of Marty, Agnes strode up to the husband. With her hand outstretched, she ordered tersely: "Give me that knife at once."

He turned from his wife and plunged his knife at Agnes, but the knife halted an inch from the brass buttons on her uniform. Her eyes were fixed on the husband's and her voice, this time, was quiet, almost conversational.

"I'll take that knife." And then: "Please."

Behind her Marty's hand had snaked toward his gun, but the knife could have been buried in Agnes before he cleared the holster. With his eyes fixed on the knife, Marty's hand froze.

The husband and Agnes stared at each other. The only sounds were the heavy breathing of the wife and a choked sob from the drunken husband. For several seconds no one moved. To Agnes and Marty these seconds seemed longer than their years in the Police Department, longer than marriage.

Abruptly the husband extended the knife to Agnes. Without turning around, Agnes passed it back to Marty.

The shaken Marty stood holding the carving knife, unable to speak.

Agnes drew the drunk over to the sofa and talked to him in a low voice. After a time, the wife sat down on the sofa too. Agnes was still in the middle. She talked to them both. Presently, to her relief, the husband and wife began talking to each other across her, and Agnes was able to fall silent. The husband no longer seemed murderously drunk. The wife was silently crying. Agnes looked over at Marty. She saw him put the carving knife down on a table. Then he went and stared out the window.

After about thirty minutes they left that apartment, but as soon as they reached the street Marty turned on her in a rage and shouted: "Don't you ever do anything like that again."

She tried to defend herself. "But, Marty, it worked perfectly."

"Maybe you've been in this job a long time, but you're a rookie when it comes to patrol. You don't know how quick a knife can work. You haven't seen the people lying on the floor that I've seen. A knife in the hands of a drunk like that moves so fast the eye can't follow it. You'd be dead before you knew he had stuck it in you. There would be nothing I could do. Don't you understand? There'd be nothing I could do."

Agnes attempted a light response. "But, Marty, I didn't know you cared."

With the side of his shoe Marty kicked at a stone on the pavement. "Of course I care. You're goddamn right I care."

In the radio car, Marty stared straight ahead.

"What would you have done?" Agnes asked.

"There's only one thing to do when a guy has a knife. You stay away from him. You keep a piece of furniture between him and you. And you point your gun in his face and order him to drop the knife, and if he moves an inch you put a bullet in him."

In a low voice Agnes said: "You don't mean that, Marty."

He wouldn't look at her after that. He parked the radio car and they went into the stationhouse. But as they were signing out Agnes said: "I respect what you say, Marty. I'll be more careful the next time there's a knife."

But that was the night Agnes realized that he cared

for her not as partner, or fellow cop, but as a woman. She hadn't been thinking along those lines at all. She had wanted only his respect and had been working hard to earn it. So she was amazed and, despite herself, pleased. She was also confused. Now that he was no longer hostile to her, she supposed he would start making sexual advances, and she didn't want that, but that was not what happened. Instead he became ever more polite, absolutely correct in all his dealings with her, and even rather shy with her at times.

That was the night Agnes realized how happy she was. She had never been so happy before in her life. She loved patrol, she absolutely loved it. She loved going into people's houses. True, every house she entered was a house in trouble, but she loved giving herself to these people and trying to help them, and she loved the education she was getting, the insights into how other people lived. There were old Jewish couples living alone on the Grand Concourse, and Blacks and Puerto Ricans living in tenements down close to the 41st Precinct, and there were all manner of peoples in between. She liked to see how the apartments were decorated, and the way the kitchens looked. She was interested in how each apartment smelled—the different odors of living. And she loved being on patrol because Marty was her partner. They had conversations in the car on all kinds of subjects. She trusted him as a cop, and she was eager that he should accept her as one, and when he occasionally praised her she glowed. The two of them were soon answering more jobs than any other radio car team in the precinct. Once the captain even remarked on this at roll call, and congratulated them. He said he wished every radio car team did as much work as they did. His praise made Agnes grin delightedly, but to her surprise Marty became embarrassed, and after that almost surly.

Being Marty's partner made Agnes realize how dull her husband was. Life to Cusack was an interminable succession of paint buckets and brushes. His work clothes were so caked with paint they'd stand up by themselves. Even their former friends bored Agnes now. Not one of their friends lived the life of excitement that had become commonplace to Agnes, and very soon most were in awe of her. When they met for drinks or a cookout in somebody's backyard in Staten Island, Agnes found that she was doing most of the talking. Nothing anyone else had to say was as interesting to the group as what Agnes had to say.

Then came the bank robbery. What happened after the bank robbery, the hours in the motel room downtown, did not surprise Agnes. By then it had seemed inevitable to her for a long time.

The days that followed were exciting. Reporters came out to Staten Island to photograph her cooking dinner for her husband. The same reporters or perhaps different ones interviewed Marty and his wife over in Queens. Agnes and Marty had gone on television together, and she had had a fight with her husband over that, a fight that she still had not managed to patch up very well.

Agnes and Marty had gone back to the same motel again. The last time Marty was worried. He said: "Every guy in the stationhouse is talking about us, Agnes. I hope you realize that."

But Agnes pulled him down on top of her, saying: "Let's not talk about it now."

She had worried about it since, but had come to no conclusions.

Now in a luncheonette on Southern Boulevard, with her hair against the plastic and an amused expression on her face, she watched Marty's hand banging the bottom of the catsup bottle he held over his cheeseburger.

Marty's face seemed to shatter, and it turned a wet and sticky red, and Agnes's first impression was that the catsup bottle had exploded in his hand. Then she heard the report of more shots, and saw Marty quiver as additional bullets struck him. She saw Marty's gore-covered face fall toward his plate. Blood filled the plate until the cheeseburger was swimming in it. Agnes never saw the gunman, only his arm and gun reaching past the side of the booth, shooting Marty. The muzzle blast deafened her.

In the instant before the shots were fired she had seen Marty raise his eyes, staring toward the front of the diner. She had seen momentary confusion in his face, but this had been replaced almost instantly by sudden awareness of his peril. From the counter a man he didn't know had raced to them and, as he reached their booth, had begun firing bullets at him from point-blank range.

Agnes, on her feet, was immobilized by too much thought, or not enough. Marty's face was gone, for no reason at all, and with no warning. She stared aghast at the top of his head, and her first coherent thought was: I wasn't able to protect my partner. What would other cops say of her now? The answer seemed too clear: that a policewoman was useless when the shooting started. All Agnes had accomplished to date was lost. She would have to go back and begin again. She had betrayed every policewoman in the department, in the world.

Most of all she had betrayed her partner. She had failed to protect her partner. That she had failed to share his fate was what she would regret most in a moment, but now as she sprang after the running gunman she was trying only to dig her revolver out. She was already in tears or close to it. She felt like screaming: Wait for me, Marty, I'm coming right back.

The swinging door seemed to swing cold night air against her face. The gunman was diving into the back of a car that was already moving and she pulled off two shots at him, missing probably, for her world had blurred and she couldn't see. With the car moving away from her she remembered to drop to one knee, holding her revolver in both hands as she had been taught, and she emptied it at the gunman, at the door closing behind him, at the car in general, four puny bullets, all she had. The gunmen were firing, too, for she could see the flashes. From the now-squealing sedan, bullets rushed toward her, like prayers that would redeem her if they struck. But she was immune to bullets though she craved them, and therefore damned. Standing, she made the target more attractive, thrusting her chest out.

The tears were streaming down her face. Her empty gun hung against her leg. She was sobbing brokenheartedly. Her life, love, career—all that meant anything to her was soaking into a cheeseburger back there in the diner. The getaway car was twenty yards away, fifty, a hundred. It squealed like a woman in ecstasy. Guns had stopped firing at her. She would not die tonight. She was condemned to face her accusers, condemned to explain, condemned to go on living.

"Kill me, oh kill me," she sobbed after the departing car. "Oh, Marty. Oh, Marty."

31

EISCHIED on the phone was screaming at the District Attorney: "Can I have my wire now? Can you see why it's important now? Will you give it to me now?"

The District Attorney said calmly: "Soothe yourself, Earl. I feel very badly about what happened last night, just as you do. But the legal justification for that tap is just as flimsy today as it was previously. My Appeals Bureau tells me it just won't stand up."

"Can you make an exception for me for once?" Eischied said, trying to control his voice. "I never asked you for a favor before. I'm asking you for one now."

The DA said: "And anyway, the chances are it's too late for you to pick up the kind of conversation you're looking for. If anyone was going to call that cleaning woman about her son, they did it days ago."

"Maybe," muttered Eischied.

"And as far as last night's assassination, you don't have a shred of hard evidence to connect that crime to the bank robberies, much less to that gunman your detective shot in the garage."

"Look, I'm begging you."

"I can't do it, Earl. I'd be severely criticized if I did it, so I can't do it."

Eischied slammed down the phone.

Lieutenant Fitzgerald came in. "The city editor of the *Daily News* is on the phone, Chief. I think he's had another note."

Eischied snatched up the phone: "Chief Eischied."

The note had been hand delivered to the guard on duty in the lobby of the *Daily News* building. The guard had been giving directions to a tourist, and when he turned back, the envelope was lying beside his hand. It had been rushed upstairs, and the city editor had just opened it.

"I'll work a trade with you, Chief," the man said cheerfully. "I'll need an hour to photograph this thing —our photo department doesn't come to work this early, because we're a morning newspaper. And, in any case, I'd just as soon that word of this doesn't get out until the last edition of the afternoon *Post* is off the press. So if you'll send a detective over here after lunch, I'll hand this note over to him."

Eischied, who had been up most of the night, said in a low, dangerous voice: "Where is the letter now?"

"Lying right here on my desk."

"Read it to me."

The city editor did so. Eischied listened to the usual rhetoric, plus the promise of more violence to come, violence which would dwarf all preceding "battles" of the autumn offensive of FEAR.

Eischied said: "I'll have a detective there within ten minutes to pick up that letter."

"I don't know if you heard me, Chief. I'll need longer than that, as I've just explained."

Eischied, separating each word for maximum effect, said: "Did you ever hear of the crime of obstruction of justice?"

From the other end of the wire came silence.

Eischied said: "See that nobody touches that thing before my detective gets there." He slammed down the phone.

Eischied hollered into his intercom for Lieutenant Fitzgerald.

Even Fitzgerald's sunny face was somber today.

"The city editor of the *Daily News* is holding the latest message from these sons of bitches," Eischied told him. "Go up there and relieve him of it, and throw the fear of God into him while you're at it. Take my car."

The Chief of Detectives imagined the scene. Red Fitzgerald—any detective lieutenant—was a pussycat to his superiors, but an awesome figure to outsiders. Fitzgerald would put on a hard expression, and that newspaper editor's knees would turn to jelly.

Fitzgerald was to hand carry the message to Captain Rolfe at the Police Academy lab. He was to wait there while Rolfe processed the message personally, and the two of them were then to report back to Eischied.

"Anything else, Chief?"

"Yeah."

Eischied paused to light a cigar. The need for the wiretap was still there in his mind. It was no great trick to tap a telephone, legally or illegally. In this case it would be a federal felony. Detectives traditionally were far more afraid of running afoul of federal law than New York State law, though jail was jail. The fear was instinctive and somewhat irrational, but the federal courthouse was foreign territory to them; they knew no one there. Whereas they had testified often in State Supreme Court and if caught could perhaps find a way out.

Eischied, whether he admitted it or not, felt the same fear. The detective who got caught would do time in federal prison. Unless during plea bargaining he agreed to testify against the commander who had ordered the tap.

To Lieutenant Fitzgerald Eischied said: "Reach

out for Detective McCluskey for me. Tell him to report to this office forthwith."

Forthwith. The word denoted urgency, and was one of the strongest in the police lexicon. Forthwith meant drop everything else.

Eischied could do no more for the moment, and he did not want to think of the bloody corpse of Patrolman Martin Delehanty anymore, so he plunged back into the normal business of the Chief of Detectives, most of it paperwork. There was the normal batch of unusuals to slog through, and the normal batch of loan applications to sign, for in the last few days the normal complement of detectives had run out of money and had decided to borrow from the Pension Fund. There was disciplinary action to consider against a first-grade detective who had failed to show up in court on three different occasions in connection with a certain case. The detective had claimed he was sick. Eischied thumbed back and forth through the report, getting the facts straight in his head. Eischied was tired. It was hard to focus his thoughts on stuff like this. Three times? Was there a payoff involved here? Corruption? Or was the detective actually sick? Or spending time with some floozy? Or just forgetful?

The report had already been endorsed by the detective's squad commander, a lieutenant; by his district commander, an inspector; by his borough commander, an assistant chief; and it now required an endorsement from the Chief of Detectives. The recommendations so far were to flop the guy back to third-grade detective. Eischied accorded the four-page report a total of about ninety seconds, then stamped it "Approved," and affixed his signature.

At 10:30 Assistant Chief Scanlon, who commanded Brooklyn North detectives, arrived to confer with Eischied about vacancies for Deputy Inspector. Recommendations on five detective captains should be forwarded to the PC for consideration. Which five?

Eischied said to Chief Scanlon, who sat beside his desk: "I count only five vacancies overall. You got to figure on at least two of them going to patrol captains. The First Dep. will probably grab two for himself. He'll want one for the Intelligence Division and one for Internal Affairs. That leaves one vacancy for the Detective Division. Who do we want to give it to?"

Scanlon said: "If we could ever get three of them, wouldn't that be something? Even two would be a hell of a victory."

This was true. The rest of the department would read that political clout had swung back toward the Detective Division. Every cop on the force would read that Eischied was strong, and that some other commander, who had been accorded less than his normal share of promotions, was correspondingly weak.

To Scanlon, Eischied said: "I wouldn't count on it right now."

He realized he would feel lucky to get even a single promotion out of this, though he did not say so to Scanlon. Instead he determined to safeguard that single promotion as much as possible by submitting one name only, but with an extremely hard recommendation behind it. Too devious to admit his thoughts even to this trusted subordinate, Eischied said: "It seems to me that the only guy we have who's been doing a really outstanding job lately is this guy who has 10th District Burglary-Larceny." Eischied on the list before him tapped the name he meant with the tip of his pencil.

Eischied was buzzed on the intercom: "Detective McCluskey is here, Chief."

Chief Scanlon took no notice of this interruption. An ordinary detective could be kept waiting all day. For a week if necessary. Chief Scanlon did not expect to have to give up his place beside Eischied's desk for any ordinary detective.

To Eischied he said: "Do you mean we're only going to recommend one guy, Chief?"

Eischied rose to his feet, signaling the conference was over. "Work up a real strong recommendation for me, and bring it over when you have it ready."

Chief Scanlon, suddenly worried about his own

political clout, f⟨…⟩
Withdrawing a ⟨…⟩
to fish through ⟨…⟩
you, Chief."

But Eisch⟨…⟩
another tim⟨…⟩

Chief S⟨…⟩
other in E⟨…⟩
His career s⟨…⟩
in ruins, and he ⟨…⟩

Eischied tilted his ⟨…⟩
his blotter, while Detec⟨…⟩
beside his desk. Blowing sm⟨…⟩
Eischied tried to decide how to pro⟨…⟩

McCluskey was a tall, heavy ma⟨…⟩
weighed over 220. He had gray hair. He⟨…⟩
complexion with permanent five-o'clock shad⟨…⟩
had not removed his topcoat, or even opened it.
his hands he held a narrow-brimmed fedora which
probably looked ridiculous on his big head.

Eischied said: "Where they got you working now,
Mac?"

"Fourth Robbery, Chief."

Eischied said: "You've been doing a good job for
me, Mac. In fact you've been working too hard. I
want you to take the next week off."

He studied McCluskey through cigar smoke.

McCluskey said: "Thanks, Chief," but his expression did not change, except that his eyes narrowed
slightly.

"How long we known each other now, Mac?"

"Didn't we work on the Wiley-Hoffa murder back
in the early sixties, Chief?"

"No, I never worked on that case."

"I know we worked one case together, Chief. You
were a lieutenant."

Eischied studied him.

McCluskey said: "Maybe it was the Anastasia case.
You remember he got hit in the barbershop when he
was under the hot towel."

Eischied said: "No, I didn't work on that case."

...ps the best opening he was going
...said: "Back in those days, if you
...you got it. We must have had fifty
... Anastasia case."

...face had turned shrewd.

...was Mafia," said Eischied. "That wasn't
...lling."

...blew smoke toward the ceiling and watched
...put in for a tap this morning in connection
...murder of Patrolman Delehanty. We'll prob-
...the tap, but I'm concerned that we might not
...on time."

...two men stared at each other. After a mo-
...nt McCluskey said: "Where would that wire go in,
...ief?"

Eischied scrawled out the name, address and phone
number of Leon Epps's mother and pushed it across
the desk toward McCluskey. While the detective
stared down at the paper, Eischied explained who
Epps was, and that his confederates could be expected
to telephone his mama to find out if she had seen him.
"The chances are," Eischied said, "that this would
give us a lead on where these bastards are. Maybe
even who they are."

Again the two men studied each other. Then Mc-
Cluskey said: "The mother is not part of any criminal
conspiracy from the sound of it, Chief. It's not a wire
that could be expected to disclose evidence of her
being involved in a crime. I'm not so sure we'll get
the tap."

Eischied said: "I'm not so sure of it either. But
without it I don't see how we're going to find these
cop killers."

McCluskey's hand reached for the paper, but Eischied's got there first. For a moment they eyed each
other. Then McCluskey glanced down at the paper,
and made some jottings in his notebook. When he had
finished Eischied lifted the note toward his ashtray
and set fire to it. Both men watched the paper burn.

Eischied said: "Like I say, you've been working too
hard. Take a week off and see if you feel better.

If you don't feel better at the end of a week, maybe
I can give you a second week off."

In a flat voice McCluskey said: "Thanks, Chief."

"I'll have you reassigned to my office for as long as
you're off duty."

Eischied came around his desk and led McCluskey
to the door. With his hand on the knob Eischied
said: "There's not a cop in the city safe until we find
those guys." McCluskey nodded. Eischied closed the
door and returned thoughtfully to his desk.

32

IN the old days, before the advent of the tough eavesdropping law, Detective McCluskey had worked many
taps like this one. Stripped to his undershirt, he was
sitting on a crate in the tenement boiler room, playing solitaire on a second crate in front of him. The
boiler-room door was locked from inside. For the
moment he felt as safe as in church.

The telephone box was on the wall above his head.
He had jimmied the cover off, found the terminals
he was looking for, and clipped on the leads to his
hand phone. This hand phone lay on the crate beside
his cards. Attached to it by induction coil was a
small tape recorder, and this would record any conversation he overheard. But so far the phone had not
rung once.

Legal taps these days were most often put in by the
security division of the telephone company. Eight or
ten taps at once could be made to terminate inside a
single office in a stationhouse. A detective could monitor that many wires simultaneously without leaving
his desk. The working-out of such arrangements, which

had been difficult both technically and politically, had been one of the great triumphs of a recent Chief of Detectives, and had resulted in enormous savings in detective manpower. It and the eavesdropping law had ended boiler-room taps forever. To a man like McCluskey this was not progress; it merely stripped from the detective job still more of its former mystique and romance.

Even though it was illegal—and therefore risky— McCluskey preferred this type of tap. He was a patient, phlegmatic man, and quite ready to sit on his crate fourteen hours a day for however many days it took. He would play solitaire part of the time, and read paperback mysteries part of the time, and though he cursed the excessive heat and bad air, the cockroaches and the rats, still this was better than some taps he had sat on in unheated tenement storerooms in winter.

Risk was slight because this was the ghetto, not Park Avenue. It was unlikely anyone would arrive to service the boiler. A ghetto boiler could go out and stay out; most likely it would be three days before anybody managed to mount a successful protest. There had been no doorman to bluff his way past, and the house did not even have a resident janitor or superintendent. McCluskey, wearing his telephone-company hard hat and carrying what appeared to be a toolbox, had merely entered the tenement, descended to the cellar and hunted for the telephone box until he found it. That the box was inside the boiler room, and that the boiler-room door could be locked—this was a nice piece of luck but not otherwise remarkable.

McCluskey was not particularly worried about getting caught. He knew he could talk his way past any cop or detective who might stumble upon him. The only danger was from the FBI or some other federal agency, like Narcotics, or Firearms. In the ghetto there was always the possibility that the feds had this house under surveillance for some reason. If so, they would wonder who he was and why he didn't come out, and would make it their business to go in after him. Or the feds could be tipped off that he was there by a suspicious resident. But the chance of that was small. Hell, for the most part these people wouldn't dare contact the local precinct, much less a federal agency.

So McCluskey was safe, he thought.

He had learned that Epps's mother reported to work at 6 P.M., and returned home about 3 A.M., at which time she presumably went to sleep. The incoming call McCluskey was waiting for would come—if it came——sometime between, say, eight o'clock in the morning and five in the afternoon. For him, a normal working day. McCluskey had brought his lunch in a paper bag. He had three bottles of beer, and the first would be cool enough but the last two would be warm. Sometime during the day he would be obliged to take a leak, which meant he would pee against the wall in the opposite corner of the boiler room. He hoped he would be out of this place before the stink mounted to haunt him.

If the job took several days, obviously some residents would notice him coming or going, and he had a series of cover stories worked out. He saw no particular risk, and he would get one week, maybe two weeks off with pay when this job was over.

And so he sat on his wooden crate, and part of the time daydreamed about where he would take his wife on this unexpected vacation, and part of the time he read these preposterous mystery novels. Once, having closed a book, he wondered why mystery writers never described detectives sitting alone for days at a time on a wiretap like this one, with no tension of any kind and absolutely nothing happening. In detective novels the hero was always a mastermind who zeroed in on the perpetrator unerringly, and moved from one exciting scene to another, including lots of fist fights and shootouts. Whereas detective work to McCluskey was sitting in boiler rooms in his undershirt waiting for a tapped telephone to ring. Often in the past McCluskey had taken part in important arrests, but the suspects were located via wiretaps, not deduction and there were no fistfights or shootouts. Arrests usually took place at five o'clock in the morning with so many detectives pouring in through windows and doors that the perpetrators offered no resistance whatever.

Suddenly Mrs. Epps's phone rang. With one hand McCluskey started his tape recorder, and with the other he slapped its induction coil to the hand phone at his ear. He was listening intently, waiting to cull hard information either from this conversation or from some later one. As he listened he felt a glow of pride. Some of the young guys wouldn't even know how to do a job like this anymore. The telephone company had to do it for them. And he also felt satisfaction. Whether or not McCluskey furnished the information that broke this case, he would have one in the bank with the Chief of Detectives when this was over, and that could prove useful.

33

EISCHIED, having called for the fingerprint card of Jonah Daniel Bell, aka Mark D. Bell, stood at his safe comparing each of the card's ten compartments to the single latent print on the scorched news clippings. There was no match that he could see. Eischied was no fingerprint expert; nonetheless, he saw no similarity whatsoever. Dropping the black cardboard flap over the evidence he turned away from the safe, and, still holding Mark D.'s card, resumed pacing.

He had not expected a match. Mark D. was twenty years old and, from his record, an ordinary mugger and stickup man. The printed rhetoric on the news clipping in the safe belonged to a bigger mind than that, and therefore the print did too, or at least this was Eischied's reasoning.

It was possible that Mark D. was the guy with the machine gun.

Mark D. was one of those who had telephoned the pants presser, according to the wiretap; so was someone referred to as The Big Man. The latent print in Eischied's safe belonged, he was convinced, to this Big Man, who was the brains of the outfit. But who could the Big Man be?

Abruptly Eischied sat at his desk and jotted down every name he could remember from the various violent groups that had been active in New York during the years of the Vietnam War; when he ran out of names Eischied culled more from the dossier on revolutionaries in his drawer. He remembered a flurry of stories about Everett Walker some months ago. The Arabs had either locked him up or kicked him out. Maybe they sent him back here, Eischied thought, and he's the one behind this. It was not impossible. He put Walker's name down. Soon he had about fifty names.

Then he put his feet up, lit his cigar, blew smoke at the ceiling and tried to think. What did he know? He knew the names of four members of the gang: Leon Epps and Floyd Fields, who were dead; the pants presser, whose name was Albert Hoyt; and Mark D., whose name was Jonah Daniel Bell. He knew approximately where in the city the gang was holed up, the South Bronx, but he had no street address. He had detectives showing Epps's picture throughout those neighborhoods, but no one had recognized Epps yet. He had McCluskey tapping Epps's mother's phone —illegally.

He had a legal tap on the pants presser, though no more calls seemed to be coming in there; and he had detectives tailing the guy round the clock. He couldn't move any closer to the pants presser yet. The rest of the gang was underground; only the pants presser moved on the surface; his status must be different and Eischied couldn't afford to lose him. The pants presser had to have room. Enough room to lead detectives into the South Bronx.

What else? Eischied asked himself.

He knew that FEAR was connected to last summer's murdered cops, for the machine gun had appeared twice. But this wasn't even important anymore. When he broke this case, he would also break that one.

His eyes closed from fatigue, and he began to rub them gently. Six customers and two countermen had witnessed the murder of Officer Delehanty last night. Eischied had interrogated these people for hours. He had not left the luncheonette until 4 A.M. By then Marty was naked on a slab in the morgue, most likely. White skin under white glare.

The eyelids that he rubbed felt caked on the inside with grit, but he forced them open again and contemplated the pile of mug shots of Mark D. on his desk: more photos for detectives to show through the neighborhoods of the South Bronx. It would have to be done, though Eischied dreaded it. Too many detectives were going to be involved; too many loose photos floating around. By tomorrow at the latest the newspapers would have got hold of one photo or both, and secrecy would go out the window. Mark D. would see himself in print and take off; the others too, most likely. We'll never find them once that happens, Eischied thought. Mark D.'s photos had been brought in by Captain Finnerty earlier. The compulsive Finnerty had aligned them not only perfectly in relation to each other, but also had set the stack exactly in line with the corner of the desk. Compulsively, Eischied reached out and mussed up the pile.

What else? he asked himself.

The press was already massed outside the 48th Precinct stationhouse. There would be pressure all day from them, from the Mayor, from the PC. He would have to figure out how to respond to each of these pressures, but felt too tired and discouraged to do it now. One thing was clear: the mood of calm he had brought to the city had been shattered. He had promised to end FEAR's reign of terror, but had failed, and today his standing was lower than it had ever been. If he were removed today as Chief of Detectives, not a voice would be raised in his behalf.

Except for his few remaining secrets, he had no muscle left at all. This morning's headlines had been, for him, disastrous. The victim, according to the papers, was not just an ordinary cop, but the bravest and finest cop in the city. Yesterday's forgotten hero had never been forgotten at all, according to the papers, and now never would be, another lie. It could have been worse, from Eischied's point of view, only if Officer Cusack had been killed too—which she probably should have been. By all accounts she had just stood there in the street while for the second time in not much more than two weeks they emptied their guns at her. Ballistics had counted more than twenty bullet holes in the parked cars behind her. That broad lives a charmed life, Eischied thought. I wonder how she does it? But at present she was hospitalized under heavy sedation. It had not been possible to question her at all, and her hysteria had been so extreme there was some fear that her mind had snapped.

What else? Eischied asked himself.

The getaway car might turn up, if it has her bullet holes in it, he thought, though in her state she might have missed completely. Witnesses said it was a late-model LTD, probably dark green. No one had got a license number.

What else?

He wondered if he should have a press conference at the 48th Precinct later, and if so, what he should say.

Just then Finnerty announced Captain Rolfe, who came in accompanied by Lieutenant Fitzgerald. Rolfe had this morning's message from FEAR inside a celluloid folder, but he dropped this on Eischied's desk, saying: "No prints. Nothing."

The message was printed in black letters on lined notepaper. Eischied muttered: "Shit."

Lieutenant Fitzgerald said: "That's exactly what I said when I heard, Chief. 'Shit,' I said."

It made Eischied want to smile, but he suppressed the feeling, glared at Fitzgerald and growled: "When I want a comedian I'll hire one from Actors Equity, for chrissake."

"There's always a bright side, Chief. A little comic relief never hurts."

"The only relief I get is at night after you go home."

To Rolfe, Eischied said: "I've got a job that I'd like you to do personally," and he led Rolfe to the safe and exposed the scorched newsprint. "I've made a list of a number of these so-called revolutionary leaders, most of whom haven't been active in years. I want you to pull their print cards and compare them to this."

He handed Rolfe the list.

Rolfe winced. "Christ, Chief, you've got fifty names here at least. That's five hundred fingers. I'll go blind."

"Start with—" Eischied checked himself, realizing that Fitzgerald was staring down at the print too.

A secret you wanted kept you shared with as few people as possible, and even Fitzgerald could not be trusted.

"That's all, Red."

Eischied wondered if Everett Walker was in jail in North Africa. In any case, he had disappeared, according to all those news stories.

"All?" inquired Fitzgerald. "Oh, I get it."

"Congratulations."

"You want me to leave. Is that what you're trying to get across, Chief?"

"There's something I want to discuss privately with Captain Rolfe."

"I was just leaving anyway, Chief." Red added, as if confidentially, "I have to go to the bathroom, Chief."

For a moment Eischied felt better. Fitzgerald always made him smile.

When Fitzgerald had scurried out, Eischied pointed to Walker's name on the list: "Start with this guy."

Rolfe glanced at him sharply.

Eischied gave no further explanation. Man, the secret animal—the detective man, most of all. "I don't want anybody to know what you're doing or why." But it wasn't necessary to tell this to a man like Rolfe.

Still depressed, Eischied rode up to the 48th Precinct stationhouse, Patrolman Delehanty's house. It was a seedy old building with an archaic switchboard and therefore an inefficient house out of which to run an investigation as big as this one. On the other hand, the presence of fifty strange detectives hustling in and out of their stationhouse was a tremendous boost to the shattered morale of the cops on patrol there, and this was important. In their hour of need they saw that the department was doing all it could to catch the murderer of one of their brothers. If the investigation had been headquartered in some other stationhouse, they would have felt abandoned.

The investigation was being conducted out of a small room off the squad room on the second floor. The scene was entirely too familiar to Eischied: detective commanders in hats and coats sitting around a table waiting; a detective in shirt sleeves and headphones answering calls from the public. The morgue photos were there too in an envelope on the table, and Eischied spread them. The corpse lay naked on the slab, and he didn't look too bad. Someone had pressed his face back together again. His mouth was closed. His upper lip looked torn, as if he had been in a fistfight. Under his lips would be several broken teeth, but you couldn't see that. That shot was the one that had killed him. There were two other neat round holes in his right shoulder, and his corpse was otherwise unmarked. There was none of the terrible surgical stitching of cops who had made it to the operating table. Marty Delehanty had been killed virtually instantly.

Eischied said nothing. Wordlessly, he replaced the photos. "What have we got going for us?" he asked.

Deputy Inspector Cornfield, commander of the Major Crime Squad, answered, even though he was not the highest-ranking commander in the room: "Not very much so far, Chief."

Eischied nodded. For a moment he considered telling these men all he knew, but this weakness passed. There was no way he could think of that his extra knowledge would help at this stage in the investigation, and to tell these men would be equivalent to broadcasting it over the radio. Instinctively Eischied felt that secrecy was still his best strength.

"Have the witnesses been brought in to the stationhouse?" he asked.

They had been, and were being kept in another room.

"All right, let's bring them in here one at a time. Let's see if they can identify any of these photos."

The identification of photos by witnesses, if it was to have any validity in court later, had to be a controlled procedure. You couldn't just show one photo. From his briefcase Eischied withdrew the album that had been prepared by Captain Finnerty earlier. It contained eight-by-ten blowups of Mark D. and all known former associates of him as well, about twenty men in all.

Eischied said: "The counterman who served coffee to the assailant—he's our best witness, I guess. Bring him in first."

The counterman was about fifty. Before opening the album, Eischied tried to talk to him amiably, but he was plainly terrified. He was a small brown man with a Hispanic name, and he spoke little English.

He recognized no photo.

"Are you sure? Would you like to go through them again?"

"I think no."

Nonetheless Eischied slowly flipped the glassine pages for him. The scared counterman was hardly glancing at the photos. He was trying to read clues from Eischied's face. He wanted to identify whichever photo the Chief of Detectives wanted identified.

"How about this one?" inquired Eischied, stopping at Mark D.

"Maybe it him. I no sure. I go home now?"

Eischied clapped shut the book. "Yes, you go home now." Opening the door he called: "Send the other counterman in."

The second counterman tentatively identified Mark D. as the shooter, and after him so did one of the customers, a twenty-five-year-old cab driver.

"He was sitting right next to me. It does look like him. Do you have a better shot, maybe?"

Eischied extracted other photos of Mark D. from his briefcase.

"That's him."

"You're sure?"

"Absolutely."

Eischied said: "Inspector Cornfield, would you take this gentleman into another room and have him sign a statement please. And you can send in the next witness too." Eischied's elation showed in his voice.

There were grins all around the tiny office, and they stayed in place even though no other witness identified any photo.

The phone rang. It was Captain Rolfe asking for the Chief of Detectives. Cornfield passed Eischied the phone.

"Are you on a secure line there, Chief?"

Eischied glanced around him. "No, I'm not."

"Maybe you better call me back, Chief."

Eischied went into the precinct commander's office, closed the door, and dialed Rolfe's number.

"Chief, that gentleman we spoke of earlier—the print could be his."

Eischied sucked in air. But after a moment he growled: "It either is or it isn't. What do you mean, could be?"

"The latent print you showed me is only a partial, Chief. I checked it against the left thumbprint of our friend. There are three bifurcations that match, and none that don't match."

Eischied said bluntly: "Then it's him."

Captain Rolfe cautioned: "Not in a court of law,

Chief. You have to have eight points of similarity for it to stand up in court."

There was a silence. These men were cops, not lawyers. Three matching bifurcations to them was solid proof.

Rolfe said: "What next, Chief?"

Eischied said: "If I knew, I'd tell you. You deserve to know. I gotta think. I'll talk to you later."

As always when under pressure, Eischied stuck a new cigar in his mouth, and for ten minutes, his feet on the precinct commander's desk, he silently mouthed the cigar. Suddenly he was faced with a great many options. Last night's killer had been positively identified. Did he announce that to the press, or to the PC, or to neither? The leader of the conspiracy had also been positively identified. Same questions.

He tried to work out the tactical advantages of each option, and he disposed of Mark D. first. Publish Mark D.'s name and/or photo, and the guy would run or hide; either way you neutralized him, which was good for the city. But you probably wouldn't catch him. Which is bad, he thought, for me.

Still, Mark D. was an easier problem to solve than Everett Walker.

Eischied picked up the phone and dialed the PC's direct line.

"Gimme the PC," Eischied told Deputy Inspector Ryan, who answered. "Interrupt whatever he's doing. This is urgent."

The PC's voice was cold, but it warmed up when he heard Eischied's news.

"The press is outside, Commissioner. They probably already know we got a positive make on the killer. I propose to confirm this now. I won't tell them his name, and I won't give out his photo. What the result will be I don't know. Possibly this way the killer won't believe we know who he is. Possibly he'll stay put until we can find him. In the meantime, the news should calm down the city, and the Mayor should be happy."

The PC was silent, considering Eischied's proposal.

The PC knew he would have to inform the Mayor at once, of course: Guess what, Mr. Mayor, good news. Pressure from there should abate somewhat. But the press conferences would be Eischied's not the PC's, which was a minus. Tomorrow's headlines would go to Eischied again, not him. Of course the case could still fall through. It was probably safer if the PC's prestige was not tied to it directly.

"You do it that way, then, Earl. Keep me informed." He rang off.

The PC had not asked a single question. Not Mark D.'s name or background, or what else was known. The PC, it was clear to Eischied, had no emotional or personal interest in this case whatever. The PC was not a curious man.

If Eischied had mentioned Everett Walker, would the PC have reacted differently? Probably he would have gone straight to the Mayor with it. What to do with a cheap gunman like Mark D. was a decision for the Chief of Detectives. But Walker was another story. Walker was big. What to do with Walker would be considered a decision, Eischied felt sure, for the politicians. Politicians would worry about possible ghetto riots in defense of their hero. Politicians would fear an outcry from civil liberties groups who preferred to consider Walker a civil rights leader rather than a murderer, and who would attack not Walker but the Police Department, number-one repressive force in our society. Three matching bifurcations were, after all, less than legal proof.

The ideas lurching around Eischied's head were giving him a headache. The subject was too complicated, he had too many options, he had had too little sleep last night—he was unable to think clearly.

He stood in the door of the captain's office staring out at cops in the muster room.

"Last night is proof it won't ever work," he overheard one cop say to another.

So he realized they were talking about Police Officer Agnes Cusack, who was still under sedation in the hospital. No cop, as far back as Eischied could remember, had ever had to be hospitalized following the death of his partner, and Eischied understood that male cops throughout the city were gloating over Agnes's crackup. They believed it meant the end of women on patrol.

The second cop said: "When you come right down to it, women don't have no balls—and I don't mean to be funny. I'll tell you one thing, they're not putting me out on patrol with no female. I'd turn in my gun and shield first."

But Agnes was a cop too, and Eischied felt only sympathy for her. Poor girl, he thought. He wished he could see some way to save her but he was too busy trying to save himself.

For the moment, he decided, he would tell no one about Walker. The secret stayed with himself and Rolfe. Secrecy was ingrained in him. It was the most normal of any course of conduct, and the most congenial. He didn't want politicians meddling. He didn't want anyone meddling. He now knew who he was looking for, and his quarry did not know that he knew. Surely this was an advantage, provided he could think of a way to exploit it.

Returning to the precinct commander's desk, Eischied put through a call to Captain Rolfe. "I want you to get together as many photos of that guy that you can find. Bring them over to my office in about an hour. Bring our artist with you."

Hanging up, he moved to complete the jobs that were left to do here.

Putting Deputy Inspector Cornfield in charge of the investigation overnight, he sent the chiefs and inspectors away.

His instructions to Cornfield were explicit. Information coming in was to be sifted. Tips from the public were to be checked out in the normal way. It was late. Tomorrow would be soon enough to organize the search for Mark D.

"Mark D. isn't our problem anyway. It's whatever genius is behind him."

"Right, Chief."

From the stationhouse stoop Eischied talked to the press.

"Yes, he's been positively identified. No, I can't tell you his name. Do you want him to take off on us?"

The press believed him. A declarative sentence was a declarative sentence, and a man of Eischied's rank at a time like this would not dare put forth an outright lie.

He could only hope that Mark D. and Everett Walker, plus whoever was the machine gunner, would think he was bluffing. If they took flight the case was lost, and so was Eischied.

"All I can add at this time is that we are pursuing numerous other leads. No, we do not know where the gang is hiding out at this time."

He moved through the mob toward his car.

Rolfe was able to produce five photos, and an hour later Eischied had them spread on his desk and was staring down at them. The only beardless photo showed Everett Walker as a juvenile offender, aged fifteen. In all the rest he wore the heavy beard that had been his trademark. To the police artist, a detective who worked out of Forensic, Eischied said: "I want you to make me a drawing of this guy minus the beard. I want it to look a lot like he must look without the beard, but not exactly like him. Remember that he's now about thirty-five years old. He's six feet tall and weighs over two hundred. Get to work."

"Here, Chief?"

"Yes, here," said the Chief of Detectives.

The artist began making sketches. Rolfe and Eischied stood on either side gazing down at the sketch pad as the drawing took shape.

Eischied was satisfied with the second drawing, but made the artist do three more, hoping for something better.

Rolfe said: "I'd go with number two, Chief."

"I agree with you." To the artist, Eischied said: "You're a detective, right? Do you like being a detective?"

"Yes, I do, Chief."

"If what you've been doing here this afternoon gets out, you'll be back on patrol so fast you won't even have time to take a leak first."

When the artist was gone, Eischied collected the four rejected drawings and went through into his toilet, where he shredded them above the bowl. For a moment the pieces floated on the water. Then he flushed them away.

Rolfe he sent down to the printing section with the one remaining drawing. Rolfe was to have this photographed and to order two hundred copies sent up. Presently Captain Finnerty came in with this pile, which he aligned as precisely as the Mark D. pile, but on the opposite corner of the desk. This time Eischied was too tired to react.

"Will that be all, Chief?"

"Yes. You can go home, Finnerty."

"Well, good night, Chief."

Eischied at his desk began to toy with the idea of releasing to the press the drawing and physical description of Everett Walker, though not his name. This additional pressure might serve to panic Walker, but without driving him over the edge. It might cause him to make a mistake. He would not be sure how much the police knew—perhaps they were only guessing. Out of bravado, or in an attempt to hold his gang of thugs together, Walker might choose to ignore the drawing and its implications. He might stick to his original plan, giving Eischied an unknown amount of extra time in which to find and arrest him. Or Eischied could give out Walker's name and photo and wait for tomorrow's headlines. They would be big ones. Would this not have the effect of mobilizing the entire Police Department, plus eight million honest New Yorkers in the hunt to find and capture Everett Walker?

It might. On the other hand, it might only stimulate Walker to ever greater precautions. It might cause him to move up the timetable of whatever outrage he was currently planning. Releasing his name to the press might ensure holocaust rather than prevent it.

Besides that, the man had doubtless managed to change his appearance. He might have let his hair grow out wildly, or shaved it off. He had certainly got rid of the beard that had once been so famous. He was five years older than the last time anybody had seen him.

Eischied did not know what to do, and the temptation was very strong to inform the PC—who would be obliged to inform the Mayor—and let them decide. But if Eischied did not know what to do, how could he trust them to know, when they were lesser men than he was?—or so he believed.

What to do?

Give out the unidentified drawing, or—

Give out Walker's name and photo, or—

Let the PC and the Mayor decide, or—

Wait for whatever additional information might come in.

These were the only alternatives Eischied could think of tonight. He did not know what he should do, or would do, tomorrow. He would keep his options open—and his mind open—till then. He was feeling confused, uncertain and very, very tired. Also, he was annoyed that he had not sent Walker's print to Latent weeks ago when it first came in. But Latent never would have been able to identify him from it, Eischied told himself. No one would ever have thought to check Walker's card against that print, any more than I thought of it myself until today.

Was he so sure this was true? Or had he indeed made a terrible and quite unforgivable mistake at the very start of this investigation, a mistake that the press —and the PC—would hang him for if they got wind of it?

His outer office was empty except for his night-duty sergeant and the faithful Louie. Eischied went downstairs and got into his car, and Louie drove him home through the now dark streets and the last of the theatre-hour traffic. He had survived one more day as Chief of Detectives.

34

THE next day was one of the worst yet, though it began well enough.

When he got to work Eischied found Lieutenant Maher, who headed the Hotel Squad, waiting in his outer office. The man was jubilant. "We scooped them all up at dawn this morning, Chief."

That was the first Eischied remembered that two days ago he had given Maher permission for the hotel arrests.

The PC would find this good news, Eischied hoped, and he invited the lieutenant into his office, sent a detective out for coffee and Danish pastry, and probed for details the PC could present at a press conference.

The lieutenant opened his briefcase and took out photos of jewelry. Eischied gazed down at a ring whose diamond was the size and shape of a Chiclet; at emeralds big as prune pits, at necklaces thick as rope. All these jewels had belonged to a single victim.

"You should see this broad, Chief. They call her the Duchess. She lives in this fabulous suite on the top of the hotel, and I understand she has been the girl friend of extremely rich and important boy friends. All of them rather decrepit, by the way."

Eischied was amused. "Tell me more."

"Some of the donors of these pieces are so old I was surprised they could even do it anymore, Chief. Then I got a look at this broad. What knockers!"

The lieutenant said: "What she really is, Chief, is the most expensive whore in New York. She's got all these old guys buying jewels for her, sometimes several of them at once. She's what they call a cinder shuffler. She's supposed to be able to manipulate the

324

muscles of her vagina in a certain way so that these old guys can sustain an erection long enough to come."

Eischied, grinning, said: "I don't think the PC will want to mention such details in his press conference."

"We got that from several informants, Chief. They said it was really quite extraordinary what she could do with her vaginal muscles." Lieutenant Maher began adding specific details. Detectives, reflected Eischied, can think only in specifics.

But he was intrigued. "You got a picture of her there?"

Maher did. She wore an evening dress and a tiara. Other jewels hung from neck and knuckles. She was statuesque in build, and her face contained a rather cold, striking beauty.

Eischied, studying the photo, said: "What did you call her, a cinder shuffler?"

"That's right, Chief. It's because of these tricks she knows how to do. She milks these old guys like milking a cow."

"Sounds like a very unusual talent."

But Eischied's mind was on the other case; he was not interested in hotel thieves or expensive whores today, though he hoped the PC would be. The PC liked press conferences.

But the PC proved not interested either. "You're not very politically sensitive, are you, Earl?"

Eischied stood before the PC's desk.

"I mean how would it look to the men? I'm up there bragging about saving some woman's jewelry and their brother officer hasn't even been buried yet."

"You're probably right, Commissioner," conceded Eischied hastily.

"How would it look to the city, for that matter? No one's interested in hotel thieves today. All anyone wants to know is what we're doing to find this FEAR gang." He fixed Eischied with a cold eye. "That's what I want to know too."

"I'll have more for you on that later in the day, Commissioner," Eischied promised, backing toward the door.

"On the hotel thieves, have Public Affairs send out a press release," the PC called after him.

Defeat number one for the day.

Defeat number two was not long coming. Cornfield phoned. "Our guys have lost the pants presser, Chief. He slipped the tail."

"Oh, for chrissake."

"Yeah, and it turns out he owns a car matches the description of the getaway car, too."

This meant the tap on his phone had gone dead as well. Though his phone might ring, he was no longer there to answer. Where then was new information to come from? From Detective McCluskey sitting alone in a tenement boiler room? Eischied doubted it.

He put his face in his hands and massaged his eyes.

An hour later he rode up to the Police Academy toward a promotion ceremony that would be defeat number three.

Attendance by headquarters brass had been ordained by the PC, and now Eischied, seated on stage with his peers, watched the swearing-in of sixty-seven new sergeants who had passed the civil service exam, and of five new deputy inspectors who had been selected and promoted directly by the PC. None of the new deputy inspectors was a detective, not one. Eischied had learned this bitter news only minutes before the ceremony, and was still in a state of shock as the five former captains, none recommended by him, were named and stepped forward. Always, in the past, promotions had been distributed according to a rather rigid ratio; Eischied could not remember the detective division ever before being ignored completely. There was only one way to read this. The PC had chosen to insult his Chief of Detectives deliberately, specifically and publicly. His message was unmistakable to everyone in the department, and the humiliated Eischied gazed from the stage out over the crowded auditorium and felt the blush start at the nape of his neck and creep up toward his ears.

The PC in his speech to the promoted men and

their families then promised that the killers of cops would be hunted down relentlessly, with every resource the department possessed. But he did not refer to Eischied or detectives in any way. The PC got a big hand, then went off to meet with the Mayor, or whatever he did, leaving the bitter Eischied to cope with the city's crime for him.

Eischied was sitting at his desk staring at a cigar, lacking even the spirit to ram it into his mouth and light it, when the photo of the cinder shuffler, wearing her diamond tiara, caught his eye. It was half hidden by other papers; but he separated it. A trick vagina indeed.

After a moment, using his private phone, Eischied dialed the hotel where she lived, and once she had come on the line, identified himself. She had a pleasing low-pitched voice. He gave her the good news about her jewels and listened to squeals of girlish delight—though she must have been forty, he guessed. Eischied explained that the recovered jewelry had to be held until after the trial, but he suggested that they meet later in the evening, when he would be in the position to give her more details. She sounded delighted, and he rang off feeling less despondent than before, even curious now about what the rest of the day would bring. Maybe he would check out this cinder-shuffling business, he thought, not really believing he could get that far—or would want to.

At least he wouldn't have to get through the evening alone.

His luck seemed to change almost immediately. The next call was from Detective McCluskey: "Did you ever hear of Koch Street, Chief?"

"Koch Street? Yeah, it's in the South Bronx. Why?" But Eischied knew why, and his heart started to race.

"Some broad called up. Said her name was Cookie. Said that this Leon Epps used to be around her place on Koch Street a lot, but they hadn't seen him in a few days."

McCluskey paused, a dramatic silence, no doubt

savoring his triumph, waiting for Eischied to beg for additional information.

People used information like clubs, Eischied more than most, and he didn't really resent it from his detective now, he only recognized it, and as a result felt weary.

"Come on, come on, what else?" he demanded.

"That's all, Chief."

"No number?"

"No number, Chief. The mother said she hadn't seen her son in a month, or heard from him, and that he was no good. She didn't care if she never heard from him. The broad sounded kind of surprised. Then she said 'Thank you' and hung up."

After a moment's thought Eischied said: "That's the call I was waiting for. You've done a good job, Mac. Why don't you go on home now, before somebody finds you there."

"I don't mind staying, if you think it would do any good, Chief."

Eischied, though he had never seen the boiler room in which McCluskey sat, had seen very many just like it. He visualized McCluskey in his undershirt, visualized the slow passage of the hours, visualized the total absence of tension, or pressure, or danger. Of course McCluskey would be glad to go on sitting there.

"Pack up your gear and get the hell out of there. Take a week off, and then come and see me. And Mac—"

"Yeah, Chief?"

"Well done, Mac."

Eischied hurried downstairs and climbed into his car.

"Forty-eighth Precinct," he told his driver.

Paula, a receptionist in a doctor's office, had left work early, claiming illness. At the moment she stood in the middle of her living room staring down at her telephone, trying to muster the nerve to ring the police.

In truth she did feel sick, sick in the stomach and

the heart. They had all watched newscasts following the murder of Patrolman Delehanty, the women solemn, the men chortling with pride. One newscast had featured interviews with Delehanty's tearful widow, and with the oldest of his orphans, who was only seven. These interviews moved Paula to tears so that Butch, after nudging Charles, had called out: "Paula, what for your eyes leaking water?" The Big Man then had told her to leave the room.

In bed that night Paula had buried her face in her pillow and silently wept for the orphans and the widow and for herself, surrounded by these terrible people who had invaded her home and who would not leave.

The day after that there had been interviews with Chief Eischied and other detectives, and news of a massive manhunt. These had frightened Paula, because she saw the police closing in on her home, and burning it down.

Paula had once been a prostitute. Although only twenty-four, she was the mother of three children by three different men. Her children lived with their grandmother in South Carolina, but she went to see them when she could, taking presents. For a time when she was younger she had been under psychiatric care—she went ten months to a walk-in clinic. She was a small, slow-speaking girl. Her psychiatric report rated her below average in intelligence. But she also had a strong moral streak that had lain dormant too long. She wanted these men out of her house because they were bad men, and because she wanted to be able to watch her own programs on television, not theirs. She wanted to be able to sleep in her own bed too, not upstairs in the dormitory with the other women. Paula was not interested in any revolution; she was interested in the new clerk in the grocery where she shopped, but she could not bring him home, with all these people crowding her place.

In addition she feared what would occur when the police finally came. It would be like the World War, she supposed, bullets and bombs going off, and although she could not really imagine the scene, she knew she would be terrified, perhaps even killed. She was certain these men would shoot it out with the police no matter how large a force came to take them.

She did not know what her lodgers were planning next. The women had not been told. But she knew it would be horrible, because of the weapons. She had handled the grenades herself. There would be more widows and orphans for sure. It would be so bad they might decide to kill her too so she could not ever tell the police anything.

There was a special phone number in the newspaper. She had read all the stories, and therefore the number, many times. The paper said to call that number if you had information about the murder of Patrolman Delehanty, and at work earlier this day, between patients, Paula had stared at the number so long and hard that it seemed now engraved on her brain.

Stooping, she grasped the receiver, but then she changed her mind and clapped it back down again, as if it had stung her.

Suppose Charles walked in while she was telephoning the police, or the Big Man, or Mark D., her former boy friend, who never came near her no more?

She began to cry. If only all this had never happened. If only by dialing that number she could make it all go away. The tears were streaming down her face because she knew she wasn't brave enough to telephone—one of the men would surely catch her in the act.

The TV set was on. She turned it up loud, and it partially captured her attention. By the time the program ended her weeping had stopped, though she was still sniveling. The cheap wristwatch she wore said it was four o'clock in the afternoon. Lately the house was empty all afternoon. Lately when she got home at five the house was still empty, and then they would all drift in for supper about six-thirty.

She told herself that if she phoned now it would only take a minute. If she heard someone come in she could slam the receiver down. No one would suspect she had been phoning the police.

She blew her nose. With the back of her hand she wiped her wet eyes. Suddenly stooping, she snatched up the telephone and dialed the number which, without even wanting to, she had memorized earlier. It had just occurred to her that she needn't even give this address. She could give the address of her office. She would talk to the police there. That way, when the police came to Koch Street to capture Charles and everyone, she wouldn't be caught in the middle of the shooting.

At the other end of the phone a man identified himself as a detective. Paula, sniveling, gave the doctor's address. "If you want to know who did it, go to that address. Ask for Paula."

The detective sought to hold her on the telephone longer, but Charles might come home at any moment.

She banged the telephone down and in frantic haste ran out of the apartment. In the street she flagged down a gypsy cab and gave the address of the doctor's office. She would wait there. She was sure the police would come right away, because she could tell them what they wanted to know.

At that moment the young man known as Frank was playing basketball in a schoolyard. Stripped like Detective McCluskey to his T-shirt, Frank was standing off two other nineteen-year-olds in a half-court game. His arms, neck and face glistened and his T-shirt was sodden. He was beating them. They couldn't stop him. Today everything Frank threw at the basket went in. He played, wearing a permanent fixed grin. The other boys clawed at him from both sides; repeatedly he spun the dribble through their legs, dived between them, and dunked it in. He felt himself a superb basketball player. If he had gone to college, he saw himself an All American by now, coveted by the pros. Unfortunately most of his brief schooling had taken place in homes for wayward boys, where college scouts do not search for talent. He graduated to purse snatching, for he was fast on his feet, then street muggings and liquor-store holdups. At Attica he had attached himself to Charles. He related to Charles.

He was still with Charles. He followed where Charles led. Between crimes he prowled from one schoolyard to the next, looking for youths to pit himself against. He liked to imagine that each schoolyard was Madison Square Garden; he liked to imagine the crowd screaming his name.

Now one opponent lunged from the left while the other lay back. Frank avoided the lunge, dribbled into the corner and, as the second youth came flying at him, feinted, leaped and tossed in a looping one-hander. He was hot, man. Swish. It went through so cleanly it barely disturbed the net. The sweat was dripping down over Frank's cheekbones. The grain of the leather fit cunningly into the circle of his fingertips. He arched it toward the basket. Swish again. Frank was giggling. He was happy. Later he would go home and eat.

Mark D. was chalking his cue in a money game in a poolroom on Boston Road. He had been playing for about four hours, taking on one opponent after another. Most were youths he had known since childhood and who knew him as Jonah Daniel Bell, but some months before he had instructed them to call him Mark D., and they did so, no questions asked. He was careful to keep his private life mysterious. This added to his allure. The other youths waited their turns to play pool with Mark D., and he always paid. Sometimes they played for money, but whenever Mark D. would win a few dollars he would give it back to them in sodas and candy bars.

It seemed to him that his friends accorded him a new respect these last couple of days. He himself felt more confident and had begun to walk with something of a swagger.

Now he listened to the clack of the balls as his opponent, a youth named Leo Stewart, ran off six straight. Stewart, proud of himself, said: "Go on, beat that, Mr. Mark D. Go on."

Stewart, with the tip of his stick, slid six beads along the wire.

Mark D., concentrating hard, ran off the next nine

balls. He cleared the table. Except for the cue ball, conspicuous as a navel, the table was naked.

Stewart wanted to play another game, but Mark D. said: "Got to go, man. Got business to attend to."

Stewart said: "What business you in, Mr. Mark D.?" He studied Mark D., who today wore a green pin-stripe suit and matching green suede shoes.

Stewart knew Mark D. had been in prison. Stewart said: "You into stickups, or what?"

Mark D. said: "Used to be. I's into something heavier now."

"Banks?" inquired Stewart.

Mark D. boasted: "No, I done give up banks. Heavier."

Stewart, giving a dry laugh, said: "Only thing heavier is icing pigs."

Mark D. looked proud. He gave a wink. "Killing pigs is a man's work, man."

Stewart watched Mark D. swagger out of the poolroom.

Stewart had no more money, and no one else invited him to play. For the next hour he lounged against the poolroom wall, partly watching games, mostly brooding. Mark D. didn't work but wore new threads every day. Stewart had a narcotics charge pending, and in his pocket he carried the phone number of the detective who had arrested him, and who was urging him to work the case off by becoming an informant. Presently Stewart left the poolroom and, after many anxious glances over his shoulder, entered a drugstore, dropped a dime in the slot, and dialed the detective's number.

35

EVERETT Walker and Charles were parked in the pants presser's car outside the church in Queens from which, the newspapers said, Patrolman Delehanty would be buried the following morning.

Walker was elated. Unlike the one in Staten Island, this church roof looked perfect.

No one had entered the church in thirty minutes. There was no sign of police interest in the place.

Walker said: "Let's check it out."

The church, when they entered it, was gloomy, and lit principally by candles burning in front of shrines.

Charles was wearing high-heeled, wedge-soled shoes, and as they approached the sanctuary these rang on the marble floor, alarming Everett Walker, who whispered: "Can't you walk quieter than that?"

Up front they knelt to pray.

An open door led presumably to a vesting room. From the altar rail they glanced as well as they could into this room. There was no sound. The church seemed absolutely empty.

Returning to the rear of the church, they mounted soundlessly to the choir loft. Walker was ready to identify himself to any priest or choirmaster as a detective. But suppose he met a real detective?

But the loft was as empty as the rest of the church. Inside what looked like a closet he and Charles found an iron ladder leading to a trapdoor in the ceiling. The trapdoor was locked but Charles withdrew a cutting tool from the satchel he carried and snapped the hasp. The Yale lock fell to the floor of the closet. It made a loud noise.

They listened, but no feet came running. After a

moment they climbed up through the trap, emerging into a hollow steeple.

The steeple was so narrow that two men could barely stand in it at the same time. A narrow doorway—the door was metal and held shut by spring hinges—gave access to the roof. Stepping out into daylight, they saw that the rectangular roof was empty. It was also bordered on all four sides by a stone parapet. The parapet was low, but high enough. A man crouching up here would not be visible from the street. He would not be visible from other rooftops either—there were no other rooftops, this being a street of one- and two-family houses.

Perfect, thought Everett Walker, surveying the roof and terrain it commanded. Just what he had always hoped for. He was no longer angry at Mark D. for bungling what was supposed to have been a double execution. This was better than Staten Island.

The church roof was as narrow as a tennis court, though longer. In its center rose a huge glass dome which reminded Walker of a female breast, even to the nipple on top, out of which rose a gaunt modernistic cross.

From the dome the roof sloped gently toward all four corners for purposes of drainage.

Walker paced the roof, like an artist getting a feel for his canvas, but he walked as softly as he could, and stayed well back from the parapets. From one edge he could see Shea Stadium rising from its barren wasteland of parking lots, and also structures near to it that were left over from the World's Fair. To the northeast, dimmed by distance and smog, rose the stanchions of the Whitestone Bridge.

"Come here," said Walker to Charles.

He had risked a glance down onto the rear street. "Do you see what I see?"

Charles peered down. The tree-lined street behind the church was bordered on one side by a chain-link fence. The fence separated the street from the eastbound lane of Grand Central Parkway.

Charles pointed at the parkway. "And that's the way out when it's done."

"Would you mind stepping back out of sight?"

Charles said: "We throw a rope over the side, and down the wall we do go." They stood near the center of the roof, working it out.

"We slip through a cut in the fence to a car waiting on the parkway."

"They gonna wreck a lot of police cars trying to drive through the fence after us."

It was about a three-story drop to the street below. To reach this street, cops in front of the church would have to run all the way around the block—the church was sandwiched in between its school on one side and its rectory and convent on the other. How long would this take them? A minute? Two minutes? More than enough for Walker and Charles to slip down the rope, dash across the street and dive through the chain-link fence into the waiting car.

Walker said: "It's even better than Staten Island. It's perfect."

Next, half hidden beside the steeple, Walker risked a glance at the tree-lined front street where the funeral would begin. Dusk was deepening. Nonetheless Walker's imagination supplied bright morning sunlight, plus five thousand penguins wearing white gloves, and the hearse rolling toward the curb. The massed gold and silver shields would shine like a monstrance. The gloves would swoop up in salute, and then, as the coffin rose to the shoulders of the pallbearers, the first grenades would rain down, followed by the terrible rockets, the random searching bullets. In seconds thirty or forty of the highest-ranking officers in the country would be down. He and Charles would sprint to the rear of the roof and drop by rope to the ground.

Walker was glad the act would happen here. The church itself would seem to supply the destruction, rather than a common apartment house as in Staten Island. Previously he had accepted the necessity of the apartment-house roof. He had adjusted his original plan. He had reconciled himself to his disappointment, which was more bitter than he had imagined possible. But this was a thousand times better and more proper. The prodigal spilling of lives demanded a ritual setting. Killing on such a scale was sacred.

Walker was a mystic. In another age or country he might have tried to start a new religious sect.

He murmured: "The day of reckoning is at hand."

Charles said: "Amen, brother, amen."

Charles gave him five. They slapped palms. Walker spread his arms in benediction. "Out of war will come peace," he intoned. "Out of death will come life."

"Color the scene red, brother," said Charles, "color it red."

"The world will be a better place afterward." This idea seemed sound to Walker. "Three centuries of injustice will be reversed in a single day, and a new era of brotherhood will become possible."

Each in turn entered the steeple and descended the ladder. Charles, who was carrying the satchel, went first. Behind him Walker pulled the trapdoor into place. The broken lock on the floor he placed in his pocket. They made as little noise as possible. In the choir loft they paused to listen, but heard no sound.

Still without being observed by anyone, as far as they could tell, they strolled out of the church and across to their car.

For the next hour they circled the neighborhood, waiting for darkness. When it came, they drove the car onto the verge of the grass behind the church and pulled up close to the chain-link fence. Through it they watched parkway traffic rush by, headlights blazing.

The driver's door opened against the fence. From his satchel Charles withdrew the heavy-duty cutting tool, and without leaving his seat stretched it across to the fence and began to work. Each link in turn snapped easily.

A few cars came down the residential street passing them. Each for a moment pinioned them in its lights. As soon as each car was gone Charles resumed work.

He cut links up to a height of about four feet, then stopped. The bottom part of the fence could be swung to and fro. Under any pressure at all, it flapped.

It seemed unlikely that anyone would notice this before tomorrow's funeral. Even if it was noticed, it could not be repaired in time.

"A good day's work," said Everett Walker. He was elated, but trying not to show this to Charles. Charles was his accomplice, not his brother. Charles was a tool. Charles would act, yes, but for the wrong reasons. Charles did not live for the future, and certainly not for the future of others.

Walker contemplated this future. Ahead of him stretched a period—perhaps lasting years—of running and hiding. But his influence would grow, and one fine day—

Or tonight's sunset might be the last he would ever see. It was possible. Even if he got killed, he told himself, this would be a proud act to leave behind him. The country would be a purer place, with so much bad blood spilled, and his people would take courage from what he had done, and begin to fight for their rightful place, all of them, united for the first time behind the ideal that had been himself.

Charles, after handing the cutting tool across to Everett Walker, slammed his car door shut and engaged first gear. Very gently, so as to leave no tire tracks in the grass, he bumped down into the street again. To Walker Charles said: "Where to?"

Walker answered: "Koch Street."

36

"KOCH Street," Chief Eischied said, pointing. A map of the streets of the Bronx hung on the wall of the small office. Eischied's finger traced the course of Koch Street. "It starts here, and ends—here. Unfortunately, it's a fairly long street. They're in there somewhere—or were. That's my information."

The six commanders crowded around studying the map. Each had rank, though none as much as he.

Just then the phone rang. All eyes turned toward the detective in headphones, who pressed his switches and lifted the phone to his ear. "Police operator," he said.

Eischied and the other six commanders watched the spools turn. The detective made notes in his log. They heard him say: "Do you have a last name, Paula? Wait a minute, Paula, let me check that address again," but evidently the caller had hung up, for the detective put his phone down.

"What was that?" Eischied asked.

"Some broad snuffling and sniveling. She gives an address and a name, Paula. If you want to know who shot the cop, come see Paula. Sounded like some nut."

The detective was writing the information out on an assignment form.

"What address did she give?"

"Not Koch Street, Chief. Sorry."

There was a wire basket piled with assignment forms. The new one went to the bottom of the pile.

The commanders, all still wearing hats and coats, conferred in low voices around a table. Each time the phone rang they fell silent while the detective in headphones answered.

"This one is for you, Chief."

Eischied took the phone and listened to the voice of a narcotics detective, who had just been contacted by one of his informants. The informant had overheard a guy bragging in a poolroom about killing a cop. The detective apologized for bothering the Chief of Detectives. He wasn't sure whether this information was significant or not.

Eischied said into the phone: "No, you did right to call. But you're tying up the public's phone. Give me your number and I'll call you back."

On the other phone Eischied spoke ten minutes with the detective, making notes. The other commanders, watching silently, heard Eischied say: "Bring the informant in here, if he'll come with you. If he won't come, make arrangements to meet him in a safe place later, and you come in here."

Eischied hung up. "The name Jonah Daniel Bell, aka Mark D., just popped up again," he muttered to his colleagues. "He was bragging in a poolroom about killing a cop."

Instant excitement pervaded the stuffy little office.

"With these people," Eischied said soberly, "the usual rules of common sense don't apply. Killing a cop is such a prideful and good thing that they have to tell everybody."

Eischied was convinced that this case was beginning to break wide open. So were the other detectives. They had seen it happen so many times before. The grins had come on.

"The idea of solidarity is really strong with these people," muttered Eischied. "Thank God they're not like us, or they'd have sense enough to keep their fucking mouths shut, and then we'd never find them."

Now Eischied surrendered to the elation of his colleagues. He too grinned. Though you got nowhere for weeks, suddenly bits of information began to come in, and then suddenly you had enough so that you could act. Eischied lifted two stacks of photos out of his briefcase. The stacks were bound with rubber bands. He dropped one on the desk.

"This is Mark D.," Eischied said. "Fifty photos. Fifty detectives are going into Koch Street tonight and try to root this guy out of there. That's point number one."

He dropped the second stack on the desk. "These drawings represent the leader of this gang of murderers. There are a few things I haven't been telling you, and one of them is this guy's name." He paused. "Does the name Everett Walker mean anything to you men?"

Deputy Inspector Cornfield whistled. The others were all shocked.

"We got a partial print off one of those notes," Eischied explained. But he was suddenly uneasy.

Excited questions came from many parts of the room, but Eischied was watching Cornfield.

"Does the PC know?" inquired Cornfield.

"I just found out myself," lied Eischied. "I haven't even had a chance to tell him yet."

"He better be told," said Cornfield firmly. "A guy as big as that he ought to know about."

"You're right," said Eischied. They eyed each other.

"Another thing," Eischied said after a moment. "In the last hour or so Captain Rolfe has been able to match machine-gun bullets from the Southern Boulevard bank robbery to bullets dug out of those cops last summer."

There were more low whistles.

"The detectives going into Koch Street should be told about the bullets so they will understand what they're up against, and how dangerous these bastards are." Eischied paused. As if they didn't know already, he thought. "As for Walker, I don't want anybody told his name—except the PC of course." He stole a glance at Cornfield. "Give each detective a drawing, with no name attached. They see anybody looks like that, they grab him. They don't need to know his name. He isn't going to be carrying identification on him anyway."

Cornfield said coolly, "Maybe we should do it the other way. Maybe we should give Walker's name and photo to the press. Then eight million honest citizens can help us find him."

Eischied on the defensive, muttered: "First of all, that's what he wants. He wants to be a hero. And, second of all, if his name gets out he'll take off—it will be that much more difficult to find him. Plus there's always the possibility that his appeal is broader than we think, and that every ghetto thug in the city will rally to his side as soon as they know he's in town. As far as he's concerned he's not killing cops, he's fomenting a revolution. Who are we to say he's wrong?" Eischied calmed down. He did not have to explain himself to Cornfield. "It seems to me the safest course right now is to say nothing to the press, and very little to the detectives. We just go into Koch Street from either end, house by house." Eischied's confidence returned. They were detectives. They would do what he said until the PC overruled him.

He began to outline procedures for the house-to-house search. He wanted Koch Street to swarm with detectives. "But I want supervision. I want one sergeant for every five detectives." He wanted precinct radio cars parked conspicuously in the side streets. "We got no warrants, and we can't get warrants. We can't go into any of these houses without probably cause. All we can do is ring doorbells, show our photos and ask questions. We're looking for a group of men who don't work and who keep to themselves. Maybe we can get close enough someone will tell us something. Or maybe close enough somebody will take a shot at a detective. If that happens, I hope to God he misses."

Somebody had to head the search squad and, although he wanted the job himself, Eischied abruptly decided to put Inspector Cornfield in charge. It was personal insurance Eischied was thinking of. It would make Cornfield less likely to knife him in the back; and the PC, inasmuch as Eischied could not be accused of trying to hoard all the glory for himself, would be less likely to countermand the search.

There was even the possibility that, with the low-ranking Cornfield in charge, the manhunt would escape the notice of the press, and this was important. The object was to trap the perpetrators in there, not drive them out into the city. The press was no ally tonight.

"I want all of you other men to go home or back to your offices. Is that clear?"

He would have to leave now himself to prove he meant it, though every instinct screamed at him to stay.

He stood up. "If anything happens, Cornfield, you can get me on the radio, and if I'm not in my office or my car I'll be wearing my beeper."

He strode out through the press to his car, and drove away from the only place in the city he wanted to be.

At headquarters Eischied found that the PC was away making a speech; he would not be back in the city until late. To protect himself, Eischied decided to telephone First Deputy O'Connor, to whom he outlined the latest information, together with details of the house-to-house search.

O'Connor grunted: "Keep me informed," and hung up.

Eischied lit a cigar. He had been a detective a long time. He knew no operation was predictable. This one could end in an hour, or last all night. It could produce multiple arrests, or a shootout, or nothing at all. A good executive was one who went about his normal business and let his men get on with it, and Eischied was a good executive. Still he didn't want to be in headquarters. He wanted to be up in the Bronx with his detectives.

Unknown to Eischied or any policeman, the pants presser was in the custody of the FBI. He had been picked up for questioning, brought to 69th Street and left alone in a room to cool while McGovern went out to bring in Vincente Cuomo. The pants presser would not now lead anyone to Koch Street. He would not even be asked any questions about Koch Street, or searched for papers that might give up an address there, for the FBI had not been informed about Koch Street, though detectives had by now started into it from both ends.

Cuomo proved hard for McGovern to find and it was not until ten o'clock at night that the gun dealer peered through a viewing mirror at the pants presser in the next room.

Cuomo turned to McGovern: "What did you bring me down here for? I never saw that guy before in my life."

"Are you sure?"

"Of course I'm sure. I told you the other guy was little. He had these black eyes. Meanest-looking little prick you ever saw. And he's much younger. Early twenties. I'm going home."

McGovern and also McGovern's supervisor sighed.

"Why don't you stick around awhile, Cuomo?"

"Not me."

"Yeah, you."

"What is this?"

"Just on general principles, Cuomo."

McGovern, pleased to make Cuomo wait alone in an empty room for an hour or two, went in and began interrogating the pants presser.

"How you doing, pal?"

"I got nothing to say to you."

McGovern wasn't too sure who the pants presser was. The FBI had a file on him as a political extremist in the sixties, but nothing since. He had never run afoul of federal law. The pants presser, from his sheet, was a street criminal who became a party official, and then disappeared from federal view when the party came apart. The cops must have a recent file on this guy, McGovern thought. Maybe we should ask them.

"I see you've been clean since the last time you got out of the can," McGovern said.

No answer.

"About five years almost. Congratulations."

Still no answer.

But a guy like this was probably still involved in something, McGovern reasoned. The cops might know.

"Are you getting hungry?" McGovern asked.

"What you want with me?"

"Oh, we just want to ask you a few general questions."

"I know what my rights is, man. I ain't answering no questions. Not a single one, hear. I'm not even going to say what my name is—"

McGovern thought: We should tell the cops these guys are floating around the city looking for hand grenades; probably by now they've got them. That's the cops' responsibility, McGovern thought. It's their city. The murder of cops is their worry, not ours.

He said with expression: "We know perfectly well what your name is."

"I got a right to a lawyer. I want a lawyer."

McGovern said: "I think you've got it a little wrong. You only have a right to a lawyer if you're under arrest, or are being detained on some sort of criminal charge. But you're not under arrest. We just want to ask you a few questions. It's in connection with your car. Who you been lending that car to lately, anyway?"

"I don't answer nothing. I want a lawyer."

McGovern saw it was going to be another long night.

"Why make it hard for yourself? If you just answer a few questions, we'll let you go home. If you don't answer, I have to go on asking the questions for the next few hours, say until one or two or three in the morning. Because, if I don't ask you the questions that long, I'll lose my job. So you can count on sitting here that long at least, getting hungrier and hungrier, unless you want to answer a few of these questions right now. And then you can go home."

McGovern and the pants presser stared at each other across the table.

"So who you been lending your car to lately?"

No answer.

McGovern sighed. "Okay, if that's the way you want it."

37

WHEN Louie pulled up outside the cinder shuffler's hotel Eischied reached for one of the three microphones that hung from his dashboard and called: "Car number four to Central. K."

After a moment Central answered: "Car number four. K."

"This is car number four, Central." Eischied had plucked his beeper from the glove compartment. "Will you give me a check on my beeper please?"

A moment later the instrument in his hand emitted a noise so high-pitched as to be ear-splitting.

"Thank you, Central. I am leaving my car at this time. I'll be on my beeper if you need to reach me."

To Louie, Eischied said only: "I'm going into that hotel." One owed no explanation to chauffeurs. A chauffeur was a chauffeur, and stayed with the car.

Louie, asking no questions, would park in a bus stop, or in front of a fire hydrant, pull his hat down over his eyes and doze. The doze might last five minutes or five hours. Louie never knew in advance, or seemed to care.

Eischied, in an elevator, ascended at great speed but in absolute silence toward the penthouse. He was trying to close the Koch Street manhunt out of his mind. He was focused totally on the cinder shuffler, or thought he was. What kind of woman was this to become so opulently rich at a trade other women performed for very little profit? Could she really do special tricks? Assuming she could, what would those tricks feel like?

Eischied, ringing her doorbell, was not so much excited as expectant. He had switched his curiosity from the whereabouts of Everett Walker—about which he could do nothing—to tonight's date with the cinder shuffler. If he could not be there, then he would be here. There were answers to be found out in both places.

She answered the door herself. A tall woman, nearly as tall as he. Lustrous red hair. When she led him inside, Eischied saw that her hair was of a voluptuous thickness and length. It reached almost to her ass. The long dress, sparkling with rhinestones or perhaps diamonds, fit her like a condom. Her breasts were extremely large.

Turning, she bumped him with one, so that in his surprise he blurted out: "Excuse me."

Strapless dress. The slope of bosom was flawless, white. Rings on both hands. Bracelets. Diamond-and-ruby necklace. Lipstick that was thick and red. False eyelashes blinking at him.

Eischied, smiling, glanced from her face down the length of her, thinking: What secret musculature is concealed behind that dress, and what cunning uses does she know how to put it to? Maybe she can be induced to give the Chief of Detectives a personal demonstration.

She stood before him absolutely drenched in jewelry, so that he thought: There must be something special about her.

Intellectually the idea made sense to Eischied. She owned the equivalent of the vocal cords of a great soprano. She could hit high notes. High notes were rare and cost money.

In her sitting room she stood gushing pleasantries while Eischied appraised the décor. Antique French furniture. Upholstery all in damask. Paintings on every wall. Eischied guessed the rent on this penthouse at about $75,000 a year, which this broad didn't pay herself.

She said: "I've never felt so flattered in my life." She had a low, sexy voice. "That the Chief of Detectives himself should bring me such good news in person—"

Skillfully she prepared two drinks. As she handed him his, her chatter never missed a beat.

"Why don't you and I have dinner together tonight?" Eischied suggested.

He had found it best to present invitations unexpectedly early. If the woman began to bore him or otherwise got on his nerves, he could always invent urgent police business and take off. And to pop such a question early put women at a disadvantage. They had no excuse ready. They weren't prepared.

The cinder shuffler hesitated just long enough for Eischied to say: "It's settled then. I know just the place."

He did, too. The owner would treat him like royalty, and there would be no check.

With mock coyness the woman said: "Is it safe for me to go out with you wearing my best jewels? Can you protect me? Are you armed?"

Eischied, responding with the smile that was expected of him, patted the bulge at his belt.

"Let me feel it," she cried, and her hand slid from his ribs to his waist as she sought and found his piece, the most voluptuous patting-down he had ever imagined. Eischied was so surprised that the skin tingled up and down his back.

It was a sexual act, no question about that, and to Eischied this seemed to promise other sexual acts later.

"May I see it?" she begged throatily. "Can I touch it?" She sounded like a virgin parked in Lover's Lane in the dark.

Drawing the revolver from his belt, Eischied flipped the cylinder open and ejected the five shells into his palm. Then he snapped the cylinder closed again and handed the gun to her. She took it gingerly—like a girl fingering her first dick, Eischied thought. He counted the shells in his hand a second time to make sure.

"Have you ever actually shot anybody with it?" she breathed.

Eischied, grinning, said: "Not this year."

"You must be very brave."

Eischied thought: Well, what kind of conversation did you expect from such a broad as this?

She said: "I guess I would be safe with a man like you."

She kept wetting her lips with her tongue. Her tongue was very red, and kept darting in and out. She had fine small teeth.

Replacing the bullets, Eischied shoved the gun down into his belt.

The woman said: "What's that bulge on the other side?"

Eischied pulled his jacket back to reveal his beeper.

"You're absolutely full of bulges, aren't you," she said.

Eischied staring at her bosom, answered: "You protrude nicely in a few places yourself."

She took his arm and hugged it to one of them, saying: "You're a fun man to be around, I can tell that."

Eischied was beginning to feel confident. She was impressed by his rank, by the good news he was bringing her—and perhaps even by himself. There was sexual excitement between them already, and perhaps he should make his play now rather than waiting till after dinner. Maybe it was not necessary to take her out and get her loaded, which was the plan he had tentatively scheduled.

Close together on a sofa that probably cost $10,000, they sipped their second drink, or perhaps their third. Photos of the recovered jewelry lay on the coffee table close to their glasses. Eischied was recounting in great detail how the robbers had been tracked down and arrested and her jewelry recovered. She kept probing for more detail, and in the face of her interest Eischied continued to embroider and exaggerate. He attempted to give the impression that, although he was too modest to say so outright, he had stalked the robbers in her behalf dangerously, devotedly, virtually singlehandedly.

When his tale was finished she hugged his arm again, laying her head against his shoulder. He found himself staring down her cleavage. Her tits looked big as melons. He imagined they must weigh ten pounds each.

She said: "If every police officer in New York was like you, I bet there wouldn't be any crime at all."

Eischied, grinning broadly, answered: "As long as there are dolls like you running around the city, there's bound to be rape."

She giggled.

Was she a little drunk? Eischied, intent on being charming, had not been counting the refills. Nor had he noticed whether she matched him drink for drink or faked it. Never mind. When it came to drinking, he was confident that he could match anybody.

Presently they left for dinner, a tactical decision by Eischied. The seduction, it seemed to him, was going beautifully, and he did not want to risk scaring her off. He would wine and dine her first because it seemed safer, and also because the excitement had given him a powerful appetite. The solution to the riddle that now tantalized him—what tricks this woman could perform that were worth so much money—seemed breathtakingly close.

He had to help her into her coat, a beige mink. It was heavy. It reached the floor. Her evening slippers peeped out, and as he accompanied her to the elevator Eischied saw to his astonishment that they had rubies for buttons. Rubies that matched that thick red hair, which she wore inside the mink, so that it seemed to rise up out of her collar like a cowl. Her ears were close to her head, and so delicate they seemed almost translucent. But the most significant thing about her, Eischied cautioned himself, did not show—the secret things she could do that no other woman could do, or at least very few, for which men lavished jewels upon her, even to the rubies on her shoes.

Downstairs he led her to his car. Louie was alert

enough to see them coming, and leaped out to open the door. Eischied and the cinder shuffler—her name was Doris, he kept reminding himself—slid into the back seat, where Eischied immediately felt uncomfortable. The mikes were up front, and this was an unaccustomed spot from which to survey his city. Louie behind the wheel betrayed no emotion of whatever kind, the perfect servant. Eischied reflected: The last of the servant class in America are patrolmen and detectives. They are as patient and as faithful, as uncomplaining and as predictable as any aristocrat could wish. This made Eischied one of the prime aristocrats in the world today, for he had three thousand of these people anxious to serve him.

After giving the address of the restaurant, Eischied said to Louie: "Any calls for me?"

"Not a thing, Chief."

Louie said nothing more, did not smirk, did not glance around at his passengers, and his face in the rear-view mirror showed no change of expression.

They rolled through the streets with Eischied wondering what was happening on Koch Street.

Mark D., still wearing his green pin-stripe suit and green suede shoes, came up to Koch Street as night was falling. It was swarming with men who could only be cops. The double-parked cars were all unmarked and the cops were not in uniform, but Mark D. recognized cops when he saw them.

He went rigid.

There were eight detectives, leaderless. They were waiting for a supervisor to come up who would tell them what to do. They had not yet heard of Mark D., but he didn't know that.

His hand had snaked toward his gun. He stood ready to yank it out and fire. Blow all them muthas away. Sweat had popped out on his face, but he didn't know that either. His fingers caressed the serrated wood of the instrument that would save him.

The scene was framed by people from the neighborhood, who watched from windows, who congregated silently on stoops. Several more arrived. Kids in ragged sneakers darted forward, then back. To them this was a lark, whatever it turned out to be. The adults knew better.

The detectives huddled in groups, as if for protection. They were aware of the hostility of the locals. They could feel it. They were like troops in a conquered city; no one wanted them here. In their discomfort they kept glancing nervously this way and that. A single glance in Mark D.'s direction might have started a gun battle, leaving many dead. But no such glance fell. The detectives were closed in on themselves. Believing themselves safe in their numbers, they were not afraid. They were simply not at ease. Their eyes moved, but saw nothing. They were looking only for a sergeant or lieutenant. They wanted to know what this was all about.

The detectives waited in pools of lamplight. The people of the neighborhood watched, mostly from the shadows. They noted the detectives' discomfort, their nervous mannerisms, and mistook this for arrogance, which it was not, though it would soon be transformed into something very similar. Once committed to ring doorbells, ask questions, their discomfort would make the detectives overly aggressive, some of them even abusive.

Mark D.'s mood had changed. He sidled over to a doorstoop and gripped the railing. The courage born of panic was gone; in its place was the panic born of fear. Mark D. wished to become invisible. He wished to run, but could barely stand. More of them might be coming—he could run right into them. He wished he could ditch the incriminating gun, but no method occurred to him. He wished he could work out a plan, but his imagination, never quick, felt frozen solid.

He was still dangerous.

The detectives stood now in a single group, ignoring the locals. The locals in smaller groups were chatting guardedly among themselves. Groups shifted. One began to coalesce around Mark D. It was as if the locals sought comfort in numbers too, and perhaps

they did. Mark D. felt the weight of the streetlight
that fell on the chest and shoulders of his green suit.
He felt conspicuous. Any moment the locals would
recognize him as the cause of tonight's invasion of
cops; after that the cops would recognize him too.

A quarter hour passed.

Still another car bristling with aerials drew up. Men
jumped out, and one ran around to the back and threw
open the trunk. With another surge of panic, Mark D.
mistook these people for cops also, and saw himself
surrounded. The well-dressed one he accepted as their
commander. The others, rough men, roughly dressed,
would be detectives.

But he was wrong. When the trunk lid slammed
down, it disclosed a man with camera gear hooked
to his shoulder. The squad of "cops" had become a
TV news crew. Mark D. had seen TV crews before,
and people who got shot and killed on TV were always
still alive afterward. The well-dressed fellow must be
the commentator. The other two men carrying gear
were technicians—an electrician, a sound man.

Hand-held lights came on, and the cameraman
began photographing the detectives, who glanced
around at the TV crew in surprise. The detectives
immediately formed into a tighter group. They blinked
into the lights.

"Hey, man, over here," a voice called from out of
the darkness. "Take my picture. I ain't never been on
TV yet."

The TV crew ignored the voice.

"Shut that thing off," a detective ordered harshly.
Like any arrested felon he was holding his hat in
front of his face.

The lights went out. The TV crew backed away and
in darkness commenced to wait as indecisively as the
detectives.

Mark D.'s legs were working again. He approached
the electrician. "Hey, man, what's this all about?"

The waiting detectives did not yet know the answer
to this question, but the electrician replied: "The
story we heard is that the guys who killed the cop

are in there. As soon as they get the signal about fifty detectives are going in after them."

This news freed Mark D. at last. Feet, take me out of here, he said to himself.

Mark D. melted silently back into the darkness.

At the restaurant the owner came forward all smiles, greeting the Chief of Detectives effusively. "So pleased to see you, Chief—and madam."

Eischied, obliged to perform an introduction, said: "This is Doris—" He didn't bother to give her last name. Doris showed all her pearly little teeth.

Owner and headwaiter both escorted them to their table. Both were smiling with apparent pleasure, and at other tables many heads lifted to watch such a grand entrance.

Doris, once they were seated, whispered: "You make me feel like I'm on a date with a film star. You must be very famous."

"I was able to do the owner a favor once."

"Tell me about it," she purred.

"The Mafia was all over him. I was able to help him out."

She pouted. "You never tell me the interesting details."

Eischied said: "I caused a little investigation to be done. And then I locked up four of those mobsters."

"Where are they now?"

"In the can."

"Your language is so rough sometimes."

Eischied, amused, thought: In the trade you're in, I imagine a broad hears much worse.

Owner and headwaiter both hovered while waiting for drink orders. Eischied, supposing Doris would be offended by anything less costly, demanded champagne. What did he care about price? In this place champagne would cost exactly the same as a highball, namely nothing.

Doris said: "I do love champagne."

They drank the stuff from fluted crystal that winked at them. After the second bottle the owner's face seemed to lose its rosy glow, but the third appeared promptly nonetheless. Doris ate daintily, but with voracious appetite. Eischied ate hungrily too. Dessert was the restaurant's special cheesecake, followed by tiny cups of espresso.

The dutiful owner, bending over the table, asked if they had enjoyed dinner. But his smile appeared pasted on. Eischied said to him: "How about some of that special liqueur you serve here?"

The owner was no longer smiling. His face showed no expression at all. "Of course, Chief."

When they were ready to leave, Eischied called for the owner. "Gimme the check."

"The check, Chief?"

"You heard me."

Beaming, the owner brought it. Eischied peeled bills off a roll.

At the door stood the owner and the headwaiter. Both wore broad smiles. The owner said to Eischied: "Whatever happened to those four guys you arrested in here?"

Eischied said: "I don't know," and followed Doris out into the night.

Louie was parked at the curb. Leaping out, he held the car door.

"Anything come over, Louie?"

"Not a thing, Chief."

From the back seat, which seemed still uncomfortable to him, Eischied considered his problem. Dinner, he judged, had lasted too long, and had smothered, it seemed to him, the fine edge of sexual tension that had existed before. He decided that his job was to reanimate that tension. So he told Doris that he was obliged to look into one of the stationhouses relative to a case that was about to break. But she was invited to accompany him.

Doris expressed delight at this idea.

Eischied's thoughts were in the Bronx, where he couldn't go. Instead he directed Louie to drive to the 19th Precinct stationhouse on East 6th Street, because it was among the oldest houses active, and therefore one of the seediest. It seemed to reek of decades of crime and degradation. The building itself might excite her, like an unusual nightclub act, even if nothing was happening there.

As he swept in the door with Doris at his side, the cop on security duty recognized him and hollered: "Ten-hut!"

Cops—Eischied counted seven—snapped to attention. They were practically quivering.

Leaving Doris standing, Eischied went around behind the big desk.

Cops studded here and there still stood ramrod stiff. Eischied said: "At ease, men," and bent to sign the blotter.

In a loud voice meant to carry as far as Doris, Eischied demanded: "Who's in charge here?"

The desk sergeant explained that the precinct commander was off, and the executive officer was on meal period. So the desk sergeant was in charge. Was anything wrong? There were five or six detectives upstairs in the squad room, the sergeant said. He didn't know how many.

Eischied led Doris up the worn wooden staircase and into the squad room. The detectives there snapped to attention too, but this time Eischied was more prompt in putting them at ease.

There were three prisoners in the cage, one a woman. Eischied led Doris over, and stood beside her staring in at them.

"They're like animals in the zoo," said Doris.

"Don't waste your sympathy on them," grunted Eischied.

A fourth prisoner was being fingerprinted by a detective in shirt sleeves. Beside Eischied, Doris shuddered.

"Excuse me a moment," said Eischied.

At the nearest telephone he dialed the 48th Precinct. Inspector Cornfield came on.

"So far, nothing, Chief," said Cornfield. "We've gone about three blocks into Koch Street from both directions. As a matter of fact, I've been waiting to hear from you. The men are tired. I'm thinking of calling it off and starting again in the morning."

Eischied said roughly: "Are you crazy? You don't think this operation is still a secret, do you? If those hoodlums are in there, and we pull back now, they'll take off, and we'll never find them."

"Whatever you say, Chief."

With an effort Eischied dragged his thoughts out of the Bronx and back to the cinder shuffler. "Come on, Doris," he said, flashing her a strained smile, "let's you and me get out of this dump."

38

EVERETT Walker, who was pacing nervously, said: "Where is everybody?"

Sitting on one of the beds, Charles concentrated on his work. Pieces of the grease gun lay beside him on newspaper. He had oiled each lever, each rod, and was carefully, concentratedly reassembling the gun.

"You hear me, Charles?"

Charles looked up, but made no answer.

Cookie said: "Yeah, it's dinnertime, and there ain't nobody cooking."

Everett Walker muttered: "Where's Paula? Where's Butch? Where's Mark D.?"

Charles eyed Walker, but did not speak.

After a moment's thought Cookie said: "Maybe they had trouble getting through."

"Getting through?" inquired Walker.

"Yeah. They's a lot of cops out tonight. They didn't say nothing to me, but maybe now they's stopping folks."

On a bed across the room sat Frank, whose gaze

was fixed on the TV set on the floor. He wore his usual glazed grin. The grin moved from the TV screen to Cookie.

"Cops?" said Everett Walker. He and Charles stared at each other. Then Charles's attention returned to the dismantled machine gun. But his fingers began moving more quickly than before. There was no time for loving deliberateness now.

Walker said: "We'll go out the back."

Charles, his fingers working fast, answered: "I be ready in one minute."

Cookie looked from one to the other. "You want I should fix up some pork chops for us all?"

Walker, ignoring her, said to Frank: "Get your things. We're going out the back way."

Frank's grin looked uncomprehending, but he said: "I is ready any time."

Charles fitted the reassembled grease gun into the satchel between his feet. Walker came downstairs with a suitcase, and with a grocery bag full of hand grenades. He began to pack hand grenades in the satchel all around the grease gun. Together Charles and Walker filled a similar satchel with bazooka rockets. Frank had been instructed to carry the bazooka itself. It was still rolled in its ratty carpet. He had the carpet over his shoulder. It did not droop. With his free hand on his way past the kitchen, Frank also thought to grab a box of graham crackers.

"What we do with the long pieces?" said Charles.

"Leave them. We got no way to carry them."

"Pity," said Charles.

Frank, grinning, looked from one face to the other.

Walker, just before leaving the house, said to Sugar: "If any police come, don't tell them anything. They can't come in without a warrant. All you girls stick close by the house. Tomorrow we'll give you a call to see if it's safe to come back." He patted her silken rump softly, insistently. He devoted nearly a minute to it, so that she purred.

"The revolutionary movement," he started to tell her, "is—" But it was not something one could expect a woman to understand, so he stopped and left the house.

The three men went down the alley, scaled the fence and crossed the vacant lot to the opposite street. The pants presser's car was parked, as always, three streets away, and they moved through these streets without incident, though carrying enough munitions to blow up the entire block. They climbed into the car and the doors slammed. They were already outside the cordon, if in fact a cordon existed.

A little later Frank, who was driving, turned that irritating grin into the rear-view mirror and said to Walker in the back seat: "Hey, man, where we gonna sleep tonight?"

Walker considered Hoyt's place, but the law might be there too. "In the car."

They moved in slow traffic along a brightly lighted boulevard.

With one hand Frank broke open the box of graham crackers. "Dinner," he said with a grin.

As Eischied led her out through the muster room, Doris in a low voice enthused: "This was so exciting. I've never been in a police station before."

Eischied's eyes raked her. Was this true? It was also possible that she had started her career on the streets, and had been arrested regularly by past pussy posses. It was possible she had been in more stationhouses than Eischied himself.

He wondered at what age she had mastered the trick or tricks which had led to her present eminence, and also he wondered if tonight he would find out what that trick or tricks might be. He had begun to doubt it. The evening had somehow turned sour. He was worried about what was happening in the Bronx, and also he had come to the conclusion that Doris was a rather ordinary woman, despite those big knockers, despite her presumed magical vagina.

"Turn the radio up louder," Eischied ordered Louie.

Since she was fascinated by her brief glimpse into the sordid police world, or at least pretending to be,

Eischied resolved to fascinate her more, if he could.

"Citywide band, Chief?"

"Yeah. And the Fourth Division band, too."

This led to a discussion with Doris about police radios, into which discussion police calls intruded regularly. However, none, as they rolled along were very sensational. The city sounded quiet.

"What are all those microphones for?"

Eischied said to Louie: "Hand me citywide."

With mike in hand at the end of its extension cord, Eischied explained that this frequency went into every radio car in the city. Its use was restricted mostly to emergencies. These could be either big emergencies or small, either a major crime or else just a citizen down with cardiac arrest on the sidewalk. To show her how it worked, he pressed the button and called: "Car number four to Central. K."

The reply came back: "Car number four. K."

Eischied said into the mike: "Give me a time check, please. K."

Central said it was ten after midnight.

"It's late," murmured Doris.

"Nonsense. The night is just starting."

During the next half hour a number of calls came over 4th Division frequency. A patrolman was holding three persons in a restaurant and needed assistance. Since this restaurant, which turned out to be a hamburger joint, was nearby, Eischied ordered Louie to drive there. By the time they arrived four radio cars had already congregated, and three men were being led out of the restaurant in handcuffs.

"How exciting," murmured Doris.

The radio cracked again: "We got a peeping tom on a fire escape at 101 East 94th Street. Which car responding? K."

A car promptly answered: "Twenty-three Boy to Central. We'll take that job. K."

Under the influence of this spurious excitement, Doris seemed to warm up. Eischied had invested heavily in this evening so far; abruptly he decided to invest more. At a nightclub where he was known they watched the two-o'clock show and drank two more bottles of champagne on the house. Eischied danced with Doris twice. Those knockers boring into his chest felt hard as wood, and he began to be as curious about them as about the rest of her.

When they came out Louie still waited at the curb, though Eischied had to rap on the glass to wake him up.

"Where to, Chief?"

Suddenly the radio blared tensely: "Report of a ten-thirty in progress—"

The address followed. Eischied glanced up at the street sign, and saw they were close. "Step on it, Louie," he ordered.

"Right, Chief."

Doris could hear the urgency in their voices.

All atwitter, she demanded: "What's a ten-thirty?"

"Armed robbery in progress." Eischied said tersely, laying it on a bit.

Doris seemed to blanch. The car had lurched forward, gaining speed. They were in a side street now, rushing down an alley of parked cars at sixty miles an hour or more.

Eischied was hurrying her toward violent crime and perhaps a shootout. In a moment she could be dead. Beside her Eischied had his gun out and looked ready to shoot someone. She saw herself caught in a crossfire.

All this Eischied read in her face. As Louie swerved violently into another side street, Eischied was thrown against her.

"There he is," cried Louie.

They saw a man in a leather windbreaker racing down the sidewalk about two hundred yards ahead. This was a surprise. Eischied hadn't expected to intervene in any robbery. Louie sped after him, and had the siren on now. Louie didn't know that the purpose of all this was to impress Doris, but then neither did the guy in the leather jacket. Louie was ready to behave like a cop rather than a chauffeur. Well, okay, Eischied would too. He wasn't any virgin at this kind of thing.

Just then a radio car swerved into the block from the other end, and two cops jumped out, guns drawn. The perpetrator ran right into them and was grabbed.

Louie squealed to a stop, headlights poking into the radio car's open door and across its empty front seat. Eischied jumped out of his car, gun drawn. There was no need. The suspect already leaned against the wall, hands above his head, and one cop was tossing him for weapons with one hand. There was no need for heroics by Eischied. A bit disappointed, he held his gun on the suspect exclusively for the benefit of Doris.

The suspect was handcuffed and shoved roughly into the back of the radio car, and the doors slammed. With a squeal of rubber the radio car backed out of the side street and turned toward the stationhouse.

Holstering his gun, Eischied climbed into his car. In the back seat, Doris snuggled up to him, big boob pressed against his arm. "My hero," she whispered into his ear. "I was so scared. You must be a man who doesn't know fear."

Nosing her hair, Eischied murmured: "Nah. These punks are all alike. They don't put up much fight."

The Chief of Detectives' car rolled silently through the late empty streets. A streetlight flashing on the side of Doris's face showed her giving an elaborate yawn. "It's so late. Shouldn't we be going home?"

As they drew up outside Doris's hotel Eischied felt disoriented. He had no confidence she would invite him up for a nightcap, and if she did not, he felt this would humiliate him in front of Louie.

But he strolled confidently toward the door with her. It was locked, and a security guard, after turning keys inside, held it open for them.

Doris turned to Eischied with a false smile. Here it comes, he thought. The answer always comes long before a couple reaches the bedroom door.

"Won't you come up and have a nightcap?"

Eischied, though delighted, concealed this. He said:

"Just let me say something to my chauffeur first."

Walking back to the curb he stuck his head in the window. "Louie, you can take the car and go home. I need a breath of air. I'll walk home from here."

Like an old-world servant, Louie neither smiled nor winked. "Regular time tomorrow morning, Chief?"

Whatever time Eischied gave would be left in a note on the steering wheel for Harold, the alternate driver, to find when he came on duty at 7 A.M.

"Yeah, eight o'clock."

"In front of your house," pursued Louie, "or here?"

Was Louie being a wise guy? Louie was too dumb to be a wise guy, Eischied decided. He was merely making sure of his instructions.

"Of course I mean in front of my house. What do you think?"

The night elevator operator wafted Eischied and Doris toward Doris's penthouse, where Doris busied herself preparing highballs. Eischied, watching her movements, waiting for her return to the sofa, saw his immediate prospects as brilliant. Anticipation made him as nervous and excited as a teenager, with the result that, when she handed him his glass, also like any teenager he immediately drank off half of it.

Vaguely he realized she had made the drinks strong. He had best be careful.

Putting his glass down, he took her in his arms and kissed her. Her lips were soft, and it seemed to him that he felt half a pound of lipstick adhere to his mouth.

She said breathily: "Thank you for finding my jewels for me, and for a very wonderful evening."

Eischied, his confidence increasing, answered: "I hope the evening isn't over yet," and kissed her again, scrubbing those pearly little teeth with his tongue.

Eischied was not surprised at what had now begun to happen. Why be surprised? I did her a favor, he thought, or so she thinks, and she's used to paying off favors. For her this is automatic. For her this is a knee-jerk reaction.

"You have the most fantastic body," he said. He

stared at her bosom. "I've been unable to take my eyes off those things all night."

"It's just the way girls are made."

"There aren't many made as well as you."

She giggled, arching her back to accompany her arch answer: "Flatterer."

Eischied downed the rest of his drink.

He reached for her, but she was gone. "Let me make you another."

Her back was toward him as she mixed the drink at the sideboard, and he could not see what her hands were doing. Her own glass, caked with lipstick on the coffee table before him, had barely been sipped.

She handed his glass down to him. He set it calmly on the table and took her into his arms again.

Her body was pressing his beeper into his midsection. It must have been hurting her too, for she broke off the kiss and remarked: "That bulge in your pants is hurting me."

Eischied said with a leer: "Which bulge?"

It made her giggle. Unhooking the beeper, he stood it on the coffee table beside her glass. Then he removed his gun, emptied out the bullets, and set gun and bullets on the coffee table too. He stood the bullets up so they wouldn't roll off. Flashing the same leer, he said: "Only one bulge left now, honey."

She seemed to think this the funniest remark of her life. She buried her face in his neck, laughing, but Eischied worried about all the lipstick she would leave on his clothes.

When she straightened up she asked about the beeper, and Eischied explained that it was simply a miniature radio receiver.

"You mean someone can hear what we're saying?"

"Of course not. But if my office wants to get in touch with me when I'm not in my car, they send out a signal, and this thing goes off like a doorbell."

She said coyly: "A man can serve only one master at a time. Who will it be, me, or that beeper?" and she reached over and pressed the switch into the off position. Eischied, watching her, did nothing, though his thoughts flicked momentarily to the Bronx.

"Okay," he agreed, and began working on the catches on the front of her dress. "Anything you say, honey."

His gun was on the table unloaded and exposed, and he was now out of contact with his office though the manhunt continued, and this made him vaguely uncomfortable even as he continued to work at undoing her dress. Her bra was a self-contained thing. When the catches were undone to her waist he peeled the dress down until those big boobs popped into view. He stared at them awestricken. They stood straight out from her chest a distance of four inches or more. There was no droop to them, none. Eischied suspected surgery, or else silicone injections. He was so amazed that his mouth dropped open, and he was momentarily speechless.

He heard Doris murmur, "Naughty boy," but the remark made no sense to him.

He peeled her clothes down to her waist.

Somehow during this activity his glass had become empty again. Doris jumped up, saying she would make him a refill, and he watched her move to the sideboard. Her tits neither jiggled nor swayed. They didn't move at all. They looked as solid as the tits of a wooden figurehead at the prow of a sailing ship. Eischied shook his head to clear it. He could hardly believe his eyes.

She stood before him naked to the waist, his drink extended in one hand. He grasped the drink and took a quick gulp. "You have some pair of tits," he said, deciding to get this relationship on as carnal a plane as possible.

"Do you think so?" she asked, glancing down, appraising herself.

"Yes, I do." Maybe that fabulous bosom was her true secret. Maybe that's what all the old guys fought to give her jewels for. Maybe there was nothing in this cinder-shuffling business.

He had to find out. His face felt hot and flushed,

and he was consumed by an eagerness to know. A detective never came up against the normal, he realized yet again. Being a detective was a search for ultimates. In a few minutes the ultimate sexual experience might be his.

Rising unsteadily to his feet, he embraced her, big naked tits pressing into his shirt. When had he removed his jacket?

He tugged at his tie, and at the buttons to his shirt. When he too was naked to the waist he embraced her again. Her tits slid off to the sides and his own chest seemed to fit between them. He was disappointed. His thoughts became increasingly less coherent. Perhaps the old guys who lavished jewelry on this broad— perhaps they were short, and liked to feel those tits pressing into their eye sockets.

He led her into her bedroom, leaving behind his beeper, his gun, his bullets. He was mildly worried that when he staggered out of this place he would be in no shape to remember that his holster was empty.

In the bedroom he undressed her the rest of the way—himself too. Now she wore only high-heeled evening slippers, plus rings on both hands, bracelets on both wrists, and that fabulous necklace around her throat. He pushed her down on the bed and crawled between her legs. In a moment he would have the answer. In a moment he would know. He slid forward, expecting that in an instant the world would explode into a thousand brilliant points of light. His life would be enriched beyond all reckoning, and he would have access to a truth to which few men had ever acceded.

But she was panting like any other woman at such a time, the private recesses of her felt no different, and Eischied realized vaguely that he was again engaged in sexual congress with a woman whom he neither knew nor liked and that in some measure this was still another betrayal of his manhood.

The story was that she could milk these old guys but without using her hands. The story was that she was a cinder shuffler, and because of this rare talent had been drenched with diamonds. It was because of this rare talent that Eischied was here. He wanted to experience it. He wanted to know.

But nothing now happening was unusual in any way. Eischied was experiencing one of the keenest disappointments of his life. The breasts were indeed remarkable, as firm as laundry bags that had been packed too tight, but this was no ultimate truth, and perhaps was not even real.

Into her ear he growled: "Are you familiar with the term 'cinder shuffler'?"

Was there a reaction from her or not? Did her whole body stiffen slightly?

Perhaps by his question he had merely intruded into the house of ecstasy which she was building for herself. She was either in a state of sexual transport, or only pretending to be, no man could ever tell, could he? Perhaps he had only disturbed her there.

But she was thrusting her loins up against him now, as if trying to bring herself off, and she gasped a vulgar endearment which Eischied afterward remembered as: "Give it to me, honey."

Eischied tried, though his heart wasn't in it, only—to be equally vulgar—only his distended organ, though this sometimes believed itself to be him in person. With a final effort Eischied's curiosity reared up stronger than ever and he resolved to speak what was in his mind. There was no way he could lose now, for he had already lost, and this was the only glimmer of hope left him. He muttered into her hair: "I'm told you're the greatest cinder shuffler in New York. I'm asking you to shuffle my cinders for me. I'm asking you, please."

"I don't know what you mean," she gasped, still writhing passionately—the charade was evidently to be continued on her side, if not his.

If she had a secret, Eischied never found out what it was. An hour later he strode across Central Park South toward his apartment. The sun was rising behind the tall buildings. Here and there elongated streaks of sunlight illuminated the pavement. He had a ringing headache, and his stomach was in turmoil. He was trying to convince himself that there was nothing in that cinder-shuffling business; he had disproved it. She owned no exceptionally cunning vagina, no magical musculature, and instead the explanation of her unique success was far more simple —or far more complex—depending upon the point of view. She had somehow caught on with all those aging cloak-and-suit guys, she had somehow become the most sought-after prize in the upper echelons of their industry, so that several of those guys had begun bidding against each other, simultaneously seeking to monopolize her services by bestowing jewelry. Her vagina really had nothing to do with it, except insofar as every woman's did. In any case, there was nothing special about Doris, and the myth of the cinder shuffler was just that, a myth.

Or else she was careful to reserve her special wares for special customers. He simply hadn't been in a position to pay her enough, and so she had held back on him.

Eischied felt as disgruntled and as disgusted with himself as ever before in his life. His mouth tasted sour, as if he had been sucking on brass pipe. The hangover was only just starting, but he could tell it would be a beauty. He had had no sleep and the morning was so advanced now that he would barely have time for a shower, a change of clothes and breakfast, before Harold would be waiting out front to drive him to the funeral of Patrolman Delehanty.

Up in his flat Eischied ran a bath for himself, and while the tub was filling he put through a call to his night sergeant, who was just about to go off duty. There had been no calls for him from the Bronx all night. None.

He lay in the tub with his eyes closed. Another day's quest for the abnormal and the bizarre had ended. Once again every answer he had sought had eluded him. But what could he expect, searching as always in the junkyard of life?

A few hours from now he would stand in the cold

morning sunlight together with several thousand other cops watching the coffin of Martin Delehanty lifted out of the hearse and carried into the church. The new day would begin as grimly as the old one had ended, and for Eischied there seemed to be death in all directions.

39

AS Eischied lay drowsing in his tub Everett Walker and Charles were attending early mass at St. Bartholomew of the Sea Church in Forest Hills, Queens. The bazooka inside its rug had already been mounted to the choir loft, where it lay under a pew. At floor level the two men knelt with faces in their hands, dozing, one on either side of the center aisle, each with a heavy satchel on the floor within reach. It was just past 7 A.M. and the priest, celebrating a feast day of the Virgin, wore white vestments and looked out over his sparse congregation through gold-rimmed glasses.

When the mass ended and the faithful straggled out of the church, Charles drifted as far as the vestibule, where he lingered at the pamphlet rack, as if studying the titles there, most of which related to chastity.

Walker remained on his knees in the pew, face still in his hands, like a penitent praying hard. His drowsiness had passed, and in the darkness of his cupped hands he was alert. He was listening to sounds and movements. He could hear the priest in the sacristy putting vestments and implements away, and he heard the cheery voices of the altar boys bidding the priest good-bye and exiting via a back door that slammed. Presently the priest departed via the same door, and the church sounded empty to Walker, totally empty except for himself and Charles. The stillness rang in his ears. He heard Charles cough once, the signal.

Walker rejoined Charles in the vestibule, and on tiptoe they carried their heavy satchels up into the choir loft, where they found that the closet door concealing the roof ladder was still unlocked. Walker opened it as carefully and noiselessly as he could.

The ladder rungs were cold in his hands. Halfway up he was able to push at the trapdoor. He kept a good grip on it as he mounted, and at last could lay it noiselessly back against the wall. With equal care he climbed the rest of the way out into the steeple. The steeple was dark. He had a detective's shield in his pocket. After pinning it on he pushed the steel door very slowly open, bit by bit, scanning much but not all of the roof. It seemed empty. He stepped out onto the roof and checked out the area behind the dome. The roof was clear. To still the beating of his heart, Walker breathed deeply several times. Re-entering the steeple, Walker reached down. From below Charles handed first one satchel up to him, then the second. Walker placed them outside the steel door on the roof proper, and then reached down to grasp one end of the rug. Charles came up behind it, pushing it up through the trapdoor. His head followed.

The bazooka is a very light instrument. As soon as Walker was able to grasp it solidly through the rug, he lifted it out of the trapdoor and carried it onto the roof. In a moment Charles joined him outside.

The early-morning view was extensive in all directions. They looked around.

Walker felt like an Alpinist. He had reached the top of the world.

The sun was above the trees now, and the day was beginning to warm up. It was Walker's decision that the rug and two satchels be carried to the middle of the roof, to be deposited there behind the dome, invisible to anybody climbing the ladder and merely peering out onto the roof.

Charles scoffed at this precaution: "Ain't nobody going to stick his head out on this roof."

"Probably you're right."

"—and anybody who does gets blown away."

"Nobody gets blown away," said Walker sharply, "until we are able to do the job completely."

Charles extracted the knotted rope from one of the satchels, and took it to the rear of the roof. The rope had once hung down into the rubble-strewn lot behind the Koch Street house. Now Charles spent about five minutes tying a loop that would fit around a roof projection. With his eye he measured its length to the sidewalk below. Then he coiled the rope carefully and left it there at the base of the parapet.

Walker risked a glance down at the spot where the rope would deposit them; he studied briefly the street they would dash across and the chain-link fence that had been sliced open in one spot, and that they would dive through. The getaway car would be waiting just there, parked on the verge of Grand Central Parkway, ready to rejoin in an instant the fast morning traffic. Frank was under instructions to drive past that spot once every thirty minutes, and to be parked there starting at twenty-five minutes past nine. The funeral was scheduled to begin at nine-thirty.

Even as Walker watched, the green LTD belonging to the pants presser and driven by Frank approached from the direction of La Guardia Airport. It was slowing down, turn indicator blinking. Standing well back from the parapet now, Walker watched Frank pull off the highway and bump up onto the shoulder, and come to a stop exactly beside the slice in the fence. A moment later Frank, who had crawled across the seat, peered up at him from the passenger side and gave a wave. Walker answered with a curt nod. Frank's glazed grin seemed stuck there, as did the car, visible through the fence to anyone in the street. Irritatedly, Walker waved him back into the traffic. Frank was the weak link, Walker judged. Mark D. would have been better. Still, Frank had found the correct spot once and presumably could do it again.

With thirty minutes to wait before the next check on Frank, and about two hours before the funeral, Walker and Charles sat side by side on the roof, leaning their backs against the base of the dome, feeling the sun hot on their faces. After a sleepless night Walker took strength from this sun. It seemed to sear his hot eyes.

Sitting on the partially unrolled rug, in order to keep the blue suit clean that he would have to travel vast distances in, he began reading this morning's *New York Times* which he had bought at a newsstand and brought up to the roof inside the satchel of hand grenades.

The big headlines would be tomorrow's. The paper was of no interest today. He extended it to Charles. "Would you care to peruse this?"

Walker got his notebook out. There would be more than headlines written, there would be volumes. His thoughts and emotions, the details of these final hours, would be sought after. He began to jot them down.

His name would go into the history books for all time, because he had dared to see grandiose truths, and to act them out on a giant scale. Whether he escaped afterward or was killed was to him at this moment of no importance whatever, or so he thought. Nor did he care what happened to Charles. Charles was not a person, he was a murder weapon. Charles was a mere instrument. Instruments were never significant.

Walker jotted down this thought about Charles, but kept it cryptic, lest Charles glance sideways at the notebook.

Walker saw himself as the first man in history to attack an entire police department. He would offer the downtrodden masses of the world a vision of freedom which would take them years to encompass.

Your purpose, an interior voice told Walker, is not that at all. You only want to be famous.

All right, he thought, I admit it. I do want to right wrongs and change the future, but I want fame too.

I want to spill life out on the sidewalks. I want to spend it. I want to waste it. And be famous.

He was an honest man. He jotted these concepts down in his notebook for the historians to argue over.

He wanted to commit an irrevocable act, an act with all humanity watching. He had chosen this one because there was no other.

"Put your badge on," Walker instructed Charles.

Charles extracted a gold detective shield from his pocket and pinned it to his lapel.

New York police shields, some lost or stolen, others counterfeit, could be bought on almost any ghetto street corner. They were as easy to come by as heroin, or guns.

Charles patted his shield into place. He said: "What precinct we from?"

"I'm from the 48th Squad. I don't know where you're from."

With Everett Walker this passed for a humorous remark, and Charles gave a cold smile. It only matched Walker's own.

The dome hid the door from them, and them from the door. It would take a deliberate search to find them. Even then they would seem to be two detectives on security duty.

If they were found, what?

Bluff it through.

If that didn't work?

Shoot their way off the roof—but only as a last resort because this would mean to abort the sacred act that, at the moment, seemed to Walker to encompass the sole meaning of his life.

Walker realized that soon police vehicles and detachments would begin arriving. The commotion below would be audible to them. Fearing discovery, they would sweat out every noise. The last hour would seem to take two hours or perhaps ten.

In addition to man's ability to laugh there is one other property that separates him from animals—the ability to suffer excruciatingly while merely waiting for time to pass.

Chief of Detectives Eischied, having finished his bath, phoned his office again.

"Reach out for Inspector Cornfield for me." By now Eischied was wearing a fresh suit and he felt better. "Wake him up if you have to. Tell him I want him to phone me right away."

Obviously the Bronx manhunt had turned up nothing. There was no other explanation for Cornfield's silence. In detective work, failure was more common than success, and Eischied was not surprised. Nonetheless he was disappointed. Now we have to start all over again, he thought.

But, before any call from Cornfield came in, Eischied was obliged to leave for the church.

As he got close the street became clogged with police cars, and he had to get out some distance away and continue on foot.

Several thousand cops had already collected in front of the church. From the shoulder patches Eischied saw that many nearby departments were represented also. Cops stood in disorderly rows for two hundred yards in both directions. All were wearing white gloves, and their ranks were swelling constantly.

Eischied took his place in the street directly in front of the church doors, in the row that was beginning to form there. Eischied's row would be reserved for two- and three-star chiefs. In the row in front of them would stand the deputy commissioners and any state or local politicians who might attend—there were always a few. The Mayor, Police Commissioner and Chief Inspector would stand out in front of everybody. Behind Eischied's row in ranks would stand all the cops from Delehanty's precinct—except Police Officer Agnes Cusack, of course, who was still under sedation. The 48th Precinct during the hours of the funeral would be patrolled by cops culled from other parts of the city.

Eischied's eyes felt full of grit; he had a blinding headache and a gaseous stomach as well, but there was work to do even here and he began doing it— shaking hands with politicians as they arrived, and also with those chiefs and deputy commissioners he hadn't seen in a long time, in some cases since the last melancholy event of this kind.

The Chief Inspector, Eischied saw, was chatting in an idle way with the PC. Both were obviously waiting for the Mayor to arrive, at which point the funeral would start. The Mayor was the focal point of the show even more so than the poor corpse itself.

Presently Eischied saw Deputy Inspector Cornfield come up. The Chief of Detectives beckoned to his subordinate, wanting to know the outcome of the Koch Street search, but Cornfield either did not perceive the summons or he ignored it. Cornfield walked straight up to the PC and Chief Inspector, and the three men engaged in what appeared to be an intense conversation. Their heads were very close together, and they spoke in low, muffled voices. Not one word carried as far as Eischied, though he strained to hear.

It was not any casual chat, that much was clear. It was lasting far too long, and Eischied, watching suspiciously, began to feel extremely uncomfortable.

At last the three heads came apart. The Chief Inspector was grinning. The PC patted Cornfield on the back, and Cornfield moved off, looking pleased with himself, in the direction from which the funeral cortege would soon appear.

"Cornfield, come over here," Eischied called. "I want to talk to you." He glanced up at the church steeple, and at that portion of the dome which was visible from the street, not even seeing the killers, for his thoughts were firmly fixed down here. Eischied sensed that something had gone terribly wrong in his life, and he was trying to compose his face.

Cornfield approached. "Morning, Chief."

"So what happened last night, Cornfield?"

Cornfield said airily: "We picked up Mark D. during the wee hours." His face was expressionless, but his manner was smug.

Eischied felt the blood leave his cheeks. It was as if he had been slapped.

Eischied said in a controlled voice: "Why wasn't I informed?"

"I tried to get you on your beeper, Chief. When you didn't respond I woke up the PC. He told me not to bother you any further. He said you deserved an unbroken night's sleep."

Eischied looked into Cornfield's bland face. Cornfield realized what this meant as well as Eischied did. But Eischied said only: "Very thoughtful of you, and of the PC, too."

"He had a Browning .9 mm on him. He didn't get to use it though. Ballistics is checking it out now. The preliminary report says it's the same gun that killed the cop."

Betraying as little emotion as possible, Eischied said: "How did you happen to pick him up?"

"I had detectives staked out in that poolroom, and he came back about two o'clock in the morning, and we grabbed him."

Eischied's skull felt like it was splitting. This would be front-page news, and a triumph for the PC.

Cornfield said smugly: "The PC has a press conference laid on for noon to talk about it. He's asked me to attend."

But not his Chief of Detectives, Eischied realized. The press conference would go off in his absence, and if this detail went down without protest the PC could lop off Eischied's head shortly after.

There was nothing Eischied could say or do to Cornfield about last night. Cornfield had operated under the personal protection of the Police Commissioner. There was nothing Eischied could do or say to help himself now. He had no more options. He could only wait to feel the ax on the nape of his neck. The hairs already stood up there. The ax would be razor sharp. He wouldn't feel a thing.

The Mayor strode up, looking important, wearing gloves and a Russian hat, though it wasn't that cold. He shook hands with the PC and the Chief Inspector. Now he reached behind to shake hands with politicians and deputy commissioners. He caught Eischied's eye, and waved in a friendly way. Eischied nodded back.

From somewhere nearby Eischied heard a command called. The hordes of cops, he realized numbly, were forming up into straight ranks. Rapidly blinking his eyes, Eischied perceived about four blocks away the oncoming funeral cortege. The hearse was preceded by two cops on motorcycles. The motorcycles were moving so slowly they could barely be kept upright. Behind in solemn cadence came the honor guard, and then, following a gap, two chaplains who moved along in front of the hearse, stepping forward with almost infinite slowness. The hearse's headlights were burning, though why? What was there to illuminate? Everything was entirely too clear.

Cornfield said: "Anything else, Chief?"

Eischied thought: 'If I'd been minding the store last night instead of trying to make that broad, maybe none of this would have happened. But this wasn't really true; his problem was deeper.

What else had he forgotten to do?

He had given no orders for a security squad to check this place out, though he supposed his office had, Finnerty had. It was routine. His thoughts darted frantically about. He glanced up at the roof of the church, expecting to see a detective glaring down at him, but there was no one. He glanced back to the funeral cortege. Here came Patrolman Delehanty, with his face destroyed and a half-eaten cheeseburger inside him. Eischied was filled with such gloom that he thought: Why rub out one cop in a hamburger joint? A real revolutionary would make his assault here, with the entire police hierarchy grouped together. He could detonate a bomb under the first rows of pews inside, or pitch a bomb off that roof there.

Eischied said to Cornfield: "Do we have any of our guys on that roof?"

"I don't know, Chief," said Cornfield smugly. "That's not my department."

Cornfield, whatever his personal relationship to the PC, was only a Deputy Inspector, obliged for a while longer to obey the orders of the Chief of Detectives.

Eischied said: "Get up onto that roof and take a look for me, will you?"

It was not a question, but a command.

Cornfield said airily: "With five thousand cops in the street, what could happen? How could a guy get away?"

You don't understand, thought Eischied. Suddenly he saw Everett Walker clearly, or thought he did. These guys don't need to get away.

"Besides, we arrested the killer last night."

"Fast," said Eischied. "I want to see you up there waving down at me."

Cornfield recognized the command and its source. But Cornfield could afford to be magnanimous today.

"Right, Chief," he said, and started for the church roof. The ushers—a lieutenant and some cops from the Police Academy—waited on the church steps. In a moment Cornfield would pass among them.

Eischied put his knuckles in his eyes and tried to rub away the pain there. His life was all coming to a premature end, but he had only himself to blame. The only love he had ever believed in as a grown man was the love that had come his way from other cops. The only excitement he had known was the visceral excitement of the crime scene, the only true pleasure, too. The only drug he had ever been hooked on was the high that came from breaking whatever case he was devoting his life to at the moment. He did not see how he was going to get along without all that.

The pain in his eyes would not go away, nor that in his chest, and when he took his knuckles away and looked out at the world again he saw that Cornfield had advanced no closer to the church doors than where the Mayor stood. The Mayor was wringing Cornfield's hand and patting him on the back simultaneously—no doubt congratulating the bastard on the arrest of Mark D. last night. Eischied, glancing down the street, saw that the cortege, though moving with all deliberate slowness, was three quarters of a block closer. People, most of them kids and youths, were running along the sidewalk toward the church, hoping to get in position to watch the coffin lifted out of the hearse. Many of these individuals carried cameras. Though Eischied and the thousands of assembled cops were there to bury a brother, these people had come for snapshots.

Cornfield was still in conversation with the Mayor. Both were grinning widely. Again Eischied glanced up at the church roof. Again he imagined bombs raining down. Cornfield was plainly not going to get up there in time, and there was no one else to assign to the job except himself.

Abruptly Eischied broke ranks, and strode toward the church door, not so much because he believed the roof needed to be checked out, but because he could not bear to stand motionless in his place one second longer. Action, however useless, was preferable to the stoic endurance of so much pain.

So he entered the church, passing among the ushers on the stoop, and in the vestibule. Eischied knew all these cops by sight, for they performed the same morbid duty at all these so-called inspectors' funerals.

"How long have you guys been here?" demanded Eischied of the lieutenant. He even waited for an answer, wasting time, not believing himself on any crucial mission.

"About half an hour, Chief."

"Did you see any of our guys go up on the roof?"

"No, I didn't, Chief. The bomb squad checked out the church a while ago, though."

Eischied nodded thoughtfully, and began glancing around for stairs to the loft, which he found. They seemed to beckon him forward. He took them two at a time.

In the loft waited an organist and two overweight young singers clutching songbooks. One was male, one female.

They looked bewildered that he had erupted suddenly among them. He nodded brusquely, then crossed to the only door he could see, and wrenched it open. Inside was the steel ladder, and he reached his hands up as far as he could, grasped the rung, and started to climb.

At the rear of the church roof, constantly checking his watch, waited Everett Walker. The funeral was late, but so was Frank. Walker, invisible from the street, stood well back from the parapet, eyes fixed far up Grand Central Parkway, from which direction Frank would come.

Behind Walker, Charles still reclined against the dome with the sun on his closed eyelids. Walker, worried about time, threw a glance in that direction. Charles was like a boxer before the main event. He conserved energy. He communicated only with himself.

"There he is," called Walker sharply, spying Frank's car.

Charles's eyes opened. After a moment, he stood up.

Walker watched the green LTD approach. It was slowing down. It was in the extreme right lane, turn signal blinking. It moved slower and slower, like a player limping toward the sidelines. Drivers swerved to go around it. Walker felt two emotions. One was a kind of soaring sense of self. He was absolutely infatuated with himself and the act he was about to commit. The second emotion was scorn for these drivers, who were passing within seconds of the most electrifying event ever to happen in this city, but didn't know it. Most of them, he thought, would feel regret the rest of their lives.

The green LTD pulled up onto the grass, and Walker, approaching the parapet, risked a glance down onto the back street that ran behind the church. The street was empty, which was only to be expected. The action was all out front at the moment, and would continue to be. Historic action. A few hundred yards up the street three empty radio cars were parked under trees. Their drivers might run for these cars afterward. He could imagine them driving frantically along this side of the fence, trying to find a way to drive through.

Frank, having slid over to the passenger side, waved up at Walker.

Walker waved back.

"Let's do it now," said Charles at his elbow.

Out front five thousand cops stood in ranks; all dignitaries were in place. Both knew this.

"Absolutely not," retorted Walker sharply.

The corpse was on its way. The target would get slightly more perfect, not much.

"You gonna get us killed, waiting."

Walker sought to hold Charles under control. "We can't look down. We can't be sure everybody's there. We can't be sure the time is correct until we hear the command 'Present arms.' Then we attack, not one second before."

"You wasting time jawing," said Charles. He snatched up the bag of grenades.

"Stop. I'm talking about optimum effectiveness." But that wasn't what he was talking about at all.

An exquisite act must be performed exquisitely. There must be no flaw. That was the concept. It was a concept that would not move Charles. Would any concept move Charles?

"What about television? The television goes on when the funeral starts. You willing to miss the television?"

Charles hesitated.

"Bounce one off the coffin," suggested Walker. "Kill him twice."

"Kill him twice," said Charles with a giggle. "I dig that."

Walker registered the giggle, and realized that Charles was under tension too.

"You better wait till the coffin gets here then."

Lifting the rolled-up bazooka, Walker carried it to the front of the roof and laid it against the wall in such a way that the rug's tattered fringe could be grasped and yanked, spilling the bazooka free in an instant.

He tested this arrangement gently, and was satisfied it would work. His breath was beginning to come fast now. His body was reacting. The normal symptoms of passion began to occur. He was like a man approaching orgasm. The pleasure was almost unendurable. He was on the edge. Very soon now would come the spasms of violence, spasms of rapture. Very soon, very soon, soon, soon.

He was no stranger to this emotion. There was nearly always an almost delirious release from tension in the commission of a violent crime. With violence, Walker knew, came a high that was better than liquor, better than any drug.

Walker had reached the front parapet crouched over, hidden from the thousands of cops in the street below. Now, scuttling over behind the steeple, he stood erect and peered up the street in the direction from which the funeral cortege would arrive. He could see only the furthermost ranks of cops, the last twenty or thirty yards of them massed there, filling the street from curb to curb; he could see knots of people who stood about under distant trees, waiting. All the side streets were closed off by empty radio cars whose dome lights turned mournfully.

After the cops the street was bare for half a mile —as far as the roadblock where normal traffic was being diverted.

Returning to the dome Walker lifted the satchel full of rockets.

Charles, having unzipped the other satchel, extracted a grenade. Walker watched Charles toss it from hand to hand.

"You ever throw one of these things?" Charles inquired.

Walker said nothing.

Charles said: "For about eleven months I threw plenty. We used to throw them every time we heard a noise. Killed kids and water buffalo, mostly." His fingertip traced the deeply cut grooves. "They's forty of these little squares. They break up into forty cast-iron pieces. The pieces will scatter about as far as a man can throw this thing."

"Bring that bag to the front of the roof," Walker said.

Charles was tossing the grenade from hand to hand. "Fits the palm well, don't it?"

Walker, crouching, carried the satchel of rockets forward and set it down against the parapet. He unzipped the satchel and left it there, and then, still crouched, moved over behind the steeple, where he could stand erect.

This time he saw the cortege approaching. It was about four blocks away. There was not much time now. A few seconds more. It was going to happen.

He watched the cortege reach the most distant ranks of policemen. They received it into their protection. They engulfed it with love and grief. Walker squinted, the better to study their ranks. How straight each line, how motionless the corpse's stricken brothers. Not a police head turned. The movement of the cortege was as slow as spring rain, and as mournful. It moved with the slowness of pain.

It passed rank after rank of blue uniforms, and on each chest was emblazoned the white badge of authority. Walker's emotions conflicted. It was a hateful scene—he wanted to blow those blue straight ranks apart so they could never re-form. But at the same time it was gorgeous in its order, its simplicity, its peace. Those privileged ranks by their nature excluded him—and always had since the day he was born. He could only disrupt such serenity, never join it. It was a sense so beautiful and hateful that tears came to his eyes, for he didn't hate those men, he wished he could be one of them.

But he scrubbed his eyes. It was indeed a gorgeous, beautiful scene and he was about to blow the shit out of it—out of all he never had. He would blow it up because it needed to be blown up, and because he wanted to enter the history books and there was no other way.

Walker hurried back to the dome.

Charles had zipped the satchel back up with all its grenades presumably inside, and stood now with his .9-mm Browning in his hand. He drew the slide back, sending a shell into the chamber. The automatic now was cocked. Charles thrust the gun back into his belt. At his feet waited the satchel of grenades.

Everett Walker said: "Carry the bag up front, and lay the grenades out along the wall. Lay the grease against the wall too. The sequence is this: grenades, rockets, then the grease. Then down the rope."

Charles nodded.

"We don't even need to look over when the grenades go. Just pitch them."

"There won't be no sound in the street at all," Charles said, " 'cept maybe the widow sobbing, and then—"

Charles lifted the satchel.

Just then they heard noise in the steeple.

"Wait," cried Walker. "Someone's coming."

He clutched Charles's sleeve, but Charles shrugged him off and started toward the front of the roof.

Behind him Walker was experiencing the keenest disappointment of his life. Was it all to be spoiled now, with only seconds to go? He was as disappointed as a child. He was sick with it. He was almost in tears.

When he came to the trapdoor, Eischied had pushed it open as gingerly as Everett Walker two hours before. But it got away from him and fell back against the wall with a slam.

This noise seemed to startle someone out on the roof, for rapid footsteps approached the steeple. Eischied pushed the steel door open and stepped blinking out into sunlight. The man stood about ten feet away. He was carrying a satchel.

Hearing footsteps outside on the roof had alarmed Eischied, but now he saw it was only a detective. He saw this immediately, spying the gold shield on the guy's lapel. What a relief.

All Eischied's air escaped in a single sigh, though the detective, he saw, had eyes like the holes in a skull. Eischied didn't know him.

"I wasn't sure this roof had been checked out," Eischied said.

After a moment the detective said: "No, we're here."

Eischied became aware of several other details at once. There was a second detective on the roof, as there should be. He stood at the far end, glancing down at traffic on the parkway out back, and Eischied caught just a glimpse of his face and shield before he turned back to whatever down there had attracted his attention.

This second man looked more familiar, either a detective he knew, or—Eischied couldn't be sure. The single glimpse was not enough.

Maybe I'm seeing ghosts, Eischied chided himself. The man had drifted out of sight behind the dome.

There were a number of other details fighting their way up from Eischied's subconscious, so many he could not immediately sort them out. There was one satchel close to the front edge of the roof, and another in the detective's hand, which seemed to be heavy, for Eischied watched him set it carefully down.

Eischied said: "What's in the bags?"

After a moment the detective said: "This one is his. I don't know what he's got in it. It feels like bricks."

But his eyes never left Eischied's. His voice betrayed no emotion. Neither did his face, and Eischied realized dimly that there was something wrong in this. Ordinary detectives did not encounter the Chief of Detectives every day, and most of them, when in his presence for the first time, were to a greater or lesser degree nervous. Not this guy.

Eischied said: "What's in your bag?" Without taking his eyes off this detective, Eischied pointed in the general direction of the other satchel.

"Change of clothes. I got a big date tonight."

Eischied nodded. "What's that old rug lying there?"

"I got no idea. It was laying there when we came up here."

At the other end of the roof the second detective drifted into view again. The sun struck both men in the chest, and for an instant Eischied was caught in the cross-eyed crossfire of their glaring gold shields. It made him blink.

But, after a single glance toward Eischied, the second man turned his back and stared down at the traffic once more.

Eischied studied the detective closest him. Eischied said: "Where are you guys from?"

"Forty-eighth Squad, Chief."

Eischied nodded. The squads had recently been disbanded. The 48th Squad, now a part of the 7th Detective District, no longer existed. Still, cops were traditionalists. They tended to keep using designations they were familiar with. It was not this detail that suddenly knifed through to the surface of Eischied's consiousness, but another. Every cop down there in the street was wearing a black mourning band around his shield, but these two on the roof of the church were not, and with that Eischied saw his own extraordinary peril. These men could shoot him down here— he was surprised they hadn't done so already—and then chuck those satchel bombs, or whatever they were, down into the street at their leisure.

"Did you know the deceased?"

"He was a good guy."

Eischied had bluffed his way out of tight spots before, and would do it again if he could just control his voice—and his knees.

He said: "I want you to stay up here until an hour after the funeral ends." Did his voice sound okay, or not? "I don't want you leaving this post until all the cops and dignitaries have left the scene. Is that clear?"

After a moment the man said: "Yes, sir."

"Good," said Eischied, and spun on his heel and strode toward the steeple. If he could reach it alive he might continue to live, but he could not run. It was five paces away, four, three. Eischied kept expecting to feel a bullet crash into his backbone. What would that feel like, how quickly would he die? And, after him, how many others down there in the street would die?

Each step nearer the steeple seemed to him a miracle, gave him hope for more of the same. He was carefully working his hand through the lining of his raincoat—perhaps one miracle could be compounded with another. His fingers found the stock of his gun, they grasped it and began to work it clear of his belt. At last the gun broke loose—his finger poked through the hole and curled around the trigger. He saw no chance of getting the gun clear of his pocket in time. It would tangle in cloth. If he was lucky enough to get off any shots at all, he would have to fire through his raincoat. He was still expecting a bullet in the back any second, but it might not kill him outright and he had begun to hope he might return a shot or two before dying, perhaps even delay their plans until help could come.

Although all these ideas flooded his brain at once, another part of his mind was still analyzing, dissecting. It stood apart on the other side of the room, as if watching someone else. He even realized how clearly he was thinking, and was proud that his immense fear had not immobilized him. He was not going to whirl to shoot it out with them; he was going to step inside that steeple first, if he could reach it, for the steeple represented cover, and a chance to go on living. In two more steps he would be there—one if it was a big one. But no, he controlled his feet perfectly, knowing he had no choice. He might lunge or dive into the doorway faster than the wind, though slower than any bullet. Instead his progress had been the measured stride of the Chief of Detectives, whose questions had been answered satisfactorily and who suspected nothing.

He was at the steeple. His hand grasped the doorknob. He pulled the door open, his gun still hanging free inside his raincoat in his other hand, his back still waiting for the bullet.

He stepped inside the steeple, even remembering to avoid in his panic tramping down on the hole in the floor. As the steel door swung shut, darkness closed in on him and also terror. He couldn't move, think or even cry out.

The inside doorknob hit him in the back, and this freed him. Yanking his gun free of his coat, he kicked the door open.

The "detective" stared at him, gun in hand—and

it was not a police gun. It was an automatic of some kind.

"Freeze," cried Eischied. The sound of his own voice terrorized him more than anything yet, for it made him realize that he did not belong here. He was a middle-aged, three-star chief. Shootouts were for younger men, even though they would be no more prepared for them than he was, even though none were available now to take his place.

He had to kick the door again to make it stay open, exposing too much of himself.

He saw the other man's gun come up, and Eischied fired. He fired at a man wearing a detective's shield. As he fired he was suddenly not sure again, so that he had only a single thought: I hope to God he's not a cop. It was as desperate as a cry and transcended his own fear: Please God he's not a cop.

Eischied fired again, and then again. The detective was kneeling as if in prayer, though struggling to rise. He was struggling to raise the automatic too, though it had become too heavy for him. In fascination Eischied watched the muzzle come up. Somehow he had stepped out onto the roof; the steel door was shut behind him. The muzzle was pointed at his head, and he found he could neither move nor fire again. He was peering straight down the hole, as if watching to see some kind of answer issue forth that would solve his whole life. Instead, the muzzle seemed to rake a line down Eischied's exposed body, still without an explosion. The muzzle descended all the way to the tarpaper, which it touched, and the man after it, crumpling, and the answer, if there was any answer, remained unspoken.

Below on the staircase and in the choir loft Eischied heard heavy footfalls running. But the steel door at his back remained closed, he was still alone on the roof with a second detective to face, and in his confusion Eischied thought he was still under fire from the first man, and that his gun was empty, though it was not. His heart was pounding, his knees were ready to genu- flect, the blood had left his face, and he thought he would pass out from fear. Now the footfalls were clomping up the iron ladder. Thank God, Eischied told himself. Help was almost at hand. A cop would be saved from cops by cops.

There was still another man out there, he realized, who in an instant would attempt to kill him, but Eischied could see no one, and in his terror had crouched close to the door, his puny little gun waving, pretending menace to the air. Now he heard shoes inside the steeple. At the same time from across the church roof came a fearful scream and other running footsteps.

The second detective was running straight toward him. He had a gun that waved as uselessly as Eischied's but his eyes were focused on the satchel beside the crumpled heap of the other man, and Eischied to his amazement saw that this second running detective was crying. He had dropped to his knees beside the satchel, and was trying to claw it open.

Eischied recognized him now or thought he did: Everett Walker.

How long and hard I have looked for you, Eischied thought.

There were cops pouring out of the steeple behind him, and they forced Eischied forward. They were all ushers from downstairs and now were immobilized by a scene they found impossible to comprehend: a corpse; a detective searching an open satchel; the Chief of Detectives with his gun out, but issuing no orders.

With so many men at his back, Eischied's terror vanished. His gun hung at his side, and he watched Walker with amazement. Walker's gun lay on the tarpaper, Walker's hands dug inside the satchel, only to emerge clutching hand grenades. There was a crazed look in Walker's eyes, and he was sobbing. Eischied thought: There is no suitable object for his rage anymore. The only person left to kill is himself.

Eischied shouted again: "Freeze!"

But Walker, clutching his hand grenades, lunged sobbing toward the parapet.

Eischied shot him, or perhaps only imagined he did. Everybody shot him. Everett Walker lay on the tarpaper and the bullets made him bounce.

One of the grenades had rolled toward Eischied's foot. After a moment he picked it up but stared at it unseeing. How quickly life and death interchange, he thought.

There were police officers standing over both men. Others kneeling, stared into the two open satchels. There were about twenty uniformed men on the rooftop now, all milling about and crying out to each other with their discoveries.

One was a lieutenant. Eischied said to him: "Go downstairs and find Deputy Inspector Cornfield. A crime scene needs to be established. Tell him he's in charge and to get up here. Get on the radio and call for Forensic, the DA, the medical examiner, the works."

"Anything else, Chief?"

Eischied thought about it.

"Yeah. You'll find a lot of reporters and TV crews down there. Once the funeral starts, send them up here through the choir loft, quietly." He glanced around the rooftop. "This thing needs to be documented."

"What about the PC, Chief?"

Eischied thought: Let the PC read about it in the papers. But what he said was: "I'll tell him myself in a little while, once you've done all those other things I asked you to do. Move."

"Okay, Chief."

Eischied stepped to the parapet. Most of the faces were turned up at him. Some men had their guns out, though at the sight of the Chief of Detectives the guns went back. The PC and the Mayor stared up aghast.

The hearse was parked at the curb in front of the church. Its rear door hung open. The six policemen who were pallbearers awaited the signal to withdraw the coffin and heave it onto their shoulders. These men too stared up at Eischied.

He nodded down at everybody. This was not the

signal the pallbearers were expecting, but they accepted it, and slid the coffin out and hefted it.

The lieutenant who served as master of ceremonies at funerals, and who stood at the church doors, cried out: "Ten-hut!" And then: "Present arms!"

At that five thousand white gloves in the street and Chief of Detectives Eischied on the roof saluted their slain brother and watched in solemn silence as his body was carried into the church.